Catherine Cookson was born in Tyne Dock, the illegitimate daughter of a poverty-stricken woman, Kate, whom she believed to be her older sister. She began work in service but eventually moved south to Hastings, where she met and married Tom Cookson, a local grammar-school master. At the age of forty she began writing about the lives of the working-class people with whom she had grown up, using the place of her birth as the background to many of her novels.

Although originally acclaimed as a regional writer – her novel *The Round Tower* won the Winifred Holtby award for the best regional novel of 1968 – her readership soon began to spread throughout the world. Her novels have been translated into more than a dozen languages and more than 50,000,000 copies of her books have been sold in Corgi alone. Many of her novels have been made into successful television dramas, and more are planned.

Catherine Cookson's many bestselling novels established her as one of the most popular of contemporary women novelists. After receiving an OBE in 1985, Catherine Cookson was created a Dame of the British Empire in 1993. She was appointed an Honorary Fellow of St Hilda's College, Oxford in 1997. For many years she lived near Newcastle-upon-Tyne. She died shortly before her ninety-second birthday in June 1998 having completed 104 works, nine of which are being published posthumously.

'Catherine Cookson's novels are about hardship, the intractability of life and of individuals, the struggle first to survive and next to make sense of one's survival. Humour, toughness, resolution and generosity are Cookson virtues, in a world which she often depicts as cold and violent. Her novels are weighted and driven by her own early experiences of illegitimacy and poverty. This is what gives them power. In the specialised world of women's popular fiction, Cookson has created her own territory'
Helen Dunmore, *The Times*

BOOKS BY CATHERINE COOKSON

NOVELS

Kate Hannigan
The Fifteen Streets
Colour Blind
Maggie Rowan
Rooney
The Menagerie
Slinky Jane
Fanny McBride
Fenwick Houses
Heritage of Folly
The Garment
The Fen Tiger
The Blind Miller
House of Men
Hannah Massey
The Long Corridor
The Unbaited Trap
Katie Mulholland
The Round Tower
The Nice Bloke
The Glass Virgin
The Invitation
The Dwelling Place
Feathers in the Fire
Pure as the Lily
The Mallen Streak
The Mallen Girl
The Mallen Litter
The Invisible Cord
The Gambling Man
The Tide of Life
The Slow Awakening
The Iron Façade
The Girl
The Cinder Path
Miss Martha Mary Crawford
The Man Who Cried
Tilly Trotter
Tilly Trotter Wed

Tilly Trotter Widowed
The Whip
Hamilton
The Black Velvet Gown
Goodbye Hamilton
A Dinner of Herbs
Harold
The Moth
Bill Bailey
The Parson's Daughter
Bill Bailey's Lot
The Cultured Handmaiden
Bill Bailey's Daughter
The Harrogate Secret
The Black Candle
The Wingless Bird
The Gillyvors
My Beloved Son
The Rag Nymph
The House of Women
The Maltese Angel
The Year of the Virgins
The Golden Straw
Justice is a Woman
The Tinker's Girl
A Ruthless Need
The Obsession
The Upstart
The Branded Man
The Bonny Dawn
The Bondage of Love
The Desert Crop
The Lady on My Left
The Solace of Sin
Riley
The Blind Years
The Thursday Friend
A House Divided
Kate Hannigan's Girl

THE MARY ANN STORIES

A Grand Man
The Lord and Mary Ann
The Devil and Mary Ann
Love and Mary Ann

Life and Mary Ann
Marriage and Mary Ann
Mary Ann's Angels
Mary Ann and Bill

FOR CHILDREN

Matty Doolin
Joe and the Gladiator
The Nipper
Rory's Fortune
Our John Willie

Mrs Flannagan's Trumpet
Go Tell It To Mrs Golightly
Lanky Jones
Nancy Nutall and the Mongrel
Bill and the Mary Ann Shaughnessy

AUTOBIOGRAPHY

Our Kate
Catherine Cookson Country

Let Me Make Myself Plain
Plainer Still

Catherine Cookson

The Dwelling Place

CORGI BOOKS

THE DWELLING PLACE
A CORGI BOOK : 0 552 14066 X

Originally published in Great Britain by
Macdonald & Co. (Publishers) Ltd

PRINTING HISTORY
Macdonald edition published 1971
Corgi edition published 1973

25 27 29 30 28 26

Set in 10pt Linotype Plantin by
County Typesetters, Margate, Kent.

Corgi Books are published by Transworld Publishers,
61–63 Uxbridge Road, London W5 5SA,
a division of The Random House Group Ltd,
in Australia by Random House Australia (Pty) Ltd,
20 Alfred Street, Milsons Point, Sydney, NSW 2061, Australia,
in New Zealand by Random House New Zealand Ltd,
18 Poland Road, Glenfield, Auckland 10, New Zealand
and in South Africa by Random House (Pty) Ltd,
Endulini, 5a Jubilee Road, Parktown 2193, South Africa.

Printed and bound in Great Britain by
Cox & Wyman Ltd, Reading, Berkshire.

*To Mrs Lilian O'Nions and her staff
at the Hastings Public Library
for their invaluable help,
which is always given me
with such good grace.*

Contents

BOOK ONE

The Dwelling Place

1

The cottage had two rooms. It was one of ten in the hamlet of Heatherbrook in the County of Durham, and, up to two hours ago, it had housed thirteen members of the Brodie family; now three of them were dead.

Cissie Brodie stood in the dim light of the death-smelling room and looked at the bodies of her parents, dressed in white calico shifts, lying side by side on the platform bed; and at their feet, hardly longer than their four bare soles, lay the baby; and her fifteen-year-old brain was refusing to take in the situation.

That the fever should take her mother she could well understand, for with each child she had gotten weaker, and the one born two days ago had been too much for her, together with the fever. But that the fever or any other ailment should kill her father was something that she could not understand; for, as far back as when she was four, she could hear him bragging about his strength, for he was head and shoulders bigger than any agricultural worker for miles around. When three years ago the fever had taken John, aged eleven, Nancy, aged ten, and Peter, aged eight, her father had said it was because they had no constitution, they had taken after their mother. He had pointed to Cissie, saying, 'You had it and it didn't take you; no, because you take after my side, and we are strong, we Brodies.' But he hadn't said this in front of her mother, because his nature was kind.

And now he was gone – strength, constitution and all. What was she to do? What was to become of them? Besides herself, there were nine of them left; the eldest, Jimmy, was only ten and the youngest, here in her arms, was but eleven months. How was she going to feed them? She didn't think about housing them, her father had been bonded by the year and the house was part of the contract.

As if the thought of food had been conveyed to the child, it started to whine; and she shook it up and down in her arms, saying under her breath, 'Ssh! There now. Ssh! There now. Ssh! Ssh!' while all the time she stared at her parents.

Last week Farmer Hetherington had let them have all the turnips they could eat and two quarts of skimmed milk a day, but she was sensible enough to know that the farmer's generosity was forthcoming only because he expected her father to be back at work this week.

A section of her mind, planning ahead, thought, Perhaps he'll take Jimmy on the farm, not just stone-picking or crow-scaring. But on this she sighed, knowing there was little chance, as they were standing grown men off all around.

'Cissie.'

She looked down at the child tugging at her skirt and whispered, 'What is it?' and Charlotte, aged five, her brown eyes wide, her lips trembling, said, 'I'm gonna be sick.'

On this, Cissie's eyes ranged helplessly around the half circle of children, all facing the bed, Jimmy, Mary, William, Bella, Sarah, Charlotte, Joe, and Annie, in that order. Then, her eyes coming to rest on Charlotte again, she hitched Nellie further up into her arms before she said softly, 'Go down to the burn and get a drink. You go with her, Sarah. Go to the clean part, mind, where it comes out of the rock; don't go near the river, mind, not even to put your feet in.' The river, Parson Hedley said, was where you caught the fever.

Sarah, a year older than Charlotte, nodded her thin face, so like that of the man lying on the bed. Then, taking her sister by the hand, she went towards the door; and, as she reached it, it opened and a woman entered and, going up to Cissie, said under her breath, 'Get rid of the lot of them. Here's Matthew Turnbull from Benham come over to measure them.'

Cissie looked at Mrs Fisher, who acted as midwife and layer-out of the dead not only for Heatherbrook but also for the other hamlets within a radius of three miles, and she nodded her head once; then, turning to Jimmy, she said, 'See to them, Jimmy, will you?' and he, as if marshalling a flock of sheep, spread his arms wide and guided the silent children through the doorway and past the big broad fellow who was standing waiting to come in.

Matthew Turnbull had to stoop his head to get into the room, and he sniffed audibly and coughed as he glanced towards the bed. Then he turned and looked at the girl with the child in her arms. At this point, Mrs Fisher, twisting her apron straight on her hips, said, 'Ah well, I'll leave you to make your own arrangements.' She nodded from one to the other, then went out.

Cissie looked at the man. She hadn't seen him before. Mr Proctor, the carpenter who usually made the coffins for round about, had died of the fever three days ago. She swallowed deeply before she asked, 'How much do you charge?'

He stared at the lint-white face before him, the two round brown eyes seeming to be lost in their sockets, the nut-coloured hair sticking wet to the forehead, the child's hand alternately opening and shutting over the point of the small breast beneath the faded print bodice, the bodice and skirt themselves hanging as if on a clothes prop, so thin she was.

They had told him that she had been left with nine bairns to see to; well, she wouldn't manage that for long, the workhouse gates would open wide for the lot of them. It was the first time he had seen her but not the first time he had heard her name. Parson Hedley had mentioned the name now and again to him. 'Joe Brodie,' he had said, 'there's a man who would have done things given the chance.' 'And a compassionate man,' he had said. Had he not found his wife when she was twelve years old working in a coal pit in West Riding? She was a distant relation of his, half cousin, but he had brought her from that life, and not only brought her, he had bought her from her people for a golden sovereign and had fetched her to his home, a cottage on the outskirts of Jarrow, and there she had stayed until she was sixteen working in the fields, which must indeed have appeared Elysium after her experiences down a coal mine from the age of seven. And on the day she was sixteen Joe Brodie had married her. Joe Brodie, Parson Hedley said, had always wanted to learn and had been determined his sons should too. He hadn't been bothered about his eldest girl because, after all, there was really no necessity for a girl to read, but the two eldest boys he had sent every Sunday to listen to Bible readings preparatory to their learning their letters. But now all that would be ended.

He looked from the bed to the girl. For the plainest coffin that would hold only until it got into the ground he charged ten shillings. He shut his mind to his father and his mother and his own particular troubles and gave her the answer to her question. 'Five shillings each,' he said.

She moved her head slowly, and when she spoke her voice was just above a whisper. 'I haven't got it, not right away I haven't. I could pay you off in bits, or—' she turned and looked at the mantelpiece where, on the narrow ledge above the open fire, stood a clock. 'If you would take that,' she pointed, 'it's worth a bit – it came from my grandmother's house in Jarrow and her father brought it from foreign parts; it's worth a bit.'

Yes, he could see that, it was an unusual clock. It was about eighteen inches high, with a painted face, and on its floor was a little man with a hammer waiting to strike the hour. Yes, he'd like that, it was a nice piece, but he guessed its value to be more than ten shillings, more than a pound in fact. He turned from her, saying, 'We'll see about it later; I'll get the business over first, leave it to me.' He jerked his head towards the door, and after a moment she turned from him and walked out and into the street.

It was about two o'clock in the afternoon and the sun was high. It hadn't rained for two weeks now and the mud road appeared like a ribbon of ridged rock running between the cottages. On each side of the road were five cottages, two pairs attached and one standing singly. The fact that their own cottage stood by itself had always given her the feeling that they were different, that their family was slightly superior to the rest of the hamlet, and this feeling had been borne out by her father's attitude both inside and outside the house, for she had never known him raise his hand to her mother, like Mr Taggart did, and Mr Snell and Mr Patterson. Very likely this was because he didn't drink. Her father had been an unusual man, inasmuch as he had been determined that none of his children would work full-time before they were ten – picking in the fields in season was nothing. Mr Fisher and Mr Martin, whose sons all went down the mine when they were seven, said he was barmy and where would it get him, but Mr Martin and Mr Fisher were not really of the hamlet, they lived about half a mile up the road; all those in the hamlet worked on the three farms roundabout, the Hetheringtons, the Woolleys, and the Thorntons, who were all tenants of Lord Fischel, so the families in the hamlet had in a way always felt protected, even in spite of riots and wage troubles.

She herself had felt protected until yesterday, for, as some of the women in the place said, she didn't know she was born. There she was, a big lump of a girl of fifteen and had never been to work in either a mine, a factory, or a farm household. All she had done was look after the house, and which one of them when young wouldn't have chosen that and thought themselves blessed . . . And yes, she supposed she had been blessed, for as they said, all she'd had to do was to look after the house, her mother, and the bairns since she was seven. There had only been six of them then, John, Nancy, Peter, Jimmy, Mary, and William. But after William was born her mother's legs had become so swollen that she couldn't put them to the ground and had to lie abed for months on end. But every year she'd had a bairn, except the year she missed between Joe and Annie, and she should have had one then but it came away too early.

Cissie had loved looking after the house and the bairns and prided herself that she kept both cleaner than any other woman in the hamlet. And unlike the rest of the women in the hamlet, who worked in the fields all day or in the farmers' houses, because that was in their man's bond, she didn't have to leave the cleaning and washing until the Sunday, but twice a week she would take the big bundle down to the stream, and if the children weren't picking they would help to beat the clothes on the stones and spread them out on the bushes to dry. But she was always thankful when there were only little Joe, who as yet was only four, Charlotte, and Sarah to help her, for that meant the others were earning.

But over the last two months she had washed nearly every day, as her mother was unable to hold anything, and if she left her for two days the place smelled. The kitchen had always smelled a little, because her mother's bed was there, also the shakedown that held Annie, Joe, and Charlotte, but again she prided herself it wasn't a stench like that which came from the other houses, it was just a smell.

But now there would be no need to wash every day except the bits and pieces that the bairns dirtied. What was to become of them? She looked at the child in her arms. Nellie had fallen asleep. She was plump and well fed; that was because she always cried when she was hungry and therefore was served first. But now there was hardly any food in the house; they were down to two loaves and some pig fat, and the children could go through two loaves quicker than lightning through a haystack. If she intended to keep them together, and she did intend to do so, where was she going to get the money for food? The thought, forcing itself up from the depth of her mind into the open, caused her to jerk her head to the side and answer it by saying. 'Me da said they were never to go down the pit.'

She walked abruptly over the road, past the end cottage, and on to the fells towards the river, and as she went she thought, William's afraid of the dark. Jimmy is an' all, and she knew that the mine represented to them, as it did to all the children, Parson Hedley's hell. This had no doubt come about by her mother telling them of how she was taken down first when she was seven and helped her da to fill the bogies, and some days she was down for fourteen hours.

When she came in sight of the children sitting quietly on the bank of the burn that ran into the river, a spot where they usually played and plodged, she stopped and, looking helplessly about her, muttered aloud, 'What am I goin' to do?' Of a sudden she had the desire to drop on to the heather and cry her heart out. But her da had always said that tears were a waste. Tears, he was fond of saying, were a woman's weak kidney. Cry and you'll have the whole house crying; laugh and they'll be with you. He was right, he had always been right; they had laughed a lot in the house. He had a way of making people laugh, seeing the funny side of things. He had even made her mother laugh, and her as bad as could be. But oh, at this moment she wanted to cry.

17

Jimmy turned and, seeing her coming, got to his feet, and the others followed him. Another time, when they came up with her, they would have yelled and shouted and danced round her, demanding, 'Come on, our Cissie, have a game,' but today they just looked at her for reassurance.

Seeing to them, organising them, would be nothing, she had done that for years; it was where to get the money to feed them that was the problem. She looked at Bella, who was staring at her unblinking. Bella was almost herself in miniature, at least outwardly. She said to her, 'Take Sarah, Charlotte, Joe, and Annie and go to the wood and gather as much kindling as you can.'

'Are you going to bake, our Cissie?'

She looked down at Joe. Joe was always hungry, his devilishness seemed to give him an appetite. 'Perhaps, later,' she said; then turning to Jimmy, Mary, and William, she added, 'You come back with me.' And so they split up, the smaller children going across the fell in the direction of the wood while the older ones, walking docilely behind Cissie, returned to the hamlet.

It was as they came round the hump and in sight of the cottages that they saw the carriage outside the door, and they all stopped and looked at each other, but didn't speak. Then they made their way down the road, Cissie still keeping a step ahead.

When she reached the door it was to see four men standing just inside it. One was the carpenter who was seeing to the coffins, and another was Parson Hedley, but the other two men she hadn't seen before, and the sight of them filled her with apprehension.

It was Parson Hedley who spoke. 'Ah, Cissie,' he said. 'Ah, well now.' Following this, he bent his tall, thin figure slightly sidewards and looked back into the room in the direction of the bed. Then joining his hands, the fingers of one hand overlapping the palm of the other, he pressed them together, and this created a sucking sound. He now brought his length bending towards Cissie, saying in an undertone as if conveying a secret, 'This is Mr Riper.' He slanted his eyes towards the smaller of the two men. 'And this, his clerk, Mr Fuller. Mr Riper is a . . . well, sort of representative, Cissie, if you know what I mean.' He paused here as if to give her time to take in this statement. 'He . . . he has come to help you about the matter of the children.'

Cissie now stared at the plump figure of Mr Riper, thinking the while that he was very much like his name, ready to burst out of his skin.

Mr Riper returned Cissie's look. His eyes had already taken in her thin body. But then that was nothing to go by, the thin ones, like racehorses, were often the stayers. But there was another nine of them, four up to five, he understood, and one, as he saw, still in arms. Well, they'd better get on with it. He said in a thin voice that was in contrast to his plump body, 'Give us the names and ages of the children.'

'Why?'

'Why!' He glanced from his clerk, who had a pencil poised above a thick sheaf of papers, and, looking at Cissie again, he screwed up his small eyes and repeated, 'Why?' then went on swiftly, 'Because, girl, they are to be put in care of the Poor Law.'

'NO! Oh no, they're not!' She pushed past Parson Hedley and the carpenter and, the child clutched tightly against her, she backed towards the table until her buttocks were resting against it, and from there she stared at one face after another before exclaiming, 'They're not! You'll not. They're not goin' into the house.'

'Now, Cissie. Cissie.' It was Parson Hedley coming forward. 'You cannot hope to look after the family now your father is gone. It is happening all about us; all the families who have lost their menfolk are going into care, that is unless they have relatives willing to take them.

Have . . . have you got any relatives you could go to?' He asked the question but he already knew the answer.

Her mind racing, she searched for relatives, but there were none. Her father's people had died of the typhoid when he was eighteen. Her mother hadn't seen any one of her family since she had left her home all those years ago, and anyway they were in West Riding at the other end of the world. But if they had lived across the road, would they have taken nine of them, ten with herself?

'Well, there now, what can you do, child?' Parson Hedley's voice was soft. His hands were joined together again as if he were suffering, as indeed he was, for this was the fourteenth family he had been to today in the three villages and five hamlets that made up his parish. But of all of them, he had dreaded coming here most, because this family had always been different, inasmuch as they were united and loving and clean, as far as it lay in their power to be so, and if they could have stayed together he was sure that this girl would have seen that nothing was altered, because she was of the same mould as her father.

'I'll work; Jimmy, Mary, and William, they can work an' all,' she was gabbling now. 'And Bella, she's seven, she can start. We'll all work, but we're not going to the house. I'm tellin' you we're not goin' to the house. Me da wouldn't rest if he thought we were going there.' She turned towards the bed and looked towards her father's face, stiff, white, and more clean looking than she had ever seen it before, although he was always washing himself in the river.

'Ungrateful. Ungrateful.' The thin voice brought her head round to the fat man. He was wagging his finger at her now, saying, 'You should be thankful that the town is willing to take on the responsibility of feeding and housing your family. If you change your mind it might not be so easy for you to get in, I'm warning you. Come.' He jerked his head at his clerk; then, turning to Parson Hedley, he said, 'I'll leave this to you; I've three more to see in Brockdale. Are you coming?'

Parson Hedley nodded, then turned and looked sadly at Cissie and said softly, 'My dear, we must talk about this. If I can't come back tonight I'll see you tomorrow after the funeral. Wait . . . wait for me then.'

She looked now at the coffin-maker. He was still standing within the doorway, his face turned towards the three men entering the coach, and not until it moved off did he look at her. Her face was even whiter than before, if that was possible; she looked all eyes and hair. He found her gaze disturbing, as if she were blaming him for the situation. There was fear in her eyes besides defiance.

He had made coffins over the past two weeks for a number of families who had lost their men, and he had seen that fat pig, Riper, dispose of the children with less feeling than a man sending sheep to market. Riper was a draper with aspirations. As was the rule, he held the term of office as Custodian to the Poor Law for a year, and any money he issued for relief was rarely spent at his shop since food was the first necessity, and this disgruntled him, and he had been known to give only two shillings in cash and a shilling ticket for draperies.

He blinked his eyes twice when she said loudly, 'They'll not do it, I'll not let them.'

'How will you manage?'

'Somehow. The boys'll get work. Do you know anybody?'

He thought a moment, then shook his head. He'd had no need to think, the question had been asked of him dozens of times lately.

'Do you want anybody yourself? Jimmy's small, but he's ten and strong; he'd be good at carpentry.'

He moved his tongue over his full lips then drooped his head slightly to the side before saying, 'I'm sorry, but ours is a small concern, we're not carpenters, we're wheelwrights. There's only the two of us. Another man, he came in when my dad got hurt. We can just keep going.' His voice trailed away and he looked down towards the floor. He didn't know why he was standing here explaining things to her. He should be on his way and getting on with the job else those boxes would never be ready for the morrow morning. He moved uneasily from one foot to the other; then, glancing towards the mantelpiece, he said, 'Don't worry about the money, I'll take the clock.'

She didn't thank him but just stared at him, and after nodding twice at her he went out and closed the door behind him. She remained standing stiffly for a moment. Then, going to the side of the fireplace, she put the sleeping child into the wash basket on rockers, which formed a cradle, and when she straightened up she stood with her toe working the rocker and all the while staring at her parents. And now again she wanted to cry, and she could because there was nobody to see her.

When she sat down at the table, her face in her hands, the tears didn't come – the pain in her chest which was swelling and swelling seemed to be blocking their escape – yet her mind was not dwelling on the loss of parents now but was ranging widely around the word 'work'. If she could only find work, somewhere where she could have Nellie with her. But that cut out factories such as the Rope Works and the Pipe Works. In any case, they were in Shields and that was too far away, about four miles, and she'd never be able to walk there and back each day and see to the rest of them. If only she could be set up in some big house, or farmhouse roundabout, but she knew there was little chance of that. Dilly Taggart down the Row had been trying for such a position for over three months now with no luck; everybody was sitting tight, nobody was changing. The only hope of jumping into anybody's shoes was if they took the fever or the cholera and died.

Things had gotten worse over the last year. Everybody put it down to the Jarrow pit strike, and Tommy Hepburn. Tommy Hepburn they said was a great man, but she herself couldn't see anything great about a man who organised strikes, because strikes to her mind meant less food and not only for pitmen. But she remembered it as an awful time for the miners for the troops had come from London and turned them out of their cottages, and, because anybody who took them in was letting themselves in for the sack, there was no place for them to go except the fells. Even when the strike was over some of them were never set on again, and these took to the open road with their families. The few who braved the winter on the fells were less in number when the spring came. The farmers, too, roundabout had taken a high hand at the time; her father had said that some of them were more uppish than Lord Fischel himself. They were controllers of food and such men could act like God. Farmers Woolley and Thornton were like that, she thought, but not Farmer Hetherington. Tomorrow, when it was all over, she would go to him; if anyone would help her he would.

But now she must think of a meal for them. She had only those two loaves left. She looked towards the open cupboard. She would get twelve slices out of each if she cut them thin; but one must be left for the morrow. She would also keep the bit of pig's fat for the morrow. Tonight she would boil the turnips and spread them on the bread. That should fill them. Another thing she must do as soon as the boys came back was to get the mattresses out of here and into the other room. It wouldn't do to let the young ones sleep in here tonight, for the smell now was really turning into a stench.

2

The two coffins were on the dung cart. The high sides had been left on but the back had been taken off. The women of the hamlet stood at their doors in respectful silence while the Brodie family took their places behind the cart. Jimmy and William first, Mary and Bella next; behind them Sarah and Charlotte; and lastly Cissie, and by her side Mr Snell, the only man, besides the driver, present. He was there only because he was recovering from the fever and wasn't strong enough as yet to return to work; the other men in the hamlet couldn't lose a day's work to go to a funeral unless it was someone in the immediate family; and it wasn't proper that women should attend. Mrs Patterson and Mrs Taggart had both voiced their disapproval to Cissie for allowing the girls to go. Charlotte, at the ripe age of five, had been left to take charge of Joe and Annie; Mrs Robinson had taken the baby.

'Gee-up!' The old horse moved and the cart swayed and the funeral procession began.

The road from the hamlet lay straight for about a quarter of a mile with open fells on one side and low-walled farmland on the other. When the farm cart rounded the first bend in the road there lay ahead a long slow rise, and it was ten minutes later when they reached the top of it. The road on the high ground was rougher and the cart rocked and the coffins moved from side to side in the foot leeway they had, and the children slipped and stumbled and broke the orderly formation of the procession until Cissie's outstretched hand pushed them into place again.

The sickness in her chest deepened as she looked over

24

the heather-clad hillocks to the right of her and into the distance where lay the river and Jarrow, for it was up here that her da used to bring them on fine Sundays, and he would sit on the highest point and talk to them, always looking towards the river, broadening it for them from the silver thread, which was all they could see, to a vast water on which ships, filled up to the scuppers with coal, set their great sails and went with the wind to London. They followed them on their journeys and all the way back until, filled now with ballast, they could come into Shields and tip it on the foreshore.

One memorable Sunday her father had brought the scene to life for herself, John, Nancy, and Peter. It was the year before the children died. Setting off at six o'clock in the morning, they had walked all the way to Shields shore and had the most wonderful day of their lives. Not only had they seen the town and the life of the river and watched great sailing ships sailing out into the North Sea, but, strangely, the pinnacle of the day for her had been when, on the return journey, their father had led them through Westoe village where the houses of the great were, dozens of them, and they had seen at least twenty beautiful coaches going in and out of drives or standing before glistening brass-adorned doors. It was on that night that the dream had first come to her and she'd seen her whole family living in the most beautiful house; it was low and white with thick walls and the sun was shining on it so brightly that it hurt her eyes to look at it. The dream had since come to her often, and it had never changed. After a weary day, as sleep was overtaking her, she would often say to herself, 'I hope I have it the night.' But it didn't always come. She had told no-one about her dream, not even her da, not because it was silly but because it was too precious to share, and she had the feeling that if she ever spoke of it she would never dream it again.

They were now going downhill and the road was so

rough that Jimmy and William had to steady the coffins on the cart.

They passed through Benham and Brockdale, and people stared to see so many children at a funeral and their expression said it wasn't right. Cissie knew what they were thinking but it didn't matter. Her da and ma were going to have a funeral with people at it, and who better than their own family. If it hadn't been such a long way to the cemetery she would have brought the lot of them.

They passed Rosier's pit just as a shift was coming out and the men, black with red-gapped mouths, stood still until they had passed; then they went through Rosier's village and the stench from the middens engulfed them like a cloud.

Fifteen minutes later they reached the cemetery gate and here they had to halt, for another funeral was going in and they all stood and stared at it in wonder. The coffin was in a glass box drawn by four black horses, and following it Cissie counted twelve coaches, and behind them almost a hundred people on foot. They had never seen such a spectacle. Jimmy turned his dark, thin face towards her and gazed at her in silence, and she returned his look.

When the last of the long cortège had gone through the gates, the driver got down from the cart and led the horse forward, not up the main driveway but along a side path and to a distant corner of the cemetery, and there, waiting at the end of a long line of open graves, was Parson Hedley, with a single gravedigger standing beside him.

Parson Hedley watched the small procession come towards him and he too shook his head at the sight of the children. But then he thought Joe would have wanted it this way and she, better than anyone, would know that. But still it wasn't right. He now went up to Cissie and touched her lightly on the arm and nodded at her twice but didn't speak before turning to Mr Snell and saying, 'I'm glad you managed it, John.' And John Snell said piously,

'Out of respect, Parson. Out of respect.' Then the driver of the cart and the gravedigger, with no ceremony whatever, pulled a coffin from the cart and placed it over two ropes. When they had taken up the ends they looked at Parson Hedley, and he, indicating to Cissie with a wave of his hand that she place the children round the grave, opened the Bible, and the service began.

Parson Hedley wasn't a good preacher. It was said that his sermons were the best 'sleeping dose' one could have, but it was also said it was with works and not words that he carried out his Christian duties.

As they placed the second coffin on the first, Mary began to cry loudly and Cissie, reaching out, drew her tightly against her side, but all the while she stared down into the grave, and as she stared she wondered what was the matter with her. Was she going funny in the head? Because, instead of crying like Mary, she was wondering if her ma was lying on top of her da or the other way about, and in which coffin they had put the baby; likely with her mother, but then you never knew, not for sure. When Parson Hedley's voice droned 'Ashes to ashes' she put her hand over her mouth because her mind was reciting the parody that her da used to say, 'Ashes to ashes, dust to dust, if the Lord won't have you the devil must.' What was the matter with her? She had no feeling in her chest now, she felt numb all over. Was she going off her head?

When William sniffled and coughed, then made a choking sound as he drooped his head forward on to his chest, she put her free hand on his shoulder and gripped it tightly. Now Sarah started to cry, but her crying was quiet. Like her nature, everything was toned down.

When the gravedigger started to shovel the earth rapidly on to the coffins, the hollow sound of the lumps of clay hitting the wood reverberated against Cissie's temples and she had the terrifying desire to jump into the hole and throw the dirt out again.

'Come away. Come away.' She allowed Parson Hedley to turn her from the grave. The children were tightly gathered around her now, even Jimmy, and Parson Hedley, putting his hand on one head after the other said, 'Leave your sister for a moment. You go on with them, Jimmy' – he nodded to the dry-eyed boy – 'I want to talk to Cissie.'

They stood aside and let her walk from their midst, but their eyes remained tight on her. Parson Hedley stopped at the end of the path and, bending forwards, said, 'Now have you thought about what you are going to do, Cissie?'

She wagged her head several times before she spoke. 'Yes, Parson.'

'You're going to let Mr Riper deal with it?'

'No, no, Parson, we're not goin' there. We might all be separated, might never see each other again. I'll look after them.'

'How?' He moved his head slowly from side to side, then added, 'You've got to be sensible, Cissie. How can you possibly provide for nine children?'

'As I said, Parson, we can work. If I can find work and see to them I will, but failing that I'll find something for the three top ones.'

Oh, dear Lord. Dear Lord. Parson Hedley now joined his palms together and made the sucking sound in the characteristic attitude that was his when troubled, and he looked up into the low sky that was threatening rain; then, as if finding another question there, he brought his head down to her again and now asked, 'But where will you live?'

'Live?' As her eyes sprung wide her mouth went into a gape; then she spoke as if addressing someone slightly stupid. 'Well, where we are, of course, Parson.'

'Oh child, don't you realise it's a tithe house; Farmer Hetherington will want to put his next man in there.'

It seemed that all the muscles of her face were twitching

now and she couldn't control her lips in order to speak. This was the thought she had been clamping down on for the past two days, this was the thought that had been frightening her. But she had smothered it with another thought: Farmer Hetherington was a kind man. But now she had to ask herself if he would be kind to the extent of letting them stay on in his house when he wanted it for another worker. He must, he couldn't turn them out. She was bridling inside herself. She said firmly, 'He won't turn us out, not Farmer Hetherington. I'll go and see him the morrow.'

Parson Hedley stared at the thin slip of a girl, and in this moment he envied her the quality that made her blind to obstacles, and he hadn't it in his heart to say to her that he already knew the family that Farmer Hetherington was putting into the house towards the end of the week, a man with six children, one of at least two dozen men who had been on the farmer's doorstep for the job before Joe Brodie had been cold.

'Have you any money, Cissie?' His voice was soft.

When she made no answer to this, only stared at him, he put his hand into his pocket and took out a shilling which he handed to her. She did not protest politely and falsely as her mother would have, saying, 'Oh, I couldn't take it, Parson,' her hand going out at the same time, but she took the shilling from him and muttered, 'Thank you, Parson. Thank you.'

Mr Snell, passing at this moment, observed the exchange and she knew he would be expecting a drink out of it. It was usual to give the mourners a drink and a meal; that's why a lot of men went to funerals. But he would get no drink out of this, this would keep them in bread and fat for two days.

'I have to go now, Cissie.' The Parson looked towards another cart which was coming up the pathway. 'I will call and see you tomorrow.' By which time, he considered, she would have seen Farmer Hetherington and know finally that her case was hopeless, and then he would contact Mr Riper again. Oh, how he hated getting in contact with that man. Would that God could make him love every man as his neighbour.

'Goodbye, Cissie, and God bless you.'

'Goodbye, Parson, and thank you. Thank you indeed.' She waited for the children to come up, and when they reached the main gate Mr Snell was waiting. She looked him straight in the eye and said, 'Thank you for comin', Mr Snell; it was kind of you.' Then not waiting for an answer from him she walked on.

They had gone some distance along the road towards home when the cart rumbled past them and the driver, stopping, asked brightly, 'You wantin' a lift?' and quickly she answered, 'No! No, thank you. No.' She couldn't tolerate the thought of them all huddled together in the cart where the coffins had lain but a short time ago. As she looked at the cart rumbling away she thought, 'Eeh! that's got to be paid for. I wonder who ordered it?'

When the first drops of rain came she looked behind her to where Mary, William, Bella, and Sarah were dawdling now, silent, their feet trailing, and she said briskly, 'Put a move on, else we're goin' to get wet,' and with Jimmy walking by her side she set the pace.

It was as they were entering Rosier's village that Jimmy, speaking for the first time, said, 'What'a' we goin' to do, our Cissie?' and she, evading the question said practically, 'Get bread or flour. Parson give me a shilling.'

They both turned now and looked in the direction of the women queuing outside the tommy shop, the iniquitous retail business attached to most mines where the miner's wife was forced to spend the main part of her husband's wages if he hoped to be kept in work, and she said, 'But I'm not goin' there.'

'You goin' to Benham then?'

'No, not there either, we're goin' to Brockdale.'

'Brockdale? But that's a mile and a half out of the way.'

'It might be, but there's a difference of a penny in a quarter stone of flour at Nesbitt's.'

'Me ma used to say it was nothin' but chaff.' He was looking straight ahead as he spoke and she, her gaze directed in the same way, answered, 'It might be but it's fillin'.'

When they reached the place where the roads branched, one to Heatherbrook, one to Brockdale and the other to Benham, they turned up the Brockdale Road but stopped as they saw a flat cart coming from the direction of their hamlet being driven by the wheelwright, Matthew Turnbull.

With the children about her, Cissie awaited the cart's approach, and when it was level with them Matthew pulled it to a halt and she looked up at him and said, 'You can come for the clock any time, Mr Turnbull.' She wondered if he had already been to the house to collect it.

He replied quietly, 'That's all right, there's no hurry.' He now took his eyes from her and looked at the faces of the children all staring up at him; then jerking his head in the direction of the hamlet he asked, 'Aren't you making your way home?' and she answered, 'No, we're going to Brockdale first, to the shop.'

When he didn't remark on this, Bella, who was a born opportunist, said, 'We're goin' for flour; it's cheaper there but it's a long tramp.'

Cissie cast a hard glance towards Bella. She knew what she was after; Bella was never backward in coming forward; Bella would never die for want of asking. It was strange; she was so like herself in looks, having the same colour skin and chestnut hair, but there was no similarity at all in their ways, nor was any other member of the family as forward as Bella. But Bella, as usual, achieved her end, for Mr Turnbull was now inviting them all up on the cart. He jumped down, saying, 'Just a minute, I'll move these,' and picking up two sheep cribs, a hay rake, and a wooden milk bucket, all looking startlingly new, he said, 'I'm goin' that way, I've got to deliver these to Bamfords.' He was addressing Cissie solely now and went on by way of explanation, which seemed slightly shamefaced although she couldn't understand why, 'Make these odds and ends when things are slack. People are running their carts on the rims this last year or so.' He gave a huh of a laugh, then added, 'There now, there's plenty of room for you all. Up with you!' He took Sarah by the armpits and lifted her well back on to the cart, then Bella and Mary, while William and Jimmy climbed up themselves. Then there was only Cissie, and he stood looking at her for a minute, but before he could extend his hands towards her she had swung herself on to the tail board.

'You'll be all right there?' he asked as she settled herself.

'Yes. Yes, thank you.'

'It's a rough road, you'll have to hang on. You can come up front if you like.'

She shook her head quickly and turned her eyes from his. 'Ta. Thanks. I'm all right here.'

When he started up the cart they all fell together into a heap but, with the exception of Bella, none of them laughed as they would have done at any other time, and even Bella's laugh was smothered.

They had covered half the distance to Brockdale when he called over his shoulder, 'How much flour are you wanting?'

Cissie heard him quite clearly but did not answer until William, giving her a small poke in the back, whispered, 'Our Cissie, he's askin' how much flour you're wantin'.'

A number of seconds elapsed before she could say, 'A quarter stone,' and then she knew that her voice would not carry to him. It was Jimmy who called, 'Quarter stone.'

Matthew made no comment on this and they had almost

reached Brockdale when he said, 'If you wouldn't mind a little longer ride I would take you to the mill, Watson's mill. I know him; you'd get more value for your money there.'

Cissie twisted round and looked towards him. He had his head turned on his shoulder as if waiting for an answer and she said clearly now, 'Thanks, we wouldn't mind the ride.' She'd drive another ten miles to get more value for her money.

He turned the horse from the main road on to a narrow track and at one point the going was so rough that it bounced Cissie off the end of the cart, but she dropped on to her feet and quickly signalled to the children not to call Mr Turnbull's attention to her.

As she walked with her hand on the end of the cart she saw the mill before the others did, and for a moment she saw it as the house in her dream. Then the impression was gone because the millhouse, although whitewashed, was tall and higgledy-piggledy.

She had heard of Watson's mill but this was the first time she had seen it for it must be all of five miles away from the hamlet, and inland, and her father had never taken them inland but always in the direction of the main river.

Matthew drew up the cart in the middle of a big paved yard and, getting down, he came to her and said, 'Wait here a minute,' then crossed the yard and went towards a round house, while the children, now scrambling down from the cart, looked about them in surprised excitement, saying, 'It's a flour mill, Cissie. Cissie, it's a flour mill.'

Sarah was standing with her back against Cissie's hip as if afraid to move into this wonder world but the others edged quietly about the yard, their eyes darting here and there. Then William came scampering back to her, saying breathlessly, 'The sails are 'round the corner. Come on, have a look, Cissie.'

Her eyes on the round house, she said sternly, 'Stop moving about. Bring them here, and behave.'

When Matthew came into view again he was accompanied by a man who had a film of white over him. He was a big man of indeterminable age but the covering of flour made him appear very old, and he looked them over before he said, 'Ah, well now, there you are. And so you're after flour, are you?'

Cissie's voice was small as she answered, 'Yes, Sir.'

'An' I hear you want all of a quarter stone.' He was laughing at her, making game of her, and she didn't reply but her face became stiffer and she straightened her shoulders. This reaction wasn't lost on the miller and he laughed louder now, saying, 'Never sold less than half a sack afore, never been asked for less, come to that, but now you want quarter stone. Well, well.' He thrust out his great hand and punched Matthew on the arm. But the blow didn't shudder Matthew, not even to make him move a step, but he laughed with the miller, at the same time keeping his eye on Cissie.

'How much do you pay for a quarter stone in Brockdale?'

The miller was speaking again and she answered, 'Ninepence for seconds.'

'Ninepence for seconds! Do you hear that?' He again punched Matthew on the arm. 'Daylight robbery. Seconds she said, mostly boxings. Well, well. But now we must see what we can do for you, eh? If Matthew says you want help, then help you'll have. Now, I'll give you seconds and good seconds, three parts white, and I'll give you a full stone for your ninepence. What do you say to that?'

The stiffness slid from her face, her shoulders slumped, her lips moved into a gentle smile and she said, 'I'd say thank you, Sir. Thank you very kindly.'

'Civil spoken, girl, civil spoken.' Before he had finished speaking he was again looking at Matthew; and now he added, 'I'll see to them, you go on 'round beyond, and if I'm not mistaken Rose'll be havin' a mug of tea at this minute. I'll take this squad and show them inside.'

'I'll do that.' Matthew was about to turn away when, through a door in the far wall, a woman appeared. Cissie thought at first it was the miller's wife, then when the woman came nearer she didn't think she'd be old enough, though she wasn't all that young, over twenty she thought. The woman was big, her head on a level with the wheelwright's, her body as broad as his, but it was the face of the woman that Cissie looked at. It was plain, she had never seen such a plain woman. She was plain to ugliness. Her nose was broad, her eyes small, very like the eyes of the miller with deep glints in them, and her skin was thick like that you'd see on some man, and she had a big mole on her chin. Then she smiled at Matthew, and Cissie's eyes became concentrated on her mouth showing now a set of beautiful white teeth. The smile made her look different and her voice was pleasant as she said, 'Why, Matthew,' and there was pleasure in the sound of it and Cissie thought, She likes him, she likes him very much. When the woman looked enquiringly at her and the children, Matthew said softly, 'They're the Brodies from Heatherbrook; they've just buried their parents.'

'Aw, poor things.' Her glance swept over them and came to rest on Cissie, and after a second she turned away, saying, 'They'll be for the house I suppose?' And Matthew turned with her, but Cissie could not hear what he answered.

The miller now beckoned them all towards him, saying, 'Come on along with you and I'll show you something I bet you've never seen afore.'

Clustered together, they went through the brick piers that supported the mill itself, past the cart that was standing near the central post, having sacks let down to it from the floor above, then, leading the way to a ladder set almost vertically against a post, he said, 'Think you can climb that? No need to be afraid, stones aren't workin', runner's being dressed. The top mill stone—' he patted Jimmy on the head – 'the one that does all the work.'

When, after scrambling and slipping, they all reached the first floor they stood, still close together, looking about them in amazement, and they stared in wonder at a man who grinned at them while smearing a long flat piece of wood with soot, after which he began rubbing it over the surface of a great stone.

'Ah! that surprises you, doesn't it? Soot in a flour mill, eh?' The miller was shouting now. 'But nothing like soot for sorting out the dents. Picks up a flaw as small as a pin head, it does. An' do you know something? Mill stones are like women, did you know that?' He was addressing Cissie again. 'They are, 'cos they have eyes and eyebrows and chests, and finally a skirt. Aye, the mill stones are very like women. You put the corn in by the eye, the chest breathes it in, and the skirt wafts it out.' He looked at them all now, laughing heartily, then said, 'You all lost your tongues? Don't want to ask any questions?'

When none of them made to answer he laughed his loud laugh again, and shaking his big head he said, 'Quietest bairns ever been in here. But then, suppose it's under-standable.' His face sober now, he led the way back down the ladder; then going into a barn-like structure beyond the piers, he dipped a big metal scoop into a bin and poured the rough flour into a hessian bag and took it to a tall scale on which he weighed it, saying, 'I'm a good guesser as a rule, but I'm out the day. Pound over a stone there is there. But we'll call it straight, eh? All for ninepence. Once in a lifetime you'll get a bargain like that, me girl, and I'm tellin' you.'

When he handed her the sack she handed him the shilling, and he said, 'Ah! change you want. Well now, 'tis

Rose that sees to the money side. Leave the sack there and come away over. Go on,' he said when he saw her hesitating to put the sack down, 'nobody's goin' to steal it.' He was laughing again.

Like sheep they followed him from the mill across the yard, through a door, and into another yard, a smaller yard, private, with boxes along one wall that held flowers and in the same wall a window that opened outwards and on which were hanging white lace curtains.

The miller was shouting through a door now, 'Have you got a shive for them?' And his daughter came into the yard, saying, 'Of course. Of course.' She had a mug in her hand from which the steam was rising, and behind her stood Matthew. He too had a mug in his hand, and the sight of the mugs brought the saliva rising into Cissie's mouth. They were drinking tea. It was over a month since she'd had a sup of tea and then it had been the cheap stuff at tuppence farthing an ounce. She had made that ounce last a week, just a teaspoonful a day, but stew it as she might, after the first brew it had come out like water, whereas if they had been able to afford the pekoe it would still have had colour in it at the end of the day. But then the time was far behind them when they could afford to pay fourpence an ounce for tea.

'Come in. Come in.' Rose Watson moved backwards and waved them towards her, and they stepped over the threshold and into what Cissie thought was her first glimpse of heaven.

The room was a great stone-floored kitchen, low-ceilinged with black beams criss-crossing it, the plaster showing as white as flour between them. The walls, also beamed here and there, were whitewashed, and around an open fire with an enormous bread oven at each side hung an array of shining copper pans, and on the broad rough oak mantel-shelf a graded line of brass candlesticks. The dresser, laden with crockery, was against one wall, a black

37

settle against another, and in the middle of the room stood a long white wooden table, and on it a wooden platter on which lay a big loaf with a knob on the top, and beside it a piece of cheese that must have weighed all of three pounds.

Without exception, they all had their eyes fixed on the table. Cissie had at first looked about the room, but now, like the children, her gaze was concentrated on the food, and the big woman, beginning to cut thick slices off the loaf, said, 'You like cheese?'

They were so dumbfounded they couldn't answer, not even Cissie, and the miller, roaring again, cried, 'They've lost their tongues. Of course they like cheese. Just you try 'em.'

Rose cut hunk after hunk of cheese and placed one on each slice of bread, then handed them round. Serving Cissie last, she asked, 'Would they like milk or tea?' And without hesitation, Cissie said, 'Tea, please.'

The miller's laugh again filled the kitchen. 'They're not daft. They're not daft. Tea please, she said. How often do you have tea?' He poked his head towards Cissie, and she answered quietly, 'Not very often, Sir.' And he repeated, 'Not very often. An' that's the truth you're speakin', I'll bet.'

Cissie had never tasted tea like it. It was hot, strong, and sweet, and with each swallow it seemed to bring new life into her. She couldn't help but empty her mug quickly, and when Rose asked, 'Would you like another?' she bit on her lip and moved her head in two small jerks, and although she couldn't see anything funny about it, this action of hers sent the miller into a choking fit of laughter; and all the while Matthew stood by smiling.

When the last of them had finished their bread and cheese and drunk their tea, Matthew buttoned his coat and said, 'Well now, I'll have to be getting along, I'm a workin' man.' This caused the miller to guffaw again, and

38

his daughter said, 'We'll be seeing you on Saturday then, Matthew?'

He nodded at her and replied, 'Saturday, Rose, Saturday.' And on this she smiled, showing all her teeth again. Then she turned to the table and with an abrupt movement swept up the remainder of the big loaf and the cheese and, taking a piece of linen from the delft rack, she bundled them up in it and thrust them at Cissie, saying, 'There, they'll be hungry when they get home.'

Cissie clutched the bread and cheese to her breast and stared into the broad plain face, and the tears that she had suppressed over the last trying days threatened to engulf her, and her voice broke as she said, 'Thank you. Oh thank you, Miss.' Then, her glance took in the miller and Matthew, who was unsmiling now, and she muttered thickly, 'You're all so kind.' And on this she turned and hurried to the door, and the children followed her.

When they were all settled in the cart she was able to lift her head and look at the woman and say calmly, 'And thank you for the tea an' all. It was lovely, beautiful tea.'

'You're welcome.'

'Bye-bye.' They were all waving to the woman and the miller, and as the cart rumbled out of the yard Matthew turned and raised his whip and when Rose Watson called, 'Goodbye, Matthew,' he called back, 'Goodbye, Rose. And thanks, thanks for everything.'

As the cart joggled on its way the children began talking about all they had seen and she let them go on until she heard Bella say, 'That bread, it was lovely. And we'll have another shive when we get in.'

'You'll not, you know.' Her eyes were slanted across her shoulder and her voice was sharp as she looked at Bella. 'You've had your share for the day; there's the others.' She was sorry she had to say this but Bella had to be kept down; Bella could only think of her stomach. But wasn't that all there was to think about when you were hungry?

William, his fair head resting against the back of her arm, said, as if to himself, 'That woman, she was kind, wasn't she?' and as Mary answered, 'Yes, there aren't many like her about,' it occurred to Cissie that it wasn't really the woman, or the miller, they had to thank for the kindness they had received today, but him driving, Mr Turnbull. If they had gone to the mill on their own, she guessed they would have had short shrift; the miller liked Mr Turnbull, and the woman, Rose, did an' all. Oh yes, it was clear for all to see. Perhaps they were courtin', very likely, and she wanted to please him. Still, no matter what the reason, she was grateful to them, but most of all to Mr Turnbull. Oh yes, she was grateful to him; she didn't know what they would have done without him these past two days.

Matthew stopped once so that she could buy a pennorth of yeast, and he did not put them all down where the roads met but took them to within ten minutes' walk of the hamlet. And when they were standing on the road she said to him, 'We've taken you out of your way,' but he shook his head as he replied, 'There's a path across the fells; that will get me to Benham in no time.'

She stood now gazing up at him, her brown eyes deep and soft with gratitude, her lips parted and moving wordlessly before she could begin to thank him. 'I . . . I don't know what to say, you've . . . you've helped us so much. The clock is there any time . . .'

His eyes moved over her face. The milk of the skin round her mouth merged into pink on her cheek-bones. There was no hollow under the eyes, the skin went tautly up to the lower lids, where the lashes curled back on to them like fringes. Her hair, escaping from the black kerchief round her head, was lying damp on her brow. There came over him a most weird sensation as if he were being lifted out of himself and standing aside from all past experience. It was disturbing, for he was a practical fellow. He had the impression that all her features were merging into one and he could see nothing but a silver light that grew brighter and brighter. He blinked his eyes and shook his head, and the light faded and he saw her eyes staring at him in some surprise now, and quickly he explained the spasm that had passed over him by saying, 'I've, I've got a toothache, it gives me the jumps now and again.'

'Oh!' The exclamation was full of understanding. She knew what toothache was. 'I'm sorry,' she said. 'Mustard's a good thing.' And to this he answered, 'Aye, it is. I'll plaster it when I get in.' Then turning abruptly from her, he said over his shoulder, 'I'll call within the next day or so for the clock'; and, mounting the cart, he started up the horse and turned it on to the fells, but he didn't say goodbye or wave. She understood this, and so did the children for they'd all had toothaches.

They went along the road, walking closely now and silently, and as she got nearer to the hamlet the sorrow deepened in her, and she realised that she had almost forgotten it during the past two hours. She comforted herself with the thought that at least they were set for the next three days; she had bread, cheese, and turnips, and with the tuppence she had left she would get a pennorth of pig's fat and a pennorth of skimmed milk, and she'd make the latter do for a couple of days. Oh, she'd manage. And she must remember what her da was always saying, never give up hope for it was that and not an empty belly that would kill you.

When they had found the farm labourer from Pelaw dead in the ditch outside the hamlet last year her da had said he hadn't died so much of hunger but from loss of hope; so she must go on hoping, and something would happen to change things.

It did the following morning.

She stood in the muddy farmyard, the glar coming over

41

the uppers of her patched boots, and she said in a whisper laden with fear, 'But where will we go?'

Farmer Hetherington moved his heavy lower jaw from one side to the other, then pursed his lips before saying, 'There's only one place and you know it. You should have let Mr Riper arrange it t'other day. It'll be a lesson to you if you can't get them in there after all and have to go on the fells. You're not the only family left like this, there's dozens around the countryside and it's ten times worse in the town 'cos the fever got a hold there; you should have jumped at the chance when you got it.'

She couldn't believe that this was Farmer Hetherington talking, he had always been kindly, giving nothing for nothing, except turnips, which he had so many of he buried them, but nevertheless he had always been civilly spoken.

An hour ago when he had sent the herdsman to tell her that they must be out the day after the morrow because another ploughman was coming into the house she had yelled at him, 'He can't, he wouldn't do it to us, me da was bonded to him.'

'Aye,' said the herdsman, 'but he took his wage weekly, that makes all the difference, ya can't eat your bread an' have it.'

'I'll go and talk to him,' she had said.

And she had talked, she had begged, almost prayed to him. Her hands were still joined in front of her waist as if in supplication, but all to no avail. The longer he talked the harsher his voice became; finally he offered her help in the way he considered best by saying, 'I'm going into Jarrow shortly. I'll get into touch with Mr Riper for you if I can.'

'No!' Her voice was low, her expression bewildered, but she went on, 'They're not going to the house. As you say, we can go on the fells as others afore us have done; but there's one thing sure, we're not goin' there an' be separated.'

When he just stared at her, saying no word, she stared back at him, and now with a dignity that made him grind his teeth together she said, 'Me da always spoke well of you, Farmer Hetherington.' And on this she turned and made her way across the dung and mud morass of the yard.

It had rained heavily in the night and the caked ridges of the road had flattened out and the ruts and hollows were now pools. Unheeding, she made her way around them and between them, all the while crying deep within her, 'Oh Da. Oh Da.' She didn't think with regret of her mother; her mother had been weak and helpless and evoked her pity, but her da had evoked her admiration and love because he could always find an answer to everything that concerned them.

She didn't know at first why she stepped off the road and climbed the bank on to the fells; it wasn't until she found herself skirting a disused quarry that she realised where she was making for, and when she reached the place she stood and gazed at it. It was a hollow within an outcrop of rock, not large enough to call a cave but deep enough to shelter eight people from the rain, and with room to spare. She remembered the last time they had all been here. It was Easter Sunday and her da had given them each a paste egg; he must have cooked them when they were asleep so as to give them a surprise, and he had put dandelion roots and bark into the water to colour the egg shells. Each of them had carried his egg in his hand as if it were made of gold and then they had stood at the top of the rise over there, below which the land sloped steeply away. They had stood in a row on the rim and her da had shouted, 'Ready, set, go!' and they'd all rolled their eggs down the hill and run, screaming gleefully, after them. But before they could come up the hill again it had started to rain while the sun was still shining, and they had scrambled into here and peeled their eggs and their da had sprinkled salt on them, and as they ate them they nearly choked with laughter at the funny things he kept saying. It had been a wonderful day.

She walked nearer to the entrance and looked down at a patch of black earth. Someone had been here recently and had made a fire, likely a road tramp. She walked under the shelter of the jutting rock and gazed at the dim interior; then with deliberate steps she paced the distance to the wall. It was four steps in depth and five in width, which was larger than the room at home. She would take the wooden beds to bits and rig them up at each side, leaving the middle free. And that would hold the table. The clothes box could go to that side at the foot of one bed and the chest of drawers at the foot of the other. She wished the entrance weren't so high; it was going to be difficult to rig up something to keep the rain out if the wind was this way. They'd have the fire outside and concoct something on which to hang the round-bottomed kale pot. But she wouldn't be able to bake, she'd have to buy bread . . . But what would she buy bread with?

She walked into the open again, across the flat shelf of shale to the edge of a long slope which dropped to a rough road. The slope was covered with early foxgloves, saxifrage, and parsley fern. When she saw it last it had been dotted with patches of shy headed cowslips. She turned to her left and walked off the edge of the shelf and on to a grassy rise that ended in a hill, and from the brow she looked in the direction of Jarrow and the river. But she wasn't seeing the village or the little shipbuilding yard, she was seeing the mine.

'I can't help it.' She spoke the words aloud, as if she were answering her da, and on this she walked rapidly away.

When, ten minutes later, she entered the house on the point of a run she startled the children by saying, 'You, Mary; gather all the dishes together and the pans and put

44

them in the cradle. Everything that will go in put in the cradle. And you, William; bundle up the beddin' . . . Where's Jimmy and Bella?'

'Jimmy's out gettin' wood and our Bella went out to play down by the burn.'

'Charlotte.' Cissie turned to the five-year-old child and said harshly, 'You go down and tell Bella to come back here this minute, she's wanted. And you, Sarah; gather the clothes up from the other room, everything. Bundle them big enough for you to carry.' Then turning to William again, who was standing staring at her, she said, 'Before you start, go and find Jimmy.'

'Where we goin', Cissie?' William's voice was small and she answered, 'I'll tell you all about it when you bring Jimmy back. Now go on.'

Within five minutes Jimmy came running into the house with William behind him, and straightaway he asked the same question as William had done, 'Where we goin', Cissie?'

Before she answered him she went and picked up Nellie from the floor, and she was holding the child with one arm astride her hip when she said, 'The cave near the quarry. We've got to get out by Friday; it's either that or the house.'

The two boys stared at her, their lower lips sagging, and she looked from one to the other now and said, 'And that's not all; you'd better come in here a minute.'

She went into the other room and they followed her, and after saying to Sarah, 'Take that lot out into the kitchen,' she closed the door on her. Then turning to the boys, her voice harsh again, she made a statement. 'There'll be no work for us until the tatie pickin', will there?'

After a moment Jimmy shook his head and said, 'No.'

'Well then, how do you think we're goin' to live?'

Their eyes seemed to grow wider as she looked at them.

'Will any of the farmers take you on 'round here?'

To this Jimmy answered, 'What's the matter with you, our Cissie? What you gettin' at? You know we can't get set on, we've tried.'

'Well, where could you get set on?'

They remained quiet for a moment, and it was William who said in a very small voice, 'You mean the pit, Cissie?'

To this she answered, with her eyes downcast and her voice low now, 'I can't help it. Me da said he would never let you, but what are we goin' to do? It's either that or we go into the house, and you know what that means . . . And they would send you to the pit from there anyway, or up the flues, Joe they'd surely send up the flues 'cos he's small.'

It was William who spoke again. 'Johnny Fisher, he's only nine and he told me he got four and six a week and their Sam seven and six. But he's eleven.'

Cissie looked at William. The prospect wasn't frightening him . . . as yet, but it was Jimmy, Jimmy who was afraid of the dark. But he had pluck, had Jimmy. She said to him now, 'What do you say, Jimmy?' and looking back at her he said soberly, like an adult man. 'If it's the only way, it's the only way, isn't it?'

It was settled then.

'When we get all the things out,' she said, 'we'll go down and ask Mr Martin or Mr Fisher how to go about it.' Then turning abruptly and opening the door, she added, 'We've got to take the beds to bits; we'll need every bit of wood we can get our hands on. Let's get started.'

She put the child on the floor again and set about organising their removal.

3

No matter how warm the day, it became cold around three o'clock in the morning. They might all go to sleep with their legs straight out but in the early dawn they were huddled together in a fleshy heap. Cissie had woken up when the stars were still bright in the sky and she had warned herself not to go to sleep again. She had no way now of telling the time except by the dawn, for the last thing she had done before leaving the house was to send Jimmy with her clock to Matthew Turnbull's in Benham. To her surprise he had returned with Jimmy and stood aghast as he looked at the cave and the odds and ends of their household goods lying around the mouth of it, and he had exclaimed grimly, 'You can't live here,' and as she busied herself putting the planks together for the bed she had answered him, saying, 'It's a dwelling, it's a dwelling. It'll do until I can find something better.'

Then he had surprised her further by stamping away as if he were in a temper. But he had been back every day since, and had never come empty handed. He had even brought her a packet of tea, a full quarter, and yesterday a bag of pig's chitterlings. These had been better even than the tea; she had made such a meal as they hadn't had in weeks.

And today the boys were starting work. Mr Martin had been very helpful, but at a price. For getting them set on he was claiming a shilling out of each of their first week's wages, and he had warned her that they might not be paid for a fortnight or even three weeks. They didn't bond the boys, he said, unless they were workhouse apprentices for they weren't employed by the mine owners but by a

47

buttie. This, he explained to her, was a man who contracted to bring the coal from the coal face to the shaft bottom and who would take on as many youngsters as he could get, and he liked them small and thin like Jimmy because they could get through the narrow low passages. He said Jimmy could start straightaway putting, and the standard wage for putters was six and six a week, but if he cared to do double shifts and work hard he could make as much as twelve shillings, whereas William, he said, being on the broad side and bigger than Jimmy, although only eight, would go in as a trapper. He also put her wise to the fact that they might have to take part of their wages in a food ticket, and that if she wanted a sub on her brothers the buttie would advance her the money at the rate of a penny in the shilling. The ordinary shift, he said, started at five and finished at five.

Jimmy had been sick yesterday but William had been excited and kept larking on and making the others laugh.

She got off the straw-filled mattress that was resting on the wooden platform and, shivering, hastily pulled on her clothes over her petticoat and under-bodice which she had slept in. When she was dressed she groped her way across the uneven floor to where Jimmy, William, Joe, and Annie were sleeping, and, her hands feeling among their heads, she fondled Jimmy's smooth, dark hair and William's crisp, fair hair and shook them gently, and when they grunted she whispered, 'Come on, get up.'

They made shivering, spluttering noises, then Jimmy coughed and said in a small voice, 'What time is it?'

'Coming up to four as near as I can guess,' she answered; 'the sky's lightening. I'll blow the fire up and you'll have a drop of tea afore you go. It'll warm you.'

There was no more conversation, not even when presently they huddled round the fire and drank the hot, weak tea; not until they were ready to go did she speak again, then handing them each three slices of bread and fat tied up in a bait rag she said, 'Make it spin out, it'll be a long day. But I'll have something ready for you when you come in . . . Come on.'

The light was breaking as they climbed the hill and stumbled across the half mile of hillocky land towards the main road and she didn't leave them until half an hour later when they could see each other's faces plainly. Then she nearly brought them all to tears with what she later termed to herself a daft action, for with a swift movement she flung out her arms and hugged them to her, and they clung to her like Annie and Joe would have done until she thrust them off and, turning from them, ran back up the road . . .

They walked for another half hour before they reached the pit. Only once did they speak; that was when the pulleys came in sight and William said in a high, excited voice, 'You frightened, our Jimmy?' And Jimmy, lying bravely, said, 'No; are you?' And William said honestly, 'I don't know now whether I'm frightened or just excited but me belly's wobblin'. Like we'll know more the night.' He laughed his warm laugh but Jimmy did not respond. He already knew what he would know the night.

Inside the yard they were lost amid a bustle of men and boys, some to their joint surprise much younger than themselves and none of them looking as if they had been washed for weeks. Jimmy started and turned 'round quickly when he heard a small boy address the man he was walking with as da. There were three boys with this man. He thought to himself, they must be all like the Fishers and go down with their das. To his fear now was added a deep sense of aloneness and he had the horrifying feeling that he was about to cry. He said to a man, 'Where's the office, mister? We've got to go to the office.' And the man, pointing, said, 'Ower there, lad.'

A man sitting at a narrow, high desk said, 'Yer name?'

and he answered for both of them, saying, 'Jimmy and William Brodie.'

'Who's yer buttie?'

'What?'

'Yer buttie, the man you're workin' for?'

'Oh, I think his name's Pollock.'

'Well, don't stand there; you won't find him here, he'll be at the shaft bottom.'

They went out and joined the crowd standing beneath the pulley way, then they never knew how it happened but they were crushed with four other boys into a small wire cage that suddenly fell into the earth at a terrific speed, causing their stomachs to come up into their throats. When there was a bump they all fell together and tumbled out into what looked like a tunnel, but strangely not an entirely black tunnel. The roof, a few feet above their heads, showed criss-cross pieces of wood holding up big boulders of rock and these pieces of wood were kept in place by nothing more than slender props dotted here and there along the tunnel. In the middle of the tunnel was piled skip on top of skip of coal reaching to the roof.

Jimmy said to one of his cage companions, 'Who's Mr Pollock?' and the boy said, 'Come along o' me.'

Mr Pollock was an almost naked, coal-dusted, under-sized man with two pin-points of light for eyes. He held a lantern above Jimmy's head and said, 'You . . . you the older?' and Jimmy nodded 'Aye, Sir.'

On this the boys who had been in the cage with them all laughed, and the man actually spat on them, then he said, 'You'll go to number four gallery with Harry and Pat here.' He indicated two of the boys. 'They'll show you the ropes. And it's rope you'll get if you don't pull your whack, understand?'

Jimmy did not now say, 'Aye, Sir.'

'Anyroad I'll see how you make out by the end of the day; they'll let me know.' He again nodded at the boys.

'And now you.' The lantern hung over William's fair head. 'You're trappin', young 'un. I'm goin' back up the road; I'll show you yer place. Important job you've got. Aye, 'tis that, important job.' Again there was laughter.

They all began to walk up the road, which still appeared to Jimmy like a tunnel, and they had gone about a hundred yards when he was pulled roughly aside by the man, and he gaped at the sight coming towards him. A boy harnessed by ropes and a chain between his legs was on his hands and knees tugging up the incline a low bogie filled high with coal, while, behind, two small black creatures, heads down, bodies almost horizontal, pushed at it.

'There! them's workers for you.' The buttie's voice was loud with praise. 'Double shift they've done and still goin' at it. But they'll have somethin' to pick up. By lad, aye, they'll have a weighty packet come pay day.'

Jimmy stumbled on, his eyes now standing well out of their sockets, and he started as the man said, 'Here comes the partin' of the ways. This way, me lad,' and he turned to see William being thrust through a low door.

It was in the darkness behind the door that William knew it wasn't excitement that was filling his belly, but swirling, galloping fear. The man now pushed open another low door and here William, who loved noise and laughter and chatter felt the quietness of the grave drop round him like a shroud.

The man was pointing to a rope attached to the door. 'You sit there,' he said, 'and when anybody comes down the road' – he thumbed up the long narrow tunnel – 'you pull on the string and open the door. Then close it again. Now I wasn't funnin' when I said this was an important job, lad. These are the air doors, the life's blood of the mine so to speak. You understand?'

William made the slightest movement with his head.

'Good enough, then. You'll be finished at five the night.'

'Mister?' His voice was a mouse squeak. 'You not goin' to leave me the lantern?'

'Leave you the lantern? What you want to do, read? You're a funny little bugger, aren't you?' The man's laugh seemed to ricochet along the tunnel in an eerie wailing sound, and then he went through the door and William was left with the rope in his hand and in darkness blacker than any night he had ever imagined. The tears were now raining down his cheeks and he whimpered aloud, 'Oh, our Cissie. Our Cissie.'

4

They had been in the cave three weeks and Cissie would have said they were managing, and finely, if it weren't for the picture ever present in her mind of the two small figures spending the long days in the bowels of the earth.

Of the two, she was more concerned for William, for William the merry, as her da had called him, was no longer merry. Never as long as she lived would she forget the sight of them that first night when she had gone to meet them. Both of them as black as climbing boys, they had come stumbling towards her, Jimmy hardly able to speak, so weary was he, his knees and the cushions of his thumbs bleeding. But it was William who had troubled her most, for he had laid his head against her and cried, and she had put him on her back and carried him as if he were a baby.

William no longer cried; nor did he laugh any more, not even on a Sunday when he was free. Strangely he spent most of his Sunday in the river sitting up to his neck in water. Even when it rained he would sit there until she pulled him out. Jimmy, too, washed himself in the river, but afterwards he would sleep nearly all day.

Yet, on the whole, things were working out and looking brighter, for this week, besides them all picking the early taties, she had got Mary settled into a good place. For this she had Parson Hedley to thank. The house was some way off, outside Felling, and was owned by two maiden ladies called the Misses Trenchard; they weren't rich but they were class and they were going to train Mary to be a general. They employed no other servants. Mary was to have a shilling a week and a half-day off once a fortnight and one Sunday a month and, glory of glories, a whole attic bedroom to herself. She was to rise at half-past five in the morning and she would be finished at half-past seven in the evening, after which she could do needlework if she liked. The Misses Trenchard indicated they were doing Cissie a great favour in taking Mary, and that the girl had fallen on her feet. And so thought Cissie.

Another important thing was, with Mary's going, it made one less to sleep in the cave.

Cissie felt very tired on this Sunday morning for she and Jimmy had spent hours during the night trying to arrange the table and the box, the four wooden chairs and the chest of drawers in such a way that it would keep out the worst of the gale that had blown up with the twilight. Having arranged the table end up on top of the drawers and box, they had to dismantle them again when the wind threatened to topple the lot back into the cave and on to the beds.

Parson Hedley's church bell was ringing, which told her it was a quarter to eight. They were all still asleep and she was going to let them lie for another hour. She had made a pan of porridge and it was simmering between bricks on the smouldering fire.

After the storm, the morning was bright and fresh and gave her the urge to walk and stretch her legs, and so she decided not to wait until one of them was awake to send him for the skim but to go herself; it would only take twenty minutes each way. So, taking her mother's black shawl out of the box and picking up a pail, she went out and in the direction of Thornton's farm. Hetherington's was nearer but she had resolved that she would rather walk a hundred miles than spend a farthing with him.

At the top of the rise she stopped for a moment and looked about her. The whole world looked clean; the fells were soft and young in the morning light, their rocks made tender and warm with a dusting of lichen. She could see smoke rising from the chimneys in the hamlet and she felt no bitterness at the sight; for one thing, up here it was free of the stench. She had laid down the law about that the first day they had set up house in the cave; there was no doing it just anywhere, she had warned them; even for number ones they had to go to the holes she had dug. Not one of them had questioned this inconvenient arrangement; it was just as if their da were talking to them.

She had seen only two women from the hamlet since they had come up here. Mrs Snell had brought them a pan of broth on the second day, and Mrs Robinson had given her a loaf of bread, and because one of their hens had died on them she had brought her the head and feet to flavour the turnip soup. The thought had been kind but the result hadn't been tasty.

After a while she dropped down on to the main road. When she came to the high wall of Lord Fischel's estate she continued along it past the North Lodge, then branched off up a narrow cart track to the farm.

She thought afterwards it was a lucky day right from the start, for not only did old Martin serve her and give her a pint extra, but he gave her real milk, and a bit of pig's fat into the bargain.

As she walked back she wondered what it would be like never to have to worry about food, to be able to look at sufficient food to last them all for a week. If that day ever came she would know she had landed in heaven.

While skirting the edge of the quarry she decided that she would bring them here this afternoon and they could have a bit of play as they had done the Sunday before last.

It was as she passed the place where they had sat and saw the remains of the wall that Joe, Charlotte, and Sarah had built when they were playing houses, that the idea came into her head with such abrupt force that it jolted her to a stop, and some milk lapped over the side of the pail.

That was it, walls. That's what she would do, she'd

build walls, three walls round the front of the cave. Hadn't she helped to puddle mud when her da was building the midden in the yard?

She laughed aloud. Why hadn't she thought of it before? All these stones here, hundreds and hundreds of them, they just wanted carting. And they wouldn't have to go down to the bottom of the quarry either.

Now, with the bucket held stiffly outwards to steady it, her legs going between a walk and a trot, she came to the cave and startled them all awake by crying, 'Come on! Come on, the lot of yous. Come on, get up. I've thought of something. You, Bella, push Jimmy.'

'What's it? What's the matter?' Jimmy was sitting bolt upright, his eyes sleep-laden, his mouth agape; William was resting on his elbow; Bella, her knuckles in her eyes, was rubbing sleep away; Sarah had not moved although she was awake, but Charlotte and Joe were kneeling up; only Annie and the baby remained asleep, and, standing before them, the milk pail still in her hand, she said, 'We're going to build walls round on the outside, three walls. An' not dry stone ones either 'cos they could be knocked over. Real ones.'

When no-one asked any questions but just stared at her, she put the pail on top of the chest; then, dropping on to her hunkers and bringing her eyes on a level with theirs, she said, 'Don't you understand? We can build walls round the front.' She flapped her hands backwards. 'It'll keep the rain out and give us more room.'

Sarah pulled herself up slowly from under the patched quilt and asked quietly, 'Will it be a real house then, our Cissie?'

'Well—' her head drooped a little to the side – 'not quite a real house, but . . . but it'll be a dwelling place of sorts. And we can stay here the winter and won't have to worry. And we could make a fireplace inside, eh Jimmy?'

Jimmy blinked, his face thoughtful; then he said, 'It'll

be the roof. How you goin' to put a roof on? Rafters and that; we haven't any wood.'

They all looked at her as she thought for a moment. Presently she said, 'They'll be cutting trees down at Lord Fischel's place come September. The carpenters and coach builders and people like Matthew have picked their trees, and the sawers cut them down and branch them. An' if you know anybody there you can always get bits and pieces. Matthew'll get us some. Anyway, we'll leave that until we come to it; it's gettin' the walls up that's goin' to be the thing. To start with, we'll all carry stones from the quarry and when we get a fair amount I'll put Joe and Charlotte on puddlin' mud down by the burn. You'd like that, wouldn't you—' she bent down towards them, her face bright – 'plodging in mud?' And they laughed and said, 'Aye, Cissie, aye we'd like that.'

'And then the time you, William, and you, Bella and Sarah, are carryin' stones, Jimmy and me will be puttin' them up. We'd do most on a Sunday, but if there's plenty of stones gathered I could be gettin' at it during the week on me own . . . Come on.' She bounced to her feet. 'Get into your things quick and have your porridge and then we'll get started.'

Their eagerness as they tumbled out of bed was shown in varying degrees, and not all enthusiastic.

A few minutes later, Jimmy, pointing to the shale, said, 'You won't be able to do it, our Cissie, 'cos you can't dig in that sort of foundation.'

She stared down at the rock, her face blank now, then said, 'We'll stick plenty of mud on, then set the first stones in it. That should do it.'

When he made no answer to this she looked at him appealingly and muttered under her breath, 'Our Jimmy, we've got to try something. Remember last night, and the winter isn't on us yet; we've just got to try, even if it does blow down.'

57

'Aye, Cissie, aye,' he said.

It had sounded like fun when she suggested their carrying of the stones, but the actual work proved an impossible task for the young ones; even Jimmy and William could only carry medium-sized ones over the distance. It was after the dinner of rabbit and turnips that Jimmy got the idea of using one of the pit methods for conveying the stones from the quarry to the cave. He took a nine-inch board from one of the beds, which meant they would have to sleep head to toe. He sawed it in two and nailed the pieces together; then, burning a hole in each end with a heated poker, he slotted a length of rope through, and on to this rough sledge he tied the biggest and flattest pieces of sandstone he could find, and with the aid of William he pulled them over the rough ground.

It was late in the afternoon, after they had stacked up about forty pieces of stone of varying sizes, when Matthew came to the cave. There was no-one about, but his eyes were immediately drawn to the heap of stones near the entrance. Then in the distance he saw Cissie staggering towards him, her arms cradling a slab that brought her body almost double. He did not run towards her for some seconds, and when he did he took the stone from her before exclaiming, 'God above! What are you up to now?'

'Oh!' She straightened her back and flexed her arms. 'We're going to build walls round the entrance to keep out the weather.'

He turned and looked at her but didn't speak until he had dropped the sandstone among the rest; then, dusting the yellow grit from the sleeves of his Sunday jacket, he said, 'But you don't intend to stay here the winter, do you?'

The smile went from her face; her eyes, looking back into his, held the defiant light he had come to know over the weeks, and her voice was flat as she asked him, 'Where would we go then?' For answer, he said, 'It's hell up here in the winter. You know it is. It's bad enough under a good roof. You'd all perish.'

'Well, if we perish we'll perish together; we're not going into the house, I've told you.'

'I wasn't meaning you to go into the house. I . . . Well, with the lads working I thought you might be able to find a place somewhere.'

Again she asked him a question, 'Where?' and when his eyes turned from hers she did not say what was in her mind, 'You know you can't get a pit house, or a farm cottage around here unless you're married. And I couldn't get a permit to go to another parish because with having no man they'd be feared we'd end up on the rates'; but what she did say was, 'I wouldn't go into the towns, either Jarrow or Shields, not into those stinking hovels. And they ask as much as three shillings a week, so . . .'

She moved away from him now, saying, 'If it's big enough we could have a fireplace inside.' Then turning quickly to him again, she said, 'Do you think you might be able to get us some branches to go across the top? We could stick mud atween them. And away down the river there's a reed bed; we could sort of thatch it in a rough way.'

He stared at her as he said, 'I'll get you all the rough wood you want. I'll be going for my timber in three weeks' time. But you don't want rough wood for up there' – he lifted his eyes to where the level of the roof would come above the opening of the cave – 'you want beams; and well battened down on supports, for a gale of wind could lift the whole lot off. And another thing . . .' He now stamped one foot on the shale and shook his head slowly as he said, 'It'll never hold. I mean you've got to have a foundation; that's the main thing.'

She put her fingers to her lips now and turned her head away, saying, 'Our Jimmy said that, but I thought that if I got a lot of mud and stuck the bricks in it, it would be all right.'

He was shaking his head again. Then, still staring at the rock, he said, 'The only way it would hold as I can see is to roughen it, use a pick on it, so the mortar'll get a purchase.'

'Would that do it?' There was eagerness in her voice now.

'It might; and if you roughed your mortar with bits of chips and pebbles and used sandy mud . . . There's a patch of it at yon side of the burn; I'll show you. It means plodging across every time but it'll be worth it in the long run . . . Have you a pick?' he now asked.

'A pick? Oh yes. And it's a good pick, it was me da's.' She hurried into the cave and came out with the pick to see him taking his coat off and laying it neatly to one side. When he took the pick from her hand, she said, 'But you're not going to . . . ?' and he replied on a laugh, 'Well, do you think I'm goin' to stand and watch you doin' it?' He was holding her gaze again. And now she could not return the look in his eyes and her head drooped and she turned away, saying, 'It's kind of you.'

He said nothing to this but asked, 'How big do you want it?' then watched her walking seven steps from the entrance of the cave. Her pacing brought her feet almost to the point of his, and when, still looking at the ground, she said, 'About here,' he did not answer or move. She lifted her head up. His face seemed to be hanging above hers; his lips were apart, his eyes unblinking, and he said softly, 'I think you're a wonderful lass, Cissie.'

The heat that swept over her body brought beads of perspiration on to her upper lip and her forehead. It brought her heart pumping so strongly under her bodice that she saw the rapid rise and fall of the buttons, and the heat brought with it a sweetness that she could taste in her mouth and smell with her nostrils. It brought with it a joy that made her want to run as she had sometimes done when alone on the fells, when the air had cut sharp against her throat and the sky was blue and endless and everything clean looking.

And then the sweat, the colour, and the sweetness seeped swiftly away to leave her cold as she remembered the woman in the mill who had given them the tea and bread, and whose ugly face had softened as she looked at him and whose voice had sounded musical when she had said his name. And she remembered also that he was Matthew Turnbull, the wheelwright, who worked to support his paralysed father, his mother, his grandmother, and his aunt. He was Matthew Turnbull who was lucky in a way to be favoured by Rose Watson, the daughter of the miller, who was a very warm man, so why was he saying to her 'You're a wonderful lass'? Perhaps because he was of a kindly nature. But the look in his eyes was not that which just came from a kindly nature; she had seen that kind of look before. Now and again her da had looked at her ma like that, sometimes after a bairn was born.

She turned slowly from him, knowing his eyes were tight on her, and she made her way to where the children were dragging the stone-laden sledge, and she had reached them before she heard the first metallic sound of the pick striking the stone.

That night she had the dream of the white house again but it was so enveloped in light that she couldn't make out any part of it.

5

The wheelwright's shop stood at the end of the village of Benham. There were about thirty houses all told in the village and James Turnbull's house was the largest, except for the inn at the other end of the street. The shop itself had the appearance of a stable, having two large double doors that opened outwards into the street. There was a window at each side, and the roof sloped up steeply above the actual shop, and under the apex, set partly in plaster, was a wheel, the hub cracked, the felloes springing out here and there from the rim. It looked, as it had done for the last fifty years, as if it were going to fall from the face of the wall.

At one side of the shop was the yard. It was a big yard and held various neat stacks of timber, besides odd piles. Two old farm carts stood in one corner and a saw pit ran along one wall. At the far end of the yard was a stable with a loft above.

On the other side of the shop was the house. It had a good-sized kitchen and scullery downstairs, besides a small parlour, three bedrooms above, and, lastly, an attic. This latter was Matthew's room, as it had been from the age of five when his grandmother and Aunt Mildred had come to live with them.

Although a six-room house with five people in it could be considered almost empty, Matthew felt the place so crowded that he was barely able to breathe in it. This impression was caused, he knew, by his grandmother's and his aunt's constant presence in the kitchen, and had been added to over the last three years by his father's prone figure in the bedroom and the fact that they all now looked to himself for survival.

Matthew's life, until the day he had been called over to Brookdale to make the coffin for a Mr and Mrs Brodie, had, he would have said, run smoothly, and this in spite of times being bad. When the prosperity of farms went down the demands for carts and wheels and repairs went down; as for households, old buckets weren't renewed but puttied. Still, he made enough to feed them, and keep on one man. And there was no need to really worry about not being able to manage, for always in the back of his mind was the lifebelt in the form of Rose Watson. He knew he had only to say the word and Rose would be his, together with all she would own when her father died, and such a decision would mean living at the mill. But that could only bring pleasure; what didn't bring him pleasure was the thought of Rose herself.

Rose, he considered, was a good lass. She was a wonderful cook and fine housewife, none better, as the mill house showed, and her nature was pleasant, at least to him, although he had heard it said she had a temper. But it wasn't her temper that would worry him, it was the looks of her, the big bulk of her. Yet, as he told himself time and time again, such women generally made admirable wives and mothers; but he also told himself that he had no feeling for her one way or the other, except that she evoked pity in him.

That was how he was feeling prior to making the coffins for the Brodies. Then he had met Cissie; and from the first moment when he had stood in that room which was reeking with death and looked at her, so young, so slight, so lovely, he had known he would never feel the same again. And that experience on the road when she had dissolved into light had set the seal on his life. And as he watched her fight to hold that squad of children together his love for her had rolled away with him, as he put it to himself, like four brand-new wheels on a wagon. Had she stood alone he would have defied his mother and his grannie and brought her into the house.

After his visit last Sunday he knew he must stop seeing her; because she was no fool, she knew what was in his mind, and it wasn't fair, seeing that nothing could come of it. He reasoned that as soon as she got the ramshackle structure up he would cut adrift, but first he must see the place right, before the winter set in.

Sunday, in his home, ran to a pattern. In the morning he drove his mother and his Aunt Mildred in the cart to church; he would sit in the back row and, except when Parson Hedley was preaching the sermon, he would think not of God or religion in any form, but of things that were of importance to him. Until recently, his thoughts had centred around his work, or the lack of it, or the injustices being bailed out to his kind. Sometimes his mind would go over what had taken place at the meeting in Parson Hedley's house the previous night, for Saturday night was the time when he and a few others went for their writing lesson, and the reading. But of late his mind had dwelt on Cissie Brodie and, not unconnected, the demanding needs of his body.

When they returned from the church the dinner would be ready – his grannie bestirred herself once a week to do this task. The dinner served, he would carry a tray up to his father and as he helped him to feed himself he would give him the gist of Parson Hedley's sermon.

He liked his father and it pained him to see him bereft of movement. It was strange how things happened. If he had had to have his back broken you would have thought it would have been while in the sawing pit where he had stood since he was a small boy pulling on one end of the saw while his father above him pulled on the other. But no, it had to be the slipping of a badly stacked tree, the stacking incidentally which he had done himself, that had brought him to this state.

After dinner, the washing-up done, the household went to sleep.

It was on this Sunday when he knew them to be resting that he took the opportunity of harnessing the horse to the cart; then he picked out several lengths of timber and placed them quietly in the cart; but when he mounted the box and made to drive out of the yard, he was checked by the sight of his mother standing grimly in the doorway.

Nancy Turnbull was a tall woman, as tall as her son, but whereas he was broadly built, she was thin to scragginess. Matthew was the only surviving child of five, and she had no love for him for she saw nothing in him that had come over from herself or her side of the family. He looked like his grandfather Turnbull, and he had a nature like his grandmother Turnbull. Her husband had that kind of nature too, close, secretive, stubborn, foolhardy; they did things that could get not only themselves but others into trouble, like the readings her husband had gone to and Matthew still attended. That kind of thing could lead you to gaol. But, after all, these were a small issue to the one plaguing him and herself at the moment, which was this tinker girl living wild in a cave.

She came and stood at the horse's head and stared up at him before she asked, 'Where you going with that lot?'

He returned her stare for some seconds before he said, 'No need to ask about the road you already know, is there?'

'You're not taking that wood out of here.'

He got down from the cart and as he went towards her he moved his hand over the horse's back, pressing hard against its skin, and when he stopped within a foot of her he said, 'Don't come the heavy hand, Mam.'

'Heavy hand?' Her voice was trembling with her anger. 'You've been cartin' stuff away week after week, all this good wood.' She swung her arm wide.

'It's not good wood.' His voice was unemotional. 'Every piece in that cart's faulted.'

'It's well enough for buckets or rakes.'

'It's not. But even if it was I'm still takin' it because' – he paused – 'it's my wood.'

Her long pointed chin drooped towards her chest, pulling her lower lip with it while her eyebrows moved upwards as she brought out, 'Your wood? You have the nerve to stand there and say it's your wood after your dad's worked here all his . . . ?'

'Dad's no longer able to work, an' the place is mine by heritage.'

'You're talkin' as if he was dead.'

'He could be, and you know it; he'll never move again. If I walk out of here the morrow what's goin' to happen to you all? Tell me that. If you thought a little more along those lines you'd know it would be a good plan to keep your nose clean. I've given you the same as me dad did, I've never cut you down. I haven't had a penny meself in wages these last two years, but them in there' – he bounced his head forward – 'they've lived the same, stuffin' their kites, sittin' from one meal to the other not liftin' a hand. And they're your people, they're not mine.'

'Have you gone mad, boy? They're your grannie and your auntie.'

'They're your mother and your sister, and they might have been dad's responsibility but they're not mine. Still, I've taken them on and they can stay as long as they and you leave me alone and don't interfere with this part of the house.' He kicked at a loose stone at his toe, and as it went pinging across the yard she moved slightly back from him as if to see him better.

And now there was just the slightest look of fear on her face. Twice she made to open her mouth, then closed it. But she wasn't wise enough to say no more, she had to blurt out what was in her mind. 'You're a fool!' she said.

'Do you hear? You're a fool; you've got the chance in a million. Any man from here to Newcastle would jump at the chance that's being held out to you. A mill, and his own business at that, the kind that will never fail because people will always want bread.'

'Aye, they always want' – he nodded at her – 'but they cannot always buy. And if they cannot buy, what about the wonderful mill then?'

'Don't be so bloomin' soft; you know for a fact it's not the poor that keeps the mill goin', it's the rich. He's got contacts in all the big houses 'round about. It'll serve you right if somebody else comes along and snaffles her.'

'They'll be welcome.'

'You're mad.' She was almost shouting now. 'Nine bairns they say, she's a scut to take them on the fells.'

'Where else would she take them? Tell me, where else would she take them?'

'There's places.' Her mouth was grim, and her eyes narrowed as she looked at him, and to this he answered, 'Yes, there are places, Mam, as you say, places such as our house. Now' – he pointed at her – 'you be careful, else I just might, and nine of them with her.' On this he turned from her and, having mounted the cart, jerked on the reins and she was forced to step aside. And she stared after him, her expression a mixture of anger and fear.

The following day he walked the horse over to Pelaw and hitched it to an old farm cart that he was bringing back for repair, and it was on the return journey that he came across Cissie and two small black figures on the verge of the road.

Cissie was kneeling beside Jimmy holding him in her arms and they were both crying; William was sitting, his legs straight out, his head bent on his chest, as if asleep.

'What is it?' He was standing over them, and Cissie, raising her head and gulping, said, 'Oh, hello, Matthew. It's Jimmy; he's . . . he's been kicked.'

67

'Kicked? What with, a horse?' He was now kneeling beside her, and she was shaking her head widely as she muttered, 'No; the buttie.'

'Let me have a look.' He pressed the boy from her and pulled down his trouser to reveal a three-inch jagged wound running over his hip bone and a number of bruises around it. It was a moment or so before he said, 'Has he used his boot on you afore?'

'Aye.'

A boot, a man's boot and steel-capped into the bargain. God! he'd like to get his hands on that buttie at this minute, just his hands would be enough; but he knew, were he to touch the man, he would land up in gaol, for who cared about a boy getting the toe of a boot in his backside? Not the keeker, or the manager, or the magistrate. He asked now, 'Why did he do it?'

''Cos . . . 'cos I wouldn't stay on, I was tired. I couldn't pull no more. When I told him he took his boot to me 'cos he said I was messin' up the team. The apprentices, they were all stayin' on. They had to, they've got no say 'cos they're from the house; he'd just knock the daylights out of them.'

Matthew bit on his lip and turned his head to the side for a moment before bending down again and lifting the boy into his arms, saying, 'Come on, we'll get you home.' On the journey he didn't speak, for he felt incensed. Why hadn't some man floored the buttie? But then the miners were like wild beasts themselves. Look at Rosier's lot going on strike, then attacking the farm labourers because they happened to be in work, and therefore eating. And this at the time of the uprising in the south when the farm labourers had stormed the squires and justices in their houses to demand a fair wage of two and threepence a day, and the cavalry and dragoons had been called out, and the gentry offered a thousand pounds to labourers to inform on their fellows! Nine men were hanged over that business, besides four hundred and fifty men and boys being transported. What was life all about anyway? Parson Hedley would have him believe it was all in preparation for the next ... Twaddle, bloody twaddle, and that was swearing to it.

Arriving at the cave, he put Jimmy down on the rough mat and said, 'It should be washed with hot water in case it festers,' and Cissie ran outside to get the fire going, giving directions to the children as she went to keep her supplied with kindling.

Left alone with the two boys, Matthew asked, 'Is it bad down there?' And Jimmy, his head falling on to his chest, muttered, 'Like hell.'

He turned his gaze on William but the boy just stared at him as if he had been struck dumb, and he remembered he hadn't heard him speak a word since they had met, and so he said softly, 'You tired, William?' and the boy made a slight movement of his head while keeping his eyes tight on his face with a look that disturbed him more than the jagged wound on Jimmy's leg, for it was like that of a dumb animal crying for help.

He got off his hunkers and went and stood in the opening. His mind was working rapidly, his thoughts presenting him with suggestions, which while they might mean the saving of the boys, would finally damn himself for life.

He looked at the walls, still no more than two feet high; he looked to where she was kneeling blowing at the embers of the fire underneath the black kale pot. He looked at the children gathered 'round her, like bees 'round their nest, and he said to himself, 'It would be two less,' and on this he went to her, and, touching her on the shoulder, said, 'Come over here a moment.'

Wiping her hands on her apron, she followed him a little way from the cave, but she turned when the baby, lying in the basket in the lee of the wall, began to cry,

'You, Charlotte,' she said, 'pick her up.' Then she walked on and joined Matthew where he had stopped out of earshot of the rest, and she waited for him to speak, all the while rubbing her hands on her apron.

He began by saying, 'His hip will be stiff, he won't be able to walk the morrow. What's more, he's frightened of going down . . .' Her voice interrupted him, harsh sounding as she said, 'You needn't tell me that; I know it, nobody better.'

'And William's scared to death.'

She moved her head slightly in bewilderment. Why was he pressing home something that was tormenting her all the time? Only today she had met Mrs Martin on the road and the woman had said, 'Me man says your lads'll never stick it, they've had it too soft. If they're put down early they get toughened to it.'

'How much are they gettin' a week?'

'William two and six and Jimmy only five shillings. They said it would be six and six or more but they docked him because they said he had slate in his corves; and then he only got half in money, the other half was a ticket for the tommy shop.'

He looked at her hard for a moment before saying, 'I could apprentice him – Jimmy; I want a lad. I could give him two shillings a week and his keep.' My God! he must be stark staring mad. If he could have afforded a lad the rate would only have been ninepence to a shilling.

As he watched the strain seep from her face and a light come on to it that led the way to a smile he said, 'But that'll not be enough for you to manage on.'

She swallowed a number of times and wet her lips before she said softly, 'Oh, Matthew, thank you. Oh, thank you indeed. I'll manage; as long as he's out of that I'll manage somehow.' Her voice stopped abruptly and the light went from her eyes. 'But there's William. He won't go without Jimmy. I'm . . . I'm more afraid for him than I am for Jimmy.'

He turned from her and looked away over the land. The bracken was browning, the heather pods were dry, the sky was low, and there was chill in the air; the land looked bleak, as bleak as his life would be if he were to voice the thought that had come to him a minute ago. Yet if he didn't voice it the obstacles between her and him were as great as ever. In the end it would be too much for him. He already knew this, so why not get something out of it for her before he committed himself finally. He looked back at her and said, 'I may be able to fix up something for William at the mill.'

She gazed at him as if he were God, then whispered, 'Oh, Matthew.' And now her hands stopped working at her apron and she put one forward, and for the first time she touched him. Her long fingers with their broken nails lay for a moment across the back of his hand, but it was only for a moment, for she felt repulsed in some way when he drew his hand away and, turning from her, said, 'I've got to go now but I'll be back some time the morrow. Keep washing his leg.'

She watched him go to the cart, mount it, and drive away before she went back to the fire and, pushing Bella aside, started to blow at it again.

He went through the kitchen, and his grandmother, an older edition of his mother, poked her long turkey-neck forward and called to him as he opened the staircase door, 'What's the matter with you? Devil after you?'

He made no answer, but mounted the stairs to his father's room and, pulling a chair close to the bed, bent forward towards the pale stubbly face, and without any lead-up said, 'I'm taking on an apprentice, Da.'

'Apprentice? What! What do you want an apprentice for? There's not enough work . . .'

71

'Things are looking up. I'm goin' into Jarrow the morrow, and I think I'll get an order for a cart.'

'But you'll have all the winter, and you and Walters can manage . . .'

'I want a boy to train, Da, as you trained me from the hub outwards, from auger-holes, mortising, to spokes and felloes.'

His father stared at him, his dry, blue lips moving one over the other. Then he said, 'If that's what you want you should get yourself a son.'

The light in Matthew's eyes darkened, his lids drooped slightly. 'I might do that an' all but it'll take time. Walter is gettin' on; I don't want to be left high and dry so I'm takin' on a lad.'

'One of that crowd from the fells?'

'Aye, one of that crowd from the fells.'

'Your mother won't stand it, there'll be hell to pay.'

He did not answer, 'I'm running things now; she'll do as I say.' And when his father said, 'It'll be a shilling a week and food, we just can't run to it,' he stood up and looked at him and said, 'I've managed up till now, haven't I? I've never asked you for anything out of the pot.' He turned his head to where an ornamental wooden kale pot, a heavy lock dangling from the lid, stood on a chest of drawers opposite the bed, then said, 'But that's another thing I want to have a word with you about. The haulers'll be collecting the trees next week and you know they want payin' on the spot. Fischel's bailiff's another one. He won't let a tree out of the wood until the cash is in his hand. I'm waiting for a number of bills to be met; if they pay up, well and good; but if they don't I'll have to ask you to dip into the pot . . . What's the matter?' He bent forward as his father slowly turned his head away from him until his cheek was lying on the pillow, and again he said, 'What is it?' and then added, 'Don't think I'll make a regular thing of it; I've never asked you afore.'

James Turnbull slowly turned his face 'round again and his expression was both sad and shamefaced as he muttered, 'There's no pot, at least nothin' left in it.'

Matthew's mouth opened and shut, his eyes screwed up and his body bent further forward before he said, 'Nothing in it? But Grandad left you fifty sovereigns. That's only seven years ago, and trade was good then.'

'Aye, it was good then, but it stopped the following year and we had three black ones in a row, an' like you I was waitin' for them to pay up. Some of them never did. They couldn't 'cos their farms were sold up. It was then I had to dip into it. There was nothing in it long afore this happened.' He pointed to his shoulder.

Matthew was speechless. He had always felt, in a way, that the business was secure because of the pot, which he thought his dad had been adding to over the years. This piece of news was like a cord 'round his neck; he felt he was being strangled, and not slowly either.

'I'm sorry, lad.'

Matthew was turning away when he stopped and asked, 'Does Mam know?'

'No; I wanted no misunderstandings; she got her weekly money, and that was that.'

When he reached the bottom of the stairs his mother was waiting for him. One doubled-up fist in the hollow of her hip, the other hand holding her chin as if it were a handle, she demanded, 'What's all the hurry for, what's happened? You seem to be in a tizzy.'

'I'm in no tizzy.' His voice was flat and he kept it so as he gave her the information. 'I'm taking on an apprentice. I went up to tell him. I'm putting him over the stable; he'll eat with us.'

'You've what!' Now she had both fists on her hips and her voice was on the point of a screech. 'Did I hear aright? You're takin' on an apprentice with things as they are?'

'That's what I said.'

'A-ah!' The exclamation came out on a long breath. 'It's one of that tribe I suppose. Well, let me tell you I'm havin' none . . .'

'You're givin' him his meat.'

'Oh! am I?'

'Aye.'

'Well, master' – she bridled – 'I suppose you'll be givin' me an extra two shillings a week.'

'I'm giving you nothing extra, you can all eat a bit less.' He swept his gaze over his grannie and his aunt sitting idly, one each side of the fire, and was making his way out of the kitchen when his mother exclaimed with deep finality, 'Well, if I don't get it from you begod! I'll have it out of the pot.'

He laughed a harsh grating laugh before saying, 'You'll be lucky. I'm going to tell you something, goin' to tell you all something. The pot's empty, an' it has been for years.'

Now he had silenced them.

He went out into the yard again. He must go to the mill when the mood was on him because if he waited till the morrow his courage might fail him. He knew that old Watson did not want another apprentice but if he picked his words and made them imply, 'You do this for me and I'll do what you've been at me to do for years,' it would work.

He was mounting the cart when his mother came through the side door and, gripping the horse's bridle, stared up at him and ground out bitterly, 'I'll go into the town and have the law put on her. I'll tell them she's a bad lot; indecent, having men up there. And I can prove that with you yourself. Don't you think you'll get the better of me in this.'

In a flash he was down from the cart and facing her, and, his voice as bitter as hers, he said, 'You lift your hand to her in any way and you'll potch yourself for life. I'll walk out of here as if you had never been, and leave the lot of you. Understand that now. Understand. I'll go off on the road, taking them all with me, and set up some place else. And don't think I can't do it, I could do it all right, any minute.'

As he drove away from her embittered gaze he thought to himself, Aye, he could do it all right, but he wouldn't.

It was late the following evening when he saw Cissie again. He had been in Jarrow all day and got the order for the cart. The man had wanted it made to his own dimensions for hawking coal round the towns, and the business and haggling had gone on for hours. He had returned home to a silent house, not only the womenfolk against him, but also his father blaming him for having given him away. And as he sat down to a cold scratched meal he thought grimly that there would be advantages in living at the mill; the food would be good, the comforts would be those he had never experienced before, and Rose would be pleasant. Her face was homely when she smiled. She had smiled at him last night. 'You'll be over on Saturday, Matthew?' she had said with meaning in both her tone and eyes. 'I'll wait the meal for you at six.' So tomorrow he would don himself out in his best coat, his good shirt and breeks and he would go to Rose and say . . . what would he say? 'Would it be too much to ask you to marry me, Rose?' He'd put it like that because at bottom he couldn't bear to hurt people, and not anyone handicapped in the way Rose was. But tonight he would go to Cissie, for besides giving her the news there'd be something he would ask of her, for the one and only time.

The dusk was deepening when he approached the cave. The children were all abed and there was no sound from them. Cissie was sitting on the stone wall. It seemed as if she were waiting; and before he got down from the cart she rose and went to meet him.

'I'm sorry I couldn't make it afore.'

She looked up at him as she said, 'That's all right.' Then

they walked together around the bluff of rock, and when he stopped abruptly, she too stopped.

'How is he?' he asked first.

'His leg's stiff,' she said. 'He couldn't have gone in any case.'

'I fixed them both up.'

She joined her hands tightly against her breast as he went on, 'Jimmy's to come to us, as I said, at two shillings a week, and William's to start with Miller Watson; but all I could get for him was one and six.' He did not say that he had had to bargain for the extra sixpence, or that the one and six a week had bonded himself for life. He saw through the dim light that her eyes were full of tears, that her gratitude was making her dumb, and he had the desire, stronger than any he had yet felt in his life, to take her in his arms, to roll with her in the heather, to . . .

When her hands came out to him, he took them both and pressed them into his chest, and when she said brokenly, 'Oh, Matthew! I haven't any words to tell you me thanks,' he drew her closer and, looking down into her eyes, he said, 'I've got to tell you, you'll hear something in the next few days that, that might upset you, it's about something I've got to do. I've looked for a way out, but there isn't one. I'm caught in a cleft stick, I've got to do it. But this I want you to know. Me heart's yours, and as long as it's in me body it'll be like that. Now—' he paused and champed at the saliva in his mouth before, his lips scarcely moving, he asked, 'Can I kiss you?'

It was some seconds before she closed her eyes and when his mouth touched hers they became still, their joined hands keeping their bodies apart, until of a sudden his arms going round her, he pressed her to him, and his lips covered her face like a ravenous man attacking food.

Then it was over as abruptly as it had begun. She was standing alone swaying on her feet and he was walking away, as he had done last night, only now he was running

76

towards the cart, and she knew that this was the end of something that had hardly begun, for the news that she would hear during the next few days was that he was going to marry Rose Watson, and instinctively she also knew that William's apprenticeship had settled a matter that had been pending for a long time.

The first Sunday that the boys came home, their faces clean, their clothes tidy, they handed her their money, and William also proudly put into her arms a sack in which there were two loaves, a bag of oatmeal, some pig's fat, and a big hunk of cheese, and she didn't thank him for it, nor tell him to take back thanks to Mistress Watson, but he fully understood – she was too overcome with the generosity of the gift to say a word. But the rest of the family made their thanks very verbal.

Part of her heart rejoiced that the boys were back to their old selves again, or at the beginning of new selves, for they vied with each other in showing off to the rest and talking of their respective trades. While William bragged of the twenty sacks of flour the mill had ground in one week, and demonstrated how he cranked the handle of the flour-boulter, Jimmy also demonstrated how he turned the great wooden wheel that worked the lathe. He talked of shell augers and spoon augers, and gave the impression that he managed the saw pit, not just standing down below guiding the great saw along the chalk mark, but up above taking full responsibility for the straightness of the cut. He spoke of the stink of elm and the pleasing smell of ash as if he had dealt with wood all his life.

It was a grand day for both of them and Cissie tried to joy with them. It wasn't until late in the afternoon when she sat on the wall nursing the baby that she looked at Jimmy and realised how much she had missed him, for he was the only sensible one of them all she could talk to – Bella was a scatter-brain.

Jimmy was twirling a brown ringlet on the baby's forehead with his finger when he asked quietly, 'You all right, our Cissie?' and she answered with forced brightness, 'Aye, of course. Why shouldn't I be? Three of you settled, and now I can get on with the wall. I must put a move on.' She patted the rough stones to her side. 'We didn't get much chance last week with gathering the last of the bilberries and the wortles, and the mushroom pickin' – we cleared twenty pounds of them . . . Oh, I didn't tell you. I went into Shields and sold them at the big houses. I had only to go to three.'

'All that way?' he said. 'Nigh on nine miles there and back!'

She laughed at him, saying, 'Well, we did it afore.'

'Aye.' He nodded; then stooping, he picked up a chip of sandstone and hurled it away into the distance, and with his back half turned to her he said, 'Matthew's gonna marry Miss Rose from the mill. Did you know that?'

When he turned and looked at her her head was level, her eyes answering his; and then she said quietly, 'Aye, I knew about it.'

Again he picked up a stone and hurled it. 'I thought he had cottoned on to you?'

It was some time before she said, and as if speaking with the wisdom of years, 'Well, how could he, with nine of us? And from what I can gather he's got his own problems.'

'Aye, he has.' He glanced sideways at her now, saying, 'I don't like his mother, nor the old 'uns, but I like him.' Then walking a few steps from her he asked, 'Did you manage to get a rabbit this week?' and after a moment she answered, 'No, I'm no good at it. I can't hit them an' finish them off. But I miss the stew. It was a grand standby.' She paused, 'Do you think you could show Joe?'

He turned to her now, his eyes bright. 'Aye, I could. He's comin' up five, he should be able to knock a rabbit out. And another thing he should be able to do.' He came up to her now, his face eager, his voice low. 'Get through a hole I've made in the bottom of the manor wall. The rabbits are gettin' fly; there's so many huntin' them on the fells that they're taking to cover, they're not daft. An' just afore I started at the pit—' he paused as if the memory alone could frighten him, then went rapidly on, 'I found some loose masonry at yon end of the manor wall that's covered with thicket, going Brockdale way, near the North Lodge, an' when I pulled the stones away I found I could get through. That's where I got the whopper, you mind the big 'un. I didn't let on, 'cos if the others had come along of me they would have made a noise and given us away.'

She was standing now; she had the baby across her shoulder and was patting its back in evident agitation as she said, 'Eeh! no, Jimmy, don't show him in there. He could be locked up if he was found catchin' rabbits on that land, the lord's.'

'But nobody'll catch him in there – it's all thicket and bramble. Anyway, if they chased him they couldn't get through the hole; I just made it big enough for me, and the gate's some way off an' the walls all five foot high and you can hardly see any bit of it for bramble. The place is a real rabbit run. I came across it one day when I saw one boltin' into the scrub and I followed through a badger run an' there was the rabbit's hole just this side of the wall, so I guessed it came up t'other side. It was then I saw that the mortar had gone in parts from atween the stones, an' it was easy to pull a few out.'

She stared at him for a moment, her hand on the back of the child's head now; then she asked, 'You sure there wouldn't be any danger of the keepers catchin' him?'

'No.' He laughed derisively. 'He would hear them comin' a mile off; it's a tangle I tell you, except for a path that runs between the bramble an' the wood, an' that's strewn with dry dead brittle an' anybody stepping on it would sound like the crack of a gun. No, there's no need to worry. Anyway, Joe's cute; he'll be smart will Joe when he grows. I'll go and get the trap.' He ran a few steps from her, then turned, and, smiling broadly now, he cried, 'I bet that once he gets the knack you'll never want more.'

As she watched him running into the cave where the trap was hidden at the bottom of the chest she repeated to herself, 'Never want more.' Because he was going to show Joe how to trap and kill a rabbit, they would never want more. She shook her head and smiled wearily.

But how was she to know that she was listening to a prophet?

BOOK TWO

The House of Fischel

1

It is a known fact that a devil of one generation can be the means of producing a saint for the next. This had happened in the house of Fischel, with one difference; it had taken a number of devils and a number of generations to produce a saint.

The long gallery on the first floor of the house showed the portraits of all the male Fischels; the first was given his title by Queen Elizabeth in 1573, together with Houghton Hall and land to the extent of three hundred acres in the County of Durham, such gift being for services rendered. The chroniclers had never stated the nature of the services, and the descendants, up to the present day, had not thought it expedient to probe this matter, although they were aware that it was only the timely death of the Queen in 1603 that saved the early Fischel from losing the generosity of his Queen, together with his head.

There was a saying come down in the family that likely had its roots in the activities of the first Fischel. It went: If a man turns his coat he must be prepared to wear it inside out. But the implication of the saying had changed, for it now stressed the integrity and honour of the family, implying that their ancestors might have been devils, but devils with honour.

The last devil had been the present Lord Fischel's grandfather and the deadliest of the bunch it was said, and John Horatio James Fischel, the present holder of the title, hadn't a doubt of this. He had met his grandfather only twice, the first time at the funeral of his grandmother, the second occasion on the night before he died. The chaise had come pell-mell to his home, which lay thirty miles from the Hall, and the steward brought the message that his grandfather was dying after being savagely kicked by one of his horses, and that he wished to see his son and his grandson. There had been no invitation for his sister, Anna, who was the eldest, nor his brother, Henry, yet that had been understandable since Henry was only four years old then. He remembered being very cold on the long ride to the Hall and then very hot when he stood in his grandfather's bedroom, for there was a fire blazing that would have roasted an ox.

It was when he had mounted the step to the bed and could see his grandfather plainly that he knew he was making his first acquaintance with the devil. It wasn't only the red face, the black eyes, the pointed eyebrows, and wild-looking grey-streaked hair; it was the shape of him, for his stomach pushed up the bedclothes into a great mound.

On the day his grandfather was buried, his father had said to him, 'He has all of eternity in which to repent, yet I doubt whether it will be long enough.' And that was the only time his father mentioned his grandfather's name to him.

But he hadn't lived at Houghton Hall a matter of days before he had the whole history of his grandfather; and if he hadn't heard it within that time it is doubtful whether he would ever have heard it at all, for within a week his father had made a clean sweep of the servants, old Taplow, the coachman, included; and it was Taplow, who had always been an ardent admirer of his grandfather, who had given him the unsavoury history.

First and foremost, Taplow had stated that His Lordship was a real man, the terror of the county not only with a horse and the bottle, but with the women. He had liked them young, said Taplow; he had always liked them young, and virgins. He'd give you five pounds if you brought him a virgin, but only a pound if she'd been used, even if she was young. In that way, said Taplow, he had kept many a family from starving come winter. And, he had pointed out, not only had you to look round the villages and the farms for the Fischel nose and the black eyes, for in more than one big house he had left his mark. And another thing: when a couple on the estate were going to be married, if the fellow was wise he'd let His Lordship do the breaking in . . . Aw, he had been a lad, had His Lordship, and there had been some goings on in the house. Send the mistress up to London, he would, to buy new clothes, and then high jinks, low jinks. Farmers threatened him with their guns. Aye, but he always got his own back on those; he had his ways, and whether they liked it or not he added one more to their stock.

It was because of Taplow's disclosure that John Fischel understood his own father. His father had always been a stern man, hard but just. From his earliest years he remembered the small family of five and ten servants meeting each morning at eight o'clock in the Hall for prayers. This was repeated at seven in the evening except when his father was away on business. Sunday was one continuous prayer, broken only at three o'clock when they had their one meal of the day.

As the years went on one trait alone of his grandfather showed in his father. This was the love of land. Yet at the beginning of the century when yet another Enclosure Act was passed, his father had openly condemned his grandfather for enclosing most of the small farms and cottages, thus enlarging his estate, which by the same method previously used had already reached six hundred acres. But it was this very land, he knew, more than the great grey stone house, that had brought his father back to his beginnings when he came into the title, and from the start he showed himself to be the antithesis of his father in that he feared God and ruled with justice, which sometimes took a whip in its hand to wipe out wickedness.

At sixteen he himself had felt the whip because he had dared to say, 'Be damned.' And the whip, delivered around the ankles of his sister while she obligingly held up her skirt the required inches above her shoes, would have guided her into a Convent had she been a Catholic. What it did was to make her the wife of a Minister more than twice her age, much to their father's displeasure, for the Minister happened to belong to the Church of Scotland.

The whip of justice took his young brother, Henry, to France at an early age and there he married a French lady of good family.

Although he himself had suffered from the whip of justice more than either his brother or sister he knew he was the only one of the three who had really loved his father. His father may have been hard but it was hardness aimed against evil, as was the hardness in himself.

Sometimes in the night his conscience would question the hardness and would ask, 'Was it because of it that his life had been shattered, that his honourable name had been dragged through the mud, and his career in Parliament choked as it was beginning to draw breath?' But the answer his conscience got was, 'No; all this was the result of his blindness in marrying a woman who, in her own way, was as evil as his grandfather had been in his.'

But now at the age of forty-eight, Lord Fischel was a lonely, embittered man, looking much older than his years and asking himself on this particular day as he dressed to go down to dinner what he was going to do with his son and daughter. The responsibility for their future, he admitted, was his but the fact irked him greatly. They had irked him since they were born. He had never liked the idea of twins, thinking that such children could only be half of their true selves. The man would have too much of the woman in him and the woman too much of the man, and this theory, he knew, had worked out in his son and daughter. His son, who should be applying himself to serious subjects preparatory to going to the University of Oxford, as he himself had done, could think of nothing but painting . . . Painting! Whereas his sister, who should be content to learn the business of running the household, together with the accomplishments of embroidery and music, and perhaps an extra language, galloped the country on a horse, never walked when she could run, talked loudly, laughed loudly, and always kept her head level when she prayed. It was a pity, he thought at times, that he hadn't used the whip of justice on them.

They had only been returned to the house a fortnight and the quiet order and routine of his life had been shattered, and was likely to be for some months ahead, for in four weeks' time he must open the London house and face the veiled looks and revived memories in order to launch them, at least Isabelle, into society.

He couldn't understand now how he had been per-suaded into the matter, but his sister-in-law, Helen, had pointed out in her letters that the girl was at an age for a suitable marriage, and in her opinion the sooner it was accomplished the better. Although his sister-in-law had the disadvantage of being a French woman who, since the revolution of 1830, had lived in Heidelberg, and had done her best during the last two years to instill into his daughter the graces necessary for social life – though he had to admit that for most of the time there was little evidence of her efforts – she was a woman of common sense and propriety.

Fate having dealt him the blows it had, he wondered why the Lord in His wisdom had not seen fit to give him children whom he could love. It was strange, he pondered, but as the years went on this feeling for the need to love increased rather than diminished. Looking back, he couldn't see one human in his life whom he had really loved, not even Irene. The feeling he'd had for her, he knew now, had never been love. Her ever smiling lips and laughing eyes had caused him to crave her body, and when he had accomplished that and found it was all she had to offer, and had turned from her constant demands, she had proffered her favours elsewhere, not discreetly, which he might have borne, if not forgiven, but openly, until her name became a byword. When she had at last left him, and for a man younger than herself, his head became bowed with shame; and even now, eight years later, he was still unable to hold it upright although he gave no outward sign of this.

As his valet helped him into his jacket he heard the sound of trotting horses coming up the drive and he turned his head in the direction of the long window and thought, 'That'll be Bellingham.'

Hugh Bellingham was his nearest neighbour, in his own class – and yet not quite in his own class, for he was in commerce, not just holding shares but actively so. Concerning himself greatly with the new railroads, Bellingham represented the powerful middle class that was clawing the power from the old reigning families, of which he considered the Fischels one of the foremost. Yet Bellingham was his only link with the outside world, the outside world in this case being London, and he was eagerly awaiting news from there, yet at the same time afraid of what he might hear.

The news that he was anxious to hear did not concern the political situation of the moment, but the gossip that surrounded the woman who was still his wife, and who would remain so until one of them died. For he considered the very thought of divorce evil. Bellingham's letter of three days before had conveyed to him the disturbing fact that his wife had dared to return to town, and this time with an Italian much older than herself who bore the title of Count and who presumably had unlimited wealth.

The situation that now troubled him was this: If

Bellingham brought him the news that his wife was aiming to set up an establishment in London, he could not possibly take up residence there; in which case what was he going to do with those two along the corridor?

The dinner was almost at an end. It had begun with Flemish soup, followed by turbot and fried smelts, after which came roast haunch of venison with vegetables. This in turn was followed by roast grouse and the meal ended with charlotte russe of which Isabelle had two helpings. She was very fond of puddings; in fact she was very fond of food altogether, yet no matter what amount she ate it did not show itself in flesh, for although seventeen in three days' time, her hips looked nonexistent and her chest almost as flat as her brother's.

As she began her second helping of pudding she made an almost imperceptible movement with her eyelid towards her brother sitting opposite, then slanted her eyes ceilingwise for a second, which caused him to cough and put his hand to his mouth.

No-one would have taken the brother and sister for twins for they were quite unlike each other in looks, nor did either show any resemblance to the man sitting at the head of the table, nor would there have been any resemblance to their mother had she been present. Clive Fischel, it was said, took after his maternal great-grandmother and was of unusual fairness, while Isabelle looked the image of her paternal great-grandfather. She only had to stand in the gallery and look at the three portraits of that notorious gentleman and she saw herself at the ages of twenty, thirty, and forty. Since she had been a child, she had taken a secret pride in resembling her great-grandfather, and only she knew that the resemblance was not in her exterior alone. Over the years she had gotten into the habit of talking to the portrait of the elegantly dressed youth and at times led herself to believe that the full sensual lips were answering her.

Only this morning, after the wearisome ritual of prayers and breakfast, she had stood in the gallery and said to the bold, dark face, with its nose seeming to protrude out of the canvas, 'I'm weary; I'll erupt if I don't get away from here. There's another month before I go to town. Heidelberg and Aunt Helen had its drawbacks but it was a wild life compared with this. What am I going to do?' She had watched the lips move and she had imagined a deep, throaty voice saying, 'Live!' And she had answered it by asking, 'But how?' And to this the portrait had only smiled.

Her home she considered to be a cross between a monastery and a convent where her father ruled like a prior, and the housekeeper, Mrs Hatton, a mother superior. She had voiced this to her brother as a rather clever quip.

She didn't like her father; but then she liked so few people. She often thought about this, her dislike of people. There was only one person in the wide world for whom she had any affection, and that was Clive; yet even towards him her feelings were mixed. She could say that she loved him, yet at the same time she hated him because he was so ineffectual. She, like her father, thought their sexes had gotten mixed up – she should have been the man; she was the vibrant one.

She looked at her brother now. She could make him laugh; she had power over him in a number of ways and he could read her every sign. Her raised eyes that had caused him to splatter had indicated her opinion of the quality of the conversation. The conversation should have been of interest to her as her father and Mr Bellingham were talking of London, but it was the political London they were discussing, not the social London. She turned her head and looked in Bellingham's direction as he said vehemently, 'That Sadler, not satisfied with attacking the enclosures, he's now pressing the Ten Hours Bill. The Second Reading was in March and if we're not careful he'll get it through. Did you ever know anything like it? They're asking for trouble; Malpass's philosophy is the only remedy and those with any sense know it. It's only through poverty and hunger that the population can be kept at balance; feed the mob and where are you? And he wants to bar the employment of children under nine . . . He wants to bring the country to ruin; burn it down in fact, for where will they get the climbing boys? They're too big over nine. And on a ten-hour day mill owners will go bankrupt. And think of the reorganisation in the mines this will cause. The man's mad. Him and his committee, he's had it running hell for leather from April, and it holds out the kind of policy that could bring this country to its knees. You've never read such nonsense as is in his report, such piffling little things as wanting to eliminate strappers from the mills. Where will you get boys to work unless they're strapped? – boys are lazy by nature. He talks about them being crippled and deformed and old at twenty. Of course they're old at twenty, they've got to be old at twenty. It's as Malpass said: "The population must be kept down, at least the populace." Moreover we know the bishop's words are right: "Everything is the will of God, and poverty and hunger is the cross the poor have to bear." You cannot understand, John, can you' – Mr Bellingham now leaned towards his host as he put the question – 'the stupidity and short-sightedness of such men as Sadler?' He did not wait for an answer but went on, his voice loud now. 'And he's not alone. This is serious. Men who you'd think would know better because the Bill is against their interests are showing sympathy with it. There's this John Wood of Bradford. He's not only employing a doctor in his mill but has put baths on the premises. Can you believe it? You'll not believe this either, but he's sent his overseer up to the committee to tell them of all the harm that can come to children employed too early and made to work over twelve hours. I tell you, things are coming to a pretty pass.' He held out his glass to his host to be refilled and ended, 'You're well out of it, well out of it, John.'

Lord Fischel moved his head twice and murmured, 'Yes, yes.' Then reaching over, he filled his son's glass with port. But there was no glass in front of his daughter to be refilled. His daughter wasn't allowed wine, although she had dared to protest to him during their first meal together that they drank nothing else but wine in Heidelberg.

He now looked at her and gave her the signal that she could leave the table, and knew a rising anger when she didn't take the cue straightaway. It was almost five minutes later before she rose and made her exit.

Going into the drawing room, she flopped down on to a deep couch before the open fire and, putting her hands behind her head, she stretched out her legs in a most unladylike fashion and muttered, 'Mein Gott! Mein Gott!' Then, her head still back, she rolled it first one way, then the other, taking in the room, the faded tapestries on the heavily upholstered chairs, the black carved Chinese cabinets, the spindle-legged occasional tables, the faded rose velvet curtains with their heavy betasselled pelmets, the carpet, thick, but the colours faded to neutrality, and overall, and in spite of the crowded furniture, the great emptiness that pervaded the room. But then the emptiness pervaded the whole house, and there was the sameness about everything, and a great heavy, weighing dullness. If she had her way she would sweep every piece of furniture and drapery into the park and have an enormous bonfire. She's bring decorators in and have the place painted in pearl grey and white. She'd put one picture on a wall and nothing more, except in the gallery, and even there she'd make a sweep. Yes, she'd make a sweep there all right, everything would go except the portraits of her great-grandfather.

When the door opened and the second footman came in with a skip of logs while apologising to her for disturbing her, she stared at him. His livery was brown, his stockings were brown, and his shoes were black. He could not be very old but he looked lifeless. When he bent over the fire she had the desire to take her foot and kick it into his buttocks and knock him sprawling over the basket of glowing logs, thinking, as she saw the picture of the incident screened in her mind, that it would take something like that to make him come alive. She didn't like servants, she had never liked servants; they whispered and talked among themselves. But of all the servants in the house there were two she disliked with particular venom, the butler, Hatton, and his wife. They ruled the place. Their faces were sombre, unsmiling. This, she thought, was because they patterned themselves on her father. She had already decided that when her father died and Clive took over she would sweep the lot of them out, as her grandfather had done, but for a different purpose.

It did not seem strange to her that she never saw Clive's wife ruling the house, for she never imagined Clive marrying. All Clive cared about was painting. She herself would marry, she was sure of this, because the feelings inside her told her she must; and she and her husband would rule here while Clive lazed his days away with his paint brush. It was all very clear in her mind.

When the door opened and her brother entered she straightened herself on the couch and waited until he was seated beside her before she said, 'Terrible, wasn't it? Ten Hour Bills, poverty, factories.' She added laughingly, 'Would you like to go into Parliament?' And he, now leaning his head back against the couch, said lazily. 'Too expensive. If you haven't a mine, a factory, or a shipyard you've got to buy votes.'

93

'Have you really?' She raised her eyebrows at this, and he nodded and said knowledgeably, 'Yes, it can cost you anything from ten to fifty thousand pounds to be elected.'

'Oh, don't bother.' She pushed him playfully, adding, 'Buy some paints.'

At this they both dropped their heads together and laughed; then she asked, 'What are we going to do?'

'Sleep.'

'You'll not, you lazy thing.'

'I'm full, replete, packed right up to here.' He placed his hand on his throat.

'Let's go out for a walk.' She pulled herself to the edge of the couch and tugged at him; but he lay supine, saying, 'Walk! Oh God, I couldn't.'

She now bent over him, her face close to his, and whispered on a wide laugh, 'You nearly let that slip in front of Father, didn't you, at the beginning of dinner?'

'Huh! yes, I did.' He pulled himself upwards now and, his long pale face dropping into sombre lines, he said, 'It's a bit much having to watch your every word; I think I'll be glad when I'm back at school.'

'Well' – she stood up abruptly – 'you've got another six weeks, and we're not just going to sit here, rising up only to pray and eat, until we go to London; we're going to do something.' Swiftly now she bent forward and, gripping his hands, jerked him to his feet, crying, 'Come on, we're going to walk right to the end of the park. We'll go and see one of the farmers, Thornton.'

'Oh, Belle.'

'Never mind, "oh Belle"; go and change your shoes, and don't come out wrapped to the eyes because you'll be sweating by the time we're finished . . .'

Ten minutes later they crossed the great stone-walled hall with the open fireplace at one end that held fire dogs three feet high and showed lead-coloured suits of armour standing like sentinels at the foot of the stairs. They went down the broad, shallow stone steps on to the gravel drive, across this and down another flight that led to the sunken lawns, then through the gardens to the park, and the farther they walked into the parkland the more wild it became until only the paths were clear, their view being checked on either side by mounds of bramble, bracken, and scrub. And the sight seemed to infuriate Isabelle, for she exclaimed angrily, 'It's a disgrace! He should have all this cleared. Do you think it's Todd's fault?'

'No, of course not. Father must have told him to let it go. Anyway, it deters intruders, and I rather like it wild like this.'

'It's gotten worse,' she said. 'Last year you could see the lodge from about here . . . What's that?' They both stopped and looked at the tangle of brambles to the side of them.

'Fox; likely got his hole in there.'

'It won't be a fox,' said Isabelle knowledgeably. 'He would have scurried long before this; and there was a squeak as if from something in a trap.'

She took her walking stick and beat at the top of the bramble, then pressed it aside with her foot, and as she did so there came another scurrying sound. And now she cried to her brother, 'Come on! Poke your stick and see what's there.'

Laughing, Clive poked his stick vigorously until it touched something soft, then he beat the bramble aside to disclose first a small fair head, then with another movement of his stick there was revealed the figure of a small boy crouched on his haunches, a rabbit lying limp across his knees, its forelegs still attached to a crude wire trap.

'Well, I never!' Clive laughed softly, while Isabelle, after a moment of staring, demanded coldly, 'Who are you?'

The small figure, all eyes and mouth, did not reply. There was no movement from him whatever; he could have been cast in stone, an ornament in the garden, so still was he.

'Answer me! Who are you? How did you get in here?'

'He could be one of the children from the farm.' Clive was still smiling.

'He's not. Look at him; he's from outside.' She reached over and down and grabbed the narrow shoulder, then relinquished it immediately, not only because the boy let out a high squeal, but because she realised that her bare hand had come in contact with a ragged soiled shirt.

For no reason that she could explain at that moment the sight of the child infuriated her. He was from outside and represented the populace, dirty, ignorant, animal-like, crippled, old at twenty, one of those who should die early to keep the population level. Mr Bellingham's theories were flashing through her mind, and she had sympathetic leanings towards them now.

'You're a poacher. You could go to prison.'

'Leave him be; it's only a rabbit, and he's only a child.'

Now she turned furiously on her brother. 'Leave him be? Don't be silly, Clive. That would be a licence to have him scaling the wall, have them all scaling the wall.'

Clive Fischel stared at his sister. Sometimes Isabelle frightened him, she was so intense, and about the most odd things. This was only a child poaching a rabbit. Likely he was hungry. Once or twice lately he had thought about people being hungry, but he hadn't dwelt upon it. It was a worrying matter and he didn't like to worry; he wanted life to be quiet, calm, the sun to shine and time to stand still, to stand still for ever so he need never stop painting. He hadn't opposed his father as yet, but he knew he was going to because he meant to paint, paint all the time. But what was Belle up to? 'Look.' He put his hand on her arm as she now took her stick and prodded the boy out of the brambles on to the path. 'What are you going to do with him?'

'I'm going to teach him a lesson.'

She had no hesitation in picking up the dead rabbit and the trap, and when, disengaging her skirt from the brambles, she turned to the child to see him sitting in the middle of the grass drive, his feet straight out, his hands tucked under his buttocks, she was not to know that this was the characteristic attitude of Joe whenever he knew he was going to get his backside smacked for some mischief. But he could not have sat in a better position for her purpose, for after deftly disengaging the rabbit from the wire, she bent down and as deftly hooked it round the boy's ankle; and at this Joe let out another scream and, hitching himself rapidly back from her, still on his buttocks and dragging the trap with him now, he yelled out a name, 'Cissie! Our Cissie!'

When her hand caught his ankle again and he screamed, scream after scream, Clive tried to pull her aside, and, shouting now, he cried, 'Belle! What's the matter with you? Stop this!'

She stood up. Her eyes still on the child and seeming unaware even of her brother, she spoke as if to herself, saying, 'Whichever way he got in he'll not get out with that on.'

'But you can't do this.' As he went to stoop down to the boy she pulled him aside with a strength greater than his and muttered, 'We'll leave him there to cool until we come back this way, then I'll let him go.'

'Cissie! Cissie! Our Cissie!'

Joe's screeching was ear-splitting now and the anguished sound brought Clive again to the child's assistance, only to have Isabelle drag at him so fiercely that she almost knocked him on to his back, the trunk of a tree saving his fall, and he stood leaning against it staring at her. Once before he had seen Belle act like this; it was on the day they learned their mother had left them. She had kicked her dog and maimed it so badly that the keeper

97

had to shoot it. He had been afraid of her on that day as he was afraid of her now, as if her attacks were directed against himself; yet on that day her attitude had created a frenzy in him, for the yelping of the dog had torn through his brain and of a sudden he had turned on her and had shaken her as their pet had been wont to do with a rat. Now as then, he was about to turn on her in defence of this dirty, snivelling creature who was not much bigger than the dog, when his eyes were lifted to the top of the wall, and there to his amazement he saw a girl pause for a moment on its crest as she took in the scene below her before dropping down into the undergrowth. She was hidden from his sight until, a minute later, she came thrashing her way through the bramble and almost to the feet of Isabelle.

She was a girl, he saw, about their own age, tall and straight but raggedly dressed, her mass of brown hair in great disorder where it had been teased by the brambles, and her hands bleeding. Her face pastel white, her eyes large and fierce were yet filled with horror.

'Who are you? What are you doing here? How dare you come into the grounds!'

Cissie stared up sideways into the haughty dark face above her while she bent down and cupped Joe's head as his hands clutched wildly at her legs. Then seeing the wire attached to his ankle she let out a cry that could have been wrenched from an animal itself, and, reaching forward, she tore at the wire until his foot was free. Flinging aside the rough piece of iron that formed the base of the trap, she glared at the girl and then at the boy, crying, 'You're devils, nothin' but devils, that's what you are, treatin' a little child so cruelly.'

'How dare you speak to me so!' The words were deep throated like those that might have come from a mature woman. 'Mind your manners, girl, if you don't want to find yourself up before the Justice. That little child, as you call him, was big enough to set a trap for a rabbit and then kill it. He was being given some of his own medicine.'

'A child's a child, a rabbit's a rabbit. You should know that.'

The two girls were facing each other now and like a flash Isabelle's arm went up, the gold-headed walking stick with it, as she cried indignantly, 'You dare answer me back!'

Even Clive couldn't believe his eyes at what followed, for he saw the girl reach up, grab Isabelle's arm and wrench the walking stick from her grasp. Then in one movement she seemed to fling the stick and Isabelle aside. The stick went hurling into the brambles and Isabelle followed it, if more slowly; three stumbling steps backwards and she fell headlong into the thicket. Then the girl, stooping quickly, gathered the child into her arms and turned and fled along the path.

When he pulled Isabelle to her feet there was a streak of blood across one cheek where a bramble had caught it, but she was unaware of this. She stood with her joined fists pressed tightly together at the front of her waist, staring along the drive where in the far distance she could see the girl still running. Without moving her gaze from the figure, she demanded, 'Why didn't you do something, stop her? She struck me. She'll be brought up for this.'

'Don't be silly, Belle. She didn't strike you, she only defended herself.'

She now turned on him in fury. 'You dare to take her part, that scut, that scum! She knocked me down.' She put her hand up to her cheek that was now beginning to smart, then looked at the blood on her fingers before thrusting her hand in front of his face, crying, 'Look!' When he made no response she cried, 'Well, if you won't get her, I will.' And pulling her skirt well up over her ankles she raced down the driveway; and after a moment he followed her, protesting, 'Don't be such a fool, Belle. Belle, do you hear?'

So quickly did she run that he did not catch up to her before they reached the North Lodge gates, and as he came panting to a standstill he heard her cry at the lodgekeeper, 'You let them through! You knew they were trespassing.'

'Aw, Miss, and young Sir.' He nodded at Clive. 'She was out through the little gate in a twinkling.' He nodded to where the iron gate at the side of the big gates stood open. 'I couldn't have stopped her if I would.'

'Who is she?'

When the lodgekeeper rubbed his hand hard over his mouth she cried at him, 'Who is she? Tell me this instant.'

'Well, Miss,' he said solemnly now, 'her name be Brodie. But she's more to be pitied than laughed at. Her parents died of the fever a short while back and she was turned adrift from her house in the hamlet, and she lives now with the children, nine of them, so I hear, on the open fells.'

When the lodgekeeper saw the young master shake his head as if in disbelief he sensed a certain sympathy from him and addressed his remarks to him only now, saying, ''Tis a sad case, young Sir; but there are many likewise.'

Clive's attention was taken from the lodgekeeper now and he cried to his sister who was making for the gate, 'Where are you going?'

She answered him over her shoulder, 'Come and find out.' And running across the rough road she made for a rise in the ground opposite the gates that would give her a view of the lower land.

From the top of the high ground she saw the girl walking now, the boy by her side, towards an outcrop of rock in the far distance, and she took note of the location before turning about and joining her brother, who was making his way slowly up the hill towards her.

It was late the same evening when she returned from a lone

ride to be greeted by Clive, who demanded, 'Where have you been? Father's been asking for you.'

'Has he?' She pulled off her long soft leather gloves as she mounted the steps to the house, saying, 'That's very fortunate because I want to see him.'

'Where have you been?'

'For a ride.'

'You haven't been after that girl?'

When she turned her head towards him but didn't speak he put in quickly, 'Now, Belle, I won't stand with you in this. She didn't strike you, but on the other hand if you had brought that stick down on her, the mood you were in, you could have killed her.'

Ignoring his remark, she said, 'Where's Father?'

'Where he always is at this time of night.'

On this she left him, throwing her gloves and crop on to the hall chair as she made for a door at the far end of a short passage leading from the hall. She paused for a moment outside the door, then knocked, and when her father's voice came to her she entered the room.

Lord Fischel was surrounded by books. Each side of the large desk was piled with them, three walls of the room were lined with them. His main occupation in life was reading, and his main interest was astronomy. He raised his head and looked at his daughter. Then the muscles of his face gave a nervous twitch as he said, 'Ah, yes. Come in. Sit down, Isabelle.'

She walked slowly across the room, but she didn't sit down. Standing at the edge of the desk she startled him by immediately asking, 'Who owns the land that runs along by the park on the east side of the North Lodge?'

'Land?' He narrowed his eyes at her. 'You mean the open land, the fells?'

'Yes.'

'It's common land.'

'You have no say about it?'

He shook his head, then gave a wry twist of a smile. 'Not as yet.'

'Are people allowed to live on it?'

'Being common land, yes, in certain circumstances, like camping. And they can graze their animals.'

'Can they build houses?'

'Build houses on the fell?' He brought himself round to face her more squarely. 'Not unless they've obtained a tenure and have deeds to that effect. Why do you ask?'

'I saw people building there.'

'What kind of people, squatters or workmen?'

'It's a family . . . there's—' she stopped herself from saying 'a girl' and added, 'There's a woman doing it.'

'Oh.' He turned his attention to the desk again. 'Likely squatters erecting a shelter. But as long as they don't dig foundations they're within the law, and anything without a foundation won't stand the winds of the winter up there.' He gave a wry smile at the futility of such wasted effort and now he said again, 'Sit down, Isabelle.'

When she had seated herself he did not look at her, but picking up a plain-handled pen he drew a star on the paper in his hand before he said, 'I'm afraid I've some very disappointing news for you. You will not be able to go to London as arranged.'

The impact of the words stunned her for a moment, and then she was on her feet again, demanding, 'But why, Father, why?'

And when, his face still turned from her, he said, 'I cannot give you the reason,' she knew it. It was her mother; he wouldn't go because he had likely heard that her mother was in town. Mr Bellingham must have brought him the news. But if she didn't go to London, where was she to go? Back to Heidelberg, she supposed, and Aunt Helen's, and the daily journey to the convent, under strong escort of course, so that she would not come in contact with the students. And there would be the musical evenings, and the decorum, and no fun, because Aunt Helen didn't believe in fun. In a way she could be her father's sister, not her sister-in-law, for her theory was that if God wished you to marry, He would send you a man; magically the man would appear, as her husband had appeared to her. But of course he mustn't be a German student. But even Heidelberg and Aunt Helen was preferable to staying here, yet she determined not to go without a protest. She said now defiantly, 'Well, I don't want to go back to Heidelberg, Father. I've . . . I've outgrown Aunt Helen.'

'Indeed!' His face was straight, and he frowned at her before he went on, 'But you need not worry, you're not returning to Germany. It so happens that I received a letter from your Uncle Henry yesterday telling me of a long-felt desire of his and your aunt's to visit India, and they intend to do this forthwith. So I'm afraid you'll have to content yourself with my poor company and the amenities of your home until further arrangements can be made.' Again there was a thin smile on his face, but it vanished when, bending towards him, she cried, 'No, Father! You can't make me put up with this all winter, it's utterly dead, and I've looked forward so much to staying in London. I . . . I want to go to London; I'll go mad if I have to stay here, there's nothing to do.'

Swiftly he rose from his seat and it was on the point of his tongue to say, 'Then we'll go mad together for I, too, cannot bear the thought of you in this house for months ahead.'

Up till they were ten he had seen little of his children, for they were kept, as children should be kept, out of sight at the top of the house. Sometimes they were brought into the drawing room to say How-do-you-do, and at such times when they stood side by side staring at him solemn-eyed he could not believe that he was the instigator of their being; he did not feel that they belonged to him. When his wife had left him he had arranged that the top floor of the west wing of the house should be given over entirely to them and the governess. A year later he had sent his son away to boarding school and the boy was fourteen before they sat down to a meal together. When his daughter was fifteen he consulted with his brother, Henry, and his wife, while they were on a visit, as to what was best for her, and when his sister-in-law suggested, as he hoped she might, that Isabelle should return to Germany with them and finish her education there, he had welcomed it.

During the last two years they had come home for the holidays, but even then he had seen little of them, apart from meal times. This year it had to be different. They were near seventeen and something had to be done; and to this end he had made arrangements which, he hoped, would take care of his daughter's future. Then that wanton, who still dared call herself Lady Fischel, showed herself on the London scene once more, and here he was having to suffer the companionship of his daughter for months ahead; and of his two children he liked her less, for not only did she look the image of his grandfather, but she had an unpredictable nature and in some strange way she disturbed him.

He said now, with studied patience, 'If you employ your time in useful ways it will not drag. I'll tell Mrs Hatton to instruct you in the running of the house. The tapestry of the firescreen in my bedroom needs attention; also Mrs Hatton has mentioned that new curtains are required for the drawing room. You can go into Newcastle and choose the material. Then you have your pastime of riding and walking . . . Your days should be full.'

Once again she was speechless, for her temper was choking her. She knew now how her mother had felt. No wonder she had taken other men. She had the desire to cry at him, 'I hate you! I hate you as much as my mother did.' Fearing she might do just that, she turned and rushed from the room, and, finding Clive waiting for her in the hall, she gripped his arm and pulled him with her to the morning room, and once inside and the door closed, she leaned her back against it and gasped at him, 'We're not going to London. He said circumstances have arisen . . . It's Mother; she must be there and he's terrified of facing her. And I'm not going back to Germany either, they're going to India. I'm to stay here all winter.' She brought her body from the door and poked her head towards him, hissing now, 'Do you hear what I say? I'm to stay here all winter!'

He himself couldn't see this as a tragedy. He would like to stay here all winter, set himself up in the old nursery, and just paint and sleep and eat.

'Well say something, don't just stand there gaping.' She now marched across the room, her arms waving wildly as she cried, 'I'll go mad. I'll do something desperate. I know I shall.'

When she turned to face him again there were tears in her eyes, and the sight was so unusual that he went to her and put his arm around her shoulder. But he didn't speak, for at the moment he had no words with which to comfort her. One needed big outsized words when talking to Belle, for everything connected with her seemed to be larger than life.

After a time he said, 'Come on up to my room and I'll give you a drink of something that will make you feel better.' He bent his head down to hers as she dried her eyes and blew her nose, and whispered, 'I've lifted a bottle of old brandy from the cellar. Come on.'

2

For four days Isabelle rode her horse along the road from the North Lodge. She would hitch it to a tree before climbing to a hidden spot from where she could watch, behind an outcrop of rock, the wall slowly rising. On the fifth day she stayed longer than usual, waiting until she saw the girl and the children leave the place together; then swiftly mounting her horse again she rode towards the structure. Pulling up some yards away she surveyed the scene: the fire let into the earth, the sooted kitchen utensils near it, the heap of wet mud. Then, turning the horse, she backed it against the wall which faced the entrance to the cave.

When the horse's haunches touched the wall it reared nervously and kicked out with its back feet; and as it made to move forward she pulled it up short and backed it again, this time digging her heels viciously into its side.

When the top of the wall gave way against the horse's haunches the animal reared up on its hind legs and almost dislodged her. Taking it forward, she turned and surveyed her handiwork. The top half of the wall lay scattered within the enclosure. Swiftly now she took the animal round to the side and repeated the performance. This time the horse did not rear; it seemed to know what was demanded of it, and not until the stones began to fall did it jump forward.

She was about to follow the same procedure with the third wall when she saw a figure flying towards her. This did not cause her to gallop away, but she walked the horse forward a little, drew it to a halt, and waited for the girl to come up. She watched her as she stared at the debris, then dashed to the remaining wall and looked over it; and she almost laughed when she turned and gaped at her, so comical was the creature's expression. Her lip curled, her head went up; then, pulling hard on the bit, she brought the horse round, its front legs clearing the ground, and galloped away.

At eleven o'clock the next morning Hatton met her as she was crossing the hall on her way out, evidently about to ride, since she was wearing her habit, and said, 'His Lordship wishes to speak to you, Miss. He's in his study.'

In the study she was surprised to see Clive already there. She had left him painting not long ago in the nursery after failing to persuade him to join her in a ride. Her father, she saw immediately, was angry; the whiteness around his mouth gave an indication of this, and she imagined that he had found out they had been drinking, for Clive had lifted another bottle from the cellar, and when, his Adam's apple working violently above the line of his cravat, he demanded, 'What is this I hear, Miss? Such conduct. Explain yourself, and at once,' she glanced at Clive; but he only stared back at her, his expression blank; and so to be on the safe side she parried with, 'I don't know what your meaning is, Father.'

'You don't know what my meaning is, girl? Do you deny you took your horse yesterday and deliberately knocked down the walls of a dwelling on the fells?'

As her eyebrows moved upwards, her lids shaded her eyes.

'It was the work of a scut. You forget yourself and the house you represent. What have you got to say?'

When she did not answer, he cried at her, 'You don't deny it?'

Now she was looking fully at him. 'No, I don't deny it, Father.'

Her boldness seemed to infuriate him and, marching to

the desk, he swept a pile of papers aside. Some floated in the air around him while he cried at her, 'Do you know you nearly killed a child? If you had had your way and knocked the last wall down you'd have buried a child lying in a basket.'

When she made no reply, he stood glaring at her. The fact that she might have killed a child really did not concern him; from what the minister had told him there were ten of them and one less would be taken in the form of a blessing. But that wasn't the point; his daughter, a Fischel, had lowered herself to retaliate against a low squatter. If the act had been done by her brother he could have understood it; but she was a girl, a young woman, and women did not stoop to such things. Her mother, wanton that she was, would not have lowered herself even to address such a person, let alone acknowledge her existence by attacking her. As he continued to stare at his daughter, she began to speak, 'I did it to teach her a lesson. It was much less cruel than reporting her and having her sent to prison for striking me.' She tapped her finger quickly against her cheek, then glanced at Clive; but he lowered his eyes as she ended, 'Also, she and her brother were poaching.'

'I know all about that.' His voice was rasping. 'The girl told the minister the full facts of the case. She admitted her brother was poaching, but I understand that she also stressed the point that the child was not five years old and that you tied him in his own trap. What is in you, girl, to do such a thing?'

'She struck me.'

As Clive's head came up quickly, her father said, 'The girl says you lifted your walking stick to her and, to prevent your striking her, she tore the stick from your hand and you fell back to the bushes. Is this true?'

'No.' Again her eyes flickered towards Clive. And now her father, his voice dropping low in his throat, said,

'Then your brother, too, is a liar, because he has already borne out the girl's story . . . Now listen to me and listen carefully. I forbid you to go near that girl's habitation again; and if you can't conduct yourself like a lady then I'll have to think up some ways and means of teaching you . . . You may go, both of you.'

When the door had closed on them he stood looking down at his desk and the papers scattered over the floor. He hesitated to ring for Hatton to pick them up and sat down heavily in his chair and, resting his chin in his hand, slowly began to tap his forefinger on his lips. The girl was going to create trouble; how was he to put up with her? What was the alternative? She was too old for school. Where could he send her? There was only Anna. But no. No, he couldn't imprison her on that stark island in the Hebrides with his austere sister and her wildly ranting husband. No, that would break any spirit; and he wasn't out to break his daughter's spirit, only to find some means of putting a great distance between them.

3

The following week it rained every day and in spite of roaring fires, even in the bedrooms, the house retained a dank odour. Some days, so dark was it, the candles had to be lit on the dining table at three o'clock in the afternoon.

So, to alleviate her boredom after dinner, Isabelle went up into the nursery and watched Clive paint; that was when the light was sufficiently good for him to work, and between times they would sip claret or port or whatever he had been able to appropriate from the cellar. His access to the wine cellar was simple; he merely waited until the servants were at meals, then went to the gun room where the cellar keys hung on a board with others, and let himself into the wine cellar, which was actually the cellar to the house, the door of which opened on to the side of the house. No-one, as yet, had seen him come or go; and if there was a noticeable reduction along some shelves, Hatton would suspect Gilbert, and Gilbert, Hatton, for the butler and the under-butler were the only two who were allowed access to the cellar.

He had this very morning managed to acquire two bottles, and now at four o'clock on this early October afternoon they were indulging in a mixture of old brandy and port and were feeling warm and very merry.

The sun suddenly making a late appearance, they sprang up and dashed to the window and laughed and shouted like children, and Clive cried, 'Look! Look, the sun. The sun! We're back on earth.'

'Let's go out.'

'It's wet.'

'Who cares? I'm hot, boiling inside.' She tore at the

neck of her dress. 'And your face is red, scarlet.' She took his cheeks between her hands and shook his head from side to side; then they fell against each other laughing. But when she pulled him towards the door he dragged his hand from her grasp, saying truculently, 'Don't, Belle; you're always pulling or pushing me. You think I'd never get along on my own, don't you?'

'Damn sure of it.'

Again they were hanging on each other laughing, and, her head on his neck, she giggled, 'If dear Papa could see us now, he'd have a fit. What do you think he'd do if he found out?'

'God knows.' Clive swung his head from side to side. 'It doesn't bear thinking about. And look,' he wagged his finger at her, 'we'd better steady up until we get well outside because I wouldn't put it past one of them to split on us. Good job nobody's allowed in here.' He turned round and surveyed the room and the bottles and glasses standing on the battered nursery table, and with a dramatic gesture he scoffed, 'Master Clive's studio, sacrosanct, the garret where he creates his masterpieces, each one stamped with his name, Clive John James . . . Rembrandt . . . Fischel, Lord of the Manor of Houghton Hall in the County of Durham in the year of God, eighteen thirty-two. Damn me, as ever was.'

Isabelle was now doubled up with her laughter, but when it got overloud Clive warned her, 'Ssh! or you'll have Mother Hatton up here.'

Making an effort to quell her mirth she opened the door saying, 'I'll get my cloak,' and he whispered, 'Here, chew a coffee bean or Nelson will smell it from you.'

'It's her . . . it's her half-day. She's gone to visit her mama in the illustrious town of Shields, in a house, I understand, from whose windows you can espy the North Sea. Just think of that.' He pushed her and she staggered forward but straightened herself at the top of the stairs and descended with exaggerated decorum to the first floor.

But her decorum vanished when, later, they crossed the hall and her laughter brought the butler's gaze on her; and behind his look of slight bewilderment was one of deep dislike. He could stand Master Clive, but the young miss, no. God prevent the day that she should ever be mistress of this house. It wasn't likely; but still one never knew. If anything should happen to the young master, and him not married, well, then there was only her to follow the master. But God forbid.

He opened the doors for them but did not immediately close them again; instead, he watched the pair of them skipping across the gravel like bairns let loose to play. They would not have acted like that if the master had been at home; he'd be back the night and that wouldn't be a moment too soon. There was something odd about both of them. He screwed up his eyes. If he didn't know it was impossible he would imagine they had been drinking. Master Clive had had three glasses of wine with his dinner, but as usual she had had none. Yet they were acting very strange, very strange.

They acted very strange across the park and to the North Lodge and through the gate to Thornton's Farm. The farmer was at market, but his wife thought the young master and miss were very skittish-like, merry, going on as if they were at a fair, leaning over the stiles and pulling the pigs' tails. Did you ever see anything like it? But, of course, she daren't say anything. If they had been her own son and daughter she would have clouted their ears and skited them across the yard. When they saw the cows being milked they went on as if they'd never seen teats pulled afore, the young miss worse than the master. It was almost two years since they had visited the farm; and if they had acted childishly then she could have understood it, but not now, when they were a young gentleman and miss.

She was glad when they left, and she went to the gate and watched them going down the road, the girl running and skipping on and off the grass verge like a young lamb when the sun first touches it.

Isabelle would not, at the moment, have likened her feelings to those of a lamb. A mixture of emotions was whirling round inside her: a feeling of excitement, a strong desire to tease, to have fun, but above all, and not fully understood by her, an overpowering urge to come to grips with someone, to master someone besides Clive.

At this point they came to a part of the road that merged with the fell itself, and to the left of them the land sloped to a grassy hollow, at the bottom of which was a mound of earth bordered by a small copse; and towards this Isabelle now ran, with Clive close behind her.

Running between the mound of earth and the copse was a long narrow pathway, probably made by sheep, and coming along it now was the girl who had hardly been out of her thoughts for days. In one hand she was carrying a milk can, and behind her was a small child.

They all seemed to stop at the same instant and remain still for some seconds. It was Isabelle who made the first move. Wagging her walking stick in front of her, and curling her lip as if she were confronting a reptile, she exclaimed in chilling tones, 'Out of the way!'

The track was too narrow to allow two people to pass. Cissie was within two yards of the end of it; there was more than twenty yards behind her. She was in her right to go forward into the open. But she would have gone back except for the fact that the girl demanding she should do this was the one who had smashed the dwelling place and nearly killed Nellie; she was the one who had tied the wire around Joe's ankle; she was a wicked creature. Her da had always said, 'A danger faced is a danger halved.' She said now in a small but clear voice, 'I'm near the end, I'm just a step off; if you'd move back I . . .'

'What! Move for you?' The point of the walking stick caught her in the middle of the chest and sent her staggering back, almost upsetting Sarah.

'Look. Go on back. It'll save you a lot of trouble.' It was the young man speaking now over his sister's shoulder. His face was red, and he was laughing.

'I'll not.' She did not look past the girl to the young man but kept her eyes fixed on the dark glaring face as she cried, 'I'm in me rights. And another thing. Don't you poke me no more with that stick, I'm telling you.'

'Rights? How dare you!' The stick came up and the milk can went flying. Then for the second time within days Cissie was struggling with the girl for possession of the walking stick.

Isabelle was stronger than Cissie; also she had the advantage of being well fed; but Cissie's thinness was a tough thinness bred of hard work and privation, and so they struggled equally for the moment while, behind them, Sarah cried, 'Give over! Give over! Eeh! our Cissie. Our Cissie.' And behind Cissie, Clive, backing into the open, laughing until his sides ached. That was until, still struggling, they came abreast of him and he saw the look on his sister's face. She was holding the stick no longer and her hands were clawing at the girl's neck.

Crying at her, 'Belle! Belle! Let up!' he tried to push himself in between them. Then one of them slipped. He thought, afterwards, that it was the girl, for when they all fell together she was on her back, he on top of her, and Belle to the side.

The girl didn't move; she seemed stunned. Nor did he move, for he too was stunned, but in a different way. One of his hands was partly under the girl's armpit and partly on her heaving breast, but the other was actually gripping the flesh of her bare leg well above the knee. He glanced sideways to the skirt and single petticoat rumpled up almost to the thighs. His glance at the same time took in

Isabelle leaning against a tree, and he saw that the rage on her face had been taken over by a fiendish mixture of laughter and glee; and as if reading his thoughts she cried, 'Well! Why don't you? Go on.'

Unconsciously, his hand had been moving along the girl's bare flesh and upwards, but it stopped when the body beneath him drew in a deep shattering breath. He looked at the face under his and saw it for a moment through the artist's eye. The skin was beautiful, the lashes on the closed eyes silken; the lips slightly open were moist. An unbearable feeling was tearing at his loins. His body was hot as if in a fever; he felt that if he didn't have release from this agony he would die. He must. He must. His sister's voice jerked his head round to her again as she cried, 'Go on! Why don't you? You're frightened. You never have, have you?'

'Go away. Do you hear? Go away.'

She made a sound like a laugh and moved from the tree, but as soon as he turned his head from her she stopped and she did not take her eyes off the figures on the ground, not even when the child came running from the track, crying, 'Our Cissie! Our Cissie! Eeh! Oh! Don't!' then stood some distance away wailing like a banshee.

It was the exploring hand and the contact of strange warm flesh that brought Cissie back to consciousness. One second she didn't know where she was, the next she was screaming aloud; and for minutes she tore and struggled with the body, first in an effort to escape, then for no apparent purpose. After that, life seemed to flow from her and she lay still, like one dead. Her eyes wide, tear-bleared, she stared upwards, conscious of the fair head nestled in the crook of her neck; but she had no energy now to push the body from her. Not even when she heard the terrible voice thundering as if God himself were speaking and the sound of a whiplash flicking through the air did she move. She only knew that the body was lifted from her as if a mighty hand had swept it aside as it would a fly. She closed her eyes tightly against an indescribable pain, not in her body now but in her heart; and when she opened them again it was to see a man standing above her. He was tall and unbending and his face was a dark bluish red; in one hand he held a whip and in the other the young man, who was trying desperately to adjust his clothes.

Her hands fumbling, she pushed down her skirt and petticoat and rolled on to her face; and when some minutes later she dragged herself to her knees there was nobody near her, only Sarah. When she got to her feet she turned her head sideways and looked towards the road where the coach was starting up. Then she picked up the milk can; she did not go towards the farm but turned in the direction whence she had come and Sarah followed her, some paces behind, not daring to speak and still crying.

4

If Lord Fischel had ever been in doubt as to the devil walking the earth he was no longer so, for he was assured now that the devil was in full possession of his daughter.

That his son should take his pleasure with a girl of the people was not out of order – the needs of the flesh must be met, God made allowances for that; and that was one of the services the common people provided; but that he should take her in the open, and in view of the road, was to be wholly condemned. Even in such acts as this a certain amount of decorum was to be observed. But that his daughter should stand and witness the process touched on something so unnatural, so evil that his very bowels churned when he thought of it.

He stared at her now, her eyes as black as coals, her face white, showing up the red weal where his whip had caught her, and he could not prevent himself from bringing his hand up and across her other cheek with such force that she staggered and flopped into the big leather chair to the side of the study window. Glaring down at her now, he hissed through thin tight lips, 'You're scum, Miss, scum, and you must be treated as such. Your unnatural action today has settled your future for you; you'll go to your Aunt Anna's in Scotland and there you will remain until you are civilised enough to return to decent society.'

'No! No!' She pulled herself on to the edge of the chair. One hand still covering her face and all the dark, fiery spirit going out of her, she begged, 'Please; no, not to Aunt Anna's, please, Father. I'll . . . I'll behave. It was because we had been drinking . . .'

'You had what!'

'We . . . we got some wine from the cellar.' She did not lay the entire blame of this on Clive. 'We . . . we did not know what we were doing.'

'You knew what you were doing when you took your horse and knocked the walls down of that girl's abode; you knew what you were doing when you tied her young brother to the trap; you know what you're doing today also. You could have stopped such action; you are stronger than he in all ways.'

She was on her feet now, pleading no more. 'I'll not go to Scotland; it'll be like going to my grave. That, that barren island . . . I warn you, Father, I won't go.'

He turned from her and rang a bell; then looking at her over his shoulder he said, 'You'll go. You'll go by coach and you'll leave the day after tomorrow in the care of Hatton and his wife. I'm sending a messenger on in the morning to give notice to your aunt.' He did not for a moment consider whether his sister would be pleased to have her niece, he only knew that he would make it so worth her while that in her straitened circumstances – her father had left her nothing in his will – it would be foolish of her to refuse. Moreover, having no children of her own, she'd likely welcome someone on whom she could inflict her doctrine of virtue through austerity.

He said to Hatton when he appeared in the doorway, 'Tell Mrs Hatton that Miss Isabelle is to be locked in her room and that she must take her meals to her. You'll also tell her to dismiss her maid. I will give her a fortnight's wages in lieu of notice, together with a reference; you will find them on my desk in the morning . . . And, Hatton . . .'

'Yes, m'Lord?'

'Be prepared to escort my daughter to Scotland the day after tomorrow. Mrs Hatton will accompany you.'

He turned and looked at his daughter, her hands to her

throat as if struggling for breath, but he felt not the slightest pity for her.

On the morning following Isabelle's departure Clive was summoned to his father's study; and when he came and stood in front of his desk, Lord Fischel wanted to rap out, 'Stand up straight, boy!' but refrained because he knew they would straighten him up where he was going. What he said to him was, 'Have a small valise packed and be ready to leave in half-an-hour's time.'

Clive wet his lips before he asked quietly, 'May I enquire, Sir, where I am going?'

'You may. You're bound for Newcastle; from there you will be heading for the Cape, East Indies, and Malaya. Where you go after that depends on Captain Spellman's charter. You will be sailing on the *Virago;* your position will be that of a deck hand. But many a man has risen from there to captain; it will be entirely up to you.'

For a moment he thought his son was going to collapse over the desk in front of him, and he was forced to say by way of some comfort, 'Captain Spellman is a good man, just and honest; he is one of the best captains in the Compton Line, in which line, you may know, we hold a great many shares.'

'Fa . . . Father.'

'Yes?'

'I'm always unwell on the sea, I don't like the sea. Would it not be possible for you to send me somewhere else?'

Lord Fischel looked at his son and there was a sadness within him. There was no fight in the boy; it was as he had always known, their natures had got mixed up. It was strange too, he thought, that he had whipped his daughter in passion on that hillside, and in this room, passion dead, he had struck her; yet when he had brought his son before him that same night he had not lifted his hand to him. He had even considered not heaping any retribution on the boy other than sending him back to school; yet he had told himself that would be unjust. He did not own to himself at that point the real reason why he was sending him and his sister away.

It wasn't until late in the afternoon when the tide was full that he stood on the quay in Newcastle in a position from which he would not be observed and watched the *Virago*, her sails set, her deck alive with scurrying figures, pass down the river; and his heart knew a strange loneliness that brought the truth to the forefront of his mind. Yet still he did not face it squarely and admit that by his supposed justice he had rid himself of their presence for some years ahead, and also made sure that neither of them would encounter their mother; but he looked upon their departure and the incidents that led up to it as the workings of God in answer to his unspoken prayers. God had ways of protecting and assisting those who obeyed his commandments.

BOOK THREE

The Child

1

'Do you hear what I said, Jimmy?'

'N . . . No, Matthew.'

'I was tellin' you, lad, why we soak the nave of the wheel in boiling water. Now look, Jimmy.' Matthew went on his hunkers before the boy. 'You've got to pay attention else you'll never learn this trade, not in seven years or seventeen. You were as eager as a calf after milk at first but something's come over you. You tired of it?'

'Oh, no! No, man . . . I mean Matthew.' Jimmy shook his head and his face worked as if he were pulling himself out of a dream. 'Why, no, Matthew, I'm not tired of it; I like it fine, nothin' better. I'm sorry, Matthew, I didn't pay attention. I will after this, I will. I . . . I heard what you said about getting the dish of the wheel, like testing the mortices for it, an' I remember what you told me about the dowels yesterday.'

'But memory isn't enough, Jimmy lad, if you don't put your rememberin' into your hands . . . You know, I spoilt a spoke this morning on the bench 'cos you didn't crank the wheel hard enough. Now you've got to take a pull at yourself . . . Aw' – he put his hand on to the boy's shoulder – 'There's no need for you to bubble. Lord, I'm only tellin' you, and quietly; I haven't clouted your ear or anythin'.'

When Jimmy turned away and hid his face in the crook of his elbow and his shoulders began to heave, Matthew pulled him gently towards him again and said quietly, 'Look, something's wrong with you. Tell me what it is. Has me mother been gettin' at you?'

Jimmy shook his head at this, but when, after a pause,

Matthew asked, 'Is . . . is something wrong up there?' Jimmy's head didn't move and after a longer pause Matthew made himself say, 'Is it Cissie?'

The boy's head now drooped further on to his chest and tears ran off the end of his nose and on to the back of his hand, but he said nothing; and Matthew, getting to his feet, put his hand on the boy's shoulder and led him into a small store room that led off the shop, and there, closing the door behind him, he looked down at him and said grimly, 'Look, Jimmy, I know Cissie's unhappy.' He stopped himself from adding, 'She's not the only one,' and went on, 'But she's young and she'll get over it. You see . . . well' – he rubbed his hand hard across his mouth – 'there's things you don't understand, things a man has to do but . . .'

Jimmy, sniffing the tears back off his nose with the aid of his thumb, said quickly now, ''Tisn't you, Matthew, 'tisn't you.' When he paused, staring into Matthew's face, Matthew asked quietly, 'Well, if it isn't me, what is it?'

Jimmy drew his bottom lip right into his mouth and scraped the teeth over the skin until his lip sprang from under them with a painful sucking snap, and then he put his hand to his head and held it there before he said, 'She was mated.'

Matthew hadn't heard aright. He said, 'What did you say?'

'She was mated.' The words were a whisper but Matthew's shoulders drew back from them. His chin pulled in to his neck, his hand came up and his fingers ran through his thick hair. His mouth opened to speak then closed again, and Jimmy said, between sniffs, 'It was as her and Sarah were goin' for the milk. She met up with the lady from the Hall – she was the one who had caught Joe nabbin' the rabbit and brought her horse and kicked down the walls – and the young master and it was in the narrow passage going round the butt near Thornton's Farm. And

124

she tells Cissie to go back and out of the way, and they were nearly in the openin' and when Cissie wouldn't she took her stick to her, an' Cissie tried to get it away and the young master got in atween them and him and Cissie fell, and Sarah said Cissie lay still . . . an' then . . .' Jimmy's eyes lowered, his head drooped, and his voice had a thin, faraway, unreal sound as he ended, 'He mated her, and the young miss laughed, and our Cissie cries nearly every night.'

Matthew sat down on a box and looked over Jimmy's head to the row of saws and tools hanging on the wall. He had the appearance of a man who had been winded. It was fully five minutes before he said to the boy who was standing looking at him in bewilderment now, 'When did this happen?'

'More than a week since but I didn't know till Sunday. She's different, Matthew, quiet, and not bothering about putting the walls up now.'

Matthew rose slowly to his feet, then went through the shop and into the yard. After he had harnessed the horse to the cart he went back to the shop door and said to Jimmy, 'When Walter comes back tell him I've been called out an' I won't be long. You sweep out, then clean the stable . . . right? . . .'

When he drew the horse to a stop on the track below the cave there was no sign of anyone about, but when he walked through the doorway of the half walls he saw her. She was sitting in the corner sorting mushrooms. Nellie in the basket to one side of her and Annie and Charlotte at the other.

Her glance met his for a fleeting second but in that time the whiteness of her face took on a flush. He stood for a moment looking at her bent head, and when the children scampered to him and clung round his legs he lifted Annie up in his arms. But still looking at Cissie, he said, 'Hello there.'

125

'Hello.' Her voice sounded throaty as if she had a cold.

He groped in his pocket now and brought from it a thin strip of barley sugar and, snapping it in two, he gave one piece to Annie and the other to Charlotte and, putting Annie down, he said to Charlotte, 'Go to the burn and find me a lucky pebble. It must be a big one mind, flat, brown, and shiny, and if you find it there's a ha'penny for you.'

Charlotte's eyes sprung wide and she made an ecstatic high noise like a whistle; then, grabbing Annie's hand, she ran out of the enclosure, and he was left alone with Cissie.

As he drooped on to his hunkers in front of her her hands went on sorting the mushrooms, the broken ones into a basin, the big flat ones into one straw skiff, the button ones into another; and as he watched her, Jimmy's tale formed a picture in his mind and he saw the whole thing happening to her; and his teeth, grinding against each other, made an audible noise. He did not ask himself how he was going to broach the subject to her, he had never been one for beating around the bush; he said thickly, 'Jimmy told me.'

His words acted like a spring, for she bounced up from the ground and ran into the cave, and he sat still on his hunkers gazing at the mushrooms for a moment before he straightened up and followed her. Standing in the doorway, he looked to where she was sitting on the low, wooden bed, her hands under her oxters, her body swaying back and forwards, and he said to her, his voice still a mutter, 'Don't worry, he'll be brought to boot. If it's the last thing I do he'll be brought to boot, Lord's son or no Lord's son that he is.'

Her body stopped its rocking; her eyes now held fear, but her voice was harsh as she said, ''Tis none of your business, leave it be. 'Tis none of your business.'

'It's got to be somebody's business.'

'Well, 'tisn't yours.' She got up from the bed and went to push past him, but his hand on her shoulder checked her, and he said quietly, 'No, perhaps it isn't. But who'll take it on if not me?'

She held his gaze as she replied, her voice calm and flat sounding, ''Tis not your place, and you'll only meet trouble if you make it your business.'

'That's my look-out,' he said; then, taking his hand from her shoulder, he went before her into the enclosure again and, looking about him, spoke as if giving orders back in the shop, saying, 'Get as many stones as you can up here afore Saturday, an' I'll bring Jimmy and Walter over with me. By Sunday night, given luck, we should have them up and a roof over. Now do what I tell you.' He turned towards her where she was standing in the opening of the cave, her hands gripped between her breasts. 'Put them all on and make as big a pile as you can.'

She did not answer him, just stared at him, her head moving slightly from side to side; and he turned from her and went down the slope and got into the cart again and drove the two miles to Parson Hedley's vicarage . . .

Young Martin let him in. Martin had once been a climbing boy and he had a mass of burn scars to prove it, but he smiled happily at Matthew; and as he went to inform his master of the visitor's presence Parson Hedley came into the hallway from a far door. Seeing Matthew, he said with evident pleasure, 'Matthew, what brings you here at this time?' then added, 'Nothing wrong I hope? Your father? Has he taken a turn . . . ?'

'No, Parson, nothing like that; they're all well. I just wanted a word with you.'

'Certainly, Matthew, certainly. Just come in here.' He led the way into a poorly furnished unheated room, saying, 'Sit yourself down. Now would you like a cup of tea? Mrs Hedley makes one about this time.'

'No, thank you, Parson; it's not long since me dinner.' Matthew had sampled the parson's tea. It was what he called faint tea, too weak to climb out of the pot, but that he should offer tea to six of them when they were at their class showed the mettle of the man – for his stipend, he understood, was ten shillings a week, and he knew for a certainty a third of that went in coppers and sixpences to those in need. It was a crying shame, when one gave it a thought, that a man like Parson Hedley was worth but ten shillings a week, out of which he had to keep up this rambling cold barn of a house, while Parson Bainbridge not four miles away got a pound and lived on the fat of the land. But then the Fischel Manor came into his parish as did the Conways and the Bentleys, and them well up in trade. And it was said, although he couldn't believe it, that the Bishop of Durham received over fifteen thousand pounds a year.

'Now how can I help you, Matthew? Have you got stuck somewhere?'

'No, Parson, nothin' like that.' Matthew smiled as he spoke. 'I've done me composition, although' – he jerked his head – 'the spelling beats me now and again.'

'It beats us all, Matthew.'

Matthew now nipped his cheek between his thumb and fingers and rubbed hard at the stubble on it before he said, 'It's Cissie Brodie, Parson. Something's happened her.'

'Oh! Cissie.' The parson nodded his head, then looked down to the floor to the side of him.

'You know about it, Parson?'

'Yes. Yes, I'm afraid I do, Matthew.'

'What's to be done then?'

Parson Hedley rose to his feet and began to walk up and down as he talked. 'What could be done has been done, Matthew. It isn't often that justice comes out of such affairs as this, but Lord Fischel is a just man. He may be somewhat unapproachable but he's a just man, a man of principle, and he has proved it.'

Matthew also got to his feet. 'He's . . . he's going to do something for her then?'

Parson Hedley stopped in his walk, his eyebrows moving upwards. 'For Cissie, no; but he has punished those responsible. It's a wonder you haven't heard. He has banished both his son and his daughter. For her part in the affair, and it was a shocking part indeed, she has been sent to the far Hebrides, to a relative there I understand. As for his son, he himself saw him signed up as a deck hand on a sailing vessel going to the Far East, to trade there. You must admit, Matthew, that it is very rarely that justice for the poor is carried to such lengths. But there, you cannot hope to please everyone for I understand that he is now being condemned harshly in some circles; for this kind of incident, as you know, is usually taken as a matter of course.'

Yes, Matthew knew this was only too true, and although in a way he was very glad that Lord Fischel had got rid of his daughter, for she had become like a bad omen to Cissie, there was still the possibility that there might be results of the incident; and what then? And this is what he said to Parson Hedley, straight and right to the point. 'What if she has a bairn, Parson?'

'Oh, Matthew, Matthew.' Parson Hedley closed his eyes and wagged his head. 'Don't contemplate such a result with six of them there still to see to. It would be disastrous. And up there on that barren place. If they all survive the winter it will be nothing short of a miracle.'

'I'm with you there, Parson; and I say again, what's to be done if she's got with a child? The House should be held responsible.'

'Oh no! No, Matthew.' Parson Hedley looked somewhat surprised that Matthew, whom he found so practical and level-headed, should be naïve enough to imagine that the House of Fischel would hold itself responsible for the result of a moment's amusement by one of its members. The head of that House had already done something unprecedented; no man would dare to ask more of him, and certainly not under such circumstances. At the moment, he was much more sorry for His Lordship than he was for Cissie, for had this good God-fearing man not only lost his wife through sin and not of his own making, but his two children also through sin.

He said on a lighter note as Matthew turned from him towards the door, 'I had a wonderful surprise yesterday. What do you think my brother sent me from London?'

Matthew didn't answer for a moment; he was angry inside, boiled up, as he put it to himself. But he must speak civilly to the parson for he was a good man. 'I've no idea,' he said. 'A cask of butter?'

'Ho! a cask of butter. No; something much more valuable to me than a cask of butter. Look.' He darted back to his desk and, picking up a book, held it out towards Matthew, saying, 'A new edition of *The Journal of a Tour to the Hebrides with Samuel Johnson* by James Boswell.'

'Oh, that's very nice, Sir.'

'This time next year, Matthew, or even before at the rate you're going, you'll be able to sit down and read that entire book; and I promise that when you're ready I will loan it to you. Now, won't that be wonderful?'

'Yes, yes, indeed, Parson.'

As Matthew walked away Parson Hedley stood for a moment at the door and watched him, thinking, He's a strange young man, Matthew. The promise of the loan of this precious book hadn't really excited him; he was more concerned about Cissie at the moment. It was right, of course, to think of other people, to be concerned for their welfare, but he should not be concerned about Cissie Brodie to the extent that it should worry him, for was he not betrothed to Rose Watson of the Mill, and this alliance had made everyone happy.

2

The third morning that Cissie felt sick she knew it was not from an overindulgence either of mushrooms or of turnips or of the sour hard apples that Joe had brought back after his scrounging expedition. She lay on her side with Annie tucked into her back and Charlotte's arm over Annie touching her waist. In the dim morning light she looked down on Nellie curled up in her basket against the wooden platform, and she thought, Dear God! she'll be just two when it comes.

The knowledge that she was actually pregnant was no surprise to her. From the day following the nightmarish experience she had known this would be the outcome, and from that moment she had known her life was blighted. No man would ever have her now, not even when she had finally got them all off her hands when she was twenty or twenty-two.

She would have said that there had been no hope in her before this happened that Matthew wouldn't marry Rose Watson, but would, in spite of the dragging responsibility, take her, together with the lot of them. She had pictured him, unable to do without her, dashing over the fells in the cart and saying to her, saying to them all, 'Get yourselves in, I'm taking you out of this place, I'm taking you home.' . . . But not now, with a bairn inside her.

Yet he had done more for her during the past month than he had done in the previous four. Hadn't he finished the dwelling place and made a surprising good job of it? In fact, it was as near a real house as you could wish, with a fireplace in it and a rough mantel above; and he had done the roof so well with thatch that not a drop of rain came through, even when it poured. And last week he had brought them a bundle of old sacks from the mill to make into towels, and a large thick clippie mat . . . *She* had sent that – she always thought of Rose Watson as *she* – but it was a godsend, because the children could sit on it near the fire and keep warm.

She got quietly out of bed, and pulled on her boots over her bare feet. Her body felt heavy, but she knew it wasn't the child, it was the weight of her heart. She was weary and sick, both mentally and physically, at the prospect ahead of her, but strangely she was no longer afraid. There were only two things, she realised, that had ever made her fearful: one was the separation of the family, the other was the daughter of the lord.

She had thought, at first, that the fear the girl bred in her was because of her power to do something to Joe, such as having him locked up for poaching, and she could have done that quite easily, because all the gentry were locking them up now since the law had come down on them for setting spring guns and gin traps in the woods; for not only were the poachers killed or maimed, but innocent folk were too. But the fear had really consumed her with a paralysing force on the day when she felt the girl's hands at her throat, and then, later, when she awakened to a different kind of terror to know that she had not only let that thing happen but also watched it.

Her da had a saying about evil. He said that God put it into the hearts of some men so that, through it, saints could be sorted from the sinners. Well, God had certainly put evil into the heart of the lord's daughter, but who was to say that it had made of herself either a saint or a sinner? The only thing certain was that from now on she would be marked.

She reminded herself that it was Sunday. She looked at the clock standing alone on the mantelshelf. Matthew had brought it back the day after he had put the roof on.

132

The clock said fifteen minutes past eight; the boys would be here by nine. She wondered what *she* would give William the day. She hoped he'd bring some oatmeal; it gave them a start with something warm in them in the morning and it saved her fourpence a week.

She opened the door and stood on the threshold looking at the morning as she wound her long plaits round on the back of her head. The fells lay before her, lonely, bleak, and desolate, yet beautiful to her because, as she put it, they were clean; and this morning they looked fresh, for a frost had clothed them in a film of silver; and the sun, breaking through low cloud, made the land sparkle and seem to move like a body pulsing below a skin.

Up till recently such a morning as this, when the world was quiet and the air biting, would have filled her with joy, for right back to when she was a small child she had been aware of joy. It had come to her in many ways: walking in the snow, holding her da's hand and he pointing to the stars and saying, 'What do you think about them for Jack, Jack shine-your-lights?' And lying in bed among the warm snuggled bodies of her brothers and sisters while listening to the wind howling down the chimney and the gale blowing outside; and the times of supreme joy, all the more precious because they were rare, when on the table was a piece of meat big enough to slice with the gully. Joy came in all forms, but she doubted at this moment if she'd ever feel joy again. She turned swiftly away from the bright morning and went inside.

Just after nine the boys came panting over the hills, both carrying sacks, and the children raced to meet them and to take possession of the sacks over the last few yards of the journey.

'Hello, Cissie.'

'Hello, Cissie.'

Jimmy and William stood before her and she made

herself smile at them, saying, 'Hello, Jimmy. Hello, William. How is it?'

'Oh, fine,' they both said together.

'Look! Look what I've brought.' William retrieved one of the sacks from Bella; and as he opened it he glanced up at Cissie, saying, 'By! Miss, she's kind, she's good; she stuffs me . . . Aw.' His head drooped for a moment and his hands became still on the sack, and Cissie said, 'I'm glad of that. Eat all you can.'

He looked up at her again, a half-apologetic smile on his face as he said lamely, 'Aye. Aye, I will, Cissie. But look.' He held up something unwieldy wrapped in a piece of paper and then, like a magician, he tore the paper away to disclose a large ham bone with a good deal of meat still adhering to it.

'Oh my!'

'Oh, look, Cissie!'

'Oh, our William!'

'Wait; you've seen nothin'.' He next drew out a raised pie, exclaiming, 'It's full of meat.' And these wonders now kept them silent for a moment.

During this time Jimmy had been standing with his hand on the other sack, and when the children turned to it, William said off-handedly, 'Oh, there's only bread in there.' And Cissie repeated to herself, 'Only bread'; and she looked at Jimmy and he at her.

Jimmy never brought anything – as he had said to Cissie, 'Matthew's mother seemed to weigh even the water' – and at this time on a Sunday morning he always felt out of it. Although he knew he was bringing Cissie sixpence a week more than their William, he still had the feeling that he wasn't contributing as much as his younger brother. But this morning he had something to give Cissie, something that would hearten her and, if it came off, give her one less to feed.

When the excitement was over and the food put away,

and the children running and jumping ahead of them over the fells towards the wood, he walked by Cissie's side as she carried Nellie in her arms; and after a while he said, 'I've got something to tell you, Cissie.'

The pause in her step caused him to alter his stride and he looked up at her face, which was white even with the wind blowing cold, and he went on, 'I think I've got a place for our Bella.'

'Oh?' She stopped and looked down at him, and he nodded at her. 'It sort of come about by Matthew making the cart, you know the new cart for the coal man in Shields. Well, this chap, he gets round the big houses in Westoe, and in one of the houses he hears they want a third laundry maid. It's a big house – well, you can tell, 'cos with three in the laundry – an' Bella could stand a chance. An' she would be trained. I'd told him and his missis about you an' us all when he took us in for a sup of tea the first time I went down, an' I told them our Bella was the next one for work, an' that she was going on eight an' a big lass. An' that's how it came about. You've got to take her down the morrow to the big house to see.'

She now put her hand on Jimmy's shoulder and pulled him to her, and for a moment he forgot he was a working man of ten years old and he put his arms about her and hid his head in her waist, and it was as they stood like this that she thought, There's no one of them like Jimmy. And it was then that she decided to tell him.

They were walking on again, he with his head slightly bent now, when she said, 'Your news couldn't have come at a better time, Jimmy, 'cos I've got somethin' to tell you an' all.'

He turned and looked at her now; but again she was looking ahead, and when she said simply, 'I think I'm going to have a bairn, Jimmy,' he stopped dead and let her walk on.

When she turned towards him and saw the look on his

face she shook her head, saying, '’Tisn’t my fault, you know that; ’tisn’t my fault.'

Aye, he knew it wasn’t her fault, but he was recalling a memory, faint, yet not so faint, for it had happened two years back when the women of the hamlet had thrown stones at Aggie Holland because she was havin’ a bairn and had no man. He hadn’t really understood it then, only that they said she enticed the men at the haymaking, but he remembered them stoning her. She left her mother’s house and he hadn’t heard her name mentioned since.

He was walking by her side again, his head bent deeply now, when he said, 'How will you manage?'

'Somehow,' she answered. 'I’ll have to, won’t I?' And to this he replied, 'Aye.'

They had gone some distance farther on when he asked tentatively, 'Can I . . . should I . . . well, what I mean is, do you want me to tell Matthew?'

She had told him because she wanted him to tell Matthew. Although she couldn’t put it into words, her silence spoke for her.

'Are you stark staring mad altogether? Do you want to potch your chance?'

Matthew had just come in the door and taken his coat off and was about to put it on the nail. Turning and looking at his mother, he asked, 'What do you mean? What chance?'

'Don’t you come the simpleton with me.' She was standing close to him now, her words low. 'You know what I mean. You’ve been over the fells again, haven’t you?'

He put his coat on the nail without taking his eyes from her. 'Yes, I’ve been over the fells again. Now what are you going to make of that?'

'I’ve said it, you’re stark, staring mad unless' – she paused and screwed up her eyes – 'you think it’s your duty to go.'

136

He surveyed her for a moment. 'Me duty?'

'Aye, that's what I said, your duty.' There was a long pause before she ended, 'I hear she's goin' to have a bairn.'

The flesh on his cheekbones whitened with the tension of his jaws, the natural fresh colour of his face deepened; but she wasn't warned or deterred by the signs, for she went on, 'Well, it would be no surprise to anybody for miles, would it, because you're never off her doorstep or her cave step, which is more like it. And the fantastic tale goin' on the wind about her bein' taken down by the young master of Fischel; why, that's a midsummer's imagining if ever I heard one.'

When his hand shot out and gripped her shoulder, she started and shrunk from him and spluttered, 'Leave go of me! What's come over you?'

'Do you know something?' His square face was close to her long, thin one. 'There's times I've asked meself however you became me mother. Do you know that?'

He watched the expression in her eyes change, and for the first time in his life he knew he had hurt her, but he went on, 'You're a mean creature. Inside and out you're mean. And your mother's mean, and your sister's mean, you're all mean; and you've crushed me dad for years. But there's one thing I'm goin' to tell you, you're not goin' to crush me. I'm not wearin' the breeches just to cover me loins. Now, you understand that! An' don't try to take them off me. You drive me too far and I warn you, I'll do what I threatened afore, I'll bring her here with the lot of them, into this house, and you'll put up with it, or get out.'

He released her with a thrust of his hand and she fell against the wall. And she stayed there as if stunned, while he tucked in the neck of his shirt and rolled up his sleeves and poured water into the wooden bowl. When he had dried himself on the hessian towel hanging from a nail by the window and turned to leave the scullery, she said,

'Wait a minute'; and when he looked at her over his shoulder, she went on, her tone slightly modified now, 'I only said what I did for your own good, for you should know that Rose has got wind of it. She was over here not an hour since quizzing, talking about going over to see the poor starving bairns for herself. But it isn't the starving bairns she wants to see, it's her.'

He made no answer but went through the kitchen, his grandmother's and his aunt's eyes following him, then up the stairs and into his father's room.

His father seemed to be waiting for him, but then he always looked like that, lost, lonely. He stood for a moment looking down at him before saying, 'No matter what you heard, I didn't give it to her.'

'I wouldn't blame you if you had, lad.'

At this the fire went out of him, and he turned away and walked to the little window and looked down on the village street; and when his father said, 'Lying here you get a sort of second sight, and I know that you're only taking on Rose because of what goes with her, but your heart isn't in it, else you wouldn't have waited this long.'

Matthew bit hard on his lower lip and closed his eyes tight.

'What's she like, the young one?'

What was Cissie like? A bright spring morning, a wood carpeted with anemones, spelling purity . . . Purity? Not any more. But that wasn't her fault. He saw the bloom of her skin, the softness of her lips and the depths of her eyes, and the heart and the spirit of her that struggled against adversity and fended for nine children on that wind-ravaged land.

He turned towards the bed, his shoulders hunched, his arms hanging limp, his head slightly bowed, and answered, 'She's a fine lass'; then he went out.

When he entered the mill yard his shoulders were back,

his head up and his chin thrust out. The miller was at the pulley, and he turned his head in Matthew's direction; and perhaps it was because his hands were occupied that he did not raise one as was usual and wave a greeting instead of shouting above the clatter and creaking of the sails.

Matthew tapped on the door as he entered the kitchen, and Rose Watson turned from lighting the lamp, looked at him, then turned back to the lamp again and adjusted the glass before saying, 'Hello there. What brings you the night?'

He walked slowly to the other side of the table so that he could face her, and when she looked at him, he said, 'I've something to say to you, Rose.'

'Aye? Yes. Well then, sit down.' She pointed to a rocking chair to the side of the blazing fire, and he said, 'I'll sit after if I may; I want to get this thing clear first. You came to the house this afternoon and had a natter with Mother.'

'Yes. Yes, I was passing that way.' She moved the lamp to the end of the table and picked up from a chair a shirt that she was making, then sat down.

'I understand that you've heard that young Cissie Brodie is goin' to have a bairn, an' you've likely heard an' all that I've been across there and finished the dwelling for them, and in spite of the fact that you've also heard tell that that young Master Fischel was sent off to sea for rapin' her you can't help, like the rest of them, in puttin' two and two together.'

'Oh, Matthew! I . . .' He lifted his hand up to silence her. 'I know, I know, you've never said it. But it's a suspicion in your mind. Well, I want to tell you that the story that you heard about the young master is the truth, an' that the child is none of mine.' . . . God that it only were! He felt for a moment that he had spoken the words aloud, but then she was looking at him softly through the lamplight, saying, 'Well now, Matthew, you can come and sit down now, can't you?'

Before he moved from the table he asked, 'Are you satisfied in your mind?' And to this she answered, 'Yes, Matthew, I'm satisfied in me mind.'

As he took his seat opposite her she bent her head over her sewing; and as she moved the needle rhythmically, she said, 'I wouldn't have blamed you for being taken with her, for she's a comely enough girl, whereas me, well' – she moved her head slightly – 'I know what I am. I have nothing to offer you but the mill when my father goes and what goes with it.'

If she had left it at the first part something in him would have responded to her and he would have said, 'You're a good woman, Rose; it's a woman I want, not a girl,' but she had added the clause to the match, the bonus that went with the bond, so to speak, the bond that tied a man to a pit, to a farmer, or to a woman he didn't love, but which offered a bonus for the hazards of the labour.

When, going off on a tangent as it were, yet her words still connected with the same theme, she now said, 'William's doing fine. Father, he says he's showin' signs of being cut out for the mill,' it was as if she had actually bound him to the chair opposite her, and he knew the irony of it was that only by marrying her could he help Cissie, for if anything were to happen to prevent their coming together then William would be sent packing, and there would be no sacks on a Sunday for the boys to carry across the fells. Furthermore, there would be no apprenticeship for Jimmy in the shop, for no-one knew better than himself that he was in no position to keep an apprentice; his trade was worsening, and without the prospect of an alliance with the mill his future, unless there was a miraculous upsurge of orders, looked bleak. She had said, 'Sit down, Matthew,' and he had sat down; and now he was bound to this armchair, hand and foot, for life.

3

It was the end of November. The days were short and cold, the nights long and cold, but inside the dwelling place there was a modicum of snugness. The fire was on night and day and the temperature inside the walls was bearable, even on the coldest days they'd had so far, and the branches of wood piled high against both end walls not only helped to support the structure but gave Cissie a feeling of security.

It was over a fortnight since Matthew had brought the last load of wood. She hadn't seen him since and she wondered whether the incident that happened that day had anything to do with his absence, for as he was unloading the cart and handing the branches down to her two women from the hamlet passed on the track. They, too, had been to the wood, as the bundles on their backs showed, and they had stopped and looked upwards to the great pile on the cart and the man unloading it, and he had paused in his handling of the wood and looked down at them; and when one made a sound in her throat like a loud derisive 'Huh!' she had seen him grit on his teeth. Well, whether the incident had kept him away or not, she knew this morning as she stood in the hamlet and faced the two women she had seen that day, that she was now stamped as a bad 'un.

She had heard through Sarah meeting Dilly Taggart that the Robinsons were killing a pig, and she had come into the hamlet to see if she could get some tripe or chitterlings. She had gone round the back way to the Robinsons' yard where Mr Robinson kept his pigs. The yard showed evidence of recent slaughter and Mr Robinson himself was in the shed cutting up the beast. He half turned to her, then turned away again as she asked, 'Have you any to spare, Mr Robinson?' And before he could answer his wife came to the house door and, her eyes hard and her voice tight, had put in quickly, 'No, it's all spoke for'; then had added, 'If I'd known you were short of a bit we would have kept you some; but then we didn't think you'd need it.'

She had stared at the woman, then at the man before turning away, and outside in the lane she had come face to face with the two women who had seen Matthew bring her the wood. They were Mrs Smith and Mrs Proctor. Mrs Proctor was the widow of the carpenter who used to make the coffins. She had no children and now lodged with Mrs Smith. After returning their stares she turned her back on them and walked away, until the mud came with a plop between her shoulder blades. Swinging round, she saw that Mrs Smith had thrown it and that Mrs Proctor was stooping down and scooping up a handful of clarts. But when she had straightened and pulled back her arm, she stopped, and while still looking at Cissie she turned her hand 'round, and the clarts fell with a sound like cows' splatter on the ground again.

Alone on the fells, she put her head down and cried, but she wiped away all traces of her tears before she entered the dwelling again, where now the room and cave seemed almost empty, holding only Sarah, Charlotte, Joe, Annie, and Nellie.

Bella had been installed for a month in Pinewood House, Westoe, in Shields, and on her two half-days she had kept them enthralled with tales of the splendour of the establishment. Nine in the family there were and fifteen servants to look after them, and the master, Mr Braithwaite, owned a brewery and other places besides; and she had said to Cissie, if she only saw the clothes the young mistresses wore she would faint right away. And did she know that Miss Catherine, who was the same age as herself, never wore less than four petticoats and the two top ones had six rows of lace on them from the waist down. And then there was the life that went on in the house; and the visitors; and the carriages coming and going. Oh, it was wonderful, wonderful. That is, she admitted after a time, except for the work. She was at the poss tub and the mangle from six till noon, but of course they had time off for breakfast. Then from twelve till half-past six at night she was ironing the roughs, which were the servants' clothes; but of course she had a half-hour for her dinner. And Mrs Weir, the laundress, had promised her that if she paid attention she would let her iron the young mistress's hankies, and that was something to look forward to.

Mary's visits were different. Mary was quiet and tired looking; she was thin, thinner even than Sarah and Charlotte; she didn't talk much but she sat close to Cissie all the while; and one day when Cissie, putting her arm around her, asked, 'Are you all right, Mary?' she replied, her blue eyes misting, 'When I'm fourteen, Cissie, and experienced, can I look out for somethin' else?' And Cissie said, 'Yes, dear, yes, perhaps afore that.'

As she had worried more over William than she had over Jimmy, now she worried more over Mary than she did over Bella, although until Bella had gone into service it was she with her forward ways who had given her concern.

Anyway, she now had only five of them to see to.

By the middle of December she had stopped being sick in the morning and felt well again, at least in her body. There was a small mound in her stomach on which she placed her hands at night, but it created no feeling in her, not even of regret or resentment; the thing was done and couldn't be undone, it had to be faced. And although she didn't want this child, it was in her and it would be born, and part of it would be her; reason it out as she might that she had taken no part in the act, part of the child would be her . . .

143

The Sunday before Christmas Day the boys did not come over the frost-hard fells with sacks; instead, they came on the cart with Matthew, and on the cart there were not only sacks holding the usual gifts of oatmeal, bread, and cheese, but also a sack with a currant cake in it, a bag of onions, and a dish of pease pudding. And that was not all. There was a great bundle of clothing on the cart, clothing belonging to Rose Watson's mother, and her mother before her, which had been stored away in the loft and which, her message said, she hoped Cissie would find useful in cutting up for the children. The woman was kind. If only she didn't know why she was being kind, she would want to bless her, for the clothes were like a gift from heaven itself.

It was weeks since she had seen Matthew, and now that he was near to her she could not look at him, nor apparently he at her. He gave all his attention to Annie, Charlotte and Sarah as they hung round him, touching him, vying with each other for his hand on their head, for he was the only man in their lives; meanwhile Joe was being playfully punched and teased by William and Jimmy, both of them, their cheeks red, their eyes bright, and overall well-looking.

When the hullabaloo died down she glanced at Matthew and said, 'Could you do with a drop of tea?' and he was on the point of refusing when he changed his mind, saying, 'Aye. Yes, it's been a cold drive, I could do with something hot.' He didn't feel mean in taking her tea for he had a quarter pound in the tail of his greatcoat pocket which he would put on the chest when she wasn't looking, and with it a pound of sugar, and that would be luxury for her indeed.

When they'd all had a 'drop of tea', Jimmy, with wisdom beyond his years, contrived to leave their Cissie alone for a minute or so with Matthew by saying, 'Come on the lot of you's an' do some choppin'. There's a barley

sugar for the one of you's who does the most, not countin'
you, our Willie.' He held up the sweet in one hand while
punching at his brother with the other. Then they all
scampered through the doorway and outside; and Cissie
went and closed the door after them to keep the cold out
before going to the top of the chest where the food had
been emptied. Touching one thing after another, she said
quietly over her shoulder, 'Will you tell her that I'm
grateful?'

There was a pause before he said, 'She knows that,' and
another pause before he asked, 'How you gettin' along?'

'Oh, finely.' She glanced at him and smiled. 'The
wood's a godsend; we'd never have been able to manage
without the wood.'

'You've got enough to last you another month or so, I
imagine?' he said.

'Oh, longer than that. The pile seems bigger than the
place.' She moved her eyes about the room. 'And I keep
pickin' to help it along.'

'You shouldn't go out pickin' this weather. Are . . . are
you feeling all right in yourself?'

'Yes, yes.' She pulled her shoulders up straight, as if
aiming to flatten her stomach.

He walked down the length of the table, then back, and
stopped in front of the little fireplace, and putting his
hands out to the blaze said, 'Do you know where to get
help?'

'Help?'

He knew that her face was turned towards him questioningly as was her voice, but he didn't look at her as he said,
'I mean, when the time comes, you need a woman.' He felt
her move away and knew that she had reached the
entrance to the cave and was standing there. 'You'll need
somebody.' He did not add, 'especially with the first one,'
but went on, 'There's a woman in Rosier's village. Her
name's Hannah Bellamy. She's rough but good-hearted.'

She remained silent, thinking. He's right, he's right. But why must it be him to tell me such a thing? And he hadn't said, 'Go to the hamlet and ask one of the women,' which would have been in order – he must have heard about the mud throwing; news travelled on the wind.

He turned to her now and said quietly, 'Well, I must be away. I drive me mother to church; she'll be waiting.'

She nodded at him and came towards the table and, resting her hands on it, looked down at them and muttered under her breath, 'You've been so kind, good, I . . . I hate to impose on you, but could you do one more thing for me?'

'Name it.'

She looked up at him, then towards the door, and said, 'I'd feel better when I was out if the bairns could lock themselves in. If I could have two sockets to lay a bar across.'

He narrowed his eyes at her as he asked, 'Somebody been after them?'

She made a small motion with her head, then said, 'There was a man came up here day afore yesterday. He offered to buy Joe.'

'God's truth! What!'

'Aye, he did. He started with three guineas, then went up to five. He's lookin' for climbin' boys. I daren't let Joe out of me sight, but he's such a live wire I never know where he is.'

Matthew took in a deep breath. There were some things that stirred him to rage. He had read in Hetherington's *Poor Man's Guardian* the farce of how the rich had their flues reconstructed, solely, they said, to provide working ease and comfort for the cleaning boys. A few decent men were trying to get an act through Parliament now to prevent a child under ten years old being sent up a chimney, so Parson Hedley said, and then at that age he must only be an apprentice, which meant a poor workhouse brat.

146

Other children weren't to be employed under fourteen years, but he himself would believe that would come about when he saw it, for up till now they still collected them at five and six. Aye, and could find plenty at that age when it meant five guineas in the parents' pockets and one less to feed. At Newcastle, not a month ago, a child had died an agonising death after dropping exhausted on to a fire. Something should be done about it, and about so many things. He was always saying this inside himself, but what could you do? If you lashed out with your hands they soon had you behind bars, or away to Botany Bay. It was only three years ago that they hanged the Lilley brothers for wounding a gamekeeper. He supposed Parson Hedley was right: in the long run education was the answer, being able to read and write. But it meant that a man had, in a way, to be extra strong-willed and put a curb on both his tongue and hands just to go on believing it.

He said grimly, 'I'll fix it for you. I'll bring it over the morrow and put it on. And I'd keep Joe tight near you for the next few days if I was you, and,' he added, 'I'll keep me eyes open for the scraper. It'll be pity help him if we meet up.'

Yet he knew as he spoke that if he did meet the scraper and he took him to the justice what would happen. The justice, who was Squire Tallen, would himself pay the man's fine on the side. This was being done all the time, because them in the big houses wanted to make out that without the climbing boys there was danger their mansions might be burned down.

He sometimes wondered why he listened to Parson Hedley at all, except when he was talking of literature, because half of his time he was putting over the goodness of God. And whose God? The God of the lords and the landowners, or their opponents for power, the factory owners and the mine owners. The goodness of God!

When he went out abruptly, saying no more, Cissie

thought there were things about him she didn't understand. But then, how could she, for after all what did she know about him except that he was kind, and had a feeling for her; but just a feeling, for if it had been love he couldn't really think of marrying Rose Watson, in spite of the numbers depending on him. But even as she thought this she knew it was the yammering of a young girl that was no more, for with a child inside her she had become a woman.

On Christmas Eve a snow blizzard covered the fells, and during the whole of the day the light was like that of twilight and they could only see each other clearly when she put fresh wood on the fire and it blazed up. But they were warm inside and out for she had cut up the old clothes and roughly remade them. Moreover, they'd had rabbit stew, together with potatoes and mangel-wurzels, for two days now. Joe had been lucky, for he had caught a rabbit on the open fells, and they were well set for Christmas Day too. When the boys had come yesterday they had brought her a hand of pork with plenty of lean on it, a big currant loaf, and a dish of pease pudding.

As it was Christmas Eve, she had done what her da always did, see that they all had a warm washdown before they went to bed. Other times it would be cold water, or the river itself, but Christmas Eve was special.

After each one of the girls was washed, she put her back into her petticoat and straight into bed, and when Joe had donned his shirt he followed them. All in the one bed, they played and teased and quarrelled until, standing at the opening of the cave, she peered through the dim light reflected from the fire and warned them, 'Now stop it the lot of you's, else I'm cookin' no dinner the morrow, mind.' They giggled and laughed at this, knowing that the threat was without foundation; then calling, 'Good night, our Cissie. Good night, our Cissie,' they settled down.

Going to the fireplace now, she sat down and took off her boots and looked at her red chilblained feet – she had worn no stockings for months. Slowly she put them into the rapidly cooling water in which she had washed them all, and, closing her eyes and letting out a deep sigh, she relaxed. And so weary was she that in a moment she had fallen into a doze.

How long she had been asleep she didn't know but she was brought startlingly awake by a tapping on the door. Wide-eyed, she turned and looked towards it. Making to rise and forgetting that her feet were still in the bowl and cold now, she almost upset the water over the floor. She grabbed at a bit of hessian and roughly dried her feet; then going to the door, she asked, 'Who's that?'

'Me . . . Matthew.'

'Oh.' She took off the bar and pulled the door wide, and he stood in the entrance shaking the snow from his hat and coat.

When he was in the room she stared into his snow-rimmed eyes and said under her breath, 'How did you manage to get the cart across in this?'

He went to the table and put his lantern on it, and the bag he had been carrying, saying 'I couldn't use the horse. I walked.'

'Walked?' It was bad enough walking over the treacherous hills and hollows of the fell land during daylight in weather like this, but at night anything could happen; you just had to slip and when they found you, you'd be stiff. She said, 'You shouldn't have come out on such a night.'

He turned and looked at her where she was standing barefooted on the rock floor, and he said, 'And you should get into your boots, you'll get your death.'

'Oh!' She made a sound in her throat, which dismissed his concern. 'I'm used to it. I've . . . I've been washin' them, I mean the bairns.' She went to the hearth and picked up the bowl of water and set it to one side; then, looking at him again, she said, 'Can I take your coat, you'll find the benefit of it when you go out?'

He paused for a moment as if considering, then said, 'Aye, you're right.' And taking the coat off and turning it inside out, he laid it across a chair, adding, 'I went to Shields Market the day.'

'Oh! I've never been to the market. Me da always said he would take us but . . . but the chance never came up.'

'Oh, it's a sight,' he said. 'And the people. You can't get stirred. But you're glad when you get out of it, and away from the town; it's too noisy, too much bustle.' He was now tipping out the contents of the sack on the table. 'I thought these would help their Christmas.' He pushed aside six oranges and a bundle of toffee apples, and pointing to a bag, he said, 'Them's tiger nuts; they'll keep their jaw goin'.' And now he separated from the rest, two parcels, one largish, the other small, and having placed them one on top of the other, he handed them to her, saying softly, 'A warm Christmas, Cissie.'

She took the parcels from his hand, looked at them for a moment, then raised her eyes to his. Her face looked blank.

'I hope they fit; I just guessed your size.'

She still stared at him until he said, 'Well, aren't you going to look and see what they are?'

She opened the smaller package first and when she laid across her hands a pair of long, brown, hand-knitted stockings, she pressed her lips together but said nothing. Then her hands were fumbling at the larger parcel; and as she undid the wrapping, the contents seemed to breathe and swell. Slowly she unfolded a fawn shawl with a pink fringe; then as she held it before her she looked as Charlotte or Sarah might have looked when confronted with wonder: a child believing yet not believing. She lifted her eyes to his but was unable to speak; a great warmth was filling her; her eyes were full of light. Never in her life had she possessed anything of colour; her clothes had always been black or brown, and never had she worn anything new. Once a year her da had taken the money he had saved for the purpose and gone to the rag market in Newcastle, and there, for five shillings, bought a pile of old clothes enough to last a year, and her mother had cut them up and remade them. But not once had her da brought back anything bright and light; he always picked serges and worsteds, knowing these to be hard-wearing. But here she had a dove-fawn shawl with a glowing pink fringe.

Slowly she gathered it into her arms and held it to her breast as if it were a child, and, her head bowing deep over it, tears rained down her face and fell on to it.

'Aw, Cissie. Cissie.' He was standing close to her, his hands gripping her shoulders. 'Ah, don't. I thought it would please you, something . . . something different.'

When her head fell lower still and the sobs shook her body his hands moved from her shoulders and slid slowly round her back; and he held her close and gentle, his chin resting on her bent head, his eyes staring at the jagged wall of rock opposite to him, from which was oozing little rivulets of moisture. Then after a moment, as if breaking through a barrier of restraint, his mouth dropped into her hair, and he moved his face back and forwards over it.

She was still holding the shawl, her arms crossed over it were like a barrier between them, and he pulled it from them and threw it on the table and, lifting her head sharply upwards with his hand, he looked into her tear-washed face and muttered thickly, 'I love you, Cissie. You know that, don't you? I love you, but . . . but I've got to go through with this other, I've got to.' He now shook her slightly. 'You understand why? Do you understand why?'

She gulped, closed her eyes, and nodded her head once.

His voice was coming like a whispering growl from his throat now. 'If it just rested with me I would take you and the horde of them . . . an'—' He jerked his head upwards before adding, 'An' the one that's comin'. I would take the lot if it was just me. But there's them back home; I'm all they've got to live by, and trade's not so good.' Not so good? He could have said it had been getting steadily worse over the past two months, that he'd had no orders since making that cart, that he'd had to put Walters on half-time in order to keep Jimmy on, and that he must have been stark staring mad to go into Shields and pay seventeen and six for the shawl. The two shillings he had given for the stockings was really more than he could afford; but seventeen and six! The money he should have paid Riley's bill with. Still, Riley wasn't waiting for it for his bread and butter, else he would have stumped it up right away. Riley was a man with four ironmonger's shops, a man who was buying property; he could afford to wait. But still, seventeen and six; how was he going to make it up? – To hell! To hell's flames. It might be the one and only thing he could ever buy her . . . out of his own money that was.

He pleaded now with her, bending his head close to hers, 'Tell me you understand why I've got to do what I'm goin' to do, just tell me, Cissie.'

She cleared her throat, wiped each cheek with her fingers, then said softly, 'I understand, Matthew.'

They looked deep into each other; then, his breath on her face, he whispered, 'Will you tell me one thing more? Do you love me?'

Her gaze did not move from his, but she did not speak. Then with a sudden movement she fell against him, and his mouth came on hers and they stood there locked together and swaying until she gasped for breath. Then they were staring at each other again. And now he drew her to the one chair that had a back to it. Sitting down, he pulled her gently on to his knees and, cradling her in his arms, he said thickly, 'Let's stay so a while; it may have to last us a lifetime.'

4

She carried the child high. It pushed out under her breasts and by the beginning of May she couldn't fasten her skirt over it although she had put in gussets. At various times the child kicked her. It seemed strong and impatient to be born, but it had six weeks more to go. She wished the days would fly for she was tired of the burden of her body; she felt cumbersome and she became weary so quickly.

It had been a beautiful spring, and it was just as well for there had been another strike at Rosier's pit. They had brought gangs of men over from Ireland and turned the miners from the cottages, and for a time she had neighbours on the fells, but at a good distance away. Yet their presence made her feel fearful, because, copying her, they had carted stones from the quarry and built shanties, and, although it was still common land, the sight of so many small stone huts could incense the gentry, and they might take the law in their hands and enclose the fells.

The sun was shining brightly today but there was a very high wind blowing and she had to hold on to her shawl, not the fawn and pink one. As she walked along the main rut-hollowed road from the farm she had to pass by the North Lodge of Lord Fischel's estate and she always hurried along this section of the road. Today she had passed the gate and was just about to leave the road and mount the fells when a carriage came rocking towards her and she scrambled up the bank and stood for a moment breathlessly looking down at the galloping horses and glimpsing through the windows the face of a man she recognised, although she had seen him only once before.

Lord Fischel, too, had seen the girl only once before but

in the fleeting glimpse he got of her standing on the bank silhouetted against the skyline he remembered her; and the glimpse had shown him more than the girl's face: it had shown him that she was with child.

As the carriage rolled through the North Lodge gates and up the driveway and across the park he sat straight in his seat, his eyes flicking along the rows of buttons in the black leather upholstery opposite as if he were counting them.

Having arrived at the house, he was met on the steps as usual by Hatton, solicitous always for his master but not presuming to enquire if he had had a good journey.

It was the valet, Cunningham, who was privileged to ask this question of his master as he helped him off with his boots, then his coat and cravat. 'I trust you have had a good day, m'Lord?' And to this his master replied, 'Fair, Cunnings, fair.'

The valet's name was Cunningham but a three-syllabled name was considered too distinguished for a servant and so had been reduced to Cunnings. Cunningham did not object to this. He was a small, thoughtful man, with the quiet, restrained manner expected of a valet; but his position in the household was unique, in that as much as it was possible he was in his master's confidence.

His master now lifted one foot up after the other so that his stockings could be pulled off. He always changed his stockings after a journey and he watched the process as he said, 'Do you remember, Cunnings, the reason why I sent my son away?'

Calmly Cunningham replied, 'Yes, m'Lord.' His Lordship was already aware without asking that he knew the reason, the whole household knew the reason – had it not been witnessed by the two coachmen? – in fact, the whole county knew the reason, and Cunningham knew that his master was thought to be insane for wreaking such vengeance on his son; girl servants were dropped every day by the sons of their masters. It was looked upon in some quarters as necessary practice for the young bloods. If there was no result of the association, well and good, and the young person might benefit by a present; but if there was a result she was sent packing. The issue of the wealthy was so mixed with the poor that he wondered, during his moments of contemplation on such matters, that the strain didn't rise above its environment and make itself evident. But perhaps it did just that, because there were men everywhere risking their livelihoods in order to learn to read and write. This in turn, in some cases, made them become pamphleteers and write against the blood that was surely in them.

Life, Cunningham often considered, was a very strange thing; but he was satisfied with his share of it, and had been for the last thirty years, during which time he had served his master even before he came into the title, and had never been out of his presence for more than twenty-four hours since. He had dressed His Lordship for his wedding; he had accompanied him on his honeymoon; and as the years went by he had suffered with him through Her Ladyship's lack of decorum. He had, like his master, but from a distance, listened to her upbraiding and talk that did not befit an ordinary woman, let alone a lady; and he had, like his master, disliked, from the very beginning, the twins her ladyship had presented to her husband.

Henry Cunningham did not believe in a God, or a hereafter, but he believed in his master's right to rule through the heritage of the Fischel family.

And now His Lordship said, 'I would like you, Cunnings, to take a walk on the fells tomorrow and make the acquaintance of a person who lives there in what I understand to be an extension to a cave. Her name is Brodie; she is with child. I want to know when it is expected.'

'Yes, m'Lord.' There was no hesitation in the answer, no sign of surprise at such an order.

His Lordship, now stripped of his clothes, even of his skin-tight underpants, lay on a straight couch placed at some little distance from the fire, and submitted himself to be rubbed down with a warm rough towel, after which Cunningham sprinkled eau-de-cologne liberally on his hands and massaged the thin almost fleshless frame.

As Lord Fischel gently sniffed the stringent odour up his nostrils he thought, It could be anybody's; they lie like rabbits. But he would know by the day on which it was born. He did not ask himself why he was taking an interest in the offspring of a girl who was, after all, only fell trash, for he could not admit to himself that he was missing his son. He had never liked his children; he had been glad to get rid of them. Singly, each had been an irritant; combined, and under this roof with him, they had become nothing short of a nuisance; yet there was that in him, if he would acknowledge it, that was crying out for his son. There was that in him that would have altered the charter of the *Virago* and brought his son back to these shores again. But there was nothing in him that desired that he should ever set eyes on his daughter again.

The gentleman was dressed plainly in black and he asked the way to Brockdale.

'Oh! Brockdale.' She shook her head at him. 'You're goin' the wrong way. This leads to the hamlet of Heatherbrook; Brockdale lies over there.' She pointed. 'And it's all of three to four miles.'

'Oh! That far?' he said.

'Yes, Sir.'

He raised his head and looked up at the sky, saying, 'It could be rain, I won't venture that far today. It's very pleasant up here.' He spoke as a stranger to these parts, and she said, 'Yes, Sir, in the spring and summer; but at the back end it's bleak.'

When he turned from his direction and walked by her

side she didn't mind. He was a gentleman, yet there was a qualifying element in her classification. Perhaps not quite a gentleman, for gentlemen wouldn't talk kindly with her like he did. But someone like Parson Hedley. And he was dressed not unlike the parson – sober, but much more neatly and very clean; his hands were whiter than any woman's she had ever seen.

As they walked along the track below the dwelling, his prophesised rain came in a sharp stinging shower and she said, 'Oh! Sir, you're going to get wet.' She turned from him as if to hurry up the rise; then looking at him again and realising he was without a greatcoat, she pointed over her shoulder. 'You could shelter if you like.' He was a stranger but she had no fear of him.

'Thank you; I'd be pleased to.' He hurried after her towards the odd-looking habitation, and when she opened the door and stood aside to let him pass, his step became slow as if he were walking into an unknown world. And such was the impression the interior made on him that his imperturbability was shattered. Three little girls were sitting on a piece of black matting before a small, rough fireplace, and in a basket was another child. The girl looked at them, then said immediately and, he thought, anxiously, 'Where's Joe?' And the tallest girl, her eyes on him, answered her sister, saying, 'He's down by the burn. He's comin'. We ran 'cos we saw it was gonna rain; you said keep dry.'

He watched her push past him now and go and stand in the rain and call, 'Joe! Joe!' and then she turned into the room again and sighed as she said, 'He's comin',' and by way of explanation, she added, 'It's my little brother.' He thought that she was very anxious that the boy shouldn't get wet, yet when the fair, bright-faced child came into the dwelling she did not attempt to divest him of his wet clothes.

'Would you care to sit down?'

'No; thank you.' He refused the only real chair he could see in the place. Opposite him was a dark hole which he surmised led into a cave. He glanced up at the lean-to roof and saw it was constructed of wooden beams with thatch across them. Then, looking about him, he shuddered inwardly at the bareness of the place. Only one thing surprised him pleasantly, and that was the absence of stench; he understood that you could cut the smell with a knife in such places. In fact the servants were forbidden to enter the Hall if they had visited a miner's or farm labourer's cottage before first being picked over and deloused in the slaughter room. The laundress did the delousing for the women and the second coachman for the men. Because of this, servants were rarely engaged from roundabout; His Lordship preferred that they should come from away so that they would need to visit their people only once a year.

He stood in silence for some time, the children staring at him. Then the girl said, 'I could offer you a drop of tea, Sir, if you'd care?'

'Oh no; thank you. Thank you very much. It's very kind of you, but the shower is nearly over and I must be on my way.'

He found he was speaking to her not in the tone he used with the servants in the House, but almost as if she were an equal.

He put on his hat and, going towards the open door, said, 'It's almost over; the sun is coming out.' Then turning to her, he added, 'Thank you for your kindness. If I happen to be walking this way again I hope I may ask after you?'

His manner was so courteous, kindly, that she smiled at him and said, 'Yes, Sir. Thank you, Sir.' She did not ask where he was from or where he was going. You did not question gentlemen; or near gentlemen.

* * *

Forty-five minutes later Cunningham stood before his master in the study, saying, 'I did not find the opportunity, m'Lord, to ascertain when the child would be born, but I have made it possible to call on her on my walks across the fells.'

Lord Fischel stared up at his man for a moment; then looking down at the paper on which he had been writing, he said, 'That is well, Cunnings. Tell me, how did you find the person?'

'Civil, m'Lord, and clean; unusually so under the circumstances.'

'The circumstances?'

'The habitation, m'Lord. It's an erection built in front of a hole in an outcrop of rock.'

'I see.' His Lordship moved his head. Then picking up his pen and looking down at the writing paper again, he said, 'You will avail yourself of the opportunity to call at regular intervals until you get the required information. Even then it may not be accurate, these things fluctuate.' He glanced up at his man, and Cunningham made a motion of agreement with his head and His Lordship ended, 'You'll continue to take your walks until the actual day.'

'Very good, m'Lord.'

With a slight movement of his hand Lord Fischel dismissed the valet and began to write, but only until the door had closed. Then he sat back in his chair. He still refused to ask himself where his interest in the birth of this child would lead him; but he did think that he was pleased to learn that the girl was clean, for the idea that the seed of his seed should be breeding in a dirty body was intolerable to him.

5

It was the middle of June and she was weary unto death and she had still another fortnight to go. Moreover, adding to her misery, it had rained for three days, only this morning fairing up.

Sarah and Charlotte had gone gooseberry picking, taking Annie with them, but she hadn't allowed Joe to go because she herself couldn't go. Last week the man had been 'round again asking to buy Joe and saying he was growing so fast he would soon be worth nothing, and she had yelled at him and told him she'd tell the justice. And now Joe had slipped out and she couldn't find him.

For the past four weeks she had felt desperately lonely and at times in the night she had cried, not for her da now, or her ma, but just for someone to talk to.

She was forever trying the impossible task of pushing Matthew out of her mind, for at times she felt bitter against him. After what he had said, and how he had acted on Christmas Eve, she thought that he would have come once in every short while, say once a week or so, but she had only seen him four times altogether since that night, and then he had stood away from her, even when the bairns weren't about. All he had asked was how she was and if she was managing. She couldn't understand him; she knew he must marry the woman, but he had said it was her he loved. If it hadn't been for the gentleman who walked across the fells and passed the time of day with her now and again she wouldn't have spoken to an adult soul for weeks, for since she had become so big, and with the incident in the hamlet still in the forefront of her mind, she sent Sarah and Charlotte to Brockdale for the few groceries that they needed; and in a new arrangement she now took William's wages from the mill in flour and she knew she benefited by it.

She slithered over the wet humps at the top of a rise from where, in the distance, she could see the outskirts of the wood and, putting her hands to her mouth, she called, 'Jo-oo! You Jo-oo!' And when there was no response to her calling she became filled with panic. If that man got Joe she would die; she would die when she was having the bairn 'cos she would have no wish to live. Joe with his impish face and lightning movements, his gay laugh, being forced up a chimney, being stuck up a chimney, being suffocated up a chimney. She held her hands to her face.

If only he would appear, dart from behind a rock perhaps where he was hiding. She wouldn't go for him; at this moment she would hug him to her.

When she had told him of the scraper he had laughed at her and said, 'I can run like a hare; no scraper man is gonna catch me.'

When she heard a cough she swung round, and there was the black-clothed gentleman at the bottom of the rise.

'Good morning,' he called up to her; and she nodded down to him and said, 'Good mornin'.' Perhaps he'd seen Joe. As she made her way down towards him the slope took her into an almost shambling run and she was about ten feet from him and trying to steady herself on the wet grass when she slipped and fell over sideways. For a moment she felt only a kind of numbness; it was when the man took her arm and tried to raise her from the ground that the pain, shooting through her, caused the whole fell to disappear in a sheet of blackness.

A few minutes later, when she got to her feet, she found she couldn't straighten up, and when the man kept asking her if she was hurt she could only nod her head.

'Oh, dear, dear; you shouldn't have run.' He was very solicitous. 'Can I help you to your house?'

'I'll . . . I'll be all right in a minute; it's . . . it's just like a stitch, you know.'

Yes, he knew. But he also knew that what she was feeling wasn't the outcome of a stitch.

She drew in a long breath and straightened up a little further and half smiled at him as she said, 'It's . . . it's going,' then added, 'Have you seen me brother, you know the little one, Joe?'

'No, I'm sorry I haven't. Has he been gone long?'

She jerked her head, then said, 'About an hour I think. 'Tisn't long that, but there's a man. He's . . . he's gatherin' climbing boys. He . . . he wanted to buy him . . . buy Joe. I'm frightened.'

They were walking now, she still bent slightly to the side, and he thought as he watched her slow progress that her concern for her family was commendable. Under the circumstances it would have been wise, he thought, to have one less to feed, besides being paid for the boy; and climbing boys were necessary; how else could you keep the chimneys clear? He understood they were trying out a new-fangled machine but he knew it wouldn't succeed because it couldn't get into the crevices, and he had heard it made a great deal more mess than the boys did.

She was a strange girl, he considered, yet very pleasing. In an odd way over the past weeks he had become attached to her, concerned for her – so much so that the reports he had given his master were a little larger than life, but all to her credit.

They were in sight of the dwelling when Joe came running out of the doorway and Cissie stopped and cried, 'Where you been? Oh, you are a bad 'un!' And when he dashed to her, his face bright and laughing, she encircled him with her arms and held him tightly to her. Then suddenly with a drawn-out groan she fell on to her knees, her body doubled in two.

'Our Cissie! Our Cissie! What's the matter with you?' Joe wasn't laughing now, and after a moment she looked from the man who was bending over her to Joe and, gripping his arm, said, 'Run . . . run to Rosier's village, you know, where Mrs Bellamy lives. Tell her . . . tell her I think me time's come. Bring her back with you. You understand?'

Joe nodded, but as he made off she checked him and after drawing in a long breath she gasped, 'And mind, don't, don't talk to anybody on the road. If you see that man, run; do you hear?'

'Aye, Cissie. Aye, I'll run.'

'Go on.' Her voice pushed him forward, and he went skipping and bounding over the wet ground like a hare itself.

'Let me help you.' Cunningham now took her arm and led her into the dwelling and when he had sat her on the chair, she said, 'Thank you. Thank you.'

'Hadn't you better go to bed?'

'Yes. Yes, I'll do that.' After a moment she got to her feet, saying, 'I'm all right. Thank you. Thank you very much.'

The 'thank you' was a form of dismissal but he still stood in the room and watched her go through the opening into the cave; and after about ten minutes, when he thought he had given her time enough to get undressed and into bed, he called, 'Are you all right?' and she answered, 'Yes, yes, I'm all right.'

Slowly he went and stood in the opening and looked down towards the floor where she was lying on a wooden structure on top of a straw mattress that had a patched quilt over it. She was still fully dressed, and as he was about to speak again he was checked by the sight of her knees suddenly coming upwards while at the same time her head was bent forward as if to meet them.

After a moment when she put her legs down and

adjusted her clothes he asked softly, 'Is it possible for me to get you something?' And to this she only shook her head. Looking about him thought what could he get her anyway in this place? He was surprised that he should find himself so deeply moved and distressed; this assignment, as it were, had turned out quite differently from what he had expected.

Over the years, taking the tone from his master, he had come to look on those who worked outside the precincts of the Hall as a form of species only a little above the animal level. Rosier's village for example was a case in point. They worked and drank and fought and bred amid stench and filth that even some animals wouldn't tolerate. A badger, for example, always kept a clean house.

'O-h G-God! O-h M-a! M-a!'

Her body was doubled up tighter now. He could see her bare thighs. He turned away in embarrassment, also in deep distress, because the sight of the girl was reviving memories that he had buried long ago for his own peace of mind.

After a while there was no sound from the room, and, seeing a bucket of water standing on a chest with a mug near, he examined it to find it was clear, and dipped the mug into the water. He now went slowly into the cave and to her side, and, bending down, said, 'Have this drink of water.'

She raised herself on her elbow and took the mug from his hand and drained it. Then, muttering, 'Ta. Thanks,' she lay back and closed her eyes.

The sweat was pouring down her face. Her hair he noticed, as he had done before, was beautiful. Her skin too, was beautiful. He took out a very white handkerchief and, assuming the position he took up when he pulled off his master's boots, he drew his handkerchief gently around her face, and she opened her eyes and gazed at him; very much, he thought, like a wild doe in agony . . .

And he had seen a wild doe in agony – some huntsmen were very bad shots . . .

Two hours later he was still with her, but looking now from the door towards the track along which he imagined the woman and the boy would come. In the last half-hour her pains had been tumbling one on top of the other and he knew that the birth of the child was imminent.

The cry that pierced his head turned him quickly about, and he went back into the cave and stopped just within the doorway to be dumbfounded by the sight before him. The girl was clutching the sides of the bed, her body arched and heaving; her knees were up and wide apart; her clothes, a mere skirt and a petticoat, were tumbled back about her thighs, and from her womb was poking the head of a child.

It must have been that her groans and cries overlaid the entrance of the woman and the boy, for he found himself thrust aside by a big creature in a black shawl who cried at him, 'Who you? What ya doin' here? Get out of it!'

When he stared at her speechless, she yelled at him, 'Go on. Bugger off! No place for you. What you want in here anyway?'

He didn't immediately obey this creature's commands but stood and watched her bend over the bed and place her big dirty hands under the child that was sliding into the world, and as he watched he became filled with bitterness and anger, for it was just such a woman, big, dirty and liquor-filled as this one was, who had killed his own wife and child, his wife to die in agony, having been poisoned through dirt. He had been twenty-two when that happened and life had ceased for him for a while, until one day, carrying on his work of assistant tailor, he had gone to measure a young man, son of a lord, whose name was Fischel.

He was brought back from the past by the sound of the boy's crying, and he put his hand on his head and turned him about and took him outside. Then, as he was about to take his leave, he remembered that he didn't know the sex of the child and he went back into the cave to hear the woman giving the explanation of why she had been drinking. 'At the mill for boxings I was,' she was saying, 'and the weddin' in full swing. Daughter marryin' the wheelwright from Benham. He's on to a good thing there. But she's not everybody's cup of tea. Still, there was no cheese parin', not only mead but gin they had, an' the hard stuff, an' it all flowin' to each an' everybody.'

He called softly to the woman, 'What is it?'

She had just cut the cord with a knife and, taking the yelling child in her hands, she thrust it towards him, pushing its buttocks up and crying, 'There! That satisfy ya? Who the hell are ya, anyway? You've no right in here.'

He ignored the woman and glanced from the child to the girl on the bed. She was lying quite still now. She looked dead, but her breast was moving up and down. He turned and went out.

6

Lord Fischel thought that if the child had been born a fortnight after the specified date from conception he would have allowed it, but it had been born a fortnight before, which could mean that she had conceived before; people in her position started very young. In his grandfather's time, looking as she did, she would doubtless have been brought to the House when she was fourteen, if not before. Yet in spite of this reasoning, the thought persisted that the date of birth could veer from the nine months, especially in the case of the first child, and with her falling.

As the weeks went by this thought kept recurring, until one day he reopened the subject with Cunningham by saying, 'You may take a stroll over the fells, Cunnings, and see that person again with a view to looking at the child. I want to know if it carries any resemblance.'

Cunningham stood looking at his master's back, and he didn't make any response until His Lordship turned on him and said sharply, 'Well!'

'There is a strong resemblance, m'Lord, I have taken the liberty of visiting the person once or twice since the birth. The . . . the resemblance is most noticeable in . . . in the nose, m'Lord. Children's features are apt to alter, m'Lord, but the bone structure I would say is that of your father. The child's face, although plump with baby fat, is long, and the head large towards the back.'

After a moment His Lordship turned away and he was sitting down before the long mirror, with Cunningham dressing his hair, before he spoke again; and then he asked, 'Would it be possible for you to bring the child here, say at night?'

Cunningham's hands became still on his master's head. His eyes looked through the mirror into the cold grey ones and he so far forgot himself as to omit the appendix as he said bluntly, 'No.' Then hastily he added, 'Well, you see, m'Lord, she's a good mother and seems very taken with the child.'

His Lordship now made a sound in his throat and after a moment he asked, 'Well, how do you suggest I could see it?'

'Well, m'Lord.' Cunningham paused to consider, then said, 'You could be out shooting, m'Lord, and happen to be passing the habitation.'

'You know that I wouldn't be shooting on the open fells.' His voice was impatient. 'And I would never be passing the habitation on foot.' The whole tone dismissed the idea as paltry, and now he went on, command in his voice, 'Tell her that I wish to see the child. She is to bring him to the North Lodge tomorrow afternoon, say at four o'clock.'

The 'but' was stilled on Cunningham's tongue. All he could do was to answer quietly, 'Very well, m'Lord.'

Up to this moment Cunningham had always been proud of his position as valet to Lord Fischel, but now, explaining it to this girl, he felt as if he were confessing to some shameful thing, and his whole manner bore this out. 'You see,' he said, 'I came at His Lordship's behest. I am his valet and, being so, he gave me an order and I had to obey. You understand?'

She had drawn back from him, her face expressing her fear. She had liked this man; she had thought he was kind; he had been the only one with her in that awful travail before the child was born; she had sensed his pity and concern for her, but now she saw him as nothing more than a spy, a lackey at best, obeying orders. She answered him over the distance, saying, 'I don't care who you are, or what you are, I'm not taking him to the Lodge, he's mine. I didn't want him, I had no part in him, but now he's mine and I'm keepin' him.'

'Please, please listen to me.' Cunningham bent deferentially towards her. 'First of all, will you believe me when I say that during the weeks I have known you I have come to respect you, and I would not willingly do anything to add to your burden? It is my hope that I might be able to lighten it.'

'By havin' him taken away? . . . No.'

'Just think for a moment.' He now joined his hands together in front of his narrow chest, and again she was reminded of Parson Hedley. 'They are powerful, I mean lords and all people who live in great mansions.' He was speaking as if he were aligning himself with her against them, the gentry. He went on, his voice just above a whisper now, 'They have ways and means to get what they want, and a position such as yours offers them numerous ways and means . . . You understand me?'

Yes, yes, she understood him; and with understanding her fear grew. He was right, they had power. For one thing they could tear her dwelling place down and turn her off the fells. They could make out she was a bad woman and take the child from her. As her fear increased her defiance ebbed.

Seeing this, he put in soothingly, 'It will only be for a moment, you needn't let him out of your arms. And there'll be no-one else there but His Lordship, I promise you.'

She said now, piteously, 'He won't try to take it away from me, will he, I mean, do something so that I won't be able to keep it?'

'No; His Lordship is a good man, a man of principle. Just think what he did when . . .' His voice trailed away before beginning again, 'He sent his son and daughter away, you know that. You have nothing to fear from His

Lordship. Although' – he moved his head slightly – 'he does not like to be crossed.'

She was staring at him now unblinking; and then she asked, 'What time?'

'Four o'clock. It is barely three yet, you have time to get the baby dressed, and . . . and yourself.' He hesitated on the last words, and she said, 'I am dressed.'

He looked at the patched bodice, the serge skirt, and the hessian apron, and he remembered that these were the clothes she wore when the child was born and he said, 'I'm sorry.'

She saw he was sorry, and to ease his embarrassment she turned from him and went into the dwelling and picked the child up from the basket and washed him, and put on a clean binder and an odd-looking nightgown that she had made out of the piece of linen Rose Watson had wrapped the cheese and bread in on the one and only time she had visited the mill, and some grey lining that she had taken from one of the old dresses; she had used the lining for the back part of the nightgown. Going to the box, she took out the fawn shawl with the pink fringe and she held it in her hand for a moment and looked down on it before she wrapped it around the child, then laid him in the basket again.

Now she washed her face and hands in the bowl, smoothed down her hair, took off her hessian apron and, going to the door, looked past the man, where he was standing patiently waiting, and called to Joe who was chopping wood, saying, 'Come and get yourself clean.' And when he came into the room she said, 'Wash your face and hands, we're going for a walk.'

'A walk?' He screwed up his bright eyes at her. 'What have I got to wash me hands an' face to go for a walk for?'

'Do as you're bid, and be quick.' Then going to the door again, she said, 'I must take him along 'cos the girls are out pickin'.' And he nodded at her, saying, 'That will be quite in order.'

Five minutes later they set out for the North Lodge. The lodgekeeper was expecting them. He was waiting by the small gate and he opened it at their approach and stared at them, but he didn't speak until he had closed it after them; then in a grave undertone he murmured to Cunningham, 'His Lordship's inside.' And his manner suggested that God had descended into his house.

Cunningham motioned Cissie to go forward while putting a restraining hand on Joe, and when she walked towards the cottage door the lodgekeeper darted before her, knocked hastily on the panel, then pushed the door open; and when she had passed over the threshold, he closed the door behind her.

She was standing in a small room, not half as clean as her habitation and smelling of musk and onions; she took in these impressions on the side, but her eyes looked straight towards the finely dressed man standing with his back to the little window. The first time she had seen his face was when she was lying prone on the ground, and she saw it again now as if it were coming at her from a distant and vague dream.

Lord Fischel took the handkerchief from his nose – the odour of the room offended him – and he, in turn, stared at the girl, ignoring for the moment the bundle in her arms. And he, too, remembered her from that distant time, but thought now, as he hadn't thought then, that she was beautiful; and he was amazed afresh that such as she could be thrown up from the dregs of the earth. She appeared clean – her clothes, although threadbare as they were, weren't befouled – but what impressed him most at this moment was the expression in her eyes. No-one of his servants would have dared to look at him like this, for her look was telling him that she could read his mind and her answer was 'No'.

171

Perhaps it was this knowledge that tempered his manner, for he did an unusual thing – he asked her to be seated.

Her back straight, the child held tightly against her breast, she sat down on a wooden seat near the table, and he, his voice still moderated to a low pitch, said, 'The child, is he well?'

'Yes, Sir, very well.'

Her mistaken form of address brought no sharp reprimand from him; instead, moving slightly from the window and still keeping his eyes on her, he said, 'Had you associated with men of your own kind before my son so far forgot himself as to take you?'

Her chin trembled, her head moved backwards and forwards in small movements and she had to force herself to swallow before she could answer him. Then, in no injured tone such as he expected from her, but her voice clear and level and her bearing dignified, she said, 'I had been with no man, or wished to. My father, he was different, he could read and write, he brought us up respectable.'

Their eyes held until His Lordship found he had to take his gaze from her, stopping himself from looking downwards only by directing his eyes to the low, smoke-begrimed ceiling. Then, his clean-cut lips working one against the other, he pursed them for a moment before saying abruptly, 'I would like to see the child.'

She did not get to her feet but she opened the fawn shawl and waited, and he was forced to step forward.

The moment his eyes beheld the child he experienced a pain. It was as if his ribs had been pierced by a sharp instrument. The child was awake and was looking up at him with eyes set in deep sockets. The nose was straight and large for the face, the mouth was his father's mouth; in fact so uncanny was the likeness, that he imagined for a moment that he was looking at the shrunken head of his father. And this impression held even when the child suddenly gurgled and, pushing out its lips, made a bubble with its saliva. Still looking down on it, he asked quietly, 'What have you named it?'

'Richard; it was me da's second name.'

His head jerked so quickly that a bone cracked audibly in his neck. This was more than coincidence surely, for his father's second name had been Richard.

His conviction now that he was being led towards taking certain steps with regard to this child was stronger than ever.

He walked away from her and to the window and with his back to her he asked, 'Will you part with the child?'

'No, no, I'll not.' Her reply came quick and from deep within her throat. 'Not for anything.'

He was facing her again, his chin out, his whole demeanour haughty. 'You'll be amply compensated.'

'I don't want nothin', only him.' She pressed the child tightly to her now. 'Nobody is goin' to take him away from me.'

He could take the child away from her by the simple matter of going to the law: the child was his grandson and the mother had no real means of supporting him. But this way would mean publicity, and he wanted no further publicity. What would have to be done would have to be done quietly, without fuss or bother.

He now took what he thought was a diplomatic way. He said to her, 'Would you allow the child to remain in my care for a while during which time I would pay you the sum of ten shillings a week?'

She closed her eyes and drooped her head and swung it helplessly from side to side. The movement was so definite that it banished any further thought of diplomacy and he said harshly, 'I will double the sum. You're in need of money; I understand you've a family to support. For as long as you allow the child to remain with me I will see that you are paid one pound per week.' She couldn't refuse that sum. No-one of her kind, and in such need as she was, would be so stupid.

She opened her eyes, lifted her head and looked at him. One pound a week. He wanted the child so much that he was willing to pay a pound a week for it. On a pound a week they could live like him, like lords, they could feed as they had never fed before. On a pound a week she could afford to go into the town and look for a house. She'd be able to get a permit to move from her particular parish if she could show she had a pound a week coming in. But what would all that mean without the child? She hadn't wanted him, even up to that day on the fells when she had slipped she hadn't wanted him, and for one moment she had hoped that her slipping might have broken his neck or killed him in some way; but now there was no money in the world that could buy him.

When he saw the softening of her face he thought he had won, as he knew money always won, until she said, 'I'm sorry; if I could do this for you I would, but I couldn't part with him, for no money could I part with him.' And it was strange that in this moment she should feel regret that it was impossible for her to part with the child, for the man before her, the great lord from Houghton Hall, was evoking her pity, because as she said to herself, he looked sort of alone, lost like.

She rose to her feet saying now, 'Will you permit me going, Sir. An' good-day to you.' She covered the child up as she turned from him, and went out of the door and looked at Cunningham, who was standing on the drive, but didn't speak to him. Then turning to Joe, who was climbing the iron gate, she said, 'Come along with you,' and together they went out into the road. And there Joe asked, 'What had you to go in the Lodge for?' And she answered, 'I had to see the bailiff; I was after a job but I

didn't get it.' And he said, ''Cos you had the bairn?' And
she answered, ''Cos I had the bairn.'

Bella came running up from the track panting; her face
was alight and she was calling over the distance, 'Hello.
Hello, all of you's.' And Joe ran towards her, shouting,
'Our Bella! . . . Looka who's here. Our Bella!'

Cissie, hurrying to the door and stepping over Nellie
where she was crawling over the threshold, stood waiting
on the rough terrace, and when Bella came up to her she
put her arms about her and kissed her, then held her at
arm's length, saying, 'By! you're lookin' bonny.' And
Bella smirked a little and blinked and smiled her broad
smile, then said, 'Oh, but me legs are achin'; it's a walk
and a half, I set off afore one. What time is it now?' And
Cissie, leading the way into the room and looking at the
clock, said, 'Gone half-past two.'

'Oh, crickey! that'll mean I'll only have an hour 'cos I
must get back afore dark. Cook skins you alive if you're
late . . . Oh!' She flopped down on the chair with a sigh,
and Joe, standing by her side now, demanded, 'You
brought us anything, our Bella?' And Bella replied
somewhat indignantly, 'You're always on the get, our Joe;
I've told you afore you can't bring stuff from there.'

Joe stared at his sister, then looked at Charlotte and
Sarah, and after an exchange of glances they went out; the
excitement of seeing Bella had vanished. They should have
remembered she never brought anything.

Cissie had been waiting anxiously for Bella's arrival, for
this was her pay day. The foodstock in the dwelling
was very low. The mushrooms were finished and there was
nothing to glean anywhere. She said, 'I'll make a drop tea,'
and as she put the kettle on the fire, she added, 'How are
you gettin' on?'

'Oh, all right.' Bella wrinkled her nose. 'But they boss
you about; there's always somebody bossin' you about.'

Bella now turned her head to the side and looked down at the child in the basket and remarked, 'By! he's grown; he's gettin' fat.' Then, her attention going off at a tangent, as was usual with her, she said, 'Do you get more stuff from the mill now since Matthew's livin' there?'

Cissie knelt down in front of the hearth and blew on the fire before she replied, 'No, just about the same.'

'Cissie.'

'Yes, Bella?' Cissie turned on her knees towards her.

'I got me pay the day, Cissie.'

'Yes, yes, I know you would have.'

Bella now put her hand down and, lifting up her skirt, took from a pocket in her petticoat a piece of rag tied into a knot and a small package, and all the while she looked at Cissie. Even when she undid the knot in the rag she still kept her eyes on her sister. Then taking from the rag two shillings and sixpence she handed them to Cissie, saying hesitantly, 'That's all I've left, Cissie. Well, you see' – she tossed her head – 'it's the tally man. He comes round and everybody buys from him, an' it's only so much a month. But . . . but I've got a petticoat . . . look.' She again turned back her skirt; then lifting her top petticoat she exposed a flimsy pink cotton garment edged with rough lace. 'It was three shillings. I only pay sixpence a month, but . . . but this month I got a hair ribbon an'' – she looked down – 'I . . . I got this brooch.' She now undid the button of her short jacket and exposed to view a gaudy piece of green tin with a red stone in the middle.

Cissie's first reaction was of deep anger. She wanted to take her hand and skelp Bella across the ear, knock her flying. She was well fed and housed and she hadn't spared a thought for her brothers and sisters up here on this bleak fell, but had spent nearly half a month's wages on trash. Yet as she stared at Bella, looking at the face that was so like her own when eight years old, she thought, She can't help it; she'll always be selfish.

176

And now Bella, sensing that the battle was almost over, proffered her peace offering. Handing Cissie the slim little parcel, she said, 'I brought this for you, Cissie.'

Cissie took the piece of paper and opened it and gazed down at a beautifully embroidered lawn handkerchief, and her eyes widened as she raised them to Bella, saying, 'Where did you get this?'

Bella got to her feet and walked to the table, and there with her forefinger she drew a number of circles before saying, 'The young mistress, she gave it to me. She's nice; she's my age and she wears beautiful clothes.' She put her head on one side now and looked at Cissie, saying, 'Aw, you should see, Cissie, silk and velvet. Aw, you should see.'

'She really gave you this?'

'A-hah.' She was drawing the circles again. ''Cos as I said she's my age, an' I'm the youngest there.'

Cissie was again looking at the handkerchief. This was no trash, this was a piece of fine lawn with an exquisite flower design worked on two corners and forming the initial C, her own initial.

Cissie was still young enough to appreciate such a gift. She forgot for a moment that they would be on short commons for the rest of the week and that she had wanted to slap Bella, for now, bending forward, she kissed her, saying, 'Thanks. Thanks, Bella. But you're sure you don't want to keep it for yourself?'

'No, no; I want you to have it. I would like you to have nice things, our Cissie. If I had a lot of money I would buy you nice things.'

Cissie now put her arms around Bella's shoulder and pulled her to her side; and then the kettle spluttered and she laughed and said, 'We'll have a drop tea.'

As she made it she thought to herself, God provides, there's always good with the bad . . .

But the following day, if she had thought about this

theory she would have questioned it, for over the fells again came the man she thought of now as 'him from the House'. She had, in a way, over the past few weeks, come to look upon him in the same light as she did the scraper who came searching for climbing boys. Yet it wasn't really him she was afraid of but his master.

There was a wind blowing which cut like a knife, but in spite of this she kept him standing outside, the door pulled closed behind her, and before he could begin she said harshly, 'It's no use, it's no good talkin', I told him, and no matter what he says it'll still be no use.'

Cunningham looked at her pityingly; he was deeply sorry for her; but he was his master's man and his master's wishes would have to be obeyed. When there came a pause in her gabbling he said quietly, 'As I said to you before, they have ways and means, and if His Lordship decides to take the matter to the justices you wouldn't have a leg to stand on . . .'

'The justices? What could they do? He's mine!'

'Yes, yes, I know; but he's also young Mister Clive's son, and His Lordship's grandson; and even if you protested he wasn't, which I know you wouldn't, but even if you did, there is the looks of the child to prove you wrong. He would only have to be held up to a portrait in the gallery and the kinship would be proved.'

'I don't care. I don't care. I won't do it. I can't, I couldn't!' She now moved her head desperately, 'He's all I've got of me own; or likely to have.'

'You'll marry.'

'I'll not!' The two words were shot at him, and he smiled tolerantly until she repeated, 'I tell you I'll not, never. I know I won't, never.' And now he was forced to take her seriously and he narrowed his eyes at her as he wondered if that one drunken act of the young master had killed marriage for her. If that were so, the tragedy was twofold.

A great gust of wind threatened to take off his hat and lift him bodily from the ground as it surged up under his cape, and he bent against it, saying, 'His Lordship has increased his offer. He said he will give you twenty-five shillings a week and find you a habitation.'

It was fantastic, utterly fantastic: twenty-five shillings a week and a habitation! But she had no hesitation in shaking her head, and, pulling the front of her bodice up round her neck because the wind was piercing her chest, she said, 'It would be all the same if he made it thirty-five, or forty-five. Tell him that.'

He looked at her sadly. She was shivering. 'Go inside,' he said; 'you're cold. Good day to you.'

When she got inside she stood with her back to the door and looked to where the children were sitting in a circle on the mat around the fire and, in their midst, the basket with the child in it. They had been playing with him, making him laugh and gurgle. He laughed easily and rarely cried. He was a happy child, and this amazed her, for during the months she had carried him her spirit had been bent down in one way and another with misery . . . And now they wanted to take him from her . . . he wanted to take him from her, that old man living in his mansion. He would pay people to wash him and look after him but they wouldn't give him love. You couldn't buy love. Twenty-five shillings a week, or all the gold in the world, couldn't buy the feeling he got from her and would always get from her.

She went to the basket and picked him up and held him tightly and wished she could press him back into her body and there keep him safe forever.

Joe said, 'What did that man want, our Cissie?' and she said, 'It was about that job again.'

Joe looked at her slyly. He didn't believe what she said about the job.

179

7

Cunningham continued to come at intervals to the dwelling, but on his visits he merely passed the time of day with her and asked after her health. He did not mention the child or His Lordship; but each time she saw him she was filled with fear, and no matter what the weather she did not ask him inside. That is, until one wild day in early December when he saw her struggling towards the habitation, the child in her arms, and a girl whom he had not seen before dragging some way behind her.

November had been wet, bleak, and bitter. She had spent nearly every day of the first two weeks gathering wood; there were no branches stacked against the wall this year. She had not seen Matthew since his marriage on the day the child was born, and she reasoned it was just as well; but some part of her heart blamed him for not sending them the wood.

Then on the Tuesday of the third week the tree carrier's float appeared on the track. It was laden with branches and cuttings and two strange men unloaded it by the simple process of throwing the wood on to the road, and they called to her, 'You'll manage, Missis?'

Going over to the track and looking down at the enormous heap of wood, she said gladly, 'Yes, yes, I can manage. An' thanks.'

It took them a full day working hard to stack the wood against the walls, and when it was done she stood back and looked at it in deep thankfulness and cried within herself, 'Oh! Matthew. Matthew.'

The following Sunday, when the boys arrived, Jimmy was wearing an overcoat. He said that Matthew's mother had made it out of an old one of Mr Turnbull's. He made them all laugh when he described how she first took him into the kitchen to measure him, but he, not knowing, thought he was going to get his ears boxed; and when she said she was going to make him a coat he said you could have knocked him down with a couple of iron spokes. He admitted to Cissie that he still didn't care for her much because she was bossy and in and out of the shop now that Matthew wasn't there all the time, but still she was kinder to him and gave him more to eat.

So, on the whole, life was bearable; she was managing, and if it weren't for the fear of that man from the Hall she would, she told herself, have little to worry her. That was, until the day that Parson Hedley came to the dwelling and said she must go down at once to Pinewood Place because Bella was in trouble.

She stared open-mouthed at the tall, gangling figure of the parson, then whispered, 'What kind of trouble?'

Parson Hedley drooped his head and shook it before replying, 'She's . . . she's been stealing.'

'Bella stealin'!' Cissie's voice was no longer a whisper, it was loud and indignant and disbelieving. 'Our Bella wouldn't steal, Parson; our da brought us all up never to touch anything that didn't belong to us, an' I've kept tellin' them all. Bella wouldn't steal.'

'But she has, Cissie.' His voice was patient, and there was a silence before she asked, 'What's she stole?'

'Garments I understand. There have been a number missing, and something was found under her bed, a handkerchief, belonging to one of the daughters of the house.'

A handkerchief. Oh God! Oh God! She turned her head and looked towards the chest of drawers. There was a handkerchief in there, a fine lawn handkerchief, beautifully worked. Oh Bella. Oh our Bella, how could you! Of all the things that had happened over the past year this was the worst. She said now, 'What will they do to her?'

'I don't rightly know, Cissie. She'll likely have to come up before the justices; she could be sent to the House of Correction. Being a girl she won't, I think, get the lash, and she's too young for deportation; it . . . it will likely be the House of Correction.'

The House of Correction! Oh dear God! Oh dear God! the House of Correction! Bella wasn't bad, just feather-brained and wanting things.

Picking up the child, she wrapped it in an old piece of blanket, over which she draped the fawn shawl. She would have to take him with her because there was his feed and her breasts were full. She put her own shawl over her head and tied a bit of string round the neck to stop it blowing off in the wind, and she said to Sarah, who had been standing listening wide-eyed to what the minister was saying about Bella, 'Look after them, won't you? And bar the door. You've got enough wood in to keep you going till I come back. And you, Joe, mind you don't go out, except to the midden, and come straight back. Do you hear?'

Joe nodded his head at her.

As she went to the door she turned again to Sarah and said, 'Warm up the broth and have half a slice of bread each. No more mind. Be good.' Her eyes swept over the five of them. Then she was outside, her head down against the wind; and when she came to the track where the minister's dogcart was standing he said, 'I can drive you as far as the crossroads, it'll be a help.'

It was three and a half miles from the crossroads to the gates of Pinewood Place and as she walked up the drive to the house she could hardly put one foot before the other, so cold was she; her body seemed frozen both inside and out, but the child was still warm.

She rounded the drive outside the front door and went towards the kitchen quarters, and when she knocked on the door and a young girl not much older than Bella opened it, she said, 'I'm Bella Brodie's sister.'

'Oh, aye. Eeh! Cook!' The girl turned round and called back into the room. 'Here's . . . here's Bella's sister.'

The cook came to the door. She was small and fat and her cheeks were red, and she said kindly enough, 'Aye. Well, come on in.' And when Cissie entered the kitchen the warmth of it almost made her faint.

'Sit yersel' down.' The cook pointed to a chair, then added, 'I'll get the housekeeper.' And as she turned to the girl and was about to give her an order, she hesitated and, looking at Cissie again, asked, 'Could you do with a sup tea?'

'Oh yes. Yes, please.'

'Aye, I think you could.' The cook scrutinised her for a moment, then added, 'Do you like sugar?'

And at this Cissie merely nodded.

'There; drink it up.' The cook pushed the mug into her hand, then watched her gulp at the scalding tea.

After a moment she asked, 'How's the bairn?' And Cissie, after drawing in a long breath, answered, 'He's all right, thank you.'

The cook now turned to the girl and said, 'You go and tell 'er.' Then looking at Cissie again, she added, 'You can take your time with that, it'll be five minutes afore she comes. She's like that; feels her position.' Bending closer to Cissie now, she said in an undertone, ''Tisn't Bella's fault; she was led away by that young Nancy Price. The things they found under her mattress, you wouldn't believe. But still, ·they haven't got them all. They only found the hanky under Bella's, but that was enough, Miss Christine has only four hankies of that kind left out of a dozen. It was the missing of the hankies that did it. You see, Miss Christine's grannie had made them, she has fine hands.'

At this moment the door opened and there entered a

woman of medium height, wearing a trim black dress and white starched cap. As she crossed the room the cook returned to her business at the table and Cissie pulled herself to her feet, and the housekeeper stared at her for a moment before saying abruptly, 'Disgraceful business.' And Cissie answered, 'Yes, Miss.'

'My name is Mrs Pain.'

At this Cissie nodded.

'You know this is a very serious business.'

'Yes.'

'The mistress is indignant; she only engaged her out of pity for your circumstances.'

'Yes, I know.'

'And it's a way to be repaid, isn't it?'

'I'm . . . I'm sorry. I never believed Bella would do such a thing; she was brought up decent.'

'Decent! Thieving?' As the housekeeper's chest rose and fell so did her joined hands lying against it. She now said, 'You are to take her back with you, but have her at the Justices' Court in Shields at ten o'clock on Monday morning. The mistress says to tell you, if she tries to run away you'll be held responsible, you understand?'

Again Cissie nodded, dumbly now.

'Come this way.' She now turned and led the way out of the kitchen and across the yard to a low door, and there, unlocking it, she looked down some steps and called into the darkness, 'You Bella! Come up here.' And like an animal emerging out of the earth Bella crawled up the ladder. She was shivering from head to foot; her eyes were staring out of her head, and her whole face was swollen with crying. She closed her eyes against the light, but when she opened them again and saw Cissie her mouth fell into a wide gape and her tongue wobbled, and she cried as she flung herself forward, 'Oh our Cissie! Our Cissie.'

And Cissie, putting one arm about her, said brokenly, 'There now. There now.' All her anger against the child had vanished; the sight of her crawling out of the dark cellar had turned it against . . . them. They were cruel and inhuman. But a dark cellar would be nothing to the treatment she would get in the House of Correction. There, she would be herded with terrible people. She trembled at the thought of such people: harlots, pickpockets, women who maimed their children so that they could take them begging, who put black beetles in half walnut shells and strapped them to babies' backs to keep them howling for pity, women who sold their children for awful purposes. Her da had told them all about the kind of people who got into the House of Correction as a deterrent never to do anything that would get themselves there. And now Bella was heading straight for it.

The housekeeper didn't allow them into the house again but ordered the kitchen maid to bring Bella's cloak and her possessions. Among the scanty few, there was the brooch, the ribbon, and the fancy petticoat she had bought from the tally man, and when Cissie saw these last articles she pointed to them and said harshly, 'She won't want them. Give them back to the traveller and tell him he can't be paid, so he'd better take them.' And on this she turned and walked across the wide yard, with Bella clinging to her skirt and crying all the while. And the housekeeper's voice followed them. 'Remember, ten o'clock on Monday morning at the Court House . . . !'

Twice during the journey home she felt she was going to faint; at one time she had to ask Bella to hold the child. Now, crossing the fells on the last stretch of the journey and the faintness attacking her again, she once more gave the child to Bella and sat down on a wet stone and drooped her head forward. It was then that Cunningham came up to her.

Bending over her, he said, 'Can I help you?' and she lifted her head and muttered, 'No, I'm all right; it's only the cold got me.'

He looked at the girl holding the child. Her face was red and tear-stained. He looked back at Cissie and said, 'I would get indoors as quickly as possible; you could catch your death of cold in this wind, and it's beginning to sleet.'

When she rose to her feet and swayed, he put his hand out and caught her elbow; and like that he walked her forward, while Bella followed behind with the child. And when they reached the dwelling and the children opened the door he led her inside and placed her on the chair, saying to them as they bustled around her, 'I would leave your sister quiet for a moment, she is not feeling very well.'

Cissie now looked towards Bella and said, 'Put him in the basket.' Then turning to Sarah, who was standing by her side anxious and disturbed, she murmured, 'Make me a drop tea, Sarah, will you?' And Sarah said quickly, 'Aye, Cissie, aye.'

After a moment she drew in a long breath and, looking up at the man said, 'Thank you very much; it was kind of you to help me.'

He knew he was being dismissed again, but he couldn't go until he had delivered his message, an ultimatum. And he was sorry to the heart that he had been called upon to do this, at this particular time, but His Lordship was getting impatient, and that was putting it mildly.

His Lordship, he felt, had become possessed of only one idea of late, and that was to have this child under his care. He had even gone to the extraordinary lengths of ordering all the nursery floor to be redecorated. This had set the whole household agog. There was one thing certain to Cunningham: His Lordship would have his grandson by fair means or foul, and so he must convey his message to her. But he must do it gently, for she was in a distressed state, that was evident, and on the point of collapse.

Merely in order to make conversation and to give her time to recover before he began to talk seriously to her, he said, 'You have walked too far. Have you been to the hamlet?'

'No.' She shook her head. 'To Shields.'

'Shields?' His eyebrows moved upwards. 'That is a long way on any day, and the wind is piercing.' He glanced towards Bella now, sensing that this child was the reason for the journey into Shields, and he said, 'Is this another sister? I haven't seen her before.' And when Bella's head drooped, Cissie explained hesitantly, 'She's been away in service. I . . . I had to bring her back.'

'Oh!'

Cissie now looked up at this man. Besides the minister, he was the only adult she had spoken to for weeks. Moreover, he was a man of some refinement, and undoubtedly he would have knowledge of the ways of the law. She would tell him about Bella, she had to tell somebody. She looked around at the children now and said, 'Go in next door, you can leave Annie. An' you, Bella; go along o' them.'

When they had obeyed her, Cissie looked up at the man and said, 'Would you like to sit down a minute?' and she indicated a backless chair by the side of the table. When he had seated himself she said simply, 'We're in trouble.'

'I'm sorry to hear that. May I ask the nature of your trouble?'

'It's . . . it's Bella. She was workin' in Mr Braithwaite's in Pinewood House in Westoe, Shields, and—' she lowered her head against the shame of it for a moment, and now, her voice scarcely audible, she ended, 'She's been stealin'.'

'Stealing?' His expression showed that he was shocked.

She nodded. 'It wasn't her fault as far as I can gather. The girl above her in the laundry had been helpin' herself to all kinds of things and she gave her a handkerchief. She shouldn't have taken it because she knew it was the young mistress's, but she took it.' She did not add that she had

187

brought it home for herself, but went on. 'And then she gave her another one. And when the things were missin' they found one of the handkerchiefs under her bed and . . . and so they sent for me. And she's got to be at the Court House on Monday by ten. What . . . what do you think they'll do to her?'

Cunningham was about to say soothingly, 'Well, I shouldn't worry. She's only a child – they won't be so hard on her; they'll likely put her in the House of Correction for a few weeks.' But he didn't say this because it came to him suddenly that this was a situation from which His Lordship could profit. The girl was unusual in that she seemed to love all these children, and they her, and he imagined that she would be prepared to do almost anything to save her sister from the punishment due to her because of her thieving.

His Lordship, although not dabbling in public life now, had himself at one time been a magistrate and dealt out justice; he knew all the ins and outs of law appertaining to local matters. Moreover, he still had many prominent friends and was held in deep respect by them. He had the power to set wheels in motion, or, on the other hand, to stop wheels turning. Very likely a word in the right place and the charge against this child would be eliminated. He would put the matter, as he saw it, to His Lordship. But now he paved the way for his master's success by shaking his head and saying, 'People in Court, magistrates and their like, have great power. Very often justice becomes unjust in that the punishment they mete out far exceeds the crime. You say it was only two handkerchiefs, whereas this other girl stole many articles, yet I should imagine they will be made to share the blame.'

He hated himself for a moment when he saw the whiteness of her face turn to grey, and, feeling slightly ashamed, he stood up to take his departure. He would leave her to stew in her worry, poor thing, then return tomorrow and lay before her the proposal.

When she looked up at him dumbly he said in a low tone, 'I'm afraid I haven't been of much help, but I haven't much power.' He seemed always to be stressing the word 'power'. 'It needs people like, well' – he spread his hands out – 'like His Lordship to make an impression on such a case as this.'

He had dropped the seed, and on this he nodded sympathetically at her and went out; and she stared at the door for some time before turning and looking down into the basket where the child lay.

There was a black frost in the night and it turned the sleet of the previous evening into moulded glass that covered every hump and hollow, hill and valley of the fells. It provided slides for Annie, Joe and Charlotte, and Nellie, who made them laugh as each attempt brought her flat on her bottom. But Sarah did not join in the sliding; she sat in the dwelling working on two flour sacks to make capes for the younger ones, while Bella sat hunched close to the fire on a low cracket, her joined hands pinned tightly between her knees; fear was imprinted on her face, and she burst into tears every time she was spoken to. That her terror was great was proved when she refused food, because above all things Bella loved food.

Cissie had risen in the middle of the night to comfort her when her sobbing had kept the others awake, and, taking her into the room and close to the banked-down fire, she had held her as she would have Annie or Nellie and said, 'There, there; it'll be all right,' while Bella had asked her over and over again, 'What will they do to me, Cissie? Where will they send me?'

Today was Thursday; there was Friday, Saturday, and Sunday to go before she would know what they would do with Bella. She'd had wild thoughts about what she herself could do. She could take her somewhere and hide her. But then, that woman had said they would hold herself responsible; and if they took her what was to become of the others? They would be taken to the House and all her efforts would have been in vain.

She had no hope in her mind that the justices would be lenient with Bella because of her age. Eight, they would say, was an age when she knew right from wrong. Just last year they had hanged a man for stealing a sheep, and two men had got five years for poaching. That was, after one of them had been shot all over by a spring gun which took out one of his eyes. But they were lucky; they could have been hanged because they were carrying a gun. But Bella hadn't stolen sheep, and she hadn't a gun, she had only taken two hankies, and they, back in the house, had only proof that she had taken one, and if they had come and searched the dwelling they wouldn't have found the second one for it was now buried two feet down in the soft mud near the river.

If only she had someone to talk to, someone to advise her. Not Parson Hedley; she felt he wouldn't be much comfort at this time because he was dealing with sin; and sin, even by the parson's standards, must always be punished. She wanted someone . . . someone like Matthew. If only Matthew would step by. If only it was Sunday and she could tell Jimmy. Jimmy would go back and tell him, then he would come. But even so it would be too late, 'cos Jimmy wouldn't see him until Monday now that he lived at the mill, and she had to be in Shields with Bella by ten o'clock on the Monday. She couldn't tell William to tell him in case *she* should overhear. William wasn't as wise as Jimmy.

She was sick with worry and striving; she felt very, very tired. She wished . . . What did she wish? That she would die in the night. Stupid thinking, weak thinking. What would become of the others if anything happened to her?

But oh, she was tired, she was so tired these days that she kept telling herself that she was tired . . .

The man came just after she had doled out the small helpings of broth to each of them. She had chastised Joe for gulping at his and not eating it slowly, warning him that there was no more for him, when there came the three small knocks on the door, and when she opened it and saw him standing there she felt for a moment glad to see him. He was, in a strange way, and in spite of her fear of him, almost like a friend. He glanced at the children standing round the table, then said, 'I wonder if I could speak to you a moment; would it be too cold for you to walk a little way?'

Her eyes narrowed slightly, and then she said, 'No; no. I'll just get me shawl.'

She went out with him and walked a few yards away from the dwelling; then he stopped and looked at her and said, 'I was greatly concerned about you yesterday and your trouble and I took the liberty of putting your case before His Lordship. As I said, it is only people such as His Lordship that have the power to alter the course of justice. Well—' He paused and rubbed his gloved hands together and seemed disinclined to go on, but after a moment, when she remained silent, her eyes fixed tight on his face, he added, 'His Lordship thinks that he could persuade Mr Braithwaite to overlook the case against your sister, but . . . but he would expect you to do something for him in return. And' – he swallowed deeply – 'I don't need to have to put that into words, do I?'

She overlapped the shawl across her neck; the knuckles of her thumbs digging into the sides of her windpipe almost stopped her breathing; then she moved her head twice, but in such a way that he did not take it as a refusal; he just waited while, unblinking, she stared at him. And the seed he had dropped last night and that had been growing rapidly in her mind sprang into poisonous growth before her eyes, and as if defending herself against something visible she thrust out her hand and backed from him, crying, 'No, no! I won't.'

He stood with his head bent, making no movement. After a while he looked at her and said sadly, 'I . . . I did my best. I was only trying to help you. And . . . and I must give you a message. His Lordship wished it. He said that if you consented, the offer he made to you in the beginning would still hold good. You would have twenty-five shillings a week as long as the child remained with him.' He half turned from her now; then looking at her across his shoulders, he said, 'There's not much time left. If . . . if your sister isn't to come before the justice on Monday then His Lordship would have to set wheels in motion by tomorrow. If . . . if you should change your mind you've only to come up to the House. The porter at either Lodge will admit you.'

She watched him walking across the slippery earth towards the track. His shoulders were stooped and his body conveyed a sadness to her that was reflected in herself a thousandfold.

Bella cried in the night again, and Cissie got out of bed and dragged her away from the others and into the room, and there she shook her, while hissing at her, 'Give over! Will you give over?' until Bella stopped and, her head hanging back on her shoulders, whimpered, 'I'm frightened, our Cissie, I'm frightened.' At this Cissie slowly lowered herself on to the chair and stared at her. Then reaching out, she took her hand and said, 'Go on back to bed . . . it'll be all right. I'll think of something.' And Bella went back to bed somewhat comforted because it was the first time that Cissie had indicated that she would put things right, and like Joe, like them all, she believed that their Cissie could put things right . . .

It was raining when at eleven o'clock in the morning she

went out of the door with the child in her arms. The drops hit her face like pellets of ice, the wind lifted the shawl from around her shoulders and whirled it over her head and would have taken it off but for the string round her neck. Over the top of the child's shawl she had put a sack to keep the rain from soaking through.

She made her way to the North Lodge because it was nearer. The porter let her through the gate without a word, and she did not speak to him. She walked up the long grass drive between the high tangle of brushwood along the side of the wall and the wood itself. She passed the place where she had climbed the wall that far-off day, the climbing that was the cause of her walking towards the Hall now. She kept on straight through the park until, in the far distance, like a grey cloud on the horizon she saw the house. She passed keepers who made no attempt to stop her. She walked across a garden and up broad steps on to a gravel drive, then up more steps, and then she was standing under the shelter of a porch and before a great black oak door studded with brass nails. Here she took the sack from off the child and dropped it on to the flags of the terrace. Then she pulled a handle attached to the wall and the bell clanged.

The man who opened the door to her was grandly dressed in brown knee-breeched livery. He stared at her for a moment, then stood aside. He did not speak either, and she entered the Hall, thinking, I'm dreaming. It's like me dream of the white house; I'll wake up in a minute and everything will be all right.

The dream was emphasised by the grandeur of the place. There were life-sized iron men standing at each side of a great staircase; there were glass lights hanging from the ceiling and animals' heads sticking out from the walls, and beneath her feet was a carpet so thick that she couldn't hear herself walk. She was in a dim corridor now and staring at the back of the grandly dressed man. After he had knocked on a door, he opened it and stood aside to allow her to pass him. And now she was in a room that seemed to hold nothing but books . . . and him.

When the door closed behind her, he rose from his seat behind the desk and came towards her, and she wasn't to know that this was a most unusual procedure, nor the fact that he should turn a chair around for her to sit on. She wasn't to know that this lord, this great man, was finding this moment one of the most exciting in his life, nor yet that he felt in his heart a kind of sorrow for her.

Cunningham's reports on the girl had been of a person of extraordinary strength of character, loyalty, and kindliness, characteristics not usually found in one so young and placed as she was. He had wondered, when listening to these reports, why it was that a girl of the common people should outshine his own blood in moral qualities.

In his position it was usual for him to speak first, especially when in contact with menials, but now he found it most difficult to open the conversation; also more difficult still to keep his eyes from the child in her arms. He thought afterwards, by way of excuse for himself, that the best and most glib people are reduced to inanities now and again, for he broke the silence by saying, 'It's a wild day.'

When she made no answer to this, simply continued to stare at him, he turned from her and, going 'round the desk, sat down, hoping that from here he would feel more in charge of the situation. He took up a pen and wrote the date at the head of a piece of paper: Saturday, December 5th, 1833. Then, his eyes still cast down, he said, 'I understand that your sister is in trouble?'

'Yes, Sir.' She heard her voice coming as if from a long distance away.

'She was in the employ of Mr Braithwaite of Pinewood Place, Westoe?'

'Yes, Sir.'

'Well, you have no need to worry any further about the unfortunate business. I have already been in touch with Mr Braithwaite and he is willing to drop the charge against her.'

She did not say 'Thank you, Sir' now; she just stared at him across the desk and held the child more tightly to her. Perhaps she held it too tightly for it began to whimper, and this brought His Lordship to his feet again and, coming slowly 'round the desk and looking down at her, he said, 'May I see him?'

She pulled the fawn shawl back from the child's face, and then the undershawl; and now he struggled to free his hands, and when he had pushed one up over the edge of the shawl he lay still, gazing at the face looking down on him; and then he smiled at it.

There was a slight constriction in His Lordship's throat. He moved his thin blue lips one over the other; then dragging his eyes from his grandson's face he looked at the mother and said gently, 'You need have no more worry concerning him, except for his loss and I wish you to believe me when I say I understand how you feel about this matter. But he is my grandson and it is my wish that he be brought up as such.' He paused, then went on, 'The agreement was that you should have an allowance of twenty-five shillings per week; this will be paid to you in advance every month starting as from today. Is there anything you would like to ask me?'

Although she wanted to say, 'Will I be able to see him?' she shook her head, for she knew that this was a fruitless question; once they took him from her arms she would never see him again; he'd be in this fortress surrounded by scores of people, all making sure that she never saw him again.

Lord Fischel stared down at her. He had been prepared to ask her to put her cross to a paper that he had roughly drawn up, but he saw that she was in great distress and emphasising such a finality might make her cause a scene, even attempt to go back on her word. The best thing to do was to get the child away from her. Once this was done, the business would be ended. He stretched out his hand and rang the bell, and when Hatton answered the summons he said, 'Fetch Mrs Hatton to me, please.'

Mrs Hatton came into the room within seconds and His Lordship with a small wave of his hand indicated that she should take the child.

When the woman stooped down, her hands out-stretched, she paused, for the look in the girl's eyes was like a knife cutting into her, and when she put her hands under the child she had to give a slight tug before the girl released her hold on it.

As the housekeeper walked towards the door Cissie now asked in a whisper, 'Can I have his shawl?' and His Lordship, again with a motion of his hand, indicated that the housekeeper should remove the shawl, thinking at the same time that it would be one less article to be burned.

Impatient now that she should be gone and that he could go and see the child, hold the child, His Lordship rang the bell again, saying, 'You must have some refreshment before you return. Hatton will take you to the kitchen.'

A moment later Hatton came into the room and received the order from his master; and Cissie, hugging the shawl to her, rose to her feet, but once she was standing upright she had the strange idea that she was about to sink into the earth. And then she knew she was going to do just that, for a great void appeared in the floor and as she fell forward into it she grabbed at His Lordship and tried to take him with her while shouting at him, 'All for two lawn hankies! . . . You got him for two lawn hankies.'

Two hours later, the general coach, used for luggage and such work, drew up on the path below the habitation, and Cunningham, getting out, assisted her down on to the muddy road; then with his hand on her elbow helped her over the fell and into the dwelling. After sitting her down he spoke to the tallest girl, saying, 'Look after your sister. She needs to rest, she's not feeling well.' Then patting Cissie on the shoulder, he stared at her in deep compassion for a moment before turning away.

When the door had closed on him the children gathered round her, the older ones not asking where Richard was, but Annie, with no inhibitions and not old enough to sense the tragedy, demanded, 'Where's our Richard, our Cissie? Where've you left him?' And Cissie, the muscles of her white face twitching, looked down at Annie but didn't answer her; then after a further moment of gazing at her closed fist, she slowly opened it and there on her palm lay five golden sovereigns, and as they all stared at them in unbelievable wonder, for this was real money, a great, great deal of real money, her mind lifted her back to the day when Jimmy said, 'I'll teach our Joe to set a trap an' you'll never want more.'

8

Matthew heard about Cissie Brodie handing her baby over to the big house when Straker, the miller's carrier man, returned from delivering the weekly flour and oats to the Hall. He could barely wait to get William out of the mill on an errand so he could tell his master the gossip.

Matthew was loading sacks on to a low dray cart; he was walking from the scale bench to the cart, the sack on his shoulder, then at one and the same time he saw Rose pause just within the wheelhouse. She had a can in her hand full of steaming tea for Straker and William at their break, and she was brought to a stop, as he himself was, when he heard Straker say excitedly, 'Place is agog with it. Took the child up yesterday mornin' an' handed it over, then, they tell me, fell flat on her face, dead out at His Lordship's feet. They say it's been goin' on for months. The valet's been the go-between. His Lordship got the place all ready for the bairn weeks ago, then nothin' happened. Nobody knows as yet what brought it to a head. They say she seemed chary, but was only likely waitin' for him to raise the price. They say she went out with a handful and she was sent home in the coach. Think of that now. A drab from the fells being sent home in the coach.'

Matthew flung the sack off his back with such a vehement toss that the heavy cart bounced beneath it and it brought Rose's eyes round to him, and she stared hard at him for a moment before walking to the bench and putting down the can. Then going to her father who was making no laughing retort this morning to Straker's tale, she said, 'How do you be now?' and he answered dully, 'So-so. I think I want a good dose of physic.'

As she left him and came across the mill floor again, she passed behind Matthew and said, 'Your drink's waiting.'

He did not answer her, not even to incline his head, but went on loading the dray, because when this was finished he'd be able to go. It was the arrangement that he would work until half-past nine in the morning at the mill. This meant he had done a good three hours' labour before he returned to the shop and started on his own work. His three hours' labour was his means of buying a share in the mill. Miller Watson, for all his laughter and joviality, had a business head on his shoulders.

Matthew scraped the slush off his boots on a grating in the wall, then wiped them hard on a mat inside the door before entering the kitchen.

Rose was standing at the table buttering a large brown bannock. She did not look at him until after she had been to the hob and brought the teapot and poured out his mug of tea; then pushing the mug and the plate across the table to where he was sitting she said, 'She sold her bairn then?'

When he didn't reply, just stared at her, a hard, cold look in his eyes, she leant over the table towards him, her voice low but her words grating, and repeated, 'I said, she sold her bairn then? Didn't you hear me? An' got a tidy sum for it, I understand.' When still he didn't speak she went on, 'Why look so thunderstruck if what you said was true. You said 'twasn't yours . . . You don't know whose it was, do you, yours, his, or anybody else's . . . ?'

She didn't finish, for the hot mug of tea went spinning across the table and the contents over one of her hands, and as she cried out and held her hand tightly under her oxter he stood gripping the edge of the table. His shoulders hunched, he cried with deep bitterness, 'I tell you again it wasn't mine, but God! if I'd known what I know now it would have been. Do you hear? It-would-have-been!'

She was still holding her scalded hand under her armpit

as she hissed at him, 'I'll tell me father you're not doing your duty by me. I will, I will.'

'You do that. You do that.' He made to go towards the door, when she now demanded, 'Where you goin'?'

Turning slowly, he looked at her, saying, 'It's me time for going, isn't it? I've done me stint.'

'You know what I mean, Matthew Turnbull. You know what I mean.'

Yes he knew what she meant. He stared at her. She was his wife, and he knew what she meant. Her skin was blotched blue with anger. Aye, and frustration. That was his fault, he supposed, but, God above, he couldn't help it. He had tried; no man had tried more, but he just couldn't give her what she wanted; as much as his own body cried out for satisfaction he just couldn't take it from hers. After that first week he had been sickened to the soul of him. If he had continued to take her it would have been as an animal did, and he was no animal. Even the sight of her face on the pillow beside him turned his stomach. But he wasn't crying out loud about anything, he had only himself to blame for the pickle he was in . . . Aye, and his folks, and young William, and young Jimmy, and the other seven of them back there.

She said now, 'If I was to tell me father he would cut you out, I know he would. There's no written agreement; he could do it an' you'd be back in your little tinpot shop. And what's more, he'd make you support me; besides which he'd send William packin'. Aye, he would that.'

He gave a mirthless, derisive laugh now as he said, 'Well, if he did, that would be no hardship to her now, would it, for if she's sold her bairn and been well paid for it, she can afford to keep the lot of them. Funny, isn't it . . . ?' His bitterness now making him cruel, he poked his head forward and ended, 'And to think it was because she couldn't afford to keep them that I married you.'

He turned from her vicious yet deeply hurt look and

200

went out; and, going into the open barn, he lifted his coat from the rack, put it on, donned his tall hat which he pulled down well over his brow, and mounted the cart and, crying briskly, 'Gee-up there!' took the horse out of the yard at a trot. He hadn't spoken to the miller, which wasn't unusual; but the miller hadn't spoken a word to him, and that was unusual.

He did not make for home but took the fell road. Twice he had to dismount and get behind the cart and, yelling at the horse to pull harder, help ease the wheels out of mud-filled pot holes. The farther he went on the fells the more grey and desolate the scene became. There was a deadly body-chilling bleakness everywhere that matched the feeling inside him.

As he mounted the slope he saw Joe and Sarah carrying armsful of wood into the dwelling. In the noise of the wind they hadn't heard the cart draw up, nor had they observed him mounting the slope, so they closed the door after them. He hesitated before knocking and it was Cissie herself who opened it, and he read on her expression surprise and what he could only translate as disappointment, and this latter emotion was borne home to him by the sudden drooping of her shoulders.

'Hello,' he said.

She did not speak, but bowed her head and stood aside so that he could enter. Then the children were around him, all but Bella and Sarah; Sarah because she didn't like Matthew Turnbull as she once had done – she hadn't liked him since he had married the woman from the mill instead of their Cissie – and Bella because she was still in a state of shock and dread, and she couldn't as yet take in the fact that she wasn't going to the House of Correction.

As the children scampered about asking him questions about William and the mill, Cissie knelt before the fire and thrust potatoes into the hot ashes. Her heart was beating rapidly. This was the first time she had seen him since his marriage. He looked older, grey in the face, but that could be the bleakness of the weather. When the knock had come on the door she had thought it was the man and he had come to ask her to go back to the Hall because they couldn't get the child to stop crying. All night she had prayed that it would cry and wail its loss of her, as she was crying and wailing inside because of her empty arms, her empty life. She had six of them here to look after but without the child they no longer seemed her kin, her flesh. She prayed that this feeling would pass and she would love them again as she had done before she had gone through the Lodge gates and over that park; she prayed that she would not hate Bella, that she would be able to keep her hand off her when she did stupid things.

Although her heart was beating painfully there was no joy in her at seeing Matthew. He was standing to the side of her now; she could see his feet out of the corner of her eye and when he said, 'Can you step outside a minute?' she sat back on her haunches, dusted the ashes from her hands and replied simply, 'No.'

There came a quietness on the room for a moment; then Sarah began to bustle, pushing at one and then another. Saying, 'Come on, you's,' she shepherded them out of the room and into the cave, Annie protesting loudly the while, 'No, our Sarah! I want near the fire.'

Matthew, dropping on his hunkers and his voice low pitched, said, 'I just heard; I'm sorry.'

At this she put the palms of her hands together and nipped them between her knees and rocked her body gently backwards and forwards.

'What made you do it? If you were that hard up you should have told William to tell me on the quiet; you know I would have come up with something.'

Her body still rocked.

'Cissie!' His arm flashed in front of her and gripped her shoulders and swung her round to him; and now, his face

202

close to hers, he whispered, 'Don't hold it against me, girl. I had to do what I had to do. I told you, I warned you, an' if it's any satisfaction to you I'm paying the price for it. Hell couldn't be worse. Look at me.' His voice was a thin, hard whisper, and when she raised her eyes to his he saw they were glazed with tears and when slowly they spilled over her lids and down her cheeks he wagged his head from side to side and gritted his teeth. After a moment he swung off his hunkers and dropped on to his knees in front of her, and his hands slid down from her arms and brought her hands into his, and he asked gently, 'Couldn't you get him back?' And when she shook her head, he said, 'What straits were you in to let him go then?'

Her voice a low mutter, her head still bent, she said, ''Twas Bella; she stole. She was due to go before the justice on Monday. They would have sent her to the House of Correction. She . . . she was terrified out of her wits, an' . . . an' then him in the Hall. He'd been after the child for weeks but I wouldn't let him go. Then . . . then I was told that he could get Bella off, and would do, but only if I let him have the bairn.'

She looked at him now. His jaws were tight clenched, his brows meeting low over his nose, but he said nothing, and she turned towards the fire again and, reaching out, turned one of the potatoes, and when she sat back on her haunches she said on a deep sigh, 'If he hadn't of got him that way he would have some other. He was going to take it to Court to claim him.' She lifted up her eyes to his again and, not knowing that her words were like knives being thrown at him, she said, 'I loved him so, an' I miss him. I don't feel I'd just had him five months. It's funny, but it's as if I'd had him all my life. And now there's nothing more to live for.'

His head was down and his cheekbones were showing white through his weatherbeaten skin. He had never seen the child and he'd had no wish to, and in the deep socket of his heart he knew he was glad she had lost it. Yet her loss created an agony inside himself. He wanted to comfort her, just hold her, stroke her hair, say her name, gently over and over again as he did in the night, 'Cissie! Cissie! Cissie!' He bent close towards her again, saying, 'I'll call in from time to time. It may be late on when I manage it, but . . . but I'll manage it somehow.'

Her reaction to his proposal startled him, for she jumped to her feet and reaching out to the mantelpiece she turned a little wooden box upside down on to her palm, then thrust out her hand holding the five sovereigns saying, 'We'll not be stayin' here all that long, we'll be gettin' a house out of it. Look; I have that every month. As long as he has the child I've got that. It's a fortune . . . isn't it? A fortune.' There was bitterness in her voice; there was accusation in her eyes.

They stared at each other for a time. Then he rose, turned slowly from her and went out.

It was three o'clock in the afternoon when William came panting into the wheel shop and, holding his side, gasped at Matthew, 'She says . . . Missis says you've got to come, the master's bad,' and immediately Matthew mounted the cart and, having pulled William up beside him, rode pell-mell back to the mill.

The light was fading as he entered the yard and Straker was standing under the platform of the threshing floor, but he didn't move towards them to take the horse, nor did he speak; and Matthew ran across the yard and entered the kitchen.

The lamp was lit and in its light he saw Jess Watson lying full length on the wooden saddle set at right angles to the fireplace, and by his side in the leather chair sat Rose. When she turned her face towards him, it looked twisted as if she were crying, but her eyes were dry and as he slowly approached her she said, 'He's dead. He . . . he came in, he said he had a pain, he . . . he couldn't bear it, it was in his chest, and then . . . and then he lay down and . . . and he just died.'

In this moment Matthew was as shocked as she was. He stood looking down on the miller, his hair and face still covered with flour, his mouth open, his eyes staring upwards. He thought, he cannot be gone, he was all right this morning. Then thinking back he remembered him complaining about his stomach. But he could not believe the evidence of the staring eyes and the gaping mouth and he laid his ear against the floured chest, but there was no movement. Then he stood up and looked at Rose, and she at him, and, putting out his hand and raising her to her feet, he said gently, 'Come away. I'll get the doctor.'

At this, she said low in her throat, 'It's too late for that,' and he replied, 'In cases like this, you've got to have him. Come into the parlour an' sit down, I'll see to things.'

Five days later they buried the miller. It was a well-attended funeral, for he was widely known and respected; and after the mourners had eaten and drunk their fill in the parlour, they lingered on, curious to know what the miller had left to his daughter. But the lawyer did not read the will until they had all left, and there was only the miller's daughter and her husband present, for the miller had been an only child as the miller's daughter was an only child.

The will had been drawn up six years previously and the miller left everything he possessed to his daughter. The mill and two acres of land, which was freehold, seven terraced houses in Shields, a row of cottages in Jarrow and, what even came as a surprise to Rose, three houses in Newcastle, which were situated in Mosley Street where the Theatre Royal and the post office were. The houses were each of four storeys; one was leased to a bank. These three houses, the lawyer pointed out, were of substantial value and were in fact equal to all the rest of the property put together, including the mill. He congratulated Mrs Turnbull in being placed in very favourable circumstances.

The lawyer gone, the house quiet, Matthew took a lantern and walked round the mill. He went up on to the threshing floor and held the lantern high. He walked round the grain store, the weighing room, the stables, then he crossed the yard and walked along the icy road to the full extent of the land. Still on the road, he skirted the house and, again swinging the lantern high, he looked up and down its face which held eight good windows; then he went in through a side door and along a passage and into the little room that Jess Watson had used to hold his bills and receipts, together with the strong iron-bound box that he took into Newcastle once a quarter and emptied the contents into a bank. He held the lantern up to show the small sloping-lidded desk, the leather chair, the empty fireplace, and above it on the wall the long pipe rack holding up to fifteen clay pipes. Finally, his eyes rested on the blank wall facing him. It was made for book shelves. He'd bring his books in here; this would be his office.

He was now the miller, he was now master of this house, and not only this house but the property stemming from it. He, Matthew Turnbull, was a rich man. Jess Watson may have left his fortune to his daughter, but his daughter was married to him and a wife's property was her husband's property . . . He was a rich man. Moreover, he'd have the vote now.

He put the lantern on the floor and sat down in the chair, and slowly his elation seeped from him and he saw again a palm held out with five golden sovereigns in it.

Jess Watson had not died soon enough.

BOOK FOUR 1836

The Return

1

'Grandpapa.'

'Yes, Richard?'

'You said I have a papa and he's in a big ship.'

'Yes, I did.'

'When will the big ship be coming back?'

'I'm not quite sure, Richard; but soon, soon. Do you like your new rocking-horse?'

'Oh yes, Grandpapa. Watch me. Look, I can gallop. When will I be able to have a real horse, Grandpapa?'

'Oh; let me see. When you are five years old you shall have a pony.'

'How long will that be, Grandpapa?'

'Oh, not so very long, two years.'

'Two years? How long is one year, Grandpapa?'

'A year is three hundred and sixty-five days long. You go to bed and get up three hundred and sixty-five times and then you have completed a year.'

'When shall we visit Elizabeth's house, Grandpapa?'

'Oh, some time next week.'

'Elizabeth has a mama and a papa . . . Where is my mama, Grandpapa?'

Lord Fischel drew in a deep breath. He had been waiting for this question for a long time now. Perhaps it had been a mistake to have Bellingham's daughter come visiting with her child; but what could he have done? – it was a matter of courtesy. She was on a visit to her father, and the fact that her child was the same age as Richard had prompted her to suggest that she should bring her over; but during the two days that had elapsed since the visit, Richard's childish conversation had been continually punctured with remarks, not about Elizabeth, but about her parents, especially her mother. And now he was holding his arms out and while asking to be lifted down from the rocking-horse he was saying, 'Nannie is not my mama, is she, Grandpapa?'

Lord Fischel did not immediately answer, nor did he put the child on the floor, but, holding him in his arms, he looked into the face that had brought him new life, new interest, and a love that he had never experienced before, which love, he knew, was what a man should feel for his own son; yet his children had, at no stage of their lives, brought forth anything akin to the feeling he possessed for this child.

The child looked every inch a Fischel. Yet, in the depth of him, his lordship admitted that its nature was other than that of a Fischel, for it was of a happy nature, warm and loving. He never allowed his thought to travel to the source of these qualities, although he was aware through Cunningham that the mother still lived in the ramshackle dwelling on the common land. Her continued presence there had at first annoyed him, even worried him, for he had imagined, with the generous allowance he paid her, she would have found a better habitation for her family. Still, she had not gone back on her bargain, which was in her favour, although it would have availed her nothing if she had attempted to. The child was his and would always remain his; and this was confirmed through not only his love for the boy but the boy's love for him.

'Grandpapa!' The child now traced his finger along the top of the white moustache and, concentrating his eyes on it, he asked, 'How big is my mama?'

How did one answer such a question as this? Lord Fischel put the child down on the floor; then taking him by the hand, he said, 'Come with me, Richard.'

'Are we going into the park, Grandpapa?'

'Presently; but first I want to show you a picture.'

'In a book, Grandpapa?'

'No, hanging on the wall.'

Suiting his steps to the child's he descended from the nursery floor into the passage that led to the gallery, and then, having walked its length, he stopped before a door leading into the railed balcony which overlooked the ground-floor hall. Pointing upwards to an enormous painting which filled the space between the top of the door and the high ceiling and which covered a third of the wall, he said, 'Do you see those figures up there, Richard?' and the child answered, 'The ladies with wings, Grandpapa?'

'The ladies with wings are called angels, and they are in heaven. You know where heaven is?' He turned about and pointed towards a long window set deeply within the stone wall. 'Heaven is up in the sky where God is; you know that, don't you?'

'Yes, Grandpapa.'

'You remember when your little dog died and was put in a box?'

'Yes, Grandpapa.'

'Well, your mama died like that once, and now she is in heaven with those angels.' He pointed upwards again, and the child, his head back on his shoulders, his dark brown eyes wide, gazed at the picture of Christ's ascension into heaven, then he drew in a deep breath before letting it out on a sigh and asked quietly, 'Won't I ever be able to see her, Grandpapa?'

'No, Richard, because she's in the sky in the House of God and you can't go there until you die, and you won't die for a long, long time. Now' – he jerked gently on the child's hand and brought his attention to him – 'it is eleven o'clock; you will have your milk and then we will go for a drive.'

His Lordship turned his head slightly to the side and made a small motion with it, and the young nurse who had been standing at the far end of the gallery, having followed her master and the child, which was her duty, came hurrying forward and His Lordship, without looking at her, said, 'Have Master Richard dressed for a drive by half-past eleven.'

'Oh, Grandpapa, are we going to see the ships?' the child cried, and His Lordship answered, 'Yes, if you would like that. Run along now.'

As he went to go through the doorway Hatton met him. He had a long envelope in his hand, and as he held it out he said, 'This came by special messenger from Newcastle, m'Lord.'

It was nothing to have a letter by special messenger from Newcastle; he had various interests which were centred there. It could be concerning stocks and shares, shipping, or mines; yet from the moment of taking the envelope in his hand he knew a feeling of apprehension. He passed the butler, went down the main staircase, crossed the hall into his study and, sitting down at his desk, slit open the envelope.

He had not recognised the writing on the envelope but when the letter began 'Dear Brother-in-Law,' his face stretched slightly; then, as he read on, it began to contract and by the time he had reached the end of the short epistle his face muscles were taut.

The letter told him that his sister was dead but expressed the hope that he would be in time for the funeral, and ended with, 'You will no doubt wish to discuss Isabelle's future.'

Staring at the letter, he did not think, Anne is dead – poor Anne, who had spent most of her life on one or another of those bleak islands, and with a bleak man – but he thought, Isabelle's future. What if she now insisted on returning home? He had warded off the idea for years, for the thought of her in the house again was intolerable; she had been unbearable as a girl, but now she was a woman what would she be like? He could but hope that the years with Anne would have improved her, but whether or no, he did not want her under this roof, especially now, when he had the boy.

Life over the past three years had been as akin to heaven as ever he hoped to get. The child had not only altered himself but the whole household; right down to the meanest servant everybody seemed happier, lighter. Sometimes he thought this was because the house had been redecorated and most of the fabrics renewed; yet the basic reason, he knew, lay with the child. And what effect would Isabelle have on the child, and . . . the child on her?

He admitted to himself in this moment that he had hoped that she would make an alliance with someone in her present environment; he hadn't been concerned with whom, relying on his sister's austere good sense to guide her. The situation was so unexpected and portended much annoyance.

What he had been expecting for some time now was news of the *Virago*. The last he had heard of the ship was that it was on its way to India, but that was months ago. He knew that some day Clive would return, must return; and part of him was eager that he should return, for he wished to have his signature on certain papers that would seal and ensure for all time this particular grandson's claim to his heritage and, consequently, the title.

But now, before him lay the long bleak journey to the far side of Scotland and the thought that he might be forced to entertain his daughter's company on his return.

It was two weeks later, on a warm, still day at the beginning of August. The young nurse and her charge had played ball, they had played blind man's buff, and now they were playing races and the nurse saw to it that her master always won.

The playing of races, the nurse had found, took the tedium out of the daily walk around the park. The walk started at the sunken lawn, continued through the trees, then along by the wall where it had been cleared of bramble right up to the part that faced the edge of the wood. Here the bramble and brushwood had been left, she understood, as a deterrent to anyone climbing the wall, because here their entry would be obscured by the wood itself. The broad path between the wood and the bramble-faced wall was kept cropped, but she had orders not to take the child along this path, which led to the North Lodge, so she always brought their racing to a stop when she came to the place where the bramble began; then she walked along by the edge of the wood, through the ornamental gardens until she came within sight of the other wall, glass-edged, this one, for it had only been built within the last fifty years.

She was very careful to follow her instructions exactly, for who knew but that someone might be watching her from the House through a spy-glass; even the master himself, for he had a number of spy-glasses up in the observatory on top of the east wing.

The three sides of the square completed, she would take her charge indoors, wash his face and hands, change his dress should there be a spot on it, and, afterwards, would attend to his dinner, which was brought up and served by the second butler. Following these tasks she would endeavour to see that her charge rested for at least an hour before once again being dressed and taken down to the drawing room at half-past five, there to have tea with his grandfather.

Today, the routine went as usual, for although His Lordship and Cunningham were away she did not dare diverge one inch from the daily plan, not with Mrs Hatton about. But at the end of the walk there was a diversion. It was caused by the coach coming to a stop on the drive opposite the front door just as she brought her charge up the steps from the sunken lawn.

The child, seeing his grandfather's face through the coach window, tugged his hand from that of the nurse and, running round the back of the coach, was just in time to see his grandfather descending the steps. Throwing himself forward, he cried, 'Oh, Grandpapa! Grandpapa! Where have you been? You've been a long time.'

His grandfather did not speak but took his hand and drew him aside; and then the child saw the coachman helping a lady down the steps and the lady looked up at the house for a moment, then she looked down at him. The lady was tall and her eyes were big and dark and her face was white. She was not smiling, but he smiled at her; then, glancing at his grandfather, he did what he had been trained to do when visitors came to the house: he walked forward, looked up at the lady, while bowing slightly from the waist, and said primly, 'How-do-you-do, Ma'am?' From experience, he knew this form of address always pleased the ladies, and they smiled at him and patted his head and told his grandfather that he had a clever boy; but this lady didn't smile or pat his head, nor did she speak; instead she turned from him and went up the steps, and the swishing of her skirts sounded like the whips they used to make the horses go.

The dinner was served, the servants had gone, and they were alone together, as they had been in the coach hour after hour, jolting, juggled, falling against each other, but never speaking. And now her father, his hands placed on the table at each side of his plate, leaned his stiff body slightly forward and said, 'This sulking silence will not benefit you any, Isabelle.'

Slowly she turned on him a deep, fiery glare, but asked calmly, 'What would you like that we talk about?'

When he bowed his head slightly, then gnawed on his

215

lip, she went on, undeterred by his signs of anger. 'You'll understand that I'm out of touch with your type of conversation; I can discourse at length on any part of the Bible from Genesis to the Chronicles and the Song of Solomon. Oh no!' She made a slight movement with her head. 'Not the Song of Solomon. Aunt Anne never read the Song of Solomon; she could never bring herself to say aloud, "Let Him kiss me with the kisses of His mouth for thy love is . . ."'

'Be quiet, girl! How dare you!'

'I dare, Father.' She was leaning towards him now, her voice low and weighted with anger. 'And one thing I must remind you of: I am no longer a girl, I am a woman whom you've had toughened by wind and weather; I've been fed on the Bible for the good of my soul, and the food I got for my body your scullery maid would have thrown in your face; and I dare further to say this to you now, I owe you nothing, respect or anything else, for you would have left me there to rot if Aunt Anne hadn't died. You sent me there so that my soul could be chastised, you did not consider the ruination of my body . . . Uncle appeared as if he wished to be rid of me, did he not, but at this moment he's back there in that squalid stone cell of a house eating his heart out. I was a great temptation to Uncle . . .'

'Leave the table!'

They stared at each other, their hate rising like a mist between them.

'You heard what I said.'

Slowly she pushed her chair back and rose to her feet, and before she turned away her lips moved into a sneering smile and she asked him, 'What do you think you're going to do with me?'

He did not answer for a moment but glared at her, and he had the urge, almost overpowering, as it had been once before, to strike her.

'Kindly leave the room.'

He watched her turn and walk slowly down the room, her back as straight as a ramrod, her head held high; and when the door closed on her he put his hand up and covered his eyes.

Isabelle walked across the hall and up the stairs; she looked neither to right nor left. She walked across the landing and to her room. It was her old room but no longer dull and gloomy; the curtains were green, the carpet was green; the wallpaper was a pleasing grey and the bed draperies a soft pink.

Four years ago the room would have delighted her; today she didn't see it, for her body and spirit were still in the stone house that was filled with God and hate, she hating both her uncle and her aunt, her aunt hating her because her husband desired her but unwilling to let her go because the money that she represented made all the difference between genteel starvation and ordinary living. Her uncle wouldn't let her go because he couldn't bear to think of life without her; it was only her threat to expose him to his hard, puritanical parishioners that forced him to ask her father to bring her away. And now she asked herself the question she had asked him a few minutes earlier. What would he do with her? A season in London in the hope that some man would marry her? It would be a brave man who would marry her, she knew that, for the wild animal in her was now reflected in her face and manners. Given scope and ordinary living over the past four years it might have become tamed, but that house on that island had chained it up, and it was common knowledge that if you wanted to make a dog ferocious you put it on a short chain.

But she was back. She would have to remake her life somehow; she would have to try to live like a civilised person. She went to the window and opened it. The garden was beautiful, the park was more open; they must have cleared it. She would ride again. What would it be like to feel a horse beneath her once more? That might bring a sensation of pleasure.

All of a sudden her head was jerked upwards as a child's laugh floated down from a window somewhere above. The sound brought her to face the room again. There was that to contend with too. Clive's son, the reason why she had been banished.

When her father told her that he had taken the child she had looked at him in amazement and although she was curious to know why he had done this she would not ask him. But she thought it was the last thing on earth she would have expected him to do, take under his wing Clive's bastard, the result of that mad drunken episode.

When a tap came on her door she said curtly, 'Come in!' And there entered a young servant girl who dipped her knee and said hesitantly, 'Mrs Hatton sent me, Ma'am . . . M . . . Miss. She says to maid you until one comes.'

To maid her! She'd had to maid herself since the day she left this house almost four years ago, even wash her own underwear. She was on the point of saying, 'I don't need your assistance'; but no, she'd take from life everything she could get from now on. It was her right, and she would wallow in it. She walked to the dressing table and, sitting on the stool, she looked at the girl through the mirror and said, 'I wish my hair to be brushed.'

'Yes, Miss. And Miss, I have to say that tea will be served in the drawing room at half-past five . . .'

Her hair piled high on her head, her gown changed, she went out of the room and across the landing, and at the top of the stairs she met the child with his nurse. Her whole body stiffened as he ran towards her and caught hold of her skirt and, looking up at her, cried, 'Are you my Auntie? Nanny says you are my Auntie. Are you?'

She stared down at the child, then her eyes flickered towards the nurse, who was watching with a tentative smile on her face, and she knew that whatever answer she gave to the child would be news below stairs within minutes. She would one day be mistress of this house – the thought had returned to her mind as if it had not lain dormant for four years – she must set the pattern for that day, no matter how she felt inside; and so her answer was, 'Yes, I am your Aunt Isabelle.'

'Oh!' When the child's hand was thrust into hers and she was forced to walk downstairs with him, her whole being revolted against the feel of the small warm fingers. At the bottom of the stairs he stopped and, smiling up at her, said, 'Elizabeth hasn't got an auntie, she's got a mama but she hasn't got an auntie.' He was drawing her on again in the direction of the drawing room, still chattering. 'My mama is in heaven with the angels. Grandpapa showed me the place. It's in the gallery.'

His mama in heaven with the angels! The figure of the girl rose before her as it had done many times during the past years. When her hate of everything and everyone dragged her down into the depths of despair it was then she would see the girl, not as she had last seen her lying on the ground but as on the day she had first struggled with her on the drive. His mama in heaven. She wished her in hell, and she would never cease to wish her there because it was this girl, and she alone, who was the cause of all that had befallen her . . .

After tea they went into the park, her father, the child and herself, and a small part of her was ironically amused that her father couldn't hide his surprise, even amazement that the child had taken to her.

The clearance of the place was more evident as she walked across the park. Never before had she seen the actual bricks of the wall that surrounded the north boundary. She imagined that their destination was the North Lodge, but as she entered the drive her father said, 'We don't go any further.'

She walked a few steps before she turned and looked questioningly at him, and he said, 'It . . . it is too enclosed; it is better that he should keep to the open.'

She stared at him. Had someone tried to snatch the child?

He gave no explanation, for he could not say that at the end of the drive were the North Lodge gates and that one day the mother might look through them and, seeing her son, cause a disturbance.

Isabelle watched her father walk away, the child dancing before him. There was a rustle in the undergrowth to the left of her, which made her turn her head. It was just such a noise on that far-off day that had caused her to poke her stick into the brushwood. She guessed that she was practically standing on the spot where it had happened. One day she would come here and she would set light to this tangle. She'd clear the whole place, the wood too, and she'd build the wall higher and put glass on the top of it. She heard the movement again. If she'd had a stick she would have thrashed at the bramble with it; as it was, she took her shoe and gave one ineffectual kick at it, then slowly walked away and followed her father.

2

In four years the dwelling had altered, and Cissie thought it was odd that the smaller her family grew the bigger the dwelling became. On the right side of the room, fronting the cave entrance, another room had been built. It was a small room but had a wooden floor where flour and oats, barley and potatoes could be stored in safety. On the other side of the room a larger building had been erected. This was called the wood house, for the walls were always kept lined with chopped wood. It was different from the other two rooms in that its doorway was much larger and its middle was always kept clear, a clear enough space in which to turn a horse.

She had only four children at home now: Nellie who was five, Annie six, Charlotte who was nine, and Sarah ten. Joe was working at the mill with William, Jimmy was still in the wheelwright's shop, and two years previously she had taken Mary from the tender mercies of the Misses Trenchard and had got her and Bella set on in the kitchen of a big house on the outskirts of Newcastle, and was hoping to get Charlotte, too, established there soon. Sarah she demurred about sending out, for Sarah was peaky, having a cough all the time, and tiring easily.

The money that she received from those who were working she spent mainly on their clothes, and with the five sovereigns a month she saw that the others were well fed and clothed. Moreover, there had been added to the house bed linen, new pots and pans, and mats for the floor. Even so, she did not spend the full amount, and a shilling or so often found its way back to the hamlet, to the Taggart family.

But her new prosperity didn't enhance her in the eyes of the people in the hamlet. Only a few days after the child had gone, a woman, walking past the dwelling with a bundle of wood on her back, had called out to no-one in particular, 'I'd be hard pushed if I had to sell me bairn to eat. I thought whorin' paid well.'

It had been almost a month after Miller Watson died before Matthew came to see her. He did not come in the cart but riding on a horse, and not bareback either. He was the miller now and the saddle was the outward sign of his prosperity, although Miller Watson had always used a trap. The day was bitter and the children were crowded round the fire, and Cissie sat with them and she didn't open her mouth to him.

But the next night, when the children were abed and it was almost on eight o'clock and she was about to go and join them because the candle was almost down to the saucer – even in her present affluence she wouldn't allow herself more than one candle a night – she heard the neighing of the horse outside, and she stiffened as she waited for his knock on the door, and a full minute elapsed before she opened it. Then he had walked past her and gone straight to the fire, and when she had walked towards him because he was standing near where her seat was, he said in a whisper, 'I've got to talk to you, Cissie.' And when she didn't answer, he ground out low, 'Look at me, 'cos I'm near mad.' And when she looked at him she saw that he could be right, for the flesh seemed to have dropped from him and his face looked craggy and thin.

'Cissie!' He caught hold of her hands, and she let them lie in his as he said, 'I've got to see you now and then. That's all, just to see you, talk with you, sit with you, like this.' He suddenly sat down in the chair and went to pull her on to his knee, but at this she resisted and, tugging her hands from him, she whispered hoarsely, 'No, no! I've had enough. Don't you know I've had enough! I can't stand no more.' Then bending down towards him, her face within inches of his, she hissed, 'Sit with you, you say? Aye, sit with you. And you know what they're sayin' about me? I'm a whore. Sit with you, you say? Aye, and have another bairn. If that happened I would do meself in. Do you hear? I would do meself in.'

'Cissie!' He had shaken his head at her. 'Listen to me.' He pulled himself to his feet and, gripping her shoulders, stared down into her face before he went on, 'I love you, Cissie. With every beat of me heart I love you, an' I wouldn't bring you no harm. God Almighty! there's nobody knows more than me that you've had double your share for your years. Cissie, believe me, lass, I'd never bring you harm. But . . . but I just want to be near you now and again, to sort of help me meet the days, just talk to you, touch you, just your hand, it'll be enough. If I can't, then God knows what I'll do because back there I feel desperate. It's worse now, since the old man's gone. She's fightin' for the trousers and I feel like murder, aye, like murder.'

As she looked into his eyes she became weak with fear for him.

He saw her weakening and he persisted, 'Just now and again, Cissie, when things get too bad. I won't make it regular, no set pattern.' And when she bowed her head on to her chest, he bent forward and kissed her hair, then said, 'I'll go now, else the horse will be frozen. Thanks, lass.'

She had not lifted her face until he was gone, and then she bolted the door and leaned against it, and another hunger was born in her . . .

He had said there would be no set pattern and he had kept to this. Sometimes she didn't see him for two or three weeks and never, after that night when he unburdened himself to her, did he speak of his wife, and only once did he mention his changed circumstances. It was as he sat in the trap on the road below the dwelling; he was well put on in knee breeches and gaiters and a long cord velvet jacket. She had looked up at him and said, 'You're going into Shields?' And he had replied with a flourish of his whip, 'Not Shields, Cissie, Newcastle. I'm goin' to a meeting of the millers and visit me bank, then on to the Groat Market and pick up some books.' Bending down low towards her, he had ended, 'I'm a man of consequence, Cissie, a rich man. Now fancy that.' There was both laughter and bitterness in his face, and he had held her eyes before whipping the horse into a gallop. As she watched him drive away she had thought that he had not only retained his own trousers but had stepped firmly into the miller's . . .

It was during the second year of his prosperity that he suggested she build a room on either side of the dwelling; and he had sent Jimmy over to help her for a full week; then he and Walters had come and put the roofs on and the floor in the storehouse.

It was shortly after this that Rose Watson came across the fells for the first time.

It was a day of high rough wind, a drying day, and Cissie was in the wood room possing the clothes in a new tub and with a new poss stick that Matthew had had made for her, when the opening was blocked by the figure of a big woman. She was wearing a brown cloak and a black bonnet and her hair was blown across her face. Cissie's heart leaped upward when she saw who the visitor was; and for a moment she thought something had happened to Matthew. She stood drying her hands on her apron while staring at the woman and the woman at her. Then Rose Watson took in a long breath, lifted her head, and looked round the mean habitation before bringing her eyes back to Cissie and saying, 'So this is it?'

Cissie had found her voice enough to say, 'Do . . . do you want something?'

'Yes, I want something.' The big woman walked

towards her. 'I want me man back. I've come to give you a word of advice. It's just this. If you don't stop 'ticing him away I'll have you hounded out of the place, an' I can an' all. Where is he? in there' – she nodded towards the other room – 'sleeping it off?'

'M . . . Matthew isn't here.'

'You're lying!'

'Well' – Cissie straightened up – 'go and look for yourself.'

Rose Watson turned away and went to the opening of the door, and there before her was Matthew striding up from the track.

Standing with her back to the poss tub, Cissie put her hand to her throat and gripped it as she saw him bend forward as if about to spring. Like this he stopped for a moment, then walked slowly up to his wife; and after staring at her while a bitter silence enveloped them, he said, 'Get away home.'

'Why should I? It's free land, I'm out for a walk. You're not the only one that can take walks.'

'Get yourself away home.'

When she didn't move, he cried at her in a terrible voice, 'I'm warning you, Rose. And remember what I said last night. I'll carry it out to the very letter. Do you hear me? 'Cos I have power over every penny, and I'll do what I said.'

At this her body jerked as if she had been prodded from behind, and, her mouth in a straight line and her chin knobbled, which emphasised her ugliness, she walked past him and across the slope to the road where she had left the pony cart, and he, standing looking helplessly at Cissie, said, 'I'm sorry. But I can promise you it won't happen again; she'll never come this way again.' And at this she had become afraid and, gripping his hands, she had begged him, 'Matthew, please, don't touch her. It . . . it isn't her fault. If you touch her it will only worsen

225

things, you know it will; it'll really be the end then.' And he had soothed her, saying, 'Don't worry. I won't lay a hand on her; I have other weapons, the money. I've threatened to sell everything up an' go off. And you know, it's a funny state of affairs, but I'm empowered to do just that. She has no say over what she's got; I'm master over the mill and the money, and the property; and she thinks more of the mill than even she does of . . .' He didn't finish but looked down; then after a moment he said, 'Don't let it worry you. You've seen the first and the last of her here. Believe me on that now.'

And she did not see Rose Turnbull again; nor did she see Matthew so frequently: a month would pass before he came. But now there was a difference about his visits, for when he came at night he always took her in his arms and kissed her, and she did not repulse him for he was all she had for herself.

And then came the day when she heard the child laugh.

She had been out looking for Joe. Although Joe was nearly six and growing fast and promising to be big made, which was, in a way, a guarantee of his not being picked up by the scrapers, she still felt uneasy when he was out of her sight for any length of time. And it was another irony of fate that since she had money to buy food he had become more adept at trapping rabbits; he even came in with a hare now and again, and these fly creatures kept to the open land.

This day he had been gone for two hours or more, and although she had been up on the high ground and called and screened her eyes against the sun she couldn't see him. Then, feeling that he had been caught, she had run along the road that led to the North Lodge and towards the hole in the bottom of the wall, and it was when she was still some distance from this place that she heard the sound of childish laughter, and she was brought to a stop and bounced back as if she had come up against a wire fence.

There it came again, playful, childish screeching, the noise a child made when at play: and as the sound went ahead of her she began to follow it, and she was almost up to the place where she hoped to find Joe when the laughter faded into the distance.

Leading from the rough road there were the signs of what appeared to be a fox track disappearing into the tangle, but she knew that it was no fox track but Joe's lead to the wall, and she called softly, 'Joe! You Joe!' And when she received no answer and no sound came from the undergrowth she went up on the fell again and gazed about her. And it was as she stood thus that she saw Joe crawling from the hole on to the road, and at the sight of him she was filled with anger and, rushing down the slope, took him by the shoulders and hissed at him, 'Where do you think you've been all this time? Why couldn't you come when I called?'

When he was free from her hands he looked up at her in surprise and, hitching his clothes straight, said, 'Oh, our Cissie, I couldn't come out. I didn't do it on purpose, they were there with the bairn at the corner. I . . . I daren't move.'

Her mouth opened and closed a number of times before she said, 'You . . . you could see the bairn?'

He nodded twice.

'How?'

'From the space where the trap is. It's right near the end where they've cleared. There's a part where you can see right across into the park. I . . . I thought maybe's they were going to clear right up to the gates and they would find the hole; but they didn't, they stopped dead at the corner where the wood starts.'

'How long have you been watchin', I . . . I mean the child?'

He blinked his eyes and looked to the side and said, 'A few weeks. It happened when I came in the afternoon to

227

see to the trap, not in the mornin', 'twas then I saw him.'

Her voice was quiet as she asked, 'Why didn't you tell me afore?'

He kicked at the dust on the road, he looked at his fingernails, he scratched his forehead, then muttered, 'You couldn't have got in, the hole's not big enough.'

Tenderly now she looked at his averted face. This wasn't the reason why he hadn't told her; he didn't want her to be hurt. Joe was older than his years, he knew more than a six-year child should. He was impish and full of fun but he was also thoughtful and caring; he, next to herself, had missed Richard more than any of the others, perhaps because he was a boy.

Very quietly she asked now, 'Does he come out at the same time every day?' and Joe, looking quickly up at her, said, 'Aye, when it's fine. But . . . but you couldn't get in, our Cissie.'

'No,' she said. 'No, I couldn't, I know that. Come on.' She held out her hand and together they went back to the dwelling.

The thought of the child behind the high stone wall and Joe's hidey-hole in the bramble haunted her. She knew she mustn't enlarge his entry to the undergrowth for that would give the show away; and there were times when the gentry out riding came along the road, and they had sharp eyes, had the gentry.

But after days of thinking her mind led her to an oak tree. The oak tree stood on the verge of the road with only a foot or so of its trunk exposed to a height of six feet or more, and there were ribbons of ivy circling even this part.

When one evening, in the twilight, she examined the tree she saw that if she cut the strands of ivy the tangle of bramble could be pushed back from it like a door, that is if she could clear a way behind it. If she could accomplish this then she could cut a path through the tangle to the wall, and along it right up to Joe's hole, then enlarge that so she could crawl through. But one thing at a time.

It took her nearly a month to make the passage to the hole because, to be on the safe side and to make sure that no-one on yon side of the wall would hear her, she went out before first light in the morning. Only once did she meet anyone. It was the morning when she had reached the hole in the wall. When she heard the distant rustling in the thicket she thought for one panic-stricken moment that there must be someone of the same mind as herself; and when the creature lumbered forward and a badger, more scared now than she was, scampered away from her feet she lay back against the wall and actually laughed silently to herself.

The most simple part of the long process was the removing of another four stones to make the hole sufficiently large for her to crawl through, because a hundred years of weathering had perished the mortar. By the time the sun came over the horizon she had the stones out and, lying flat, dragged herself through the three-foot hole into the dim miniature glade that Joe had made for himself over the years.

Breathless, her heart pumping against her ribs, she peered through the deep gloom. Then, attracted to where the gloom lifted a few feet above her outstretched hands, she pulled herself forward over the ground and, rising to her knees, which brought her head in contact with the bramble roof, she saw the opening. It was about three inches long and at an angle that caused her to keep her head on one side. It was like looking through an elongated keyhole, and in it, pictured in the rising morning light, she saw the park.

When she shivered with the cold she brought her gaze from the hole and pushed herself backwards, and as her foot hit a thick branch sticking out of the ground and the roof above her swayed she twisted swiftly round and righted one of the supports that Joe had placed, like pit props, along the side of the clearing. A few minutes later she pulled back the bramble door near the oak tree and stood for a moment looking right and left before stepping on to the road.

When she reached the habitation Joe was standing at the door and he greeted her with a crack in his voice, saying, 'Where you been, our Cissie? Where you been? I heard you get up. Where you been again?'

She led him back into the room and, stirring the fire, pulled him down towards her and whispered, 'Listen to me. I can get through the wall . . .'

'But you . . .'

'I said listen to me. I've been workin' on it for weeks; I'll show you this afternoon how I done it. Now what I want you to do is this. When I go in there I want you to play about on the fell, and when I'm comin' out I'll whistle like a peewit, and if there's nobody on the road you don't do anything, but if there's anybody comin', you'll whistle back. Now you understand that?'

'Our Cissie.' His face was screwed up. 'It's not very high in there, you mightn't be able to turn round. You . . .'

'I've been in and I got out again. And listen to what I say. You're not to tell the others, do you hear?'

He nodded at her.

'On fine days we'll take the sack and go lookin' for wood or some such. Anyway, they know I always try to keep you in sight so they won't be made to wonder.'

Long before two o'clock that same afternoon she was lying in the bramble waiting, and when, in the far distance, she saw through the slit two figures, one tall and one small, zig-zagging through the trees, she put her hand to her mouth.

It was a full five minutes later, when her view of them was clear, that she almost cried aloud as the child, running away from the nurse, came straight towards her as if into her arms.

He was wearing a dress made of some cream material. It had a deep collar and wide sleeves and it flounced up and down as he ran. Her eyes were stiff with staring. One hand was pressed tight on her mouth to check her breathing. He was not more than three arms' length away from her when the nurse caught him and, swinging him about, said, 'No, not that way, dearie. You mustn't go that way.' And he laughed and struggled in her arms, then ran away again. The last Cissie saw of him that day was the soles of his white kid boots as he fell on his face; and when this happened and a wail filled the air she instinctively thrust her hand forward into the brambles. Then pulling it back bleeding, she held it to her mouth while she sat back on her hunkers, her head on her chest and the tears raining down her face.

This was the beginning of her daily vigil. Only when the weather was so bad that she knew the child wouldn't be allowed out did she resist crawling through the hole in the wall. There were days when it was fine and she caught no glimpse of him, and she worried in case he was ill. But quite suddenly he would appear, and nearly always accompanied by . . . him. And he was always running and laughing.

Then came the day when she saw the lady with them. She saw them afar off and she thought, He's showing him off to company. That His Lordship loved the boy she had now not the slightest doubt; it was in his face as he looked down at him, it was in his voice as he called to him. There was, she thought, a sort of pride in him concerning the child, and this puzzled her greatly. When they gradually came into her view she found herself staring at the lady, and when memories stirred she shook her head against them trying to deny what her eyes were seeing. The figure had developed; it was full and taller but the face was the same, dark, not only the eyes and brows and hair, but the expression was dark, forbidding . . .

She had come home. His daughter had come home. She was moving nearer and nearer; she was going to walk down the path. She could have put her arm out sideways through the bramble and touched her skirt.

She heard His Lordship say something to his daughter. She didn't take in what it was. Although she couldn't see her now, she knew she was standing still; she felt that she was looking at her, glaring at her through the thicket, and she slipped from her elbow on to her side, and some dry twigs cracked beneath her.

She let them get well away before she moved backwards and through the hole, and when she reached the oak tree she stood for a time leaning against it before she pulled aside the dead ivy-threaded bramble door; and having passed through it she still kept her back pressed against the tree and slanted her eyes up and down the road, for there was no Joe to give her a signal now, and hadn't been for some weeks past since he had started at the mill.

As she walked over the fells she found she couldn't stop trembling. That woman frightened her; she had frightened her when she was a girl, but now she looked even more ferocious than she had done then. And what effect would she have on the child? That the child was happy she had to admit; but would it remain happy living with that woman? And there was another thing; if she was back . . . was *he* back? What would she do if she ever came face to face with him again?

Was it too late to say she wanted the child back and put up a fight for him? But how could she fight the lord on her own? There was no-one she could turn to for help in this case, not even Matthew; for instinctively she knew that Matthew was glad she had let the child go.

3

The sailor walked along the Newcastle quay. He was tall and thin and weatherbeaten; he wore a thick blue serge suit and a cloth cap, at the sides of which could be seen fair hair that was bleached to a silver whiteness. In one hand he carried a valise, while the other hand supported a canvas bag on his shoulder.

When he reached the end of the quay he turned and looked back at the ship he had just left, which, compared with the others lying alongside it, looked a dirty tramp, and when from the top of the gangway he saw a hand go up he bounced his head once towards it.

Leaving the quay, he threaded his way through the narrow streets, up Pilgrim Street, past the inns, the flax dressers, the cheesemongers, and the open-fronted shops until he came to the corner of New Bridge Street, where three cabs stood waiting for hire. The first cabman, seeing that his fare was a sailor, and knowing that sailors were free with their money, especially when they had just come off a voyage, relieved him almost in a flash of his bags while asking, 'Where to, Mate?'

'Houghton Hall.'

'Houghton Hall?' The man stopped in his placing of the bags on the rack, and he turned his head and looked at his fare. 'Houghton Hall, you said?'

'Yes, that's what I said. Do you know it?'

'Aye; yes. Yes; but 'tis a long way out.'

'You'll be paid.'

Although the man was young, the cabby recognised that the voice held authority, as did the look in the eyes. Without further ado he opened the door of the coach and handed his passenger up, then mounted the box, and soon they were threading their way through the press of traffic in the town. But not until they had passed The Side and crossed the Tyne Bridge could he put the horses into a gallop.

They went through Gateshead, Felling, and Pelaw, and here they bypassed Hebburn and by a narrow road cut across open country. At one point the cabman drew the horses to a halt and, bending down to the window, called, 'I'm not quite sure of me way, Sir.' He did not make the mistake of using the misnomer of mate now, and his passenger, looking out of the window, pointed. 'Fork left; the main gate is about a mile farther on.'

At the main gate the porter surveyed the dingy conveyance for a moment before slowly unlocking the gates, and then as the carriage passed him and he saw the face under the cloth cap, the face that he hadn't seen for almost four years, but which he instantly recognised, he touched his forelock, shouting as the coach rode on, 'Welcome home to you, Sir.'

The sound of the approaching cab brought the second footman to the top of the steps. He was a new addition to the household, having been in His Lordship's service for only three months, and when he saw the sailor with a canvas bag and battered valise leaving what was obviously a hired cab, he stiffened and, adopting his most haughty manner, asked, 'What is your business, Sir?'

'Get out of my way.' The voice sounded weary, and after the sailor had passed the man he turned and thrust the kit bag and the valise at him, saying, 'See these go to my room.' And comprehension hitting the footman like a stone, he muttered obsequiously, 'Yes, Sir. Yes, Sir.'

In the hall he encountered Hatton; and the butler, after standing perfectly still for a moment, his lower jaw sagging, pulled himself quickly together and advanced towards the sailor, saying, 'Oh, Mr Clive. I'm . . . I'm very pleased to see you home again.'

'You are, Hatton?' The clear grey eyes had a piercing quality. 'Thank you.'

The butler stared at the roughly clad young master who didn't talk like the youth he remembered and in some strange way no longer held any resemblance to him, and whose tone had a coarseness, but a commanding coarseness, about it.

'Where is His Lordship?'

'He . . . he's up in the nursery, Sir.'

The fair brows drew together, hooding the eyes. 'In the nursery, did you say?'

'Yes, Sir. With . . . with Master Richard.'

The head came forward, the eyes became slits. The enquiry was quiet. 'Master Richard?'

'Yes, Sir.' Under the scrutiny the butler's composure was chipping, and now he added quickly, 'If . . . if you would care to go into the drawing room or, or His Lordship's study, I will inform His Lordship that . . .'

'There's no need.' The hand was flapped carelessly back at him. 'I think I can still find my way about. The nursery you said?' The head was turned over the shoulder, the eyes hard on him again, and Hatton swallowed before he answered, 'Yes, Sir.'

He went slowly up the stairs looking first to one side and then the other at the hall below. The place had been done up, it was lighter. This was a different carpet on the stairs from what he remembered. Master Richard in the nursery. What was this? It could only mean that Isabelle was married. Well, well; and so they now had a Master Richard.

Two maids, carrying slop buckets, stopped dead on the landing and gaped at the sailor walking towards them, and they stood still while he passed them, widening his eyes at them in imitation of their amazed staring. Then they scurried away.

As he mounted the nursery stairs he commented to

himself, Cream and grey; she always said she would have the place redecorated one day. When he reached the landing he heard childish laughter coming from the door at the far end. A nursemaid, not unlike the one he and Isabelle had had, came out of the doorway and she, too, stopped dead and gaped at him.

She was barring his way into the room now, and so, bowing his head towards her, he said quietly, but firmly, 'If you please,' at the same time moving her gently aside with the back of his hand. And then he walked forward into the old day nursery where he had played, and later painted and drank.

But this was not the old nursery, this place was bright with colour. His immediate glance took in a gaily painted rocking-horse, and a quarter life-sized coach; the model sprung as if the real thing and drawn by a wooden horse on wheels. There was a child climbing into the coach, but it paused on the step and, turning round, said, 'Grandpapa,' then stopped and looked towards the man in the sailor's clothes and added, 'Why look, Grandpapa, a gentleman!'

Lord Fischel straightened up, turned and saw his son, and for a moment his heart raced so quickly that he thought he was about to have a seizure.

It was Clive who spoke first. Going forward, his eyes on the face that seemed younger to him than when he had last seen it, he said, 'Good-day, Sir.'

'Clive! Why . . . why I didn't know you were in; I never heard. They should have informed me. Why, dear me.' He was flustered. He moved his hand up to his brow and with his two middle fingers rubbed it as if trying to smooth out the furrows.

The cold grey eyes moved over the now twitching face. 'I hope I find you well, Father?'

'Yes, yes, thank you, Clive. I'm very well. And . . . and you?'

'Oh, I am very well, thank you. Tough, strong,

weatherbeaten; the sea does a great many things for you.'
He nodded at his father and watched the blood slowly
recede from under his skin, then he turned and looked
down at the child who was standing staring up at him, and
he said to him, 'And I understand your name is Richard,
young man?'

'Yes, Sir; what is yours?'

'My name is Clive.'

'Have you come to play with my coach?'

'Not exactly; but it's a very fine coach, I can see
that.'

'Grandpapa bought it for my birthday. I am three.'

The fair brows moved upward again. Three was he? His
mind did some swift calculation. She must have married
almost immediately. He led up to further details by
asking, 'I hope Isabelle is quite well?'

'Yes, she's quite well.'

When his father turned away and walked towards the
nursery door he turned with him, saying, 'Whom did she
marry?'

For answer His Lordship now called, 'Nanny!' and
when the nurse appeared in the doorway he said, 'See to
your charge,' and she dipped her knee and said, 'Yes,
m'Lord.' And he walked from the nursery on to the
landing, and it was as he was walking down the stairs that
he said quietly, 'Isabelle is not married.'

'O-oh!' He suppressed the huh! So that was it. But he
wasn't surprised. Oh no; he wasn't surprised. And looking
back and remembering his sister he was only surprised
that it hadn't happened earlier, say when she was fifteen,
even fourteen.

They had reached the ground floor and were making for
the study when Clive asked, 'Is Isabelle here?' and His
Lordship, entering the room, said, 'Yes; Isabelle is here.'
Then seating himself behind his desk he said to his son,
'Be seated,' and asked, 'Would you like a drink of some

sort?' When Clive replied, 'Yes. Yes, I would,' he rang the bell.

Hatton appeared and kept his gaze focused on his master, and His Lordship said briefly, 'Bring the decanters.'

It wasn't until they both had a glass in their hands and His Lordship had sipped twice at his that he said, 'There's something that you should know right away, Clive.' He did not look at his son as he went on rapidly now, 'The child you saw is not Isabelle's, it is your child, your son.'

Clive had just taken a drink, not a sip, from his glass and now he choked on it and had to bend forward, his hand to his mouth. The water was springing from his eyes and running down his nose and he dabbed his face with a handkerchief and sat gasping and staring at his father. But he made no comment, not a word, and His Lordship, waiting until the spasm was quite passed, said, 'The child was being brought up in poverty and squalor, so I could not allow it to go on. But I made sure it was your child before I took any steps. He is the exact replica of your grandfather, didn't you notice it?'

Notice it? The child had just been a child, Isabelle's child, so he would have expected it to look like a Fischel, a typical Fischel, dark-eyed, dark-haired, long-nosed. He himself, being so fair, was an oddity or a hark back to his maternal grandfather who had been a Norwegian. He drank from his glass again. He was staggered; the wind had certainly been taken out of his sails before he had been on board five minutes, so to speak.

For days now, even months, he had rehearsed what he was going to say to his father at their first meeting. He was going to give him a detailed graphic picture of life at sea, seen and suffered through the eyes of a boy who had been gently bred, a boy who had been thrust into the stinking bowels of a ship with the deep raked scum of the earth for his companions; who had been kicked, spat on, and flogged for no other reason than that he had come from the gentry. A boy who had suffered seasickness for three long months and to such an extent that it brought him near to death, and who was alive today only because the Captain himself had called a check to his first and second mates' discipline, a discipline patterned to give the whole crew hell but particularly the youngest member.

In this tale he had intended to dwell a long time on the joy he felt as he watched the first mate, who had been swept overboard, or perhaps had been pushed, being torn alive by barracuda, and of his glee when he had seen the second mate stabbed during a fight in a brothel; and in the telling he had meant to convey his hate for the man who had brought out depths in himself that he was ashamed of. And finally he had meant to end by emphasising that the act that had caused his banishment had been but a 'God bless you' compared with the things he had achieved along the same lines during the past four years.

But now, here was his father telling him he had a son. That child upstairs was his son. But what of it? He could have many sons. His sons could be dotted all over the Far East; in every port he had docked he had left his seed in black, brown, and white bellies.

'Have you nothing to say? Didn't the boy impress you?'

'Impress me?' He made a deep laughing sound in his throat, then moved his head in a wide sweep; and he was about to speak again when the door burst open and Isabelle stood staring at him across the room.

'Clive!'

He rose slowly to his feet. 'Hello, Isabelle.'

'Why, Clive!' She was standing close to him, peering into his face, her eyes searching it as if looking for some remembered feature. This was Clive, the other part of her. 'How are you?' She felt awkward, and it was an unusual feeling for her.

'Very well. And you?'

239

'Oh' – she laughed – 'I'm alive.'

It was a strange answer and he noticed that when she said it her head made the slightest movement in their father's direction, where he sat stiff-faced behind his desk taking in every nuance of their greeting, while knowing that this was but a polite façade and what they had to say to each other would be said while out of his presence.

Yet what would he have to say to her, his sister, the being who had been as close to him as his skin? As he stared at her he could not believe that he had once been afraid of her, that he had once been weak enough, timid enough, even loving enough to follow her lead. He saw that she was vastly changed for she had the appearance of a woman well into her twenties, and what beauty she had was a hard beauty. Yet looking into the brown blackness of her eyes he knew that inside she was still the same, still a dynamic, wayward, vicious being, and perhaps more so now than ever before. He knew that during the last four years there had erupted in himself passions that were natural to her. He had got release from some of them, but what about her? Well, he supposed, being that this was Isabelle, he'd soon find out.

When she said, 'Have you seen Richard?' and he raised his eyebrows and made a slight motion with his head she laughed aloud. Her laughter brought her father to his feet, and on this she turned and looked at him, her glance cold and distant. Then turning to Clive again, her laughter higher now, her eyes glinting, she said, 'Richard and I are great friends. He calls me Auntie, but he said yesterday that he would have liked me for his mama. Now isn't that quaint?'

Clive turned to see his father walking out of the room; then he looked at his sister and, the corner of his mouth moving up into a twisted smile, he stared at her for moments before saying, 'You know, it's a funny thing about time, it can be endless, and then it is as if it had never been. I thought you might have changed but you haven't, you're still the same Isabelle.'

Her face took on a blank, dead look as she returned his stare and, her voice low in her throat, she said, 'You're wrong. Time takes its count from where you are; and on a grey island every minute is a month, and a year eternity, and the seasons chop you up and you die slowly.'

When her lips trembled and she swallowed and the bone in her neck moved up and down like a man's Adam's apple, he put his hand out and gently touched hers. She gripped it fiercely, and hung on to it; then, her head bowed, she thrust her hand through his arm, saying thickly, 'Come; let's get out of this room, we've got a lot to talk about, you and I.'

4

After only a month at home Clive was experiencing the strange sensation of being confined on all sides, even more so than when he had been incarcerated in that boat in the middle of the ocean. Yet his days were filled with riding, shooting, visiting, and, of course, walking with his son.

His son troubled him. Strange as it was, or perhaps not so strange, he was the only person in the household who wasn't worshipping at the boy's feet, for memories recurring from his own childhood caused him to object to different liberties accorded the boy. He himself had never been allowed such liberties. He had been fourteen years old before he had sat down to a meal with his father, yet this child came into the drawing room every afternoon for tea.

Months had gone by in his own and Isabelle's childhood during which they didn't see their parents. When the season came their parents disappeared to a place called London and they were left to the mercies of a nurse and a relaxed household. Even when their parents were at home, weeks would go by without their getting a glimpse of them; then perhaps for three days at a time they would see their mother. She would come up to the nursery, gay and beautiful, and want to play with them, but he himself could never play with her because he wasn't used to her.

In his childhood the nursery had been a world kept apart from the rest of the house; now the whole house was merged into the nursery. Every morning his father visited the nursery; every afternoon, weather permitting, he walked with the child; then there followed the tea ceremony in the drawing room. He doubted whether in all the land there was a child who had as much liberty as this flyblow of his.

But whereas his son irked him, the attitude of his father towards the boy angered him. He would scarcely give himself a day's shooting because he would miss a session with the child.

And now there was this business of inheritance. The child was his, he couldn't disclaim that even if he wanted to, but to recognise him legally, not only to give him his name, but to state in writing that no matter what further issue he might have this child would claim first place as his heir was taking the whole business to lengths that were not only unreasonable but fantastic.

When he put to his father the question, 'What if I marry? Do you think any woman is going to stand for her son taking second place to a bastard, for no amount of legal writing is going to alter that fact?' his father's reply had merely been, 'He is your son.'

He was standing now at the window of his room looking out over the drive and the sunken garden, and into his view came his father and the child, with the nurse walking some distance behind. The ritual was taking place again. The child's chatter, penetrating through the window to him, irritated him. He was allowed to talk without let-up; he was under no discipline; not that he was rude, for in spite of his liberty he had a charming way with him . . . This being so, why couldn't he love him, at least like him? It came to him as he watched the child running wildly here and there that he felt towards him as his own father had felt towards himself, a mixture of irritation and responsibility.

The child, too, he knew had sensed his feelings, for after the first ecstatic moments when he had been presented to him as his papa from the big ship, he had not been free with him as he was with his grandfather, or even with Isabelle . . . Now that was strange, the affection that

243

existed between the child and Isabelle. As she had said, he almost treated her as his mama, and she in turn, behind the outwardly cynical acceptance of his affection, was now as besotted by him as was his father.

What was going to happen to Isabelle? Would she marry? Bellingham's nephew seemed attracted, but he was like whey to her thick brown beer. What she needed was a master, but where was he to be found? Not in the narrow, censored circle of their acquaintances as far as he could see.

His feelings towards his sister, too, disturbed him. They were a mixture of pity that was akin to love and dislike that was akin to hate; his softer feelings towards her were aroused when she told him, as she did at intervals, of her life with the licentious, puritanical parson and their aunt, a female replica of their father enlarged still further by frustration.

He had been made to wonder at first how she had become such a good shot, for she handled a gun like a man, which was unusual. Then one night after supper when she had drunk well – their father no longer objected to her taking wine at the table – she had not only told him how she had become so expert with the gun, but had given him a demonstration, which, in a strange way, had made him shudder, for she had put her arms around his neck and slid her hands down his arms and over his hands and brought them into a firing position, and like this she had held him close for a moment before almost throwing him off her as she said, 'That is how I learned. He would knock me up at dawn, or before, to take me out shooting. He kept the table supplied with wild duck, and as Aunt cooked and served it I know she prayed that it would choke him . . . and me.' She had laughed wildly for a moment, and he'd had a clear picture of the hell in which the three had existed in the stone house on the island, and his own experiences in the bilges seemed clean in comparison.

And it had all come about because of an argument as to who had right of way in a narrow passage. His thoughts had brought him to the point from which he always shied because the picture in his mind did not actually put before him the act of his first copulation but that of a sweat-covered face out of which were staring two terrified eyes.

He turned swiftly now from the window and looked about the room, then flexed his arms wide as if to push aside the walls. He'd have to get away, not only from the house but from the grounds, and not only from the grounds but from what lay immediately outside, the land, poverty stricken, overrun with the poor and the mean and the starving.

For the first two and a half years of his voyaging he had lived not only among the poor and the mean and the near-starving but also among the dregs of humanity; and he had been brought down to their level, and had prayed the while to be delivered. And he had been delivered, in so far as during the latter part of the voyaging he had risen, first to second mate, then to first mate, thanks to the barracuda and a six-inch blade. But even then he had longed for civilisation again, a feather bed, eight-course meals, and the ebb and flow of lackeys around him. Now he had all this, and perverse nature was turning it into brine in his mouth, for yesterday he had gone into Shields and walked the waterfront and lingered on until dark when he had meandered through the taverns; and part of him had felt at home even while he had seen the earth as peopled with scum.

And what of his painting? He had promised himself that, once ashore, between eating and sleeping and drinking he would paint, do nothing but paint; for during his four-year voyage he had painted only five pictures and they during the last six months. And they weren't of seascapes, mountainous seas, or billowing sails, but of the brutalised faces of his companions. And now, here he had been almost five weeks in civilisation and he hadn't lifted a brush.

He went to the wardrobe and took down some breeches and put them on. This was another thing. He had become so used to dressing himself that he couldn't bear a man fingering him. As he buttoned up the breeches he went out of the door, across the wide landing, down a passage to where there was a window at the end, and, opening it, called into the courtyard below, 'Micky! Micky!' and when a stable boy appeared he shouted at him, 'Saddle me the Rover.' Then he strode back to his room, finished his dressing, and fifteen minutes later he was on his horse and riding out through the main gate.

He paused for a moment outside the gates. To the right and four miles away lay Bellingham's place; but he wouldn't go that way because he had refused to join the shoot. Opposite him was the road to Jarrow and Rosier's pit village, and he didn't fancy passing through that stinking hole; so he turned up the road to the left which led back towards the North Lodge, deciding that from there he would cut across the open ground towards Felling and perhaps stop at the tavern near the toll-gates because he felt like talking to someone; he did not add 'someone ordinary', but left it at that.

There was a bend in the road some distance ahead and he saw a peasant woman come running down from the fell and on to the road. She was holding up her skirts. She had brown hair which glinted in the sunshine. He wondered in passing whom she was running from or whom she was running to, for this was a lonely part, there being no habitations about. Then a surprising thing happened. When he rounded the bend and looked along the straight stretch of road that led to the Lodge there was no sign of the woman.

When the explanation came to him his chin jerked, and

he thought, She'll certainly be tickled, if nothing more painful, for she had likely gone into the thicket bordering the wall to relieve herself. He put the horse into a canter and galloped along the road.

When opposite the North Lodge, he turned the horse and mounted the fells; he let the animal have its head, and it had covered almost a mile before it tossed him. When he felt himself diving through the air from the saddle he relaxed his body before it touched the ground, a life-saving trick that an old sailor had taught him – when you're thrown almost from one end of the deck to the other, and not only by high seas, you have to learn some defence. But his horse hadn't been so fortunate. When it scrambled to its feet it was evident that it had badly sprained its fetlock. He swore as he led it back over the way they had come. But before they were in viewing distance of the North Lodge he decided that he could cut the journey short by forking to the left; this should bring him almost to the bend in the road and near the main gates.

He was some distance from the actual road itself when he again saw the woman. He saw her coming out of the tangle near an oak tree, and he mightn't have thought any-thing more but to remark to himself that it had taken her a long time to do her business but for the fact that she first looked one way along the road, then the other. If she had raised her head high she must have seen him and the horse, but she didn't. What she did now was to turn away and walk along the road; and when she reached the bend she mounted the fells and became lost to him among the hillocks.

He took the horse gently down the slope and on to the road; and when he came to the oak tree he glanced at it, then stopped. He noticed that it was covered, except for a few feet from its base, by a tangle of bramble and ivy. One thing, however, stood out: the ivy on the left hand side was dead because it had been cut.

247

Dropping the bridle and using both of his gloved hands, he pushed at the tangle, and when it fell inwards like an object without support his eyebrows moved upwards. Pushing it still further aside, he now saw through the dimness a clearing leading to the actual wall. He pursed his lips into a silent whistle. He did not venture to investigate further as he thought that would be unwise; there could be a trap somewhere, it could even be a spring trap and blow his head off. Yet why would anyone want to set a spring trap outside the grounds? No, that wasn't the reason for this tunnel; the tunnel had to do with the wall, the wall that guarded the grounds. He stepped back and pulled the bramble into place again, then thoughtfully led the horse away.

The thought of the woman and the tunnel intrigued him, and he would have returned to investigate further but for the fact that he hadn't escaped altogether lightly from his fall. He found he was bruised rather badly down one side and his shoulder was stiffening up; so when the next day it rained he took the carriage into Newcastle and presented himself at his father's club and sat drinking most of the afternoon, and although he was without company he found the atmosphere preferable to that of the house where everything seemed to be dominated by the requirements of Master Richard. The child, he thought, attracted people up to the third floor more surely than a whore did long-voyage men.

He did not rise early the following day because he had a heavy head, but when he looked out the sun was shining, and after a light breakfast he decided to take a walk.

Isabelle met him at the foot of the stairs. She had not seen him since early yesterday morning and now she looked at him through narrowed eyes, and when she spoke there was hostility in her tone. 'Is it by accident you are becoming aloof, or is it intentional?'

He gave her his one-sided smile as he answered, 'It was very wet outside yesterday, so I decided to match it' – he thumbed his chest as he ended – 'internally, so I took myself to a place where the process would be undisturbed.'

'A sailor's hostel?' Her lip was slightly curled, but he showed no offence and even laughed before he said, 'No, no. No place so sordid. I am reverting to my inherited standards; I honoured Father's club in the city.'

'I want to talk to you.'

'Well, you can do that any time. What do you want to discuss?' He thrust his hands into his breeches pockets, and the attitude annoyed her and she said, her voice low, 'It's about the child, and I can't do it here. Come to my room.'

'Huh!' He jerked his head upwards as he left the bottom step. 'The child!' And on this she grabbed his arm, saying, 'What is the matter with you? This is something you've got to face. Like it or not, he's yours and he's got to have your name. This is about the only thing I'm in agreement with Father over.'

'Oh! you are?' Their eyes held for a second before he gripped her hand that was clasping his arm and jerked it away, and the action was as if he had cut the umbilical cord that had roped them together from birth; and now he said grimly, 'Then I'm afraid there's going to be two of you disappointed.' And on this he turned from her and walked across the hall, picked a walking stick from the stand, then went out by a side door.

As she watched him go she gritted her teeth, and she wondered where that part of him had gone that she had loved; because the boy she had known to be timid and weak and easy-going was now none of these things, he had turned into a man that she almost disliked. The fact that he had no feeling for his son did not displease her, for this being so, he would have no wish to take him away from his grandfather's care and this house, even if he married, and she could see no sign of this happening because his manner towards women was dour, the exaggerated courtesy he showed them being little short of ridicule. But even should he marry she could not imagine his keeping the child in the same house as his bride. And that's where she came in. She had always seen herself as mistress of this house and slowly but very surely over the weeks she had made her position felt by gathering the reins of management into her hands. The servants were aware of this, even if her father wasn't.

If anyone had told her that within five short weeks she would come to love, with an irrational compelling love, the child of that low, ignorant fell creature, she would have laughed at him, while wanting to slap his mouth with the back of her hand in the way her aunt used to slap hers in the early days in the stone house.

Even during the first two weeks of her acquaintance with the child she had remained obdurate against her rising affection for him. Then came the day when, with his arms tight around her neck, he had said, 'Can you have two mamas, Aunt Isabelle?' And when she had laughed and replied, 'Yes, that is possible; if your first mama dies you can have a second mama,' he had hugged her close and whispered, 'Then you are my second mama, Aunt Isabelle.' And it was done.

Clive had spent some time in the stable examining the horse's fetlock, looking at the other mounts, and talking quite affably with Morris, the coachman, Bowmer, the second coachman, and Micky, the head stable boy. He felt quite at home with the stable staff and they with him. The verdict was, he was all right was Master Clive, come back a man and no mistake, and could hold his drink better than most. Now who would believe that when they remembered the nervous young stripling who had been transported, so to speak.

Half an hour later he strolled through the park, out through the North Lodge, then continued casually down the narrow road until he came to the oak tree. He had purposely put on a plain coat, the skirt of which came to his knees; and quickly now, after glancing up and down the road, he pushed aside the bramble door. Once behind it, he put it in place again, all as if he had done it many times before.

The passage to the wall was high enough to allow him to walk with only his head stooped forward, and when he reached it he made out, through the filtered light from above, that for some distance alongside it a way had been cleared. Thrusting his walking stick out in front of him and moving it from side to side, he walked slowly forward until he came to where the clearing ended. And there he stared down at what was a man-sized hole.

Well! Well! He nipped on his lip before slowly dropping on to his knees. But he had to lower his body still further before he could get through the hole, and now, still on his hands and knees, he peered about him. He was in a tiny clearing, the bramble roof held up here and there by props. He stared about him in amazement . . . and recognition. This must be the very spot where, on that faraway day, the small boy had hidden. But that was four years ago. This place was still being used, he had seen the woman come in. Why? There were no rabbit traps that he could see, there was no outlet that he could see. He turned once more on to his knees and crawled around the space, which at most was but three yards in length and two in breadth, and as he crawled he asked himself to what purpose it could be used. He was inside the grounds. Why would anyone want to sit in here? They couldn't get out, that was a certainty. His eyes began to search the dark green screen, and then his crawling suddenly stopped. He was looking through a slit. His vision was obscured by tiny branches, but nevertheless he could see into the far distance, and in the distance he saw his father and the child and Isabelle. And now he sat back on his heels, and his hand, going to his mouth, tapped it slowly.

He was about to put his eye to the opening again when a slight sound, as if a rabbit were scurrying over dry leaves, came to him; then distinctly he heard the intake of a long drawn breath as happens at the end of a run.

From the position he was in now he was facing the hole and could be seen by the girl when she came in, for instinctively he knew it was the girl and he felt cold at the thought. He had already guessed the reason for this place.

Her scrambling through the hole, although almost noiseless, cut off the sound of the movement he made in shifting his position, and as her head and shoulders appeared and she looked upwards, his arm shot out and his hand across her mouth only just stifled her scream. As she began to struggle furiously, his other arm about her like a vice, he pulled her into the clearing where, losing his balance but still keeping his grip on her mouth and shoulders, he fell to his side, and she with him. And there they lay, their bodies close for a second time, their eyes staring into each other's, hers so terror-stricken, and her heart beating against his breast so rapidly that he wouldn't have been surprised if she had died there and then.

She was still now, lying stiff, frozen, like someone being hypnotised into terror; and into the silence, broken only by their mingled hard breaths, there came the sound of a child's high voice, crying, 'Watch. Watch me, Grand-papa.' And on this her eyelids moved.

Slowly taking his arm from about her shoulders but not his hand from her mouth, he held his forefinger up to her and wagged it twice, indicating that she be silent, and accompanied this with a pursing of his lips into a 'Ssh!' Now, drawing his hand from her mouth, he pulled himself away from her and on to his knees, and as he gazed at her lying crumpled on the ground he felt slightly sick, for she looked as she had done all that time ago just a second before his father had torn his flesh out of hers.

He turned on his knees and pointed towards the slit in the brambles and motioned that she should look through it, but she made no movement, not even when she heard the stamp of the child's footsteps running past the edge of the thicket and his laughter filling the air. It was not until Isabelle's voice came to them, calling, 'Come, Richard. Come. Look, I will race you,' that she moved her eyes from his and looked up at the green tangled roof.

Minutes later, when the voices and steps had faded into the distance, he motioned to her that she should come away; and he, going first, backed through the hole. But he had to wait almost three minutes before she put in an appearance, and when he went ahead walking close to the wall to keep his coat away from the loose bramble she did not follow immediately, and again he had to wait for her.

When he opened the screen door, he surveyed, as she did, the road both ways before walking on to it; and when she was through she stood with her back tight against the oak staring at him as if he were the devil.

Now he kept his distance, almost two arms' length from her, and what he said was, 'You have no need to fear me in any way.' And when she made no answer he repeated, 'Do you understand what I am saying? You have no need to fear me in any way, any way whatever.'

He saw that she was petrified and he searched in his mind for some way to allay her fears, but he found none and went stumbling on, 'Go in there when you like, I won't give you away.'

When she still made no effort to speak he said softly, 'I'm not the devil from hell, don't look at me like that, girl. If . . . if it's any consolation to you I'm deeply sorry for what happened on . . . on that day.'

Still there was no word from her; and now he said with some impatience, 'If you care for the child so much as to risk your neck going in there, for you could be shot at by the keepers, why did you let him go in the first place? Why did you sell him?'

'I, I didn't sell him.' Her body jerked from the tree, then fell back against it again, and he was slightly startled at the vehemence of her reply.

'I'm under the impression that you did.'

'Well, you're wrong, see.' The top part of her body had again moved from the tree, but her hands at her sides were still gripping the bark.

'You are being paid twenty-five shillings a week, I understand. Is that right?'

'Yes, 'tis. But . . . but I didn't sell him. If he said that he's lying.'

'Well, if it wasn't for the money why did you let him go?'

There was a silence before she mumbled dully, her eyes cast down now, ''Twas because of Bella, my sister. She was in service and she got into trouble. She stole, she stole TWO HANKIES.' Her voice was bitter again and she raised her eyes to his. 'They were for sending her to the House of Correction, and . . . and I couldn't bear it for she was only eight, and the man, the valet, said His Lordship would put things right for her on condition I let him have the child.' She now leaned her head back against the tree and, her voice louder, she ended, 'They had been at me for weeks, months, from when he was born, but I wouldn't budge. But . . . but it was because of Bella, not the money.'

God! Two hankies. The House of Correction. Blackmail. His father had got the child on the strength of two hankies . . . Christ Almighty! He said to her now, 'The child is three years old. Why is he still so important to you?'

Her head sank forward until he could see the crown from where the brown hair flowed in a clean shining circle, and when he heard her words soft and heart-felt saying, 'He's mine; he's all I have of me own,' he had an almost uncontrollable urge to grab her hand, run her to the Lodge and through the park, pick up the child and thrust it into her arms and say, 'There! Take your own.' But after a moment, while he continued to stare at her, he said, 'Remember what I've told you, you have no need to fear me in any way.' And on this he turned abruptly and walked from her.

5

Perhaps it was, His Lordship thought, because Isabelle was confined to her room with a chill that his son deigned to accompany the child and himself on their afternoon walk.

It was the first fine day for almost a week, and as they strolled through the park, the child running before them, His Lordship, merely because he was finding his son's silence embarrassing, remarked, 'I think we'd better have Stracey over to see Isabelle if her cold is no better by tomorrow.'

The comment on this came almost absentmindedly from his son, 'Oh . . . oh yes.'

'She's hardly ever indoors, out in all weathers. I think it's unseemly, this craze for shooting. It isn't a woman's place. But there, times have changed.'

This remark bringing no response whatever, His Lordship glanced at the tall, hard thinness of the young man at his side, and he thought now as he had thought often over the past weeks that his son was almost unrecognisable to him. The boy Clive, the painter, the sensitive individual he had known and recognised as some small part of himself, but not this man. It was strange but he was finding himself more at ease in Isabelle's company than in his son's, and that was strange indeed. Yet Isabelle was deporting herself very well when all was taken into account, that is with the exception of her craze for shooting. Still, Bellingham, or at least his nephew, seemed to welcome her presence. But above all, what pleased him most was that she had taken to the child, and the child undoubtedly had taken to her. Things never turned out as one expected. He had dreaded her return to the Hall, yet daily he had looked forward to seeing his son again, and yet here they were finding it difficult to carry on an ordinary conversation. That was until his son suddenly said, 'About this business of inheritance, Father.' He nodded towards the child.

'Yes.'

'I've been thinking.'

His Lordship waited, his eyes on his son's profile.

'I think perhaps after all it would be a sensible thing to do; as it is, no-one has any real claim to him, have they?' Now Clive turned his head and looked at his father, and His Lordship moved his head slowly to the side and nodded twice before saying, 'That is right.'

'Except of course the mother.'

'Oh well, that could easily be seen to.'

'How? You have nothing in writing from her.'

'That's quite true, but she has taken my money for over three years; the courts would soon put her in her place.'

'I wouldn't be too sure of that. There was the Dunlop case you'll remember last month. They gave the custody of the child to the mother.'

'Different thing altogether.' His Lordship's head was wagging now. 'She was a lady; she had been going to marry the man but unfortunately he was killed. The mother in that case had a right to him.'

'Even when the grandfather tried to prove he was the issue of his only son and without him the line would die?'

His Lordship stopped in his walk, and, his tone barely covering his anger now, he said, 'I don't see why you're holding this case up as an example if you intend to give the child your name.'

Clive had stopped a few feet ahead of his father, and standing sideways to him with the nonchalant, disinterested air that seemed part of him now, and which annoyed his father, he said, 'I was merely stating a case in point. That courts don't always do what is expected of them; so, as you suggested, I think it would be wise to have this matter settled once and for all.'

'Yes, yes, I agree with you.' His Lordship was walking on again, his voice calmer now, but his Adam's apple, moving rapidly up and down, showed his inner agitation, and his irritation came to the fore again when his son, seemingly bent on continuing the conversation along what he considered, under the circumstances, very tactless lines, said, 'Has she ever tried to see the child?'

'No, of course not.'

'How is her money paid to her?'

'What!'

'I said how is the money paid to her?'

'I told you this weeks ago. At the beginning of the month.'

'What I mean is, does she come and collect it?'

Now His Lordship merely paused in his walk while he looked at his son, then asked stiffly, 'What is all this? Why this sudden interest in this girl?'

'She is the mother of the child, isn't she?'

'There is no-one disputing that, and least of all me.' His Lordship's anger was now evident, but it seemed to make no impression on his son.

'You didn't say how she got her money.'

'Cunningham takes it to the habitation.' His words were cold and stiff.

'The habitation?' Now Clive was looking at his father.

'She lives on the fells in a makeshift house. That is her own fault; she has enough money to rent a decent place.'

'On the fells, the open fells? Why do you think she continues to live there?'

'How should I know? These people are like rats, they cling to their homes.'

There was a pause. There was no sound between them, no sound from the child even, for he had stopped and was

258

examining a dead, blackening rowan frond that covered his two small hands. No bird sound broke the silence in these seconds, no wind in the branches of the trees; it was Clive's voice that cut it, saying with strange bitterness, 'For a rat she did rather well in my opinion.' Then, moving quickly forward, he gathered up the boy in his arms and held him above his head; and for the first time he really looked at him. And the boy, surprised by the playfulness of his papa, did not respond for a moment, not until his papa put him down on the ground and, taking his hand, ran him forward towards the end of the park to where the grass drive led into the forbidden distance; and, standing close to the tangle of undergrowth, lifted him up in his arms again and, pointing into the distance, said, 'I think that's a rabbit.'

'Where, Papa?' The child leaned forward and peered along the path.

'Oh, he's gone. Rabbits are very quick little fellows.'

He held the child in the same position until His Lordship came almost to his shoulder, saying, 'Don't encourage him to go along there. He could easily slip into the wood; it's heavily trapped.'

He put the child down now and, patting his bottom, sent him forward at a run and laughing gleefully. And then he said, apparently in some surprise, 'But I was through there last week. I never came across a trap.'

'There weren't any last week. But we found a place where they were getting in; there must have been a number of them. It could have been the scum from Rosier's village or one of the gangs that sell to the markets. Anyway, they certainly thinned the birds out; even came as far as the pens and helped themselves . . . And not a dog barked; they're elusive as vapour.'

'I understood it was illegal now to set spring traps.'

'Illegal or not they're staying. I have placed a notice on the south wall to the effect that it is dangerous to enter the woods. I have not stated that there are traps set; they're clever enough to deduce why the notice is there.'

Clive gave a huh of a laugh now as he said, 'They won't need much evidence to prove that there are traps if they show they've one leg missing, or blinded.'

'What can one do? You tell me. They're scourging the country like vermin, no man's property is safe from them. Do you know that Bellingham had a keeper tied up, gagged, then thrown face downwards in the lake to drown. And he would have but one of the other keepers had been watching from the undergrowth and managed to get him out in time. Travel may have widened your sympathies, Clive, but I would like to wager that, when you inherit, your forbearance on such matters will be wanting.'

'Very likely, very likely.' Clive was nodding his head thoughtfully now. Then he went on, 'Touching on the matter of inheritance reminds me that I've also been rather negligent about visiting Compton and getting my matters settled. You said, didn't you, that I would have around four thousand a year from the trust?'

'Yes, about that. Perhaps a little more; the investments abroad have been very favourable of late.'

'Quite enough to set up a small establishment?'

'Yes, if you go careful. Were you thinking of doing this?'

'Yes and no. My mind is rather unsettled at the moment.'

'You have given up the idea then of returning to the sea?'

'Not entirely. Captain Spellman is anxious that I sail with him again; but there's plenty of time for me to consider that because the ship is doing a coastal run, and in the spring, when the sea's open, he'll be trading to Bergen, so I understand. Anyway, he'll be near enough at hand should I change my mind.'

'What if he should have taken on a permanent first mate in the meantime?'

'Oh!' Clive's tone was airy. 'He'll arrange matters.' He paused before ending, 'You know, you made a deep impression on the Captain, Father.'

His Lordship's face took on a slight tinge of pink and when the child came running back towards them now and flung himself against his father's legs and hugged his thigh he hoped with a deep intensity that his son would, in the end, decide to return to the sea, and for more reasons than one.

6

It was early November. For eight days now they had seen no sun; the fog shrouded the grounds in a white mist in which the trees floated and men's heads appeared in the distance as if disembodied.

In almost every room in the house a fire was blazing. The whole place was warm, even the great hall and the stone passages, and the atmosphere was light, almost gay. The servants bustled and looked happy in their bustling; all day long there were men and women carrying big skips of wood and buckets of coal, or big copper cans of hot water for baths. The master, Miss Isabelle, and the child bathed every day; only Master Clive had no use for daily hot baths. Up till a fortnight before he had taken his bath in the river. In the opinion of the indoor servants Master Clive was a funny one; they would even have dared to say not quite a gentleman any longer, for he didn't have a valet, and he had the plebeian way of thanking servants for doing him a small service. This latter might go down with some, but servants of long standing knew that these weren't gentlemen's ways.

On this morning of thick fog and air so chill that it penetrated even the thickest clothing and probed the skin, Clive left the warm comfort of the house and took a walk. No-one had enquired as to where he was going. His father was closeted in the study with his bailiff and Isabelle was playing with the child.

Once outside the North Lodge he turned right along the road until he came to the oak tree, and there he stopped. She would not have been here for days. How intense must have been the hunger that brought her here in the first place, that made her create the hidey-hole and run the risk of discovery.

He walked on sharply now and mounted the fells at about the place where he had remembered her going up the bank. Away from the shelter of the wall and the sunken road the air caught at his breath and made his chest heave. He could see no farther than sixty feet ahead; and for the first time since leaving the house he asked himself a question: 'If I do see her how will I bring the matter up?'

Long before he had gone into Newcastle the week before to sign the deed claiming that the child, christened as Richard Brodie, was his son and rightful heir and would henceforth take the name of Richard John Horatio Fischel, he had known what lay behind his change of attitude; but he also knew it would take time before he could present it to the girl in an acceptable fashion, time in which he must convince her that he was up to no trickery, that his one aim was to recompense her for the wrong he had done her.

Each night since he had surprised her in the hidey-hole he had gone over the incident second by second. It was much clearer in the dark, much more real; he felt her body close to his for the second time in his life. He saw the blood press to the surface of her face where his fingers squeezed her mouth. He saw the creamy film and the texture of her skin, and he smelled the smell of her, that woman's smell that her old shabby clothes could not smother. He had smelled it on the day he had taken her, and never had he smelled it since on any other woman. Women all had particular smells, but there had been none like the odour that came from her; and there, as he had held her pressed tightly to him while their child laughed and called on the other side of the bramble fence, he had been more aware of the odour of her than he had been of the strangeness of the situation.

He knew that he could wander about up here for hours, even go round in circles and never come across a living soul. After some time he took out his watch and peered at it and was surprised to see it was only a quarter to eleven, little more than an hour since he had left the house. He felt he had been away from the confines of the Hall for days.

When the fog lifted for a moment, and he saw in the distance the figure of a woman, he stopped. The woman had seen him, and she, too, had stopped. He couldn't make out in the swirling fog if it was the girl or not, but when the figure came hurrying towards him he knew it wouldn't be the girl. The woman stopped within twenty feet of him. There was a look of surprise on her face; it was as if she had thought she would see someone else. He saw that she was a big, ugly woman but not poorly clad; and when she turned and almost ran back the way she had come, he remained standing, puzzled by her appearance and quick disappearance. It was evident she had not expected to see him.

After a moment he, too, turned and retraced his steps the way he had come; but fifteen minutes later, when he hadn't reached the road, he realised he had missed his way. Then ten minutes later still he came on the dwelling.

It seemed to rise out of the ground like an eruption. It was akin to something he imagined a man would build if wrecked on a desert island; it looked like a number of poor cow sheds at different levels stuck against the outcrop of rock. He saw it was in three sections but that only the middle section had a window, and there were only two doors. The larger door was open and revealed what looked like a wood shed, the other door was closed. He was staring at this door, wondering whether he should knock, when it opened and there she stood. But only for a second. At the sight of him she heaved in a deep breath, sprang back into the room, and banged the door shut. And then he heard a bar being dropped into its socket.

God Almighty! She was still all that afraid of him. Couldn't she believe that he meant her no harm, only good? If he could only get her to realise just how much good he meant her.

He knocked on the door sharply as he said, 'Open the door, please. I must speak with you.'

He heard a small voice which wasn't hers say something, and again there was silence. And again he said, 'I have no intention of going away until I can speak with you, so you might as well open the door. I have something to say to you that is of great interest to you . . . it, it concerns the child.'

Two full minutes passed before the bar was lifted; then slowly the door was opened, and there she stood, one hand gripping the door and four children standing round her, their eyes wide, with fear in them. The sight brought his head down, and after a moment he asked quietly, 'May I come in?' And now she pushed the children from her and opened the door further to allow him to walk into a room that wasn't a room, but the strangest place he had ever seen, and he had seen some strange places.

The wall of the outcrop jutted roughly into it; there were odd bits of old furniture here and there, and at the far end a tiny fireplace . . . She and the rest of them had lived here, according to his reckoning, for five years, and here his son had been born and nurtured by her until he was five months old. He looked at the children, all girls – they were grouped together now at the side of the fireplace – and turning his gaze to her, he said, 'Do you think I might have a word with you in private?'

When she went and picked up a shawl from the top of a chest, he said, 'No, no, it is bitter out. Is there no place to send the children?' And on this she made a motion with her head and the tallest girl, still with her eyes on him, sidled past him and to a door at the far end of the room, the others following her.

When they were alone he looked at her where she was standing by the far corner of the fire, her face averted from him, and he said, 'Won't you sit down?' When she made a small movement with her head he said under his breath, 'How can I convince you of what I said the other day, I mean you no harm?'

She still made no answer, but her shoulders moving up and down showed him the rapidity of her breathing, and the terror of him that was still in her; and so, throwing aside his formulated plan of slow approach, he said, 'How would you like your child back?'

Her body was slow in turning, her lips were apart, her eyes wide, and the fear had gone from her as if it had never been, but the look that had replaced it lasted only a matter of seconds; and when her shoulders slumped downwards they seemed to drag with them a veil of blankness over her face, and she said dully, 'You're just sayin' that. There's no chance; he . . . he would never let me, not now.'

'My father has no power over . . . your child.' He had almost said 'our child'. 'I am the person, who, from now on, will dictate what will happen to it.'

The eager look was creeping back into her face and she said in a whisper, 'You . . . you really mean that . . . that I could have him again?'

'Yes, yes, that is what I mean. But you would have to have a suitable place in which to bring him up.' His eyes flickered around the room. 'May I . . . may I ask you a question?' He waited a second, then went on, 'Are you thinking of being married?'

The question seemed to surprise her for she jerked her chin before turning her head to the side and looking down as she answered, 'No; an' I won't, never!'

He was surprised at the answer and the authoritative tone in which it had been given, and he allowed a moment to pass before he went on, 'Well, now what I have in mind is this. I will settle a sum on you that will enable you to take a house in a respectable healthy neighbourhood, say on the outskirts of Newcastle, and when he reaches the age of five, you will send him to school. It could be a day school, but a good one. I would wish him to be known as Richard John Horatio Fischel; he has recently been registered under this name.' He stopped as he saw her hands going out towards the table, and gripping it as if for support; and then, her gaze still cast downwards, she asked, 'Why . . . why are you doing all this?' to which he answered quietly, 'Isn't it evident? I wish to make reparation to you for the harm I brought on you, and I wish to settle it before I return to sea.'

She raised her eyes to his now and stared at him, and she saw him, for the first time, not as a demon but as a young man of pleasing appearance, with an expression that was serious, and grey eyes that were kindly, and she couldn't associate him with the other being, who on two of the three occasions they had met, had held her to him and created in her fear-tearing panic.

When she asked softly, 'What of your father? I . . . I think he is very fond of the child,' he paused before answering because, deep within him, he knew that he should ask the same question of himself as she had in reply to his former question, 'Why are you doing all this?' and if he were to be truthful he would answer with another question: Why should his father have it all ways? He had banished him for raping a young girl, hadn't he, and yet had himself been quite prepared to enjoy the fruits of that act? Moreover he had taken upon himself a halo for his clemency. Clemency! when, as she had said, he had got the child, not for money, but for two lawn handkerchiefs.

His answer to her was now checked by the door opening and a thick-set powerful man entering. He stared at the fellow and the fellow stared at him; then she, in great agitation, exclaimed, as she moved down by the side of the table towards the man. 'Oh! Matthew! I didn't think to see you the day.'

Matthew came slowly into the room, and after glancing at her he returned his gaze to the visitor and, his voice grim, said without preamble, 'What's your business here?'

'Whatever my business I cannot see what it has to do with you, Sir.' Clive's voice was no longer that of the sailor, or the pleasant individual who talked to the outside staff, but that of a Fischel, a man who demanded respect and obedience as his right. 'Now, perhaps you'll allow me to ask you the same question. Who are you?'

'Everybody knows who I am. I'm Matthew Turnbull, the miller, from Brockdale.'

Clive now cast a glance towards Cissie. She was staring at the fellow, pleading in her eyes. Hadn't she said she was not going to be married, nor ever would be? Then who was this man who spoke as if she were his property? Well, it would be easy to find out, he was the miller at Brockdale.

He turned and looked at her, saying now, 'You'll be hearing from me again. In the meantime good-day to you.' He made no motion of farewell to the man who had his eyes fixed hard on him but went out through the door and into the mist; and as he walked, the face of the miller intruded on to a picture that had formed in his mind when he had said to her, 'You will take a house on the outskirts of Newcastle.' The picture had shown him returning from sea and going to the house to visit his son . . . and his son's mother . . .

'Who's he?'

Cissie closed her eyes, rubbed her hand all 'round her face, and finished by smoothing her hair back; but even then she didn't answer Matthew's question. Sitting down on a chair, she joined her hands tightly together before looking up and saying, 'It's . . . it's him, His Lordship's son.'

'What!' Matthew looked as if he were going to bound towards the door, and she leaned swiftly across the table and grabbed at his arm, saying, 'No, no! It's all right. Let me tell you. I've . . . I've got somethin' to tell you. He . . . he didn't come lookin' for me, plaguing me; he came to tell me I . . . I could have Richard back. Aye, he did.' She moved her head slowly at him. 'You see, it was like this . . .' And now as he stared stiffly down at her she told him what she had kept to herself for years, and had made Joe keep to himself, the hidey-hole from where at intervals she had watched her child grow, and she finished, 'He . . . he could have given me away but he didn't; instead, he's gone about makin' it possible for me to have the bairn back.'

And now Matthew asked the question she had asked of Clive, 'Why?'

''Cos' – she looked down and wagged her head – 'he's, he's sorry for what he did.'

'Huh! God!'

She brought her eyes quickly up to his. 'He is, Matthew, he is. I . . . I was terrified of him, scared out of me wits at the sight of him, until . . . until a little while ago when he stood there an' I seemed to see him not as a devil any longer but just like, well, anybody else.'

'But he's not like anybody else, an' you know that. You know it only too well. And if he says he's goin' to do something for you let me tell you, Cissie, he's not doin' it for nothing. They don't, not them lot. You be careful, it could be some kind of trap, an' I'm warning you.'

'What kind of trap could it be if he gives me the bairn back?'

'I don't know, I haven't had time to think, but I tell you, be on your guard; what he did once he could try on again . . .'

She pushed her chair back and got to her feet, staring at him the while, and he said defiantly, 'Well, I'm sorry, but . . . but I don't trust any of them.'

She turned away and when there was a silence between them she muttered, 'Will you have a drop of tea? it's fresh made.' Then, 'What brings you over at this time of day?'

Now he sat down and, bending forward, stared into the fire and said, 'I think she's goin' out of her head. I . . . I came over 'cos William told me that he had seen her as he and Straker were coming back in the cart from Gateshead. He saw her mounting the fells in this direction, and . . . and I was afraid.' His head went lower and his voice went into a low growl as he ended, 'I'm afraid all the time now . . . Cissie' – he turned round – 'why don't you move? Look, I can get you a place, in Jarrow or Shields or anywhere roundabout.'

She stopped with the teapot in her hand, but she didn't look at him as she said, 'I could be movin'. If I get the bairn back he says I've got to move into a respectable district and . . . and have him educated.'

'And he'll pay for it all?' He was on his feet now.

'Well' – her head was up and her voice was harsh – 'it stands to reason that *I* can't, doesn't it?'

'Look.' He put out his hand and pointed his finger at her. 'I'm warnin' you. You be careful; men like him don't promise houses to people like you – now that's putting it bluntly – unless they're after something.'

'He's only trying to pay for what he did.' She was shouting at him.

'That's what he says. Oh my God!' He held his brow for a moment; then asked in a quieter tone, 'You want to get away from here?' And she said softly now, 'Aye, Matthew; I'm sick to the heart of me at the thought of another winter.' And when he came and stood close to her and said, 'Well, let it be me who'll fix it for you,' she looked up at him and said quietly, 'Not if I take the child with me.' She could have added, 'And not if I don't either, not as long as you're married, and her almost going off her head as it is.'

He swung round from her now and marched towards the door while thrusting on his hat, but when he had opened it he turned to her once more and said, 'Keep the door bolted, and keep a look-out. And I'm not only meaning with regards to her.' And on that he was gone.

7

Clive went into Newcastle to see the solicitor – not his father's solicitor, but one of his own choosing.

The firm of Weir and Dixon was well established and dealt with a number of county families, and Mr Weir wasn't unused to the request the young man made. It was to the effect that he should look for a house for him, a small establishment of eight to ten rooms with a garden, the whole to be in a secluded spot in a healthy district. Also, that he wanted papers to be drawn up to the effect that one thousand pounds a year was to be allotted to a certain lady in support of herself and her son. The purchase of the house, the furnishings, and the maintenance in the future of the entire establishment were to come out of a separate fund.

Mr Weir assured the young gentleman that his wishes would be attended to with the utmost speed, but it might take a few days, or even a week or so, to find such an establishment. Nevertheless, he had no doubt whatever that it could be found.

Clive impressed upon him that the matter needed speedy attention, then left, and went to his father's club, where he ate a small meal and drank a great deal; and as dusk was falling he was assisted into the coach by Bowmer and driven back to the Hall.

The following day he was late in appearing at breakfast, and was favoured by a scowl from his father as he took his seat at the table and an almost disdainful look from Isabelle, which latter amused him. His fiery sister was a very tame person these days, one could almost say a motherly person. How would she react to the news that he was taking the child away, giving it back to its rightful mother? He didn't ask himself whether she would be hurt because he didn't care if she was hurt or not; for the truth he'd had to face a long, long time ago was that he really disliked his sister, he hated some part of her, and the hate stemmed from the day she had laughed, and cried to him, 'Well, why don't you? Go on!' and had leaned against the tree and finished, 'You're frightened. You never have, have you?' Without her taunting he never would have, even then; and he knew now, even more so than he did then, that there was something unnatural, something bad in the make-up of a woman who could witness such a deed.

So, feeling like this, he saw her act of mothering the boy as just that, an act. If he had been told at this moment that he could be proved wrong he would not have believed it; it needed action on her part to convince him, and he had it later that day.

The day before, much to his father's annoyance, he had refused the invitation to join him and Isabelle in the shoot on Bellingham's estate, and his father was now demanding in a tone heavy with exasperation, 'What is the matter with you? You enjoy your shoot, don't you?' to which he replied, 'Yes, but I'm not feeling inclined that way at present. How long is it on for?'

'The week.'

'Then I may accompany you tomorrow.'

Later, Isabelle had stood at the top of the steps pulling on her gloves and she allowed her father to descend almost to the bottom before she turned to Clive and said under her breath, 'What has come over you? You're acting like a bore; you should go back to the sea, you'd be more at home there.'

'Quite right, quite right.' His lips moved into the twisted smile. 'And I'm thinking seriously of doing just that.'

Her eyes widened slightly as she said, 'Don't be

273

ridiculous; you seem to forget you have taken on a new responsibility.'

'Oh, I haven't forgotten that.'

'You surprise me! Then may I ask that during the time I . . . we are out you could force yourself to go and see the child?'

'Yes, yes, you could.' He bowed his head to her. 'I may even go further than that. I may take him for a walk; it's a very nice day.' He looked up into the bright sky. 'Yes, that's what I'll do, I'll take him for a walk.'

'Oh!' She went down the steps, her riding crop whipping against her leather boots.

He watched them ride away, then turned indoors. She had set the germ of a thought alive in his mind and he said to himself, 'Why not? why not?' It would be a prelude to the final act; it would show him the child's reaction to her and the place. Not that he would allow the child to live there; but it wouldn't do any harm for him to see it, as young as he was. Early memories left an impression; he could remember happenings in his own life right back to when he was two years old.

But he did not immediately put his plan into action. Rather, he ordered himself and the child an early lunch and informed the nurse that he would not require her to attend them on their walk that afternoon.

So it was around two o'clock when the nurse brought the child down to the hall. He was muffled to the eyes against the cold; he wore white kid boots and white gaiters. These came well up under his three flannel petticoats. He wore a blue woollen dress heavily embroidered with silks, and over this a blue melton cloth coat lined with fur; on his head was a bonnet-shaped hat to match, out of which his cheeks poked like two rosy apples.

He held out his hand to his father, saying, 'Are we going to the sea, Papa?' and Clive replied, 'No, not today; just for a walk.'

'Are we going to the farm?'

'Perhaps.'

The child looked up at him solemnly now and asked, 'Will you take me on your big ship one day, Papa?' And to this Clive answered with a laugh, 'Now that's more than likely, more than likely.'

When they reached the beginning of the drive to the Lodge he swung the child up into his arms and walked rapidly along it, and Richard, looking about him excitedly, cried, 'This is where the rabbits are?'

'Yes, this is where the rabbits are.'

At one point on the road the child said, 'Is this the way the carriage goes, Papa, when we go to the sea?' and Clive answered, 'It is indeed.' He found it difficult to talk with the child. One moment he saw him as a baby, the next as a little boy very advanced for his age, for he talked incessantly, and very distinctly; almost, Clive thought, like his father. And he was forever asking questions about everything he observed. He did not like to confess that he wasn't at ease with the boy. When the child looked at him now it was as if he were reading his thoughts, for he said quite suddenly, 'Do you like me, Papa?'

Clive blinked, smiled, and moved his head jocularly before he answered this probing question. 'Of course I like you. Why do you ask such a question?'

'Because Nanny says you're not like a real papa.'

'Oh, she does, does she?' He pursed his lips. 'Why am I not like a real papa?'

'I don't know, but that is what she said.'

'Did she say that to you?' His face was straight now.

'No, Papa. She was talking to Radcliffe while they were attending to the bath water.'

'Do you think I'm a real papa?'

He watched his son hesitate before saying, 'I don't know . . .' then add mischievously, 'but I would like to go on your ship.' And at this Clive put his head back and laughed.

They were well on the fells now. They passed the stone quarry; then, a few minutes farther on, they rounded a bluff, and there in the distance was the dwelling.

The child saw it immediately and cried, 'Look, Papa! Stables.' And Clive said, 'They're not stables, Richard, that is a house. I am taking you to see' – he paused – 'the lady who lives there.'

As he came nearer the dwelling he saw two small girls carrying water, and when they caught sight of him one of them dropped her bucket and ran helter-skelter into the house.

He was still carrying the child when he approached the door, and there she was standing framed in the opening, her eyes fixed on them as if she were beholding a vision. To put matters straight right away, he said quickly, 'We have only come to pay you a visit, we were out walking.' He watched her mouth open and close; then her head moved downwards in a nod, and she stepped backwards into the room. Now he put the child down on the ground and, taking his hand, led him forward and into the dwelling. Inside, he looked down at his son and said, 'Say how-do-you-do'; and the child, holding out his hand to Cissie, looked up into her face and, in a voice that was almost as strange to her as to be foreign, said, 'How-do-you-do, Ma'am?' And when the lady didn't make any reply, only held his hand tightly, he added, as he had been taught to do, 'I hope you are well.' At this she slowly released his hand and looked at Clive, and he again said, uneasily now, 'We were out for a walk; I thought it would be a kind of introduction.'

'Yes.' She moved up the room. Her eyes still on the child, but speaking to Clive, she said, 'Will you take a seat?' And he went and sat down and he looked at the four little girls staring at the visitor and was about to say,

'Wouldn't you like to play?' when he had the thought they could be verminous, but then dismissed the idea. She wasn't verminous – he'd lay his life on that – and she'd never allow them to be. He wondered in passing how she came to be so different from the types in the hamlets and villages; perhaps living up here in the clean raw bareness of the moor had something to do with it. Whatever it was that had made the difference, he knew in his own mind that she was different, and for a moment he saw her dressed as Isabelle was dressed and visualised her beauty enhanced a thousandfold. He also imagined she would be educable.

He said now to the child, 'Would you like to play with the little girls, Richard?' And Richard, smiling broadly, said, 'Oh yes, Papa.' He did not often have children to play with and this indeed was a surprise to him. When he held out his hand to Nellie, who was nearest to him in size, she glanced up at Cissie; and Cissie nodded to her, and she took the boy's hand and allowed him to tug her down the room and out through the open door.

When the other children rushed after them, Cissie, as if just coming awake, flew to the door and cried at them, 'Be careful! Play gentle. And don't go away from the flat. Hear me now.' Then she turned into the room again and walked slowly to the table, and standing there, she said simply, 'Thanks.'

'I . . . I thought it better he should see you before the final arrangements were made. My solicitor tells me that it may take a week or two to find a house, but I would imagine you should be well installed before Christmas.'

She now walked along the side of the table and, staring at him, her head shaking, she said, 'I don't know what to say to you'; and to this he answered, 'There's no need to say anything. I . . . I have already told you why I'm doing this.'

His eyes were looking straight into hers, and she

lowered her lids and after a moment muttered, 'I . . . I was thinkin', what if he doesn't take to me? And . . . and the change. What if he frets?'

'He's only a child, a baby; he's still young enough to forget about everything over there. And . . . and he'll have young children to play with. This he has never had. His life is peopled with adults; it is not good for him.'

'What . . . what does your father say?'

'He doesn't know yet.'

'He'll never let it be.' She moved her head slowly, and he answered, 'He has no power to stop it. He himself saw to it that I recognised the child as mine, gave it my name, and am responsible for it. He's mine to do with what I will; and I will to hand him to his mother.'

Again they were looking at each other; then again her lids shaded her eyes. She didn't know what to make of this man, who was young, yet not young. Only one thing she knew, and in a way this surprised her; she was no longer afraid of him. She didn't actually know what her other feelings were towards him, but she did know that she no longer stood in deep fear of him.

A silence fell between them, and he broke it by asking softly, 'What is your name?'

She was for saying, 'Cissie,' then she gave him the name by which she was christened and which she had never heard spoken but once, and that by her father; 'Cecilia.'

'Cecilia.' He inclined his head towards her, then said, 'It's a beautiful name.'

She felt the colour rushing over her body, up her neck, and to her hair, and she had no power to suppress it, but as she looked into the eyes fixed hard on her, Matthew's warning came back to her: He's after something; they do nothing for nothing, people like him, not for the likes of you, they don't.

She turned slowly about and moved down the room to the door and looked at her son chasing the girls gleefully

278

hither and thither on the flat rock terrace, and they were responding to him as if they had played with him all his life, and not just while he was in the cradle.

Clive now joined her, standing just behind and to the side of her. He glanced at the playing children for a moment, then brought his eyes on to her head to where the thick, brown plaits of hair were twisted to form a cap. And there came to him again the aroma from her body, and he knew that of all the things he had wanted in life, and of all the things he might want from life before he died, he would never want anything, or anyone, as much as he wanted this girl at this moment. When she turned her head quickly towards him and said, 'He . . . he looks happy, he likes them,' he said, 'Of course, he likes them. I don't think you'll have anything to worry about.' Then stepping past her, he called to the boy, saying, 'Richard! Richard! Come here.' And when the child came running to him, he said, 'Let the lady see what a big fellow you are, how heavy you are.' Then turning to Cissie, he added, 'Lift him and see what a great boy he's grown into.'

Cissie, stooping over her child, slowly put her arms about him and lifted him up; but when the child's face was close to hers she couldn't see it, and the breaking point came when the child's hands clasped her cheeks and his small voice said in concern, 'Why are you weeping?' And, his own voice breaking, he turned to his father, saying, 'Papa! Papa! the lady's weeping.'

Clive took the child from Cissie's arms and with his hand on her shoulder he turned her about and pressed her gently through the open door into the room again. And the children gathered round the door and watched the unusual scene, and so no-one noticed the two riders on the road at the bottom of the slope.

Isabelle had had an enjoyable day. She had brought down a number of birds and evoked the admiration of Arthur

Bellingham. She had been pressed to stay to dinner at the Bellinghams' but had refused, as had her father; the nights drew in early and neither of them relished even a five-mile ride in the dark. Her father had gone on ahead some time ago, taking the high road back to the Hall, and she had been content to meander by side roads with young Bellingham, whose admiration afforded her some amusement, if nothing else.

They crossed farm land, taking the horses uncaringly over fields of turnips, then dropped down on to the narrow road that ran alongside the wall of the estate.

It was as they turned the bend in the road, and her head was back laughing at a weak quip her companion had made, that her eyes took in the huddle of stone buildings in the distance at the top of a slope, and the group of people standing in front of them.

It was the first time she had been on this road since she had returned home, but it was not the first time she had thought of the girl or the stone dwelling; and now there they both were, the girl, and that shanty, which she herself had tried to wreck, and . . . no! No! She must be imagining things, it must be a trick of the light, because that couldn't be Clive and the child. He would never . . . NEVER! She reined her horse in and stretched herself upwards in the saddle, and clearly now she saw her brother lift the child from the girl's arms and put his own arm about her and lead her into the place; and it was only young Bellingham's voice that stopped her from bringing her horse round and taking it up the slope at a gallop.

'What is it,' he asked, 'squatters?' His horse was prancing and he brought it to her side, and when he looked at her he was amazed to see that her face was distorted with anger; yet at the same time he was pleased to note she had a feeling for land. 'Damn nuisance, all of them,' he said. 'As Father said the other day, it wants a mighty brush to sweep the whole bang lot of them into the sea. He's right an' all, quite right, can't leave a yard of land open these days but they come up with some tin pot claim to it. You should get your father to enclose it.'

She didn't enlighten him as to the fact that her father didn't own this land; she was concerned at the moment only that he hadn't recognised Clive over the distance, for had he done so the scandal would have swept the county like wildfire. She was already aware that he had a loose tongue and gloried in tidbits of scandal.

She surprised him still further by swinging her horse about and setting it into a gallop, and she didn't stop until she reached the North Lodge, through which she was just passing when he drew up with her. She turned in the saddle and said, 'I'll likely see you tomorrow. Goodbye,' and on this she set the horse into a gallop up the drive, leaving him gaping after her.

She didn't slacken speed until she pulled up the animal on the gravel drive. Jumping from the saddle before the stable boy could reach her to take her foot, she ran up the steps and into the hall; and there she saw Hatton and demanded of him, 'Where is His Lordship?' and Hatton, looking at her in some surprise, said, 'I should imagine he . . . he is taking his bath by now, Miss.' Didn't she know that His Lordship took a bath immediately after returning from a shoot? He watched her tearing off her hat and gloves and throwing them aside together with her crop, as she crossed the hall; then he watched her lift up the dip-end of her riding skirt in no ladylike fashion and mount the stairs at a run.

When she reached her father's room she rapped on the door, which rapping indicated to His Lordship, who was immersed in his bath, that it was no servant outside. Thinking it was his son, he said to Cunningham, 'If that is Master Clive admit him.'

When Cunningham opened the door and saw Miss Isabelle standing there he immediately pulled it closed and allowed himself only a small aperture in which to stand.

'I wish to see His Lordship.'

'I'm . . . I'm sorry, Miss, but His Lordship is in his bath.' Cunningham's voice was a mere whisper, and for a moment he thought she was going to push past him. Then she said, 'Tell His Lordship I must see him immediately . . . immediately. Do you hear?' Then she raised her voice. 'It is very important.' As a maid passed down the corridor she dropped her voice to a whisper, and, leaning towards Cunningham, she added, 'Tell him it is to do with Master Richard.'

'Yes, yes, Miss, I will do that.'

'Tell him I will wait in his dressing room.'

'But . . . but, Miss.'

'Cunnings.' Her tone was louder now. 'I will wait in his dressing room. Give His Lordship that message.'

Cunningham realised that His Lordship could quite clearly hear the message and when he closed the door it was to see his master getting out of the bath; and so, going hastily towards him and picking up the warm towels that hung on the rack to the side of the fire, he enveloped him in one of them, and, taking the other, he knelt down and dabbed at his legs and feet, saying hesitantly, 'Miss Isabelle, m'Lord, she wishes to . . .'

'I heard, Cunnings. Be quick. There, that's enough. My robe.'

Minutes later he opened the door into his dressing room, and he saw his daughter with an expression on her face that he hadn't seen since the day he raised his hand and slapped it. Yet the anger and venom in it weren't, he recognised, turned against himself now. 'What is it?' he asked sharply.

'Clive.' Her mouth was so dry that she had to wet her lips before she could go on. 'He's . . . he's taken the child to that . . . that woman on the fells.'

The muscles of his face seemed to drop, then contract sharply, 'What!'

'I saw him as I was coming back. She . . . she was holding Richard in her arms. He took him from her and' – now she bit on her lip – 'he escorted her into that place, that shanty. And there were others about, children.'

He looked closely at her and was about to say, 'You're mistaken; you have become so obsessed with the child that you have dreamed this up,' because he knew she was becoming obsessed with the child, even more so than himself, and he was aware that he was jealous of the child's affection for her. Although the child was not less pleased to see him now than before, he always wished her to accompany them on their walks, and was forever touching and fondling her, and she him. But about this happening she would have no illusion. Yet he must make sure. Stepping back, he opened the door and said, 'Cunnings!'

'Yes, Sir.'

'Bring the nurse, immediately.'

He watched his daughter striding up and down the room like someone demented and he said to her sharply, 'Stop that prancing. If this is true then it has deeper implications.'

'She is a low, wanton hussy.' Isabelle, following her own train of thought, now took her fist and banged it against the top of the high-backed leather chair. 'She's scum! A harlot. After what happened she encourages him again.'

'Be quiet! Do you hear? Don't raise your voice. You don't know the ins and outs, the circumstances. On the two occasions I spoke with her she did not appear to me to be a loose creature; poor, common, ignorant, but I don't think immoral.'

'How do you know? They live like vermin.' She was bending towards him now, her aggressiveness aggravated by the fact that he should speak well of the girl in any way.

He said coldly, 'Use your sense. She could not have

283

approached him; any advance would have been made by him.' He turned and, looking at Cunningham, who was standing in the doorway, said, 'Yes?'

'The nurse, m'Lord.'

He walked now into the bedroom to see the girl standing just within the doorway, her face white, her eyes wide.

'Where is your charge?'

'Mr . . . Master Clive took him for a walk, m'Lord.'

'At what time?'

'Shortly after two, m'Lord.'

'Without having their dinner?'

'Master Clive ordered a light meal beforehand, m'Lord.'

'Did he say where he intended to take the child?'

'No, m'Lord. I . . . I thought it was just into the park. I . . . I've been waiting for them.'

'Very well.' He turned from the girl and she sidled out. Then looking through the doorway to his daughter, he said, 'Go and change and meet me downstairs within the half-hour. If he hasn't returned, then be prepared to accompany me in the coach.'

It was almost dark when he came across the sunken garden and mounted the steps to the drive, there to see a coach driving out from the stable yard, its lights blazing, and Hatton ushering his father and Isabelle through the house door and on to the terrace.

'Grandpapa! Aunt Isabelle!' The child bounced excitedly in his arms and made as if he wanted to be put down; but he held him tightly, saying, 'Now, now. Wait until we get inside.' He paused a moment at the bottom of the steps and through the lights held by the footmen he looked upwards and into his father's eyes, then watched him turn abruptly about and, pressing Isabelle before him, enter the house again.

When he went past Hatton, who was holding the door

wide, he put the child down on the floor and, tapping his bottom, said, 'Go with Hatton. Go on now.' And the child stopped and looked to where his grandfather and aunt were walking away from him across the hall; then he looked again at his father, and when his father nodded at him, he held out his hand to Hatton, and Hatton walked him to the bottom of the stairs where he handed him to Mrs Hatton. She took his hand and led him up the stairs to where the tearful nursemaid was standing, and he went with her. And there was no-one to tell about the exciting adventure he had had with his papa because his nanny kept weeping all the time and would not listen. Everyone was weeping today.

In the study Clive looked at his father and Isabelle standing almost shoulder to shoulder, for once in complete harmony in their rage against him. He did not think they knew where he had been; he thought their anger was occasioned by sheer fright at his having taken the child outside the precincts of his small world at a time when the cholera was known to be raging not only in Sunderland but also in Jarrow, which was much nearer home. But when his father, his voice trembling with his anger, said, 'Explain yourself, Sir,' he felt for the first time that the matter went deeper with them than the mere fact of his taking the child outside the gates. And then he had it, the explanation, because Isabelle, unable to contain herself any longer, spat at him, 'How dare you? How dare you take the child to that filthy hovel?'

Oh. He nodded his head at her. So that was it. They knew. How it had come about he didn't know, but they knew. And in a way he was pleased because it had saved him thinking up a way to break the news to them. Now his father was speaking, grinding out his words through his thin lips. 'Have you no decency, Sir? Have you no feeling for what is right and proper? Even after your four years' chastisement?'

Now it was Clive's turn to rear. The twisted smile went from his lips, the grey of his eyes turned bottle-hard, and his voice was the deck voice, the voice of the first mate as he cried, 'You, to talk of decency! You, to talk of what is right and wrong! You took the child away from her by force . . .'

'That is a lie.'

'All right then, you paid for it, but by playing on the feelings of a simple girl and her ignorance of law, you bought the child for two pocket handkerchiefs. Isn't that so, Sir? Not for twenty-five shillings a week, as you would have me believe, but for two pocket handkerchiefs that her sister stole. You saved her sister from the House of Correction and the payment for it was her son . . . Don't talk to me of the correct thing to do, and decency. I raped the girl. You doled out punishment for my act but you couldn't erase it from my mind, for it's been with me ever since. And now I wish to atone for it. I am going to atone for it by giving her back the fruits of my sin – as I remember your words for my act, Sir.'

'You can't! You can't! You're mad.' It was Isabelle shouting at him now. 'I won't let you. The child is . . .' and she substituted the word 'Father's' for 'mine' and went rushing on, 'He has looked after him, given him this environment; the child will die up there.'

'He is not going up there; I am providing a home for his mother and him.'

'No. No.' The words were soft, quiet, as if from someone about to faint, and the look on His Lordship's face indicated that this could indeed happen at any moment; and the tone still quiet, he said, 'You can't do this.'

'Can't I? You were very anxious, Sir, that I should prove my right to the boy by making everything legal. I did just that. The boy is my responsibility, his life is mine to order; and after consideration I think the best place for him would be with his mother. The arrangements have been in motion for some time now; they should be settled within the next week. And you, Sir, can do nothing about it.' He turned his head. 'Nor you, my dear sister.'

'You won't! You shan't! I won't allow it.' She had stepped in front of him, her bust, that had once been as flat as a boy's, big now, was almost touching his coat. She was the termagant, domineering Isabelle that he remembered, out to make him fall in with her wishes, to frighten him into doing her will. But she was forgetting to take into account his four years' education on a sailing vessel; and when she now cried at him, 'I'll see him dead before I'll let him go to that dirty, stinking whore,' his forearm came out and, with a chopping movement, hit the top of her breasts and knocked her flying. It was only her father's arms that saved her from falling full length on the floor, and when he had steadied her his own rage was subdued by the sight of his son's blazing face. He didn't recognise him or the voice that cried at Isabelle, 'Don't you dare put that name to her! Huh!' He was bending forward, all his muscles taut, his voice coarse sounding and guttural as he cried, 'On your own admission you're worse than any whore. You encouraged the antics of the parson and his straying hands, or you wouldn't have let it go on for four years. And you enjoyed torturing Aunt Anne. You've been unnatural all your life. You've only been saved from the pillory or worse because you were born in this house, and I'm sick in my stomach when I think I was in the same womb as you.'

Isabelle was standing alone now. Her father had taken his support from her when his brother-in-law's name had been mentioned, and now he stood apart as if from the whole concern, looking first at his son and then at his daughter; and the thought that he had tried to bury rose again: Why had he been plagued with such offspring?

'ENOUGH!' His voice seemed to shudder the walls.

There followed a heavy, telling silence, and it was finally broken by Clive turning abruptly and stalking out of the room.

His Lordship now walked around his desk and sat down. He felt very tired, old, ineffectual, useless. The only human being he had ever really loved in his life was to be taken from him and he could do nothing about it. And that's what he said when his daughter, leaning over the desk towards him, asked between short, hard breaths, 'What are you going to do?'

'There is little we can do; in fact, nothing.'

'There must be something.' So far was she leaning across the desk that her face was on a level with his, and he saw again, as he looked into her eyes, the face he had struck, and he wanted to put out his hand and push it from him, far, far away. Once again he wanted to push both of them far away, away out of his life.

What peace he had experienced during the past few years in this house, just the child and him. Happiness had pervaded the place, the workings inside and out had gone without a hitch. The child, he thought, had cast a spell over all his domain. He certainly had tempered his own attitude towards the peasantry, for he had made work for extra hands on his estate, he had given liberally to the charities in both Jarrow and Shields, and he knew that his generosity had kept the soup kitchens going for two winters. All this since the child had come into his life. And now he was to go back from where he had come.

'Isn't there any legal way? He is your heir once removed.'

'Yes, once removed. That is the crux of the matter: once removed. As things stand his father has legal right to him, and he is of age.' His tone was full of regret and he made a sound in his throat. 'And I was the one who insisted upon this. And you, too' – he moved his head towards her – 'were all for having legal recognition. Well, we got what we desired, we got legal recognition for the boy – and this is the result.'

She moved away from the desk holding her face in both her hands now. He watched her walk the length of the room twice before stopping near the table on which a lamp stood, and when she took her hand and passed it over the tall glass funnel, which emitted quite a severe heat, he felt himself shudder.

She walked back to the desk and her voice more controlled and her body straight now, she said, 'If you can do nothing legally, what can you do illegally?'

He remained still. The suggestion disturbed him but he did not refute it. Then, her face close to his again, she whispered, 'I . . . I could take him away.'

He got sharply to his feet, saying, 'No, no. That would be ridiculous, and fruitless.'

'Then what do you suggest? That he should just walk out of here with the child and hand him to that creature?'

As he moved to the fire and stood looking down into it she said, 'I once heard Mr Bellingham making a statement about land. Fence it in, he said, enclose it, and let them fight it out from there. Possession is nine points of the law.'

He turned and looked at her. Possession is nine points of the law. If the boy were out of reach for a time then Clive might be brought to his senses through cool argument and discussion, not in heated passion as had happened tonight. Of course he could take the matter to court under the heading of abduction, or kidnapping, but he didn't think that his son would do this, for he imagined that underneath the crude shell that his four years of voyaging had built round him, there must still remain the indolent, sensitive creature, who would take the line of least resistance and would be open to reason. He sighed now and said, 'We'll discuss this further tomorrow. In the meantime, stay with the boy as much as possible, and

289

should Clive show any sign of carrying out his threat you will, of course, inform me at once . . . and,' he added, 'make the necessary arrangements with the nurse.' He then made a motion with his head and turned from her, and she went quickly from the room.

Ten minutes later, standing before her dressing table mirror, she picked up a strand of white silk cord that was used for binding her hair before it was dressed, and slowly she began to pull out single threads as if she were drawing sinews from a body.

8

He had been into Newcastle and heard from Mr Weir that
they had procured a house for him on the outskirts of the
town with a very pleasing aspect towards Denton Burn.
Fortunately, as it happened, the owner was taking up a
post in India and the house would be vacant at the end of
the week, and although it wasn't usual that a new owner
should occupy the premises until all matters were settled,
Mr Weir had arranged that his client should take
possession right away. He also went on to state that all the
furniture was to be disposed of and suggested that Clive
should look at it with a view to purchase.

When Clive saw the contents of the house he said he
would take everything as it stood. The furniture was
more solid than tasteful, but then, he imagined, it would
be more durable under the rough handling of children.
The house, as Mr Weir had pointed out, was very
pleasantly situated and he saw its isolation as no draw-
back. There were three reception rooms, a quite sizeable
hall, and offices; four bedrooms and dressing rooms
on the first floor, and four attic rooms on the second
floor. There was a stable yard bordered by a coach
house and two loose boxes. It was a small but very
desirable residence. He complimented Mr Weir on his
choice.

Later, as he rode along the Gallowgate through the Biff
Market and the Groat Market and through the compara-
tively new Collingwood and Dean Streets which sported
flag pavements and whose shops had display glass windows, he thought, I'll bring her and show her it all. I
doubt if she's ever seen the shops in the city, and she must

be dressed. Yes, before she takes up residence she must be dressed.

He went to the Club, but only for a meal; and his drinking was moderate because he knew he must keep a clear head. He had an odd feeling that there was something afoot in the Hall; things were too quiet, his father too studiously polite, Isabelle too controlled, but not so controlled that she could cover her hate of him. But this did not trouble him too much.

He had come into the city on horseback and he had already travelled two-thirds of the return journey when he left the main road, took the side road that led to Rosier's village, then mounted the open fells. He gazed about him as he rode. The sky was low, seeming to rest in the distance on the hillocks. The ground in parts was hard and slippery under the horse's feet, while in others the animal had to plough through quagmires almost up to its knees. This, he told himself, was the scene that she looked upon all winter, had looked upon for many winters, and had survived and brought her young family through to survive. And there was now joined to the uncontrollable secret feeling she created in him a deep admiration for her.

When he reached the habitation there was no-one in sight, and when he knocked on the door there was no answer, and he knew a keen disappointment. But just as he was about to ride away she came up the slope from the track below. She was wearing a fawn shawl with a pink fringe; it was the first time he had seen her in a light colour and it enhanced her. She was carrying a wicker basket in which there were various articles of grocery, and round her were the four children, and each of them was carrying something, large and small.

He led his horse forward and she slowed her step when he came up with her, and the children sprang away as the horse flung its head up and down and snorted loudly. He said haltingly, 'I . . . I was just passing. I have some news I thought to give you.'

'Yes, Sir.' She moved her head towards him, then followed the children towards the dwelling where they stood waiting for her round the door. Taking a large iron key from the pocket of her skirt, she inserted it in the lock; and as the children went inside she said to Sarah, 'Here, take this,' and handed her the basket. Then she turned and looked at him again.

He was standing by his horse's head now and smiling gently at her. After a moment he said, 'You told me your name was Cecilia.' He made a little moue with his mouth, and leaned his head slightly to the side before he added, 'Well, mine is Clive.'

She gave no answering smile in return, nor did she speak, but once again a heat spread over her body and her face flushed. Clive, he had said. She would as soon have thought of calling God 'Bill' as calling this young man by his christian name. Her feelings at the moment were strange to her for they were a mixture of excitement, wonderment, and fear, yet the latter was no longer connected with him.

He said quickly, 'I have found a house. It is very pleasing. It is partly timbered, and isolated somewhat, being in the country, but the aspect all around is beautiful. In six days' time it will be vacant. I wonder if you would care to accompany me and view it before you take up residence there?'

He was speaking to her as he would to one of his own class. He talked of going to view, not having a look, and taking up residence, not going to live there.

When she hung her head he said, 'What is it?' and she replied quietly, 'I'm troubled.'

He took a step nearer to her, still holding the horse's bridle, and said, 'Why? Why are you troubled?'

She looked up into his face and if she had spoken the

truth she would have said, 'Because Matthew was here last night and got into a rage and called me a fool.' 'Ask yourself,' he had said. 'Have you ever known any of his kind do one good turn without expecting something back? Even their feeding of the poor in the winter is just to keep them going because they'll need them come spring and summer on the land.' Then he had taken her by the shoulders and, looking deeply into her eyes, said flatly, 'Sit quietly, Cissie, and ask yourself one question. Why is this fellow, who will one day be lord of the Hall, giving you his son, the son who he tells you he has claimed as legally his? Why? I'll tell you why. Because once you are in that house he'll be free to come and go. You can't stop him seeing his son because if you did he'd whip him away again. You'd be his kept woman, and that's how you'll be looked on in any case if you take his money and his house.' He had ended by pleading, 'Do as I say and let it be me who'll get you a place out of this.' She had turned on him then crying, 'It doesn't matter if I'm classed as your kept woman! As it is, you've made me name like clarts, and I can't go even as far as the wood now but I see your wife watching me. Kept woman! That's what she thinks I am, your . . . your kept woman. If I go to his house I have the bairn, if I go to yours I don't. And' – she had ended finally – 'I want me bairn.'

He was waiting for an answer and she said softly, 'It'll be a strange arrangement.'

'Oh no.' His voice was airy. 'There's nothing strange about it. You will be living in your own house with your own income. I can assure you everything is being done legally and proper. A temporary deed is being drawn up until the papers of register are ready, then they will be sent to you and no-one will trouble you further. For myself, I am, as I have told you, returning to sea. I may be away for months, or years, but I would, naturally, at the end of a voyage like to see my son, and with your leave I will call upon you then. That will be all.'

At the end of a voyage, and with your leave I will call upon you then. It sounded so strange, yet quite above board. No smell of the kept woman was indicated by these words.

'Look,' he now said with quiet persuasion, 'let me call upon you tomorrow, and I will take you to see the house. At least the exterior, as the tenants won't be moving out until the end of the week. I will also take you to my solicitor and he will immediately put at your disposal the income you are to have in the future . . . Then perhaps you might want to look at the shops.' He did not mention clothes, he would leave that to her, at least for the time being.

There was a long pause before she said quietly, 'Thank you.'

'That's settled then. Can you be ready about ten o'clock in the morning? Or is that too early?'

'No' – she shook her head – 'it's not too early.' Not for someone who usually rose with the dawn no matter what time of day it came.

'Till tomorrow then.' He bowed slightly towards her, and as he gathered the reins into his hand and prepared to mount she said hastily, 'Your . . . your father. What does he say now?'

He did not turn his face fully to her as he answered, 'He is naturally against it. It could not be otherwise.' And on this he mounted the horse, inclined his head downward and rode off.

His father was surprisingly civil to him at dinner. He opened the conversation with the shoot he had arranged for the week ahead, starting the next day. He spoke of his friend Bellingham, and suggested that he was likely to get better bags on the Houghton Estate than he had garnered from his own during the past week, the shortage of birds being put down to the activities of the poachers. He said he would be going out early in the morning and enquired if Clive would be accompanying him; and to this Clive replied politely that he was sorry but he had made arrangements to go into town. His Lordship had expressed regret but said there was always another day.

This conversation had taken place while the servants were waiting on the table; and although Clive knew his father was a stickler for etiquette and decorum, there had been many times, even since his return home, when, for much less reason than he had now, he had sat through the entire meal in silence.

Isabelle's attitude towards him was more comprehensible for she exchanged no word with him, excusing herself immediately after the meal was over and leaving the dining room. And he did not find her in the drawing room when he later went there; nor did he see her for the rest of the evening, and this he could understand.

The following morning he arrived downstairs in time to see the servants dispersing after prayers. He sat down to breakfast with his father and was not reprimanded for not having observed the rules of the house. But there was no small talk this morning and the meal was passed in silence; and when Isabelle did not put in an appearance there was no remark made on her absence.

Just before the meal ended he said, 'I would like to use the second coach; would that be in order?' And to this his father replied, as if the request had surprised him, 'Oh yes. Yes, certainly.'

Excusing himself, he left the table and in the hall he said to the third footman, 'Kindly tell Bowmer I will be needing the second coach immediately.'

He went up the stairs and on to the landing, and from there he saw Isabelle and her maid leave her room at the end of a corridor and mount the stairs to the nursery floor. She had not seen him, and he stopped and stared at her. She was not dressed for a shooting party but in a green corded costume suitable for travelling. The maid, too, was dressed for a journey, and across her arm she was carrying her mistress's cloak.

He walked slowly towards his sister's bedroom and, gently opening the door, glanced in. The room was orderly, there was no sign of luggage or of a quick departure. Still moving slowly, he ascended the nursery stairs, and, on reaching the landing from which six doors led off, he walked quietly to the day nursery, and with a jerk he threw open the door and startled the nurse and the child.

The child recovered quickly and cried, 'Oh! Papa. Are you coming for a walk with us?' and Clive, going to him where he sat dressed, except for his coat and bonnet, touched his hair, saying, 'Not this morning, tomorrow perhaps. Yes, tomorrow surely.'

At this the maid made a queer sound in her throat and he turned and looked at her. Her face was red and she started to cough. It was a choking cough, and he said to her, 'Take a drink of water,' and she turned from him and fled into the other room. And he stared after her for a moment, then walked quickly to the night nursery door and threw this open too, but it did not reveal his sister and her maid.

He came back to the child who, staring up into his face, said, 'Papa, can I whisper?' and Clive, bending his ear down close to the smiling mouth, said, 'Yes; what do you want to whisper?' And the boy in a conspiratorial manner, as if he were aware that this was a thing to be discussed between them alone, said, 'When will I be able to play with the little girls again, Papa?' Looking tenderly at him, his hand fondled his son's long curls, Clive said, 'Soon, my son; quite soon. Be a good boy until I return. Goodbye.'

'Goodbye, Papa.'

Out on the landing, he looked towards the other doors. If he opened them and found her there what would he say?

She was at liberty to take a drive without sanction from him. As he stood staring, her maid emerged from the staircase that led to the servants' quarters. She stopped when she saw him and her agitation almost equalled that of the nurse.

Thoughtfully now he returned to his room, donned his cloak and hat, inserted a handkerchief into the cuff of his coat, and put a bag of sovereigns into his hip pocket; then he went out and down the main staircase, across the hall, and on to the drive.

There he stood for a moment and looked up at the sky. It was high with great billowing white clouds going before the wind. As he brought his head down his eyes slid to the side, attracted by a movement in the window of his father's study, but when he turned and looked at it fully there was no-one there.

In the stable yard he saw Morris fully dressed, and he thought it strange that his father should have ordered Morris to drive the second coach for there was strict protocol as to which groom drove which carriage. Then Bowmer came from the stables leading the two bays and the second coach, and he doffed his hat and said, 'Good mornin', Sir. It's all ready.'

'Morning, Bowmer. By the way, is the first coach being used today?'

Bowmer seemed to hesitate for a moment, then said quietly, 'Yes, Sir.'

'Who is using it? I understood His Lordship was going to the shoot.'

'I . . . I don't rightly know, Sir; I only know Morris got his orders last night to stand by.'

Clive stared at the man. Morris got his orders last night to stand by? His father was going to the shoot, and Isabelle was ready for a journey . . . where? And this he put to the coachman, 'Do you know where the carriage is bound for?'

Bowmer seemed uneasy and his reply came, hesitant, 'No, Sir.' He looked at Clive through kindly eyes. He liked the young master and he knew there was business afoot to do him down. He might have strange ways but he was more human than anybody else in the house. He said now, slowly, 'I only know, Sir, that the extra luggage rack has been put on the back.' He held the young master's eyes until Clive said, 'Thank you, Bowmer,' before walking to the carriage door. Bowmer jerked forward and opened it for him, and as he closed it Clive put his head near the window and said in an undertone, 'Stop the carriage when you're two-thirds down the drive, say, near the cypress walk.'

The coachman nodded, then muttered, 'Very well, Sir,' after which he mounted the box and drove the horse over the cobbled yard on to the main drive and turned them right in the direction of the South Lodge.

Dutifully, three minutes later Bowmer drew the carriage to a halt and Clive, alighting, said, 'Wait here. I'll be back.' Then turning, he walked at a brisk pace up the drive until the bend brought him within sight of the house. Here he stopped, and, standing on the grass verge against the shelter of an evergreen hedge, he saw the coach drawn up below the steps. He saw the servants hurrying down it with cases of luggage; then he saw the nursemaid and Isabelle's own maid descend the steps, and in each hand they carried a valise, and behind them came Isabelle and his father with the child between them.

The ground was flying away under his feet. He had reached the corner of the house before they came to the last step, and when they saw him surging towards them they stopped, but just for a second. Then Isabelle, grabbing the child up into her arms, dashed to the coach. But she had only managed to thrust the boy inside before she was torn from the doorway and suffered the indignity of stretching her length on the gravel.

By the time they had picked her up he had the boy out of the carriage and in his arms. But he said not a word. The servants were all staring at him with their mouths agape and keeping their distance. His father, his face almost ashen, was levelling on him a look that was both shamefaced and condemning, but Isabelle's glare could be described by only one word: murderous.

He turned now, his eyes searching for the nurse, and when he found her cowering by the tail end of the coach, he cried at her, 'Your master's luggage immediately,' and like someone hypnotised she brought the two bags she was still hanging on to and dropped them at his feet; then, going to a rack at the back, she pointed a trembling finger at a trunk, and the coachman hastily lifted it down and put it on the ground.

The child, sensing a hostile atmosphere now began to whimper and Clive patted his back. Then glaring at the coachman, he barked at him in a manner that brooked no hesitation on his part, it did not even allow him to glance at His Lordship for leave to carry out the order, 'Get this luggage down to my coach! You'll find it down near the Lodge gates.' He now gave one last look at his father but did not deign to glance in his sister's direction before he strode away still patting the child, who was crying aloud now.

He had gone only a few yards from the seemingly mesmerised group when Isabelle, pulling herself from the support of the stone balustrade, raced after him and, clutching wildly at his arm, cried, 'You can't do this! You can't! You won't get away with it.'

When he continued to walk on she kept by his side, spitting abuse at him until they reached the head of the drive, when she hissed under her breath, 'If you take him from us I'll kill her. I swear to you I'll kill her.'

At this he pulled up and, dragging his arm from her grasp, said icily, 'That would avail you nothing: you would merely be signing your own death warrant.' And at that he left her. But her threat went with him, for, knowing his sister, he was aware that she never thought of the consequences of her actions: she just acted. A panicking fear filled him, and he knew that he must get the girl away from that habitation as soon as was humanly possible.

Within minutes they were bowling through the gates, and ten minutes later Clive rapped on the roof of the coach, and when it came to a stop he got out, and lifting the child in his arms he said to Bowmer, 'Bring the small valises and follow me. I will come back and help you with the trunk.'

'Yes, Sir.' Dutifully Bowmer picked up the two bags and followed the young master up the slope; and when they reached the top of it he could not believe his eyes when he saw the place for which they were making. As he later said to Morris, 'I was with him all the way, I still am, but I think he's gone off his rocker to leave the child in that hole, whether she's his mother or not.'

The door opened as they were crossing the flat and Cissie appeared, dressed in a clean serge skirt and shirt-waist, over which she was wearing the fawn shawl, which she only just saved from falling from her shoulders to the ground when she saw him striding towards her carrying the child and a young fellow in livery following with bags.

When Clive, walking past her into the room, said to the man, 'Wait outside, I'll be with you in a moment,' she looked from him to the child who was standing now by his side but still whimpering, his face tear-stained, and she whispered, 'What's happened?'

He replied simply, 'They tried to abduct him. If I hadn't suspected that something was afoot this morning they would have got away with it.' He drew in a long breath. 'Now listen, and listen carefully. You can move into the house on Monday, or Tuesday – the present owners will be gone by then – but in the meantime keep the child with you, don't let him out of your sight.'

She shook her head as she said, 'But what if they should come? What if he should send servants to take him?'

His answer to this was quiet and firm. 'They won't do that. I'm going back to the house now and after what I have to say to them I can assure you they won't do that.'

And in his own mind he was sure that after he had told them what the result of any precipitate action of theirs towards her would evoke, they would be forced to hold their hand.

The idea for the deterrent had come to him during the drive from the gates to this place, but it was an idea which, although only formulated within the last hour, had, he knew, been there for days past, weeks in fact, just waiting to be hatched out. And this morning's business had firmly chipped the shell.

He said now, 'I'll be back and forward during the next few days just in case, but I don't think you have any need to worry. But do as I say, don't let him out of your sight. And it would be wise not to go far afield.' He glanced about him, then asked, 'Where are the other children?'

'They're out gathering . . . getting wood.'

'Oh.' His chin jerked upwards. Then he said with a forced smile, 'Well, from Monday onwards there'll be no more need for them to go wood gathering.'

It was odd, but she had thought the very same thing that morning, and she had been about to stop them when from habit they took the sacks and went out, but then she had said to herself, it'll keep them busy. She had given them instructions with regard to their dinner and about locking the door once they were back.

She looked at the child. He was staring up at her, one finger in his mouth, his eyes still bright with tears, and she dropped on to her hunkers spontaneously in front of him and said, 'There now, there now. Let me take your coat off.' And when his hand came out and slapped her and his small high voice cried at her, 'No! no! I want Nanny,' it was as if a knife had been thrust through her ribs.

'Richard! Richard! That is rude. You must not be rude or insolent. Look at me, Richard.' He caught at the boy's hand. Then pointing towards Cissie, he said, 'You remember your mama who you thought was in heaven? Well, she did not go to heaven. This lady, Richard . . .' He now wagged his finger towards Cissie.

'Papa! Papa!' The tears were raining down the child's face now, the voice a whimper, and Clive shook his arm impatiently and said, 'Listen to me. Don't interrupt when I'm talking. This lady . . .' But it was Cissie who interrupted him now. Looking at the child's gently stamping feet and shaking legs, she said almost in a laugh, 'It's all right, it's all right,' then whipping him up, she took him into the cave, and there, pulling a bucket from the corner, she lifted up his dress and petticoats and let him relieve himself.

When he was finished she adjusted his clothes and he stared at her solemnly, and she took his hand and they went into the other room. But it was empty, and she saw through the open door Clive and the servant carrying the trunk up the slope.

The trunk, she saw, was bigger than their clothes chest and she marvelled that any one child could have so many clothes.

When Clive said in a formal manner, 'I must away, but I will return shortly,' and in the same manner took his son's hand, saying, 'Be a good boy,' the child said, 'May I come too, Papa?' And he replied, 'Not this time, I'll be back in a little while; you stay with your . . .' He looked towards Cissie, then towards the open door, outside which Bowmer was standing, and added, 'Stay with this lady, I won't be long.' And nodding at Cissie, he ended, 'He'll be all right; he'll get used to it.' Then he was gone.

She had to stop the child from running after him; and again Richard slapped at her hands, then backed from her until he came up to the rock wall, and, his lower lip trembling, began to cry loudly now.

As the coach turned into the road where the milestone was and the land sloped away to a valley bottom, Clive saw a group of riders in the far distance, and he knew them to be the Bellingham party coming for the shoot. He gauged he would have five minutes' grace in which to speak to his father and Isabelle before their arrival. And so, putting his head out of the window, he called to Bowmer to speed the animals.

The lodgekeeper showed his surprise at seeing him back so soon, but even more so did Hatton when Clive entered the hall and demanded, 'Where is His Lordship?'

'In . . . in the drawing room, Sir.'

When he walked into the drawing room he saw that not only his father was there, but Isabelle too. And it seemed significant to him that his father was seated while Isabelle was standing, but they both held brandy glasses in their hands.

Their surprise outdid Hatton's. It brought his father slowly up from his chair and caused Isabelle to take a step forward while putting down her glass on a side table.

He did not keep them waiting for him to give the reason for his quick return. He said, 'The child is now with its mother and I want to inform you, in fact, impress upon you, that should either of you attempt to take him from her care, or' – he now looked directly at his sister – 'do her an injury in any way, I will take action which will, by way of embarrassment, make the present situation pale. And my action will be simply this: I shall marry her . . . and quickly. So, think on it seriously and consider whether you want her for the future Lady Fischel, because before God I will do as I say. And I may tell you it would be pleasing to me, for she is naturally beautiful and can be made to fit the situation. Clothes will change her outward appearance; her mind can be educated; it has been done before. I think you will remember that my great-grandfather adopted this measure with his second wife.'

Neither of them spoke, they just stared at him, glared at him, and on the point of turning from them, he said formally, and speaking directly to his father, 'The person in question cannot take up residence in her new home until Monday or Tuesday, so until such time I will avail myself of your hospitality, Sir, so as to be near . . . the child.'

As his hand touched the door handle his father's voice came like an arrow at him, saying, 'Clive!' And when he turned towards him again he saw that his father was finding difficulty in speaking, for he ran his tongue over his thin lips and swallowed deeply before bringing out, 'In the meantime, may I ask you to consider bringing the child back here? I promise you there will be no further effort made to take him away, but I cannot think of him living in that habitation.'

'Thank you, Sir, but I think no. I should not worry about his health, for I understand there has been a large family brought up in that habitation and they all look quite well, considering . . . But I don't think . . .' here he paused before going on, 'I don't think there would be any difficulty if you would wish to visit the child and its mother at a later date.' And on this he went out and closed the door, and as he did so he heard the shooting party come up the steps, and he made quickly for the stairs and his room.

9

Three events tended towards the climax. The first was that His Lordship told Clive the following morning that if he was staying in his household, for whatever length of time, then he must conform to its standard, and it would be courteous if he joined the shoot, especially as his sister was indisposed.

What his words really meant was that his son's appearance at the shoot would dilute yet another scandal which was being laid on his house.

The second event was that Isabelle, presumably confined to her room with a cold, was drinking heavily. Her father being out, she ordered the decanter to be brought up to her, and such was her standing in the house now that Hatton couldn't disobey her command.

It did not need brandy to inflame her fury. She drank in the hope that it might dull it and blot from her mind the face of that detested girl. In her brain-heated musings she looked back down the years but could see no further than the day when she had caught the boy with the trap and had struggled with the girl and come off the worse. It was from that day her life had begun; it was from that day that her turbulent nature, out to conquer and domineer, had been challenged. The girl had fallen as a seed into the fertile soil of hate that lay deep within her, and in which sooner or later someone would have embedded himself. But it had to be this girl, who sprang from the lowest form of the working class, the agricultural labourer.

Not the least part of her hate was made up by a sense of indignity that she, the daughter of a lord, should have found that, for years now, some part of her day had been taken up with the thoughts of this creature. And now she must suffer the greatest indignity of all, for the girl not only had charge of the child, but she had gained the love of her brother, her twin brother. He had said he would marry her, and she believed him. Oh yes, she believed him, for the desire for her was in his eyes, the need of her was in his tone when he spoke her name. At this point she took her empty glass and flung it with all her force at the iron framework of the fireplace, and it shivered into a thousand fragments and brought the maid running to the dressing-room door, standing there with her hand to her mouth exclaiming, 'Oh, Miss! Oh, Miss!'

'Get away!' she cried at the girl; she then added, 'Bring another glass.' She stood up and walked to the window. She was quite steady on her feet. The home brew that her uncle had made had been quite potent and had seasoned her. Her thoughts flashed to him for a moment and she muttered aloud, 'Parsons! Stills in the cellar, and whores in the vestry.'

When her maid brought the glass she helped herself to another measure of brandy, and stood sipping it while she looked out on to the grey day. The sky was heavy and low, there was a feeling in the air that spelled snow. She wanted to get out, ride, walk; she wanted movement. Why shouldn't she join the shoot? She could say her cold was better. She put her hand out flat against the window pane and watched the heat from her fingers outline them on the glass, and when she took her hand away she didn't move until the last fragment of steam had evaporated and the outline was no more. Her thinking brought her round almost with a jump and she was crying to the maid, 'Robson! Come here! Robson!' And when the girl came hurrying into the room, she said, 'My riding habit, and quick now. Quick!' And as the girl ran to the wardrobe to get the habit she started to unhook her own clothes to aid the process.

The third incident took place at the mill. Matthew had just returned on horseback from Benham. As he entered the main yard he saw Straker come scurrying through the door from the house yard and at the same time he noticed that the horse was still harnessed to the flour dray, and he knew without even having to guess that Straker, who had been out delivering, had just now also delivered a bit of tittle-tattle to . . . the mistress.

Matthew was well aware that Straker, for various reasons, didn't like him – the main one being that he was now master of the mill, whereas before he had been little more than a hand like himself. Another reason was that he had chewed him off one day when he brought him a bit of gossip, and had told him that if he spent less time jabbering to the customers his journeys would be shorter and he would have more time for work. This was the day for delivery at the Hall and by the looks of things he had brought back a piece of gossip that had warranted no delay before being passed on.

He glanced in the mill and saw that William and Joe were busy on the threshing floor and he called to William to get the store cart ready and harness the horse; then he went into the house.

Rose was busy at the table, and Peggy, a woman from Brockdale village, was on her knees whitening the hearth. As he passed through the kitchen he turned his head in Rose's direction, saying, 'I'm going to change, an' I'd like a bite.' But he didn't immediately make for the stairs; instead he went along the passage to the office, and he had hardly closed the door behind him when it was opened again, and she came into the room and repeated his words, 'Going to change. An' you'd like a bite.' Then she added, 'And where you off to the day?'

'It's Friday, isn't it, the second in the month? I'm going into Newcastle, of course, to the bank, and then on to the chandler's.'

'There now,' she said mockingly, her two fists thrust into the hollows of her broad hips. 'It's only twelve o'clock. You've never left the house afore one on a Friday for Newcastle.'

'Aye, that's true enough, but I've just managed to get there on the bank closin'. I'm going earlier the day so I don't have to rush. Now what have you got to say about that?'

'Just that you might be making a stop on your journey.'

Oh, God Almighty! He gripped his head with his large hands and they trembled and the knuckles showed white through the skin.

'Well' – her voice had a careless, airy sound to it – 'I thought you might just be calling in to say goodbye, seeing she's all set to move to her mansion.'

Slowly he turned and looked at her, and she said mockingly, 'Don't tell me this has come as a surprise to you. You know all her business; surely she wouldn't keep you in the dark about this now, would she?'

His hands hung slack at his sides now and he waited, but she had to make a prelude as she always did before touching on the vital point. 'By! the trouble one body can cause. And you wouldn't mind so much if it was somebody of importance, but when they're scum, well, you've got to ask yourself, haven't you?'

He had learned to still his tongue because he knew that if that was let loose his hands would become loose too, and once they touched her they wouldn't be able to stop. And of this he was afraid.

'Didn't you know there were great doings at the Hall yesterday? My! they said never, even in the old man's time, the one afore the last one who begot half the countryside, never did he cause a scene like that of the young lord. Stopped them going off with the bairn, he did; caught them in the nick of time, kicked, lashed out, bashed, knocked everybody sprawling, then up with the bairn and takes him . . . Now where do you think he takes him? Well, to his mother, of course. It's natural, isn't it, that he should take him to his mother? But just until Tuesday. Well, that's what they say, just until Tuesday when her big house will be ready. In Newcastle it is, thirty rooms so they tell, Bowmer says, and a great stack of servants. Now it's like a fairy-tale, isn't it, from rags to riches? And you know something else? He's leaving on Tuesday an' all. And where do you think he's going to live? I'll give you a guess.'

He was near the desk, where stood a big glass inkwell. From the corner of his eye he saw the light glinting on it.

He gripped his hands tightly together in front of him and looked down at them as he said, 'Get out of me sight, do you hear! Get out of me sight!'

Now the mockery went from her voice and she cried, 'Out of your sight! You'd like me out of your sight altogether, wouldn't you? You're thinkin' of ways to get rid of me all the time, aren't you? Oh, you needn't tell me, I can see your mind working every minute of the day. But you can take it from me I'll be here when you're gone. Get that into your head, when you're pushing the daisies up I'll be here, an' I'll be ruling as is me right.' Then pulling her lips tightly in between her teeth, she bit on them before saying, 'God, why did I let meself in for you?' And he, unable to curb his tongue any longer, cried at her, 'For the simple reason I was the only one in straits dire enough to take you.'

On this her rough skin took on a bluish tinge, her small eyes became round dots of dark light; and as her hand whipped out in the direction of a brass vase used for holding pipe spills, he shouted, 'You throw that an' I promise you it'll be the last thing you'll ever throw.'

Such was his tone, such was the look on his face that her hand became still on the rim of the vase, and he went past her and out of the room and up the stairs, and, tearing off his breeches and coat, he changed his clothes. Then taking a chamois leather purse from a drawer, he picked up his tail hat and went out and down the stairs and through the kitchen, which was empty now; and William was standing in the yard with the cart and horse ready. He paused for a moment before mounting the cart; then, looking at William, he said under his breath, 'Have you had any word from Cissie?'

'You mean the day, Matthew?'

'Aye.'

'No, Matthew. Is anything the matter? Is she all right? She was all right Sunday.'

'Yes, yes, she's all right.' He nodded at the boy. 'I . . . I just wondered.' He mounted the box thinking, It could all be a story. She would never make any move without letting the lads know, and if she was going to be in so much clover it was ten to one she would take them with her. Still, on the other hand, she hadn't had much time had she, if this upset only happened yesterday? But he never thought she'd do it, and she wouldn't have done it if it wasn't for the bairn. Damn the bairn!

He shortened his route, although he knew he stood the chance of being bogged down. Taking the road to Rosier's mine, he forked right, then cut over the rough pot-holed track that led to the open fells which would bring him down to the road that skirted the boundary wall of the Hall.

It was just before he reached the road that he saw a man running hell for leather across the open fells. One minute he'd be in a hollow and the next minute on a hump, then he would jump a gully here and there. The figure was too distant for him to recognise but he thought the man was a poacher and the beaters after him. There was a shoot going on somewhere roundabout. But then no man would be so foolhardy as to poach in the middle of a shoot, unless he wanted his brains blown out.

311

As the cart continued to move forward the man was lost to his view. He rounded the bend and another hundred yards or so farther on he stopped, and, quickly jumping down from the cart, mounted the slope. One second he was hurrying forward, the next he was frozen to the spot, his eyes looking at something his brain for the moment denied seeing. Before him were three people, two of them spaced within a distance of fifty feet of each other; these were Cissie and a woman with a gun. Cissie was standing with her back tight against the corner wall of the dwelling; and lying breast pressed against a hump, a gun to her shoulder, her eye on its sights, was a strange woman; the third figure was the man who had been running, and him he recognised now as young Fischel. He, too, had a gun and he was standing dead still on a hillock some distance away. His gun was half cocked, but it was his voice he used, and he was calling now, desperately, 'Isabelle! Isabelle! Listen to me. Don't! Don't!'

Matthew saw the woman's head turn slightly to the side; then once again her eyes were concentrating down the length of the gun, and when she fired it there came the sound of a double report.

As he saw Cissie slide down the wall he heard himself screaming, 'Christ! Christ!' And then he was kneeling beside her, holding her to him, crying, 'Cissie! Aw, Cissie!'

Her eyes were open and she was breathing deeply, and she pushed him away with her hand as if to get air, and he gasped at her, 'Where? Where you hurt?'

In answer she made one small movement with her head, and then with one hand she began tentatively to feel her chest and shoulder; following this, her fingers moved to her cheek from where the blood was running and in which was embedded a sliver of stone.

He pulled her hand away and examined her face; then gasped again, 'You all right? You all right?' And she moved her head once more; and as he lifted her up on to her feet and she leaned against the wall she slewed her gaze to the side and there, about six inches away, was the place where the bullet had struck and slivered the sandstone. Matthew's gaze followed hers and he exclaimed in awe, 'My God!' Then he turned about and screwed his eyes up to bring into focus the man and woman on the mound. And again he said, 'My God!' for the woman he saw now was hanging over the mound, her arms stretched downwards, her head at a queer angle, and the man was kneeling beside her with the gun still in his hands.

Cissie, too, was looking at the figures on the mound and she groaned, 'Oh no! No. Oh, dear, dear God! Oh no!'

Sarah and Charlotte came running from the house at this moment, crying, 'Our Cissie! Our Cissie!' And Matthew turned on them and yelled, 'Get back in there! Do you hear? Get back in there and don't come out until I tell you.' They backed from him and fled inside and he rushed after them and put his hand round the door and took out the key and locked it from the outside. Then running back to Cissie, where she was moving slowly now across the open ground like a sleepwalker, he said, 'Stay where you are a minute. Stay where you are.' Then he pushed her back towards the wall and he himself went forward towards the mound.

He gazed down at the girl with the hole in her neck from which the blood had poured and soaked her fine clothes, then he looked at the young man who, up to that moment, he had hated as only a man can hate another who had taken the virginity which he thought of as his own right and who was now aiming to follow up his raping in a more legalised way. He saw that he was trying to speak but couldn't. When he swayed and put one hand to his head Matthew thrust out his arm and steadied him, then watched the young fellow's head droop forward and his face screw up into agonised contortions before he put his hand across his mouth as if he were going to be sick.

'Come on. Come away.' When Matthew went to turn him round, Clive shook him off. Blinking rapidly and with the muscles of his face straightening, he quickly knelt down and, gently turning his sister over, put his hand inside her habit. She felt warm, but there was no movement.

Now Matthew, kneeling beside him, pulled off the white muffler from under his cape, and, lifting the lolling head, wound it gently but firmly around the red-stained neck. And as he did so the strong smell of brandy was whiffed up to him and he, too, felt sick as his fingers came in contact with the warm, sticky blood. He said now quietly, 'There's a door down below. I'll bring it up.' He rose from his knees and hurried down the slope to where Cissie was standing supporting herself against the wall once more, her eyes staring from her head. He put his hand on her and said, softly, 'Go inside; you're shivering. Go on, you can do no good out here.' But she made no response until he said, 'I'm going to take the old door.' Then she followed him slowly into the wood house.

When he had picked up the door and gone out, she automatically, but still moving like someone in a dream, began to clear aside the wood that the children had been chopping earlier. Then she moved the chopping block into the corner; which done, she stood waiting for their arrival.

When they brought Isabelle in she had to grip tightly on the edge of the sawing cradle to steady herself. She stared at the dead-white face, the blood-soaked wrapping around the neck, the green velvet habit, the brown leather riding boots, the pointed toes sticking directly upwards.

The door lowered, they all stood still like hypnotised beings in a deep, heavy silence until it was broken by a child's cry coming through the wall; and Clive's head turned in its direction. Then he groaned aloud.

'Sit yourself down.' Matthew took his arm again and led him to the chopping block.

Clive sat on it and dropped his head into his hands, and after a moment, during which Matthew and Cissie looked down at him, he heaved a deep sigh. Then, straightening his back, he said haltingly, 'Her . . . her horse, it's tethered on the hillside; I'll . . . I'll ride to the Hall.'

Matthew gathered his lower lip into his mouth and gnawed at it before he said, 'Take your time . . . Sir . . . and . . . and whatever comes of it I'll . . . I'll be a witness. You had to do it.'

Clive looked at the miller. He had said he had to do it. But did he? Did he have to do it? Yes; far better him than anyone else, for if she had killed this girl she would have died anyway. When all the facts of the case were brought to the fore, the jury wasn't assembled which would dare have let her off, well born though she was. She seemed due to die in any case, and now he was going to follow her. They might not hang him but they would make him pay the penalty in some way, for wasn't this last act the result of his raping a young girl? And there were many puritans in law now who felt it their duty to make examples of rakes. Why? Why did he ever come back? Why hadn't he gone on sailing the seas? If only, in this moment, he could find himself on a heaving deck in the middle of the ocean . . . 'What did you say?'

'I was saying, Sir, to wait a while.' Matthew did not now find it difficult to address this man as 'Sir' – his hate of him had vanished. The dead one lying there had, he felt, created a barrier between the young fellow and Cissie that was impregnable. He went on, 'Cissie's gone to make a strong cup of tea. And, Sir, I've . . . I've been thinking. There could be a way out of this . . .'

Clive looked towards the figure lying on the door. It was covered up now with a black cloak. He hadn't noticed the miller doing that, he hadn't noticed the girl going out. He asked now, 'What time is it?'

'Getting on for two, Sir.'

Getting on for two. It was just over an hour since he had come out of the wood on Thornton's farm. The shooting had been spasmodic because of the light. He had left the main group and made his way back through Thornton's and was in sight of the North Lodge when he saw her come out of the gate, turn immediately right, and gallop down the road. He hadn't called to her – it would have been fruitless – and he hadn't to think twice of her destination. He had leaped forward as if he had been released from a spring; and he had taken to the open fell land without any hope of cutting her off, because that was impossible the way she was riding, but praying, as he ran, that he'd be in time to stop her doing anything mad. And in a way his prayers had been answered. He had no thought to kill her. No! No! Not that; he had aimed at her shoulder, but that slight turning of her head when he had called to her had deflected his own aim and consequently hers.

'Look. Look.' Matthew was talking as he might have done to Jimmy. 'Pay attention to me for a minute. As I said, I've been thinkin'. It was all an accident. If you hadn't stopped her she would have done for Cissie. You must look at it like that.' Matthew paused; the young fellow wasn't really with him, he wasn't listening, he was dazed. He said now, his voice louder, 'Were you out shooting, Sir?'

'Yes, yes; I was out shooting.' He spoke as if he were repeating a phrase he had learned by heart.

'Well then, look. She . . . she was likely out shootin' an' all. That could be so, couldn't it?'

'Yes, yes, that could be so.' Clive moved his head once.

'Well now, in a short time it'll . . . it'll be dark. By the way, Sir, where was the shoot?'

'Over Thornton's land towards Willey's, the west side of the estate.' His tone was weary and held a slight impatience.

'The west side?' Matthew nodded his head in a series of small movements, then went on, 'They'll have been shootin' around there all day, and accidents can happen in shoots.' He now bent down and stared into Clive's face and muttered below his breath, 'You get what I'm driving at, Sir? If she was to be found around there it could be an accident; it's happened afore, like the one at the Gallow's Dip.'

'The what?'

'The Gallow's Dip. You wouldn't know it by that name. It's a piece of land; it's actually in one of Thornton's fields. There's a hump in the ground, it runs along like a ridge. If you're a tallish fellow and walking in the hollow your head appears to anyone on the other side as if it were bobbing along the ground. That's what they said, at the inquiry when the keeper shot a poacher; the keeper said that the head was bobbing along the ground. It was bad light and he took it for a rabbit. An' he got off. It must have happened in your great-grandfather's time. But do you get what I'm aiming at? Accidents happen at shoots, keepers take pot-shots at shadows; every movement from dusk on is a poacher to a keeper. If she could be found round there . . . well, like I said, it would be taken for an accident, because after all that's how it was, you never aimed to kill her, did you?'

Clive didn't answer but he swallowed hard at the saliva sticking in his throat. He wasn't really listening to all the miller was saying, for the longing was strong in him again to be on the sea, miles and miles away from all this . . . What about the child and her, and the house he was going to visit between voyages? The thought came to him as he saw her coming through the door, a mug of steaming liquid in each hand; and when she offered him one of the mugs he took it from her and for the first time on this day he looked into her face; and he saw the cut on her cheek and the dried blood where the bullet had grazed it, and he thought, My God! as near as that, and for a fleeting moment he was glad he had done what he had done, for Isabelle had set out deliberately to murder this girl.

He sipped slowly at the tea. It was bitter, and distasteful, very much like the stuff they brewed in the galley; but he drank it as he had for four years. There came another blank in his thinking when he was unaware of the movements about him and he was brought back to the present by the sound of low sobbing and he became aware that she was crying and that the miller was holding her in his arms and stroking her hair gently, and she was resting against him as if it were her natural place. The sight made him sad, deeply sad, and he wanted to get up and go out; but he sat on looking at them and listening to the miller talking.

'Go on in,' he was saying, 'and stay in. Now listen to me. Stay in and try to make yourself forget everything that's happened. Tell the girls that an' all . . . Anyway, they didn't see anything. They didn't get round the corner, they could have only heard the narration. Go on now. And if I can't get over the night I'll be here some time the morrow. And no matter who comes you know nothing. Mind that now, you know nothing. An' you got that . . .' He touched the dried blood on her face gently with his forefinger. 'You got that from a sliver of wood, remember.'

Cissie turned from him and looked towards Clive. He had saved her life and he had put his own in peril. She wanted to run to him and clasp his hands and . . . and bring comfort to him in some way, for his eyes looked so deeply, deeply sad, he looked entirely lost. He wasn't the young, slim, commanding figure of the man who had brought the child to her yesterday. When his gaze dropped from hers she turned away and went out slowly.

And now Matthew stood looking down at the shape of the figure lying under his cloak and his mind was working at a rate it had never reached before in his life. He knew that the plan he was hatching in his mind wasn't purely altruistic, though at the moment he was both grateful to and sorry for the fellow sitting there. It was of Cissie he was thinking; and, through her, of himself. If this fellow here was brought up for the killing of his sister the sympathy of the people would not go to him, or the girl he had saved, but would be lavished on the dead, and no matter what sentence they passed on him, short of hanging him, it would be light in comparison with the sentence that would fall on a girl who lived rough on the fells, who'd had a child to the accused man and who, they would say, had sold the child to its grandfather; then when the father appeared again egged him on to have the child returned to her. Oh, he knew the pattern it would take. He had in his time been in the Shields Court and the Durham Assizes and listened to cases and marvelled at the twisting of the law men. But it wasn't the condemnation of the law men he feared most for Cissie but that of her own kind. They would hound her from the villages and the hamlets around here; and, moreover, they would drag himself into it and name him as one of her men. He could stand that, for he was so named already, but it would only go to blacken her. She'd had enough; for years now she'd been hounded in one way or another and this would be the last straw.

As Clive rose to his feet Matthew turned sharply towards him and, standing before him, he said low, 'This what I'm thinking of doing. I've got it all fixed in me mind. Now listen to me.' He was speaking again as he would to one of his own kind. 'As soon as it's dark enough I'll carry her down to me cart. I'll tie the horse to the back, an' take the road by which I came, an' when I get to the fork I'll make a wide detour circling the North Lodge, and I'll come out by Fell Gap, then make my way down the track by Gallow's Dip. Then I'll pick a spot along there where I'll say I found her. I'll leave a bit evidence of some sort so that I'll be able to take them back and show them the place. And I'll do it properly, I'll . . . I'll rough up the ground a bit . . .'

'No, no!' Clive, seeming to throw off his stupor, thrust him aside. 'Don't be absurd. I couldn't allow this. No, no; you could be caught before you got there. Do you realise that?'

'What would that signify? As long as she's away from here I could even say I found her on the road below, or any other place; but there'll be fewer questions if she's found on the place where the shoot was the day. Look, Sir; all I ask is that you go now, for the sooner you're in the house the better. Go in as if you'd just . . .'

'No.' Clive's voice was calm and firm now. 'It's very good of you, miller, but I can't accept such an offer. It's impossible.'

Matthew stepped back from him and let out a long oath finishing with, 'Christ's blood! What's the good of another of you dying? Cissie's now got one on her mind but if she should have you an' all, even if you were just put along the line, it will drive her insane. And then there's the child. Have you given him a thought? When the tale comes to him when he's older there won't be a word of truth left in it . . . It's all senseless.'

Yes, the miller was right, it was all senseless. He was a cute fellow, this miller. Perhaps he had been a poacher in his day; he was reasoning like a desperate man. Yet it was himself who was the desperate man, and he couldn't think at all. What was the plan he had suggested? She was out shooting . . . ?

It was a full five minutes later when, still listening to Matthew, he said thickly, 'If you are bent on doing this for me then I must go with you in case you meet someone before you reach the . . . the allotted place.'

'No, no, Sir.' Matthew shook his head vigorously.

'Yes!' The word was almost rapped out and it conveyed to Matthew that the young fellow was once more in command of himself; so he said, 'Well, Sir, have it your own way for the time being, but stay where you are for the minute, and I'll get the horse an' bring it here in case he should be spotted. There's plenty of room; this is where I stable mine.'

There was a moment's pause as they looked at each other. Then Matthew went hurriedly out and Clive turned his back on the black-covered figure on the door and stood staring into the deep gathering twilight.

Within five minutes Matthew came back leading the horse, and the animal snorted and reared until Clive went to its head and spoke softly to it. But it remained uneasy and trembling, conscious, as animals are, of death.

Twice during the next hour as he alternately sat and stared at the figure on the door, while sorrow cut at him like a knife, then walked the narrow space of the floor, he burst out, saying, 'Look. It's very generous but . . . but I can't go through with it, not this way.' And Matthew said simply, 'Wait, just hang on. Once it's dark it'll be all right. I'm telling you, Sir, it'll be all right.'

When the light had almost gone Matthew went and stood at the far end of the door and looked towards Clive, who, he saw, had to make a great effort before he could walk the three steps forward and pick up the other end.

Five minutes later the body was on the cart, the cloak over it, and the horse tethered by a long rope to the back. Then Matthew said, 'Get up, Sir, an' I'll lead him.' And he went to the horse's head and they started.

He had not lit his lamps and he knew that it would be very unfortunate and put a spoke in the whole business if he were to meet anything on the road before he could get on to the fell track, but he had to take that chance.

The chance came off and sometime later, as he heard a church clock in the distance striking five, he stopped the horse and lit the lamps. By half-past five they had skirted the North Lodge and come within half a mile of the Thornton land; and before he turned off the narrow track that would lead to the road running by the west wall he stopped the cart and said, 'Now, Sir, I'm all right; I'm going to drop you off just afore we reach the road, an' if you keep right you'll come to the Lodge within fifteen minutes.' He paused, and they stared at each other through the dim reflection of the lamps. Then Matthew, speaking as man to man, said, 'So far, so good. You've got nothin' to worry about; the only thing to do is to keep your mouth shut. What's done's done; nothing you can say can undo it. Think of it that way. And think an' all, what good is it going to do you or anybody else stuck in gaol for years? It's likely to kill your father an' all.'

It was strange, but in all this he had never thought once of his father – and here was the miller saying it was likely to kill him. And that was true. His daughter murdered and his son hanged, or, as the miller had just said, rotting in prison, and his grandchild taken from him. Christ alive! What had he done? If he had only left things as they were, left the child where he was, not played the Don Quixote, all this would never have happened. But then it had happened, and the reason for its happening he could trace back to his own anger and hate towards his father, for he had wanted to hurt him, have his revenge on him for those years of squalid slavery and degradation. Yet within the past two hours he had not given him a thought. But this he knew now: the miller was right, this tragedy would kill his father; fast or slow it would kill him, and strangely now he did not want him to be hurt further.

When he held out his hand and said, slowly, 'What can I say to you?' Matthew took it and they gripped hard, and when he didn't speak Clive asked, 'Why are you doing this? Why were you prepared to take this risk?' And Matthew, as always, coming straight to the point, answered, 'For a number of reasons, Sir. But if I was to tell the truth, the main one is Cissie. If this came out, if it was told as it happened, her life would be hell, because the truth is, no matter what they did to you they would do twice as much to her, with or without law. Ignorant people act ignorantly, Sir. I don't want her to be hurt no more.' Nor to be driven to some far place where he wouldn't be able to see her.

There was a long pause before Clive said, 'Nor me. Thank you. Thank you. By the way, what is your name?'

'Matthew Turnbull.'

'Thank you, Matthew.'

'You're welcome, Sir. Goodbye and good luck.'

Good luck? He'd certainly need that from now on.

As he moved away in the darkness he heard the miller click his tongue at the horse and the cart joggle forward; and he could see the figure lying prone in the back as if illuminated, and he groaned out, 'Oh Isabelle, Isabelle.'

When he rang the bell at the North Lodge the lodgekeeper came running out, holding his lamp high, and on seeing who it was, he exclaimed, 'Oh, Sir. I didn't know you were still out, thought perhaps you might've come back t'other gate. His Lordship's in this half-hour or more.'

'Got . . . got stuck in the mire, Beecham.' He pointed down to his mud-covered boots and breeches, the result of his stumbling into a ditch farther back along the road.

'Lord! Sir, you are in a mess. And you're just in time; 'tis spittin' on an' could turn to sleet. It's a bitter night and black as the ace of spades; would you like a lantern, Sir? Take this one.'

'Thank you, Beecham. Good night.'

'Good night to you, Sir.'

When he left the lodgekeeper he let out a long shuddering breath; it was as if he had got over his first obstacle. Anyway, he had talked, he had talked naturally, but how would he talk when the miller brought the cart to the door? But he wouldn't be there, he'd be in his bath. He'd take a long, slow bath and he'd fill up with whisky inside. But not too much, just enough to get him over the night. God! He stopped on the path and gripped his face with his hand. How had this all come about? He had killed his sister, he who had no real love for gun sport had shot a human being. He who, as a boy, had squirmed when he shot his first rabbit . . . Rabbit! It had all started with a rabbit, and just about there. Somewhere in that tangle was the spy-hole where she'd lain and watched the child. And one day he'd lain with her. Oh Cecilia! . . . Oh Isabelle! One as dead as the other to him now.

10

For six days the child had whined, cried, and sulked, and Cissie was desperate to know how to bring him round. He wanted his nanny, he wanted his grandpapa, he wanted his Aunt Isabelle, he wanted his bath, he wanted his walkie; he didn't like that porridge, he didn't like that broth, he didn't like that bed, and most of all he didn't like the lady picking him up; and he slapped at her whenever she attempted to do so.

He wasn't crying this morning but he was sitting close to the fire, and when she said to him, 'Come and see the snow, Richard. Come and look out of the window and see the snow,' he shook his head, then said in a whimpering voice, 'I'm cold.'

She didn't think he could be cold; he was well wrapped up and the room was warm. She had kept the fire going full blast night and day. Charlotte came to her and whispered, 'Will we take him out to play snowballs?' And she replied dully, 'No; he might catch cold.'

She said to Annie and Nellie, who were sitting on the mat looking at a little coloured picturebook she had bought them the Christmas before, 'Let Richard have a look'; then, turning to Sarah who was washing up the breakfast crockery in a bowl that was standing on top of a box in a corner of the room, she added, 'Leave those, Sarah, and read the story to Richard.' And Sarah dutifully left what she was doing and dried her hands; and kneeling on the mat between her sisters and the small boy, she smiled her quiet smile and, taking the book from Annie, began in a slow syllable-spaced way to read, 'Ma-ry-put-a-sau-cer-of-milk-on-the-mat-for-the-pus-sy-cat-and-the-pus-sy-cat-lapped-all-the-milk-up-then-Ma-ry . . .'

Sarah got no further, for the tattered-edged book was slapped out of her hand; and Richard, standing up and stamping his foot and with tears bursting from his eyes, cried, 'Don't want to hear about the pussy cat. Don't want to hear about the pussy cat. I want my grandpapa, and Aunt Isabelle. I want to go home. I want nanny and have my bath.'

Cissie bowed her head and closed her eyes, then turned away and, pulling the old black shawl from the back of the door, she went out. Keeping her head down against the snow she hugged the wall until she reached the wood house. Then she stumbled towards the chopping block and, sitting down, buried her face in her hands and began to cry. What was she going to do? What was going to happen? One thing was certain. She couldn't keep the child fastened up here. But even if they went to live in this other house, would he ever get to like her? That was the unbearable part of this business: the child didn't like her. Her own family, each and every one of the nine of them, loved her; but her own child, whom she not only loved but had adored blindly for years, he couldn't bear her touch, he struggled in her arms, he slapped at her. He was but a child of three and a half years but he acted more like Charlotte and Sarah in age; and each day did not dim his memory of what he had left, only seemed to put a keener edge on it.

By the previous arrangement she should have moved to the new house the day before. Not that she now wanted to go. She didn't really know what she wanted at the moment, for she was feeling odd. Perhaps, as she put it, she still had the shock on her. But she would be forced to go if she was to keep the child. And that was the question written large across the front of her mind. Was she going to keep him? Would he like her any better among nice furniture and warm surroundings? It wasn't furniture he was crying after, but people, his people, his nanny, his grandfather . . . and her.

She sat up and clasped her hands tightly between her knees and stared at the logs and branches of wood arrayed neatly against the wall opposite her. Matthew had come in yesterday, after the inquest. Everything had gone just as he had foretold. 'Death by misadventure' was the coroner's verdict. One good thing, Matthew said, was that they weren't going to go searching for a scapegoat in the form of a poacher. The fault lay with one of the thirty-five people who were at the shoot. These included His Lordship, his guests, Farmer Thornton and his son, the bailiff, and the keepers. It had been admitted that all of them had passed within range of the spot where the body was found sometime during the afternoon. Matthew said the coroner had asked him one telling question. Did he possess a gun? And he was thankful he could answer it truthfully. No; nor had he ever handled one in his life. He wouldn't know how.

Following the inquest, Matthew said His Lordship had sought him out and thanked him kindly for all he had done. But Mr Clive hadn't spoken to him; they had just exchanged glances. And Matthew had ended, he looked like death. He had then said to her, 'Have you heard from him?' And when she shook her head he said, 'Are you going to his house?' And she had looked at him piteously before answering, 'If I want to keep the child what else can I do?' And on this he had stared at her hard before turning away and leaving her without a further word.

She rose to her feet and, gathering up a pile of wood, she went out and was making her way back to the house when a figure loomed out of the snow gloom and came to the door just as she reached it. And she recognised the figure as the servant who had come with the child. He handed her a package, saying, 'This is from Master Clive.' His voice was stiff, his look accusing, and when she said 'Thanks,' he merely nodded once and turned quickly away.

When she went into the room she saw that the girls were sitting on the mat together at one side of the fireplace and the child was huddled up on a cracket at the other. She sighed deeply as she sat down at the corner of the table farthest away from them. She opened the big envelope and looked at the papers inside, then called Sarah to her and said, 'Do you think you can read these?'

Sarah and the others went to Sunday school every week. Parson Hedley took them for an hour and taught them their letters. She would have liked to go with them but she was too ashamed to ask; but on the quiet she had said to Sarah, 'Do you think you could learn me, Sarah? I'd like to be able to write me name.' So now she knew the alphabet and could form a few one-syllable words, but she knew no big words.

Sarah picked up the single sheet first and stared at it, then looked at Cissie and said, 'It says, Dear . . .' Then she stopped, and again looking at Cissie, she said, ''Tisn't your name.' And Cissie looked down at the paper and although she had never seen her name in writing she recognised it and said, ''Tis. It's me proper name, Cecilia.'

Sarah gave a small laugh, then began again, 'Dear Ce-cilia, The car-riage-will-call-for-you-to-to-mor-row-mor-ning. The-house-is-read-y-and-I-hope-you-will-be-happ-y-there. I-will-not-see-you-a-gain-as-I-am-due-to-sail-to-mor-row. Go-to-the-law-yer . . . whose-ad-dress-you-will-find-on-the-en-clos-ed.' Here Sarah paused and slowly spelled out the word 'document', and although she mispronounced it Cissie knew what it meant. And she said softly, 'Go on.' And Sarah finished, 'He-will-help-and-ad-vise-you. All-that-re-remains-for-me-to-say-is-that-I-pray-you-will-for-get-the-past-all-of-it-and-that-you-will-

come-to-look-upon-me-kind-ly. I-re-main-your-ser-vant,
Clive-Fis-chel.'

Sarah now looked at Cissie. She had her head bent
deeply on her chest, and after a moment she said, 'Shall I
read these, our Cissie?' And Cissie nodded and Sarah
opened the first of the two folded parchment sheets, and
after her eyes had scanned the small neat handwriting she
said, 'I couldn't do this,' and Cissie took it from her hand
and looked at it. Then she opened the other sheet and
looked at that. This was a double sheet and it was covered
all over with small writing, and had a red seal at the
bottom. After a moment she folded it up again and said,
'It'll be about the house.'

'Are we goin', Cissie?' Sarah's voice was an excited
whisper; and Cissie turned and looked towards the boy
still sitting silently on the cracket, his face white, his eyes
wide, his small baby mouth on the verge of a tremble all
the while, and she shook her head and said, 'I don't know,
I don't know.'

She gathered the papers up now and took them to the
chest and placed them in the top drawer. Then, picking up
her old black shawl again, she put it over her head and tied
the string around her neck, and over this she put the fawn
one. Then she took the two milk cans from the box and
went to the door, saying, 'I'll be as quick as I can. Keep
the door barred till I come back.'

When she was outside, her body bent against the
blizzard, she wondered why she had bothered to tell them
to bolt the door for she had no fear now of their coming to
take the child from her. And the scrapers didn't come in
the winter, not to this God-forsaken part anyway. More
and more now she was looking upon the place as God-
forsaken; and if she didn't leave tomorrow, what then? If
she carried out the distant thought hovering in her head,
what then? Winter on top of winter up here until she
was old? For she wouldn't take a house from Matthew,

not as long as he had a wife. So, should she follow the trend of her mind as it was at this moment, it would be the finish of any idea of a real home and comfort, and a different life for the girls; on the other hand if she put her foot down, asserted her right and fought him, she'd be set for life. It was odd to think of her, a grown woman now, fighting a child, and her own flesh into the bargain.

Written on those papers she had pushed into the drawer was her right to hundreds of pounds, and that to come to her every year. One thousand pounds he had said. She couldn't visualise this amount, she could only break it up into countless sovereigns, and the sovereigns into shillings, and she knew there was enough of them to last her a number of lifetimes. But she would have to get the better of the child first.

The snow had eased off, and there wasn't much on the ground as yet, only a thin powder that the wind whipped up into dusty clouds; and when she looked across the open land she saw the clouds skipping over hillocks and dropping into hollows, somersaulting into tight corkscrews, then disappearing as if wiped away by a magic hand.

The last few days, when going for the milk, she had taken a different route, so that on no part of her journey would she see the boundary of the Hall. She was crossing a wide stretch of open land, flat here, to where it joined the road, and she had only to cross this and she was in the lower field of Thornton's farm.

The field was edged with a dry stone wall. It was easy to climb, being only about four feet in height. She had the knack of pulling herself up backwards on to its broad top and swinging her legs across; the short cut saved her a good ten minutes' walk. About fifty feet away to the right of her the road turned sharply and ran through a copse; and as she was about to cross to the wall there appeared from the dark tunnel of trees darker moving objects. They were standing out in dense blackness against the white drift-covered ground, and as she stared at the oncoming cavalcade she knew a moment of panic bordering on hysteria and she almost cried aloud, 'I thought it was over.' When the servant had brought the letter from him this morning she thought it was because everything was finished and he was about to go. But now here was the funeral advancing on her and she couldn't move. The black-plumed horses with their black-clad riders, streamers flying from their high hats, seemed like figures coming at her out of hell.

When she hit the wall on the opposite side the cans clattered to the ground and the sound echoed above the horses' hooves and the grinding of the wheels on the rough road. Slowly she turned her body round and pressed her back tight against the wall, willing herself to keep still, willing herself not to cry out in fear. She was dead, dead; she was going to her burial; she could do her no more harm, yet here she was coming towards her.

She would yell. She would scream. She couldn't stop herself.

The horses were bobbing their heads, making their plumes dance, but the men on their backs were stiff, straight, and they, too, looked dead. There were six of them. Two passed her, then another two, then another two; and then there was the hearse. It was all glass, and in it the coffin lay, and she could see inside the coffin, she could see the girl. Her head was turned towards her and there was a great hole in her neck.

She opened her mouth wide but the icy air rushed into it and down into her lungs and she gasped. And now there was the first coach passing her. It had great black bows of ribbons tied to the corners, and there were two people inside. Their faces stood out from their black clothes whiter than the snow, one was the lord and the other was

. . . Even in this moment she couldn't let herself whisper his name, she could only think he was riding with his back to the hearse. He shouldn't be riding with his back to the hearse.

Then came another carriage. There were two people in this, but they were facing forward. And then another carriage; and then another; an endless row of carriages all with black bows and streamers floating from them.

Following on foot now came the long line of men-servants, headed by the bailiff, and the butler, and behind them the farmers, and the tenants. All men. And whereas no face had turned towards her out of the carriages, now every eye that passed her was slanted in her direction, all judging her, all condemning her. Had she not taken the young master away from the Hall and broken the young mistress's heart and brought His Lordship into old age? Even to the lowest of them their eyes condemned.

The haughtiness, the slights, the manner of the dead one that had not only kept them in their place but labelled them for what they were – menials – was forgotten for the moment, for the dead could do no wrong. But someone must be condemned. There were still the living; and there she was standing against the wall, brazen. If she got her just deserts she should be hounded. But she was being given a mansion, so it was said, and a small fortune was being made over to her. Who said the wicked shall not prosper?

She was still pinned against the wall when the last figure in the long black procession faded into the distance; and then she gave in to the overpowering feeling and slid down into a blackness all her own.

Minutes later she came out of the faint, and when she raised her head the world swung about her and she vomited.

When she dragged herself to her feet she remembered to

collect the cans, but now she didn't go over the wall; instead, she staggered like someone drunk across the road and made her way back to the habitation. She felt ill, so very ill.

11

The following morning she rose in the dark and attended
to the fire. She still felt ill, and would have liked to stay in
bed with a hot brick at her feet for she was cold and
shivering. Deep inside of her was a feeling that she'd never
be warm again. To try to soothe this feeling she made and
ate some hot gruel, but it didn't help.

Before she called the children she took from the middle
drawer of the chest her son's clothes and slowly she laid
them one by one on top of the others in the trunk, leaving
out only those things he would need to put on. Then she
locked the trunk and brought from the cave itself the two
valises and stood them by the side of the door. Then she
washed herself, combed her hair, put on her only other
clean skirt, also a matching clean shirtwaist. This done,
she woke Sarah and Charlotte and whispered to them to
bring their clothes into the room and get dressed.

Sleepy-eyed, they obeyed her; but when Charlotte
caught sight of the cases standing near the door the sleep
fled from her and she whispered excitedly, 'Are we going,
Cissie? Are we going to that house?' and Cissie, walking to
the shelf and taking down the wooden bowls, placed them
in a row on the table before she said, 'No. No, Charlotte;
we're not going to the house.' In the silence she peered at
the two girls through the candlelight. Both their faces
looked small and pinched, and she thought, There's still
time: I could make a stand.

Turning from them she went into the cave and woke the
other two, putting her fingers to her lips to ensure their
silence, so that they wouldn't wake the child. When they
had risen she lit the candle that was standing on a box near

her bed. She'd had to keep the candles going for hours the first three nights because he was terrified of the darkness of the cave, for his darkness had been but a twilight of night lights. And now, going down on her hunkers, she held the candle half over the bed, for he was lying on the far side close against the wall. At first he had resisted her lying with him, and when she would wait until he had fallen asleep and he would wake up and find her there, he would toss himself as far from her as he possibly could – and he still did.

She gazed down at him. His face was pink and warm looking; his brown curls were hanging over his brow and spread like a halo on the pillow round his head. His mouth was not forming a baby button, but looked tight and firm as if in his sleep he were still resisting her.

The pain was grinding deep into her bowels. She thought she could die of it and she wished at this minute she could die, just suddenly go out like she had done the day before, but finally. She was past thinking of the others. All her life she'd had to think of their wants, their needs. Now there was her own need. She needed this child as she would never need anything again in her life. But he didn't need her. He could not remember that she had carried him in her womb, nor that he had suckled at her breast. He had no memory of the anguish of his birth in this very place; he only remembered the environment that had surrounded him during his awakening to life and the people that made that environment possible.

With one finger she softly stroked the clenched fist that was lying on top of the quilt, and even that light movement made him withdraw his hand and tuck it into his neck. On this she closed her eyes, then slowly straightened up, left the candle burning, and went into the other room. There she saw them waiting for her, all looking at her, not accusingly, just mystified, unable to understand why their Cissie wouldn't move from here when she had the chance of a nice house.

At half-past ten, when Bowmer knocked on the door, she and the child were ready. The coachman's face was unsmiling. If you wanted his opinion he would have said that this whole business was wrong, crazy. But there; there was no accounting for the ways of gentry. Gaol you, put you to the lash, stick you in the pillory, deport you, even hang you for a trifle, then turn a complete somersault and give their own away and set up a fell squatter in a fine establishment. It didn't make sense.

When she said, 'Are you on your own?' he answered curtly, 'No, I've a lad with me. We'll get the things down. What is there to go?'

'Just a trunk and the two cases.'

He brought his head quickly around to her. 'What about the other things, your own things?'

'That's all that's going this mornin'.'

He now glanced at the four girls standing on the far side of the table. They weren't dressed for outdoors, and he brought his gaze back to her and said, 'You're not leaving them here alone, surely?'

'For the time being,' she said. 'I'll be back.'

'It's a long journey,' he said now, his voice gruff. 'Over two hours each way. That's if it doesn't snow.'

His tone seemed to drag her shoulders up as she said evenly, 'It won't take that long where I'm goin'. I want you to drive us back to the Hall.' She watched his lower jaw slacken and drop; she watched his head nod two or three times; then he said, his tone soft now, 'Yes, Ma'am . . . Miss. Yes, as you say, it won't take as long going there.'

The child now came towards her, almost at a run. He had been standing solemnly before the fire. He knew he was dressed for a walk, but he didn't like the walks on the bare land where the wind cut at his face. But now the word Hall seemed to bring him out of his solemn stupor, and he associated the coachman with it and he knew that the Hall was home, and he cried eagerly, 'Are we going home? Are we going home?'

Cissie looked down at him. For the first time since his father had left him he was looking at her with a look that did not hold hostility. And now catching hold of her hand he asked, 'Are we going to see Grandpapa?'

After a moment she said, 'Yes,' then added, 'Say goodbye to the children.'

He turned, but still held on to her hand as he said, dutifully, 'Goodbye.' And they answered dully in the same way, except Nellie, and she muttered, 'Tarrah, Richard.'

When the child saw the coach at the bottom of the slope he made a high, gleeful sound, and, tugging his hand from hers, ran over the wet ground towards it, and was only saved from falling by Micky. And when he steadied him the child laughed into his face and said, 'I nearly fell,' to which Micky replied, 'You nearly did'; then he lifted him into the carriage.

But it was Bowmer who assisted Cissie up; and when he tucked a rug round her knees her throat filled near to bursting, and she said 'Thanks.'

'You're welcome,' he replied. He would never have dared say that to a member of the household, but at this moment he meant what he said.

During the journey the child chatted and talked, he touched her hand and leaned against her knee, and his every action drove the pain deeper into her.

At the present time she couldn't separate the pain in her heart from the pain in her body. All her bones ached, her throat was sore, and her chest felt rough. When she breathed in deeply she got a pain below her ribs as if the air were stabbing at her. She had a great desire to lie back and close her eyes, but she kept them wide and fixed them on the child, taking her fill of him that would have to last her a lifetime.

When the carriage drew up below the steps of the Hall the big oak door opened and showed Hatton standing there and unable to hide his astonishment.

When the person came up the steps with the young master by the hand his gaze flitted from one to the other; then he pushed the door wide and stood aside and allowed her to pass.

'Oh, Hatton, where is my grandpapa?'

'He . . . he is in his room, Master Richard. But he should be down . . .' He turned and looked towards the wide staircase and to the head of it where stood His Lordship. Then the child, running across the deep shadowed hall, for the blinds in the whole house still remained half drawn, cried to the stationary figure, 'Grandpapa! Oh, Grandpapa!' Then he was scrambling up the stairs.

They met halfway; and as the child flung his arms wide and gripped his thighs, His Lordship bent down and cupped his head in his hands and made a deep sound in his throat impossible to translate. Slowly now he took his grandson by the hand and turned him round and went down the stairs to where Cissie was standing, and they looked at each other for a long moment before he said, 'Will you come with me?'

She followed him across the hall and into a huge room, and towards a great open fire; and the child danced round them and talked and chatted, telling his grandfather now, in an almost joyous form, about the little girls and the funny bed, and that he didn't like porridge. And where was Nanny? And he was going to see Aunty Isabelle.

When he made to run away from them His Lordship caught hold of his arm and said softly, 'Presently, presently. Be still now.' Then, with his other hand, he indicated that Cissie should sit on the couch opposite the fire.

It was a low couch, and when she sank into its deep upholstery her feet stuck out, and they looked ugly in her thick black boots and she brought them under her so that her skirt would hide them; then she laid one hand on top of the other on her lap and waited.

His Lordship was seated now and looking at her. He still held the boy close to him, and he asked simply of her, 'Why?'

She answered simply, 'Because he was missin' you.' And at this his head dropped forward. Then abruptly getting to his feet, he rang a bell, and in a moment Hatton answered it and His Lordship said, 'Tell Nanny she is required.'

Almost immediately, as if she had been waiting in the hall, the girl appeared in the doorway – the house telegraph was very efficient – and as soon as the child saw her he pulled away from his grandfather and, running with open arms, he cried, 'Oh, Nanny! Nanny! Where have you been, Nanny?' And she forgot herself so far as to drop on to her knees and take the child into her embrace and cry while she gabbled, 'Oh Master Richard. Oh Master Richard.'

Cissie didn't think she'd be able to bear much more. If only once he had greeted her as he had done the nurse she would have something to remember; but all he had given her, until an hour before when he placed his hand willingly in hers, had been slaps and pushed and words like 'don't', 'no', and 'I don't want to', and four other words which she couldn't bear to think of.

'Take the young master to the nursery.'

'Yes, m'Lord. Yes, m'Lord.' The girl pulled herself swiftly from her knees and almost ran out of the room with the child.

Now the door was closed and they sat in silence; she sank into the deep couch which was like no bed she had ever dreamed of, and he sat upright in a great winged chair to the side of the fireplace.

It was over, and her child hadn't even said goodbye to her. How much could one stand of such pain? If you had the choice what would you take? The cutting off of a limb, or the breaking of a heart? She moved her head slightly. Her mind was asking her very funny questions. She was in for a fever, she knew she was. It had been coming on for days. She would say what she had to say and then she would go. She put her hand under her shawl and into the pocket of her skirt and withdrew a large envelope and, bending slightly forward, she handed it to him, saying, 'I won't be needing these now. Perhaps you'll keep them, an' . . . an' give them to your son.'

He took the envelope from her and without making any comment extracted the two parchments from within it – she had kept the letter; that was hers – and he looked at them. One was a temporary deed to a house called Fieldburn Place in the County of Northumberland. It was situated in four acres of freehold ground, and its cost, together with furnishings, was eleven hundred pounds; the other was a letter to the effect that his son was leaving one thousand pounds a year to Cecilia Brodie, to be made payable in monthly instalments. He looked up at her. 'Have you read these?'

She shook her head, 'No; I . . . I can't read much. But . . . but I know what they are; he . . . he told me.'

'And you are returning them?'

'Yes, Sir.'

He stared at her for a moment. This girl had nothing, nothing in the wide world, and her future, as far as he could gather, held nothing; and yet she was willing to give up what a great many would consider a fortune. She could have closed her eyes to the child's need of him and gone on the assumption that children soon forget, and very likely in better surroundings, such as the one this deed indicated, the child would have forgotten him and this house. But because the child was unhappy she brought him back and, therefore, renounced a life which must appear like heaven compared with that which she was enduring. He folded the deeds up and, returning them to the envelope, he handed them to her, saying, 'You must give these to my son himself. It will be for him to say whether he will take them or not.'

Her eyes widened slightly and she murmured, 'I . . . I thought he would be gone. He . . . he said he was sailin' the day.'

'Not until this evening. He is to leave at noon.' He rose to his feet, and when she also made to rise he put his hand out towards her, saying, 'Please stay seated.'

Going to a row of small knobs that were attached to the wall behind the red-corded bell rope, he pulled on the third one; then walking towards her again he stood looking down at her, and he moved his tongue over his lips a number of times before he said, 'May I say that I am deeply grateful for your action, and that I understand what it must have taken for you to come to this decision. If there is anything, any time, that I can do for you or yours you have only to call on me. You understand?'

She moved her head once and said, 'Yes, Sir. And thank you.'

He still continued to stare at her; then he said, 'If my son cannot induce you to accept' – he pointed to the envelope lying on her lap – 'then I will see that provision is made for you as before.'

Again she said, 'Thank you, Sir.'

She was now attacked by a fit of coughing that racked her chest and he said with some concern, 'You must have something warm to drink.' And when the door opened at this moment and Cunningham appeared he turned to him, saying, 'Tell Master Clive to attend me here immediately.

341

Also tell Hatton to bring a hot beverage for my . . . my guest.'

'Yes, Sir.' Cunningham did not once let his eyes rest on the figure on the couch but turned swiftly and went into the hall; and after giving Hatton the order he hurried up the stairs and to Master Clive's bedroom. After knocking on the door and being bidden to enter he said, 'The master wishes you to attend him in the drawing room, Sir.'

'Very well, Cunnings.'

'He . . . I . . . I think I'd better warn you, Sir, there . . . there is a lady with him.'

'Yes, Cunnings?'

'She . . . she's brought Master Richard back, Sir. He is up in the nursery now.'

Clive stared at the man, and Cunningham said below his breath, 'I . . . I thought it only fair to warn you, Sir.'

'Thank you, Cunnings. Thank you.'

When the door had closed on the valet Clive stood still in the middle of the room. She had brought the child back. Why? *Why?* She should at this moment have been on her way to the house. Now he'd have to look on her again, and it could only add to his other torment. But why had she brought the child back? She wanted him. Crawling through that hole for years to see him, the hunger in her heart deeper than the hunger in her belly – why had she done it? He looked round the room as if searching for an answer. Then going to the valise, the same he had left the house with when he went on his first voyage, he closed it; then straightening his cravat and pulling down the skirt of his coat, he went out of the room and down the stairs and into the drawing room.

His father looked at him over the distance, and then he turned to the girl on the couch and bowed slightly to her before walking down the room. He did not pause as he passed his son but he looked hard at him; then, his back straight as always, his head held erect, he went out, and his son would have been surprised to know that the deep private thoughts in his father's mind at this moment were as near his own as was possible.

When he reached the couch he slowly sat down on it, but some distance from her, and, like his father, he asked her, 'Why have you brought him back?'

She looked at his grey, grave face. It didn't look young any more. She said, 'He . . . he wasn't happy; he was fretting as I knew he would. And . . . and what's more' – she made a slow, sad movement with her head – 'he never took to me. He even had a dislike for me.'

'Oh no! No!' He moved an inch or two towards her and bent his head forward. 'You're imagining things; he could never dislike you.' He did not add, 'No-one could dislike you . . . except, except Isabelle.'

'He did. It was . . . it was hard to stomach but he did, until this very mornin', when he knew I was bringing . . . bringing him home.' She stared into the deep grey eyes that were holding hers and some part of her was surprised that she was talking to him in an ordinary way, as she would to Matthew, not waiting for the right words to come to her, but just saying what was in her mind. She said now, 'You'll let him stay here, you won't send him any place else will you?' And he asked quietly, 'Where else could I send him?'

She began to cough again, and he screwed up his face at the harshness of it and said, 'You have a cold'; and at that moment there was a tap on the door. It opened and Hatton came in, followed by the second footman bearing a tray. Hatton now placed a small table to the side of the couch and, putting the tray on it, said, as if speaking to a member of the household, 'I hope you find all you need . . . Miss.' And she looked at him and said, 'Thank you.'

When the servants had gone and she had made no attempt to drink the soup, or eat the hot rolls and odd-shaped pieces on the plate that looked like chicken, he bent over and pulled the table further towards her and said gently, 'Drink the soup,' and handed her the bowl and the spoon, and she found herself drinking it gratefully.

She had an odd feeling about her as if she weren't really here and didn't care where she was, and the feeling was growing every minute. She did not stand any longer in awe of the servants or His Lordship, and certainly not of him sitting there. She was halfway through the soup when she remembered about the papers. They had fallen from her lap on to the couch, and she picked them up and handed them to him, saying, 'I . . . I won't need these now.'

'That's nonsense.' His voice was sharp. 'You'll need them as much as before; you can't possibly stay in that place any longer. You must accept them.'

She shook her head as she gulped a spoonful of soup, 'No, no; I couldn't. It wouldn't be right. Anyway, I just couldn't. An' . . .' she turned towards him and there was a deep sad softness in her face now as she added, 'I'd be out of me element. I wouldn't know what to do, or how to go on. And what's more I'd be among strangers.'

He was about to reply, 'You'll never be short of friends when you've got money,' but he resisted and said firmly, 'They're yours, the house and the money have both been made over to you.'

'No, no.' She was again shaking her head. 'Your father is goin' to do what he did afore, an' that'll be enough. I want nothin' more, just enough to keep the bairns – the children – warm inside and out until they're able to fend for themselves.' She took another spoonful of soup, then finished conversationally in a slow quiet tone, 'It won't be long now. Nellie's going on six, Sarah's ten. She should be out in place, but she's not strong, Sarah.'

He stared at her. She was talking as she had never talked to him, and she was more beautiful in this moment than he had ever seen her. Her face was flushed with the chill she had, he supposed; her lips were moist and tempting, her

344

eyes were deep and warm; even the scar on her cheek was like a large beauty spot. God! he mustn't think about the scar, or the cause of it. It was over, finished. He had escaped. Thanks to the miller. Where would he be now but for the miller? And the miller loved her. He was a married man and he loved her. Why hadn't he married her? There must have been a reason. Perhaps he hadn't known her long. But there was one thing certain: he knew her now and wanted her. There were all kinds and shades of wanting, there were all kinds and shades of love. Why had this girl been brought into the pattern of his life? Or, at least, if she'd had to come, why couldn't she have come as one of his own class? But what was his class now? He had fallen between two stools, and today he was climbing back on to the lesser of them, from where he'd rise, he supposed, to the glorified position of captain some day. As a captain of a ship he could have married her; as first mate he could have married her; but as captain or first mate he was still, underneath the skin, Clive John James Horatio Fischel, and heavily conscious that one day he'd bear the title of lord.

He now asked softly under his breath, 'How is the miller?' and she answered, 'He was well when I last saw him.'

'I'll . . . I'll never be able to repay him. Will you tell him that?' She made no answer to this and he went on, 'Nor to forgive myself for all the wrong I have done you.' His head was bowed deep, and she looked at it. His hair was very fair, almost silver. She had the crazy desire to put her hand out and stroke it. What was wrong with her? Was she forgetting what this man had once done to her? Yes, perhaps; anyway it wasn't good to go on harbouring animosity. She said softly and very, very gently, 'You mustn't blame yourself any more. You know, I was thinkin' in the night about something that me da said.' There she was going again, talking ordinary-like to him.

What *was* the matter with her? But she couldn't stop herself, and so she went on, 'He used to say, "Time is to the mind as goose fat to a rough chest," and so about this time next year things'll look different. And I was thinkin' an' all that it wasn't really you who started all this, it was our Jimmy. You see . . .' She now leaned her head against the back of the couch because she felt it was about to wobble. She was feeling slightly dizzy, but she continued, 'It started with him showing Joe how to set a trap for a rabbit. And yet I can't blame Jimmy, because we'd have been hard put many a time for a bite if it hadn't have been for Jimmy and his trap. No, I kept thinkin' in the night, although it seemed to start with Jimmy yet there was another cause for it. And it wasn't me ma and da dying either, because we had been hungry when they were alive, yet somehow it was being hungry.' She turned her head and looked at him. 'Yes, it was being hungry, I think, that started it in the first place. If people had enough to eat and could keep warm I don't think things would happen, do you?'

'Oh, my dear!' He moved his head in wide sweeps as she finished, 'So what I mean is, you're not to blame yourself, 'cos you know . . .' She brought her body up straight on the couch, but she bowed her head deeply forward towards him as she ended finally, 'I'm . . . I'm not sorry I had the bairn.'

When he lifted himself towards her and grabbed her hands he startled her, but she left them in his. Their faces were but inches apart, and now, as he slowly raised her hands to his mouth, her heart pounded and the noise was loud in her ears as if she were standing near the river when it was in spate. His lips were pressed against her red rough knuckles. They were warm, hot, and when they moved over her fingertips she felt it was too much to bear and she gasped and turned her head away on to her shoulder as her body stiffened against her wild, mad thoughts. She felt her hands returned to her lap. Then he was standing up; and when he spoke she dropped her head back on to her shoulders and stared at him.

'Goodbye, Cecilia. Think of me kindly, will you?' His face floated mistily before her gaze. She moved her head twice; then in answer she said one word. She didn't know whether she spoke it aloud or not, but what she said was, 'Always.'

She closed her eyes for a second, and when she opened them he was no longer there. When she heard the door close she turned her head in its direction; he was gone.

She brought her head round again and once more she leaned it against the head of the couch and stared towards the great blazing fire, and she knew he needn't have gone. If she had been scheming enough, or clever enough, she could have kept him and he would have been glad to stay. Yes, she knew that; right deep within her she knew that he would have been glad to stay, and with her, an ignorant girl, who could only just write her name.

She didn't hear His Lordship enter the room; she didn't know he was standing to the side of her until he spoke, and when he asked, 'You drank your soup?' she pulled herself to the edge of the couch, saying, 'Yes, thank you, Sir.' And now she rose, and she knew that if she didn't take a pull at herself she'd pass out, as she had done once before, right at his feet. And it mustn't happen a second time, for they would say she was just doing it. Yes, they would say that. 'I'll . . . I'll be going now, Sir,' she said.

'Very well.'

She walked slowly down the room, he by her side, and before they reached the door he stopped and said, 'May I say again how very grateful I am to you? I shall always be in your debt. Cunnings will call upon you soon and tell you of my arrangements for you.'

She said nothing to this, yet she wanted to talk, jabber. It was a strange feeling.

His Lordship accompanied her across the hall. He made a sign to Hatton who called to the coachman. Then, within Hatton's hearing and, as the butler said later he could hardly believe his ears, His Lordship bowed towards her and said, 'If you would care to call at any time I shall be pleased to see you.' He had not said 'If you would care to come and see the child,' but that was what he meant. Again she told herself to keep silent. She now inclined her head towards him, then walked from him and down the steps to where Bowmer was waiting to help her into the carriage.

Fifteen minutes later Bowmer helped her out of the carriage and then found he had to help her up the slope; and when they entered the house he put her on a chair, and she said to him, in an odd voice, 'Thanks; I'll be all right now.' Looking at her face he didn't think she would be, but that wasn't his business and so he took his leave.

12

There was a blizzard raging when Matthew made his way, by road, it being the safest to the dwelling; and when Charlotte opened the door to him he saw that her face was red with crying. He was kicking the snow from his boots and leggings as he asked quickly, 'What is it?'

'It's our Cissie; she's bad.'

Inside the room he looked to where Cissie was lying on the straw tick before the fire, with Sarah kneeling beside her. When he reached them Sarah looked up at him dumbly, fear in her eyes, and he gazed down at Cissie.

Her breath was coming in short, hard gasps, pushing the padded quilt up and down as if it were worked by a pump handle.

He said quickly, 'How long has she been like this?'

'Since yesterday, since she come back after takin' Richard to the Hall.'

'She took him back?'

'Aye. An' she's been bad since. It got worse last night an' . . . an' she told us to keep her warm. She brought the tick in here.' She tapped the bed. 'She keeps talking and yellin' and she won't let's touch her hands. We've washed her face but she won't let's touch her hands.'

He looked at Cissie's hands, tight against her breast, the fingers of one hand tucked into the other.

She turned her head now and looked up at him with a blank gaze and croaked, 'The scarf was round her neck, round the hole. 'Twas all red, just the ends white, just the ends.'

'She keeps on like that,' said Sarah; 'she keeps on about a scarf. And she was sittin' up in the night and yellin'

349

about a woman with a gun. She's gone wrong in the head.'

He turned and looked at Sarah in silence until Cissie began to ramble again, her head tossing now as she mumbled, 'She was as long as the door and her feet stuck out from under the cloak. Matthew . . . Matthew . . . he put his cloak over her, an' Clive . . . Clive . . . Clive . . .' Her voice trailed away. Then she pushed herself up on her elbow and began to cough, and Sarah held her and when she lay back she caught hold of her sister's hand and said between gasps, 'He sat on the wood block, just like her, like dead, an' . . . an' he had the same look in his eyes, when . . . when . . .' Her voice again trailed away.

Sarah said now, 'We should get somebody, a woman from the hamlet.' And he asked, 'What?' then exclaimed harshly, 'No! No!' That was the last thing they wanted in here, a woman who, listening to her ravings, would soon put two and two together, and then where would they all be.

'Is it the fever, Matthew?' Sarah now whispered, and he said, 'No, not the typhoid. I think it's a sort of pneumonia.'

'Will she die?'

'No! No!' Her question brought him up on to his feet, and he said briskly as he took his coat off, 'Get some boiling water going. And you' – he turned to Charlotte and Annie – 'stop your snivelling now and bring me some covers, top bedding. Go on.'

He rolled up his sleeves, saying to Sarah, 'We'll make a sort of tent an' fill it with the steam from the kettle . . . Put a bit of sacking round the bottom to save the soot falling off it. And get Charlotte to keep the kale pot boiling.'

'Clive . . . Clive.'

He looked down on her. She was thrashing the cover with her joined hands as she gasped out the name, and his face hardened for a moment as he thought, She must think

350

of him as that. But what odds. What odds now, for if she wasn't seen to and quick she wouldn't be able to think anything, she would die. His father had gone like this, not through his broken back but just with . . . the chill.

It snowed all day and it lay thick, and when darkness came and a keen north-east wind started to blow, it gathered into deep drifts which piled against the dwelling and muffled all sound like a great feather tick.

The heat in the room was almost unbearable. Matthew felt he was sitting in a steam bath; he was wearing only his shirt and breeches and they were both sticking to his skin. Except for the time he had galloped back to the mill he had been on his knees most of the day and under a tent-like structure held by the girls, while he supported the steaming kettle. Twice he'd had to lift her while the girls had pulled the sweat-soaked coarse sheet from underneath her and put a dry one in its place. And he had seen her body for the first time when he had rubbed it with warm towels, and he had groaned inwardly the while. Now it was close on nine o'clock and there was a long night to face, and she seemed to be getting worse with every minute of it.

Nellie and Annie were in bed in the cave. Sarah, worn out, was sleeping huddled up on a blanket between the foot of the mattress and the cave wall, and Charlotte was making a brave effort to keep awake and to hand Matthew the things he needed.

There were two candles burning on the mantelpiece and a lantern stood in the middle of the table. Although the room held sounds of Cissie's agonised breathing, the wood crackling in the fire, and the water bubbling in the big black kale pot on the low hob, the place was strangely quiet.

He himself felt very tired – sapped, in fact. There was a cramp in his leg and he was in the act of pulling himself to

351

his feet when Charlotte let out a smothered scream and he swung round to see her with her hands across her mouth staring at the little window. His eyes flicking to it, he saw, above the banked snow on the rough ledge of stone that supported the frame, a face. One second it was there, the next it had gone. Although the impression had been as fleeting as lightning he had recognised the eyes in that face.

As he rushed across the room he grabbed his coat from the chest and the lantern from the table. The next minute he was outside pulling the door closed behind him. Stretching his arm to its fullest extent he swung the lantern high and in its arch, he saw the dark, bulky figure stumbling away in the snow. He ran down the path the children had cut earlier in the drift leading to the wood house, and when he reached the end of the wall he floundered into deep snow and shouted above the wind, 'I hope you're satisified.' Then he stood for a moment before turning about and going into the house again.

When he had gone home earlier in the day he had said to her frankly, 'I'll be out all night.' She had been cutting some material on the table and had a pair of scissors in her hand. She had pulled her fingers from the handles and gripped them like a man does a dagger before plunging it forward, and he had answered her ferocious look by saying, 'If it was for that I could have stayed out nights years ago; I'm goin' because she's ill, very ill. It's pneumonia an' there's only the bairns there.'

He had watched her gulping on her spittle before she growled out, 'It's usual to get a woman to nurse another; she's near the hamlet.' And to this he answered, 'Aye, she is; but you and your like have made it impossible for her to go near the hamlet for years. Anyway, few will risk their necks over that land in weather like this.'

'But you will . . . You will.'

'Aye, I will.' He nodded at her, and on this she stabbed

the scissors point down into the wooden table. Then she said under her breath, 'I'll bring Parson Bainbridge to you and I'll get him to hold you up from the pulpit. He's done it afore to bring folks like you to heel.'

His face darkened at this and he said slowly, 'You bring Parson Bainbridge here or go to him and, I'm telling you, I'll prove your words right. Just think on that. You bring him here an' I'll not only take her but every bitch I can get me hands on. And I'll pay them well. Aye, by God, I'll pay them well. I'll see the miller's money is put to some good. Now you think on it.' And with that he had left her . . .

Back in the room, Charlotte said, 'Who was it?' and he answered, 'Likely somebody lost their way.' She stared at him, not believing him, but said nothing more, until Cissie began rambling again, croaking out words, 'Soup. Soup.' Turning from her knees she said, 'She keeps on about soup but she can't drink any. And she's at that again, pushing the back of her hand across my mouth.'

'Get by,' he said, and taking Charlotte's place he began to wipe the running sweat from Cissie's face and neck.

Her breathing now was becoming even more difficult. She tossed from side to side and moaned and croaked out the child's name. 'Richard. Richard.'

It was around two o'clock in the morning, when the crisis was at its height, that she spoke his own name. 'Matthew! Matthew!' she said, and he soothed her and whispered, 'Yes, my love?' And then she said, 'Clive. Poor Clive.'

When she pushed her hand up towards his face he gripped it in both of his and brought it down to his breast, and when again she said, 'Clive. Poor Clive,' he dropped his teeth tight down on to his lip.

Her coughing began to rack her body, and the beat of her heart raced against him as he had felt no heart race before, and the sweat ran from her pores and soaked him, and he began to use Parson Hedley's prayers, together with his own form of bargaining, beseeching the Almighty not to take her and promising Him payment in return. He could ask anything of him and he would do it, if only He wouldn't take her.

When he became aware of the four girls standing around him he knew that some time had passed for he hadn't heard them come. He also became aware that his calves were in an excruciating cramp and his left arm was dead with numbness and that his shirt was stuck to his back and his own body was running sweat. He stared down at the head lying on his arm and for a moment he thought she was gone. Then she made a sound in her throat and phlegm came out of her mouth, and he withdrew his arm and laid her back on the pillow; and more time elapsed while he and the children stared at her. Then Annie's weeping forced its way into his mind, and he turned to her, he turned to them all and said, 'She'll be all right, it's over.'

At eight o'clock the next morning when he made his way into the mill yard Straker said to him, 'What's happened the missus?' and he stared at the man a whole minute before he asked, 'Isn't she back?'

The answer seemed to surprise Straker, for he said, 'You knew she was out then?'

Again he didn't answer immediately, but his mind was moving fast. If she hadn't come back she had been out there all night, likely fallen into a drift, and that would mean – he wouldn't even let his thoughts pronounce the words, but if Straker knew the reason why she had gone out in a blizzard then there'd be talk, dangerous talk. He said now, 'Of course I knew she was out; she brought some soup over. I was with a friend who's got pneumonia. I told her I was stayin' the night. She . . . she left about nine. Have you been indoors?'

'Aye.' Straker shook his head now. 'I went in the

kitchen. The fire was still banked down, the breakfast wasn't set. I thought it was funny. I called upstairs and when I got no answer I went up and knocked.'

Matthew now hurried towards the house, saying over his shoulder, 'I'll change me things, they're wet, then we'll go and look.'

In the kitchen it was as Straker said; and he stood now gripping his chin tight in his hand. Then he went swiftly to the fireplace and picked up the kettle that was bubbling gently against the banked-down fire and brewed himself some tea; and after he had hurriedly changed his clothes he gulped the tea quickly, then went out again.

Straker was waiting for him in the yard, and the old man said, 'Where will we look first?'

'We'll keep to the road,' he said, 'to the turnpike, then cut up on the fell. That's the way she came.'

They did this, and it took them two hours before they came in sight of the habitation. But there was no sign of Rose. Nor when other searchers joined them and spent the day in the blizzard did they find her; they didn't find her until the third day when the snow had ceased falling and the gale-force wind, whirling fanatically, made unnatural valleys and hills all over the fell. It was the barking of a sheep-dog that drew the searchers to the quarry. And there they saw, uncovered by the wind, the body of the miller's wife still clinging to her lantern. She must have slipped off the edge and tumbled to the bottom; and being stunned, she had frozen to death, then was buried by the drifts.

It wasn't until after her funeral when the mourners had gone and only his mother, his grandmother, and his aunt remained that he allowed himself to realise that he was free, and what this meant. It was his mother who actually forced the realisation to the surface, for during the five days Rose had lain in the parlour he had told himself he must try and do the decent thing. For the time she lay in the house he mustn't allow himself to think of the future. It was there shining bright, but he couldn't open the door to it until she was in her grave. And not even then; there was the period of respect to be maintained . . . And then his mother had said, 'We'll move over the morrow.'

He had been sitting to the side of the fireplace while they were at the table picking at the remains of the ample refreshments that had been provided, and he was turning his head slowly towards them when she added, 'I won't bring the beds, just odds and ends.' Putting his hands on the arms of the chair and slowly pushing himself upwards he looked at her and said, 'What was that you were saying?'

'We'll move over the morrow.'

'You'll move over the morrow?'

'Are you deaf? That's what I said.'

'No, I'm not deaf; and yes, that's what you said. But that's not what's going to happen.' His voice was slowly rising now. 'You're not moving over here the morrow, or at any other time.'

They were all staring at him and he swept his eyes from one to the other. 'Get that into your head, all your heads. I don't need you here, I don't want you here, you're stayin' where you are.'

'Who's going to look after you?' His mother was on her feet now facing him.

'There's Peggy; she'll cook for me.'

'She can't run the house, and she's only a servant; you've got to have somebody to run this . . .'

'Aye, I'll have to have somebody to run this place, Mother, but it's not going to be you.'

She pressed her lips together, wagged her head from side to side, pushed out her chest, then cried at him, 'Now look you here!' But before she had finished he was bellowing at her, 'And look you here. And this is the last time we'll talk about it. You're not comin' into this house,

Mother, nor you, Gran, nor you, Aunt Millie. And something else I'm going to tell you. I don't want you even here visitin', and if you put your foot back after the day do you know what I'll do? I'll turn you out of where you are now, family or not. Ted Joyce's cottage is vacant at the end of the village. I own that. There's three rooms there an' that should be enough for you, and that's where you'll end up if you don't do as I say. Arthur Spragg is after the business, he wants to start his son up in it. He's been at me this last few months to sell him it, but he wants the house with it. He's offered me a decent price an' all. Now I hadn't any intention of telling you this but now I am telling you. You try to interfere with my life from now on and you'll end up in Joyce's cottage, the lot of you, and with your money cut down into the bargain.'

'You're unnatural.' It was his grandmother speaking, and he turned on her and cried, 'Aye, perhaps I am, but I've come from unnatural stock, from you and her.' He bounced his head towards his mother now, and addressing her again he said, 'You led me father hell for years. In a way he was glad when he broke his back and you couldn't push him any more. And you bullied and thrashed me from I was in petticoats. And since I've been a man you've tried to rule me life. But now it's finished; I don't care if I never set eyes on any of you again. Keep your noses clean and you can stay where you are, but should I hear anything like, say, detrimental to me character and I trace it back to you, you'll be down at the end of the village as if a cuddy had kicked you. So I'm warning you.'

'You'll come to a bad end.' His mother's voice was low and trembling. 'And she with you. I know why you don't want us here. It's 'cos of that trollop, that fell trollop. And another thing I'll say when I'm on. I'll bring it into the open; I wasn't going to but I will now. You can't tell me that Rose was taking that one soup, she had more likely gone to see what you were up to.'

He stared at her, then said slowly and deeply, 'I'm warning you. Go home and think whether you want to end your days in Joyce's cottage. And mind you, I don't care a damn or a tinker's cuss what people will say about me if I do it, but believe me, all of you' – he thrust his glance over them – 'that is what I'll do should you open your mouth about me or my business in the future. Just one whisper, that'll be enough to come back to me. Now get your things on and get yourselves away.'

A minute or two later they came walking out of the parlour in single file, dressed for the road, and like three witches they stared at him. But none of them spoke, except with their eyes. They went out, and not until he heard the cart crunching across the yard did he move.

Slowly he began a tour of the whole house, going from room to room, and finishing up in the attics. The place was silent, empty, but he comforted himself it wouldn't remain that way for long, for he'd soon have her here, have them all here.

How long would he have to wait? The decent time would be a year; but, God above, a year was a long time. He wouldn't wait a year, perhaps nine months; no, six. There'd be talk if he did it in six, but damn the talk.

He did it in three.

13

It was a day in early April. The sky was high, the sun was shining, the wind was fresh but not cold. It was the first day in the year that you could go outside and not shudder.

They had all been up since dawn; in fact, the children, like herself, had hardly slept. They had put on their new grey serge frocks and shining black boots and they had tied their hair with bright new hair ribbons and were ready two hours before the cart was expected.

Cissie had not put on her best clothes straightaway but had busied herself with tying up their ordinary clothes and the bedding in bundles, stacking the crockery in the basket that had been a cradle, and putting everything they were taking to the side of the door for easy fetching. And not until all was ready, with the exception of one last thing she had to do, did she dress herself for her wedding.

When she was attired in a grey alpaca dress with a cape to match, a blue straw bonnet resting on her brown hair, and a pair of black buttoned boots on her feet, she went to the top drawer of the chest and took out the long envelope and looked at it. The letter that had accompanied the envelope when she had first received it she had burned last night, and this morning when Mr Cunningham came she would hand him back these deeds that he had brought when she was ill, and then it would all be ended, at least outwardly.

When she heard the children talking, not laughing and shouting, she knew Mr Cunningham had arrived, and when he came in through the door he stopped and surveyed her and she felt herself blushing.

'How becoming. How very becoming.' He kept moving

his head slowly up and down as he advanced towards her; then gallantly he said, 'You didn't need anything to enhance you, but your dress has insisted upon it.'

She smiled shyly. She liked this man, she liked him very much. 'Will you take a seat?' she said. 'We're all upside down.'

Placing two packages he had been carrying on the table, he indicated that she be seated first, and when he sat down and his eyes had dropped to the envelope in her hand, she held it out to him, saying, 'I would like you to give that back to His Lordship, and thank him very much. As I said the other day I won't have any use for either after this.'

Cunningham now joined his hands together and leaned towards her and said quietly, 'I conveyed your message to His Lordship and he has told me to say to you the matter is out of his hands, the young master left the business arrangements with the solicitors Weir and Dixon, and it is with them you must deal. But, as His Lordship pointed out, they will be unable to do anything further about the matter until Master Clive returns – and the *Virago* might be away for years.' He paused now and surveyed her with a gentle expression before he said, 'May I offer you my own advice? You see, one never knows what is going to happen in life; circumstances change. What we reject today we long for tomorrow. So my advice to you is simply to keep them by you – they will eat no bread.'

It was his homely statement ending his pedantic way of speaking that made her smile at him and say after a moment of pondering, 'Perhaps you're right; but I'll have to put them to one side, out of sight, for Matthew'll have none of them. Still, I'll do what you say. You've . . . you've been very kind to me all along, very kind.'

'I couldn't have been otherwise.'

She drooped her head; but after a moment she lifted it and said quickly, 'But . . . but I can't go on taking the five guineas. You, you told him?'

360

'Yes, and His Lordship understands that.' He reached out and lifting from the table one of the packages he handed it to her, saying, 'His Lordship would like you to accept this as a wedding gift. He would like you to buy something with it entirely for yourself.'

She undid the parcel and before her startled gaze she unwrapped a trinket box. It was made of silver, but the lid was padded with red velvet to form a pin cushion, and when she lifted it, there, filling the box in neat rows right up to the top, were golden sovereigns. She gasped at the sight of them and Cunningham said, 'There are a hundred; I counted them myself.' His smile was prim and pleased.

'Oh.' She wagged her head from side to side and looked at him, unable to find words; and to cover her embarrassment he brought forward the second parcel, saying, 'This is a little gift from myself to you both. I hope you enjoy the contents every day.'

And now she unwrapped an elegant pewter coffee pot with a graceful spout and an ornamental lid, and all she could do now was to close her eyes tightly and try to stop the tears from welling out; and he said, 'There, there now. Please, please don't upset yourself. The miller would wring my neck if he thought I had made you cry.'

Again the homely saying brought her smiling, and, stretching out her hand, she took his and said, 'Thank you. I . . . I can't say all that I feel but . . . but thank you. And will you thank His Lordship for me? Thank him very kindly.' Then rising to her feet, she put the two gifts on the table and, resting her hands to the side of them, she looked downwards as she said now soberly, 'I have never asked afore but I'd like to know how . . . how the child's farin'.' And he replied, with equal soberness, 'He's very happy. If it's any help for you to know this, I can say he's extremely happy, and the household is almost back to normal. His Lordship was somewhat ill following Miss

Isabelle's accident; it was such a tragic accident.' She turned to him. There seemed something in the way he had stressed the word 'accident' that brought fear rushing into her, but he looked her straight in the face as he finished, 'But he's over it now, and the child is his one thought and concern.'

She nodded her head slowly and said, 'I'm glad. An' thank you for telling me, Mr Cunningham.'

Now the sound of the children calling and laughing came to them. She went to the door, and there was Matthew coming up the slope. Some of them were dancing round him, but running towards her were Mary and Bella, and she enfolded them in her arms as they both cried, 'Oh, our Cissie! Our Cissie!' and when she held them from her to look at them, they looked at her and almost simultaneously cried, 'Eeh! you look bonny, our Cissie.'

Matthew was standing behind them and amid the babble he didn't speak; he just gazed at her, then from her to Mr Cunningham standing within the doorway, and the two men nodded at each other and smiled.

As if the children had rehearsed it they all ran into the house and grabbed up a bundle each and ran down with it to the cart; and as Mr Cunningham surveyed the nine of them scampering over the slope he said to Matthew, 'Will you have room? I'm sure His Lordship wouldn't mind if we used the carriage.'

On this Matthew turned to him, and for a second a veil came over the brightness in his eyes and he said, 'Thanks all the same, but we'll manage with the cart.' Then he added with slight pomposity, 'I could have brought the trap along but I wanted them all to be together.' And Cunningham inclined his head and replied smilingly, 'It's understandable.'

Cissie went back into the room and she picked the two gifts up from the table. Then she looked about her, at this dwelling place where she had lived for over five years, or

362

was it twenty-five, or fifty? She was twenty-one years of age but she felt old, she had felt old since her illness, since the morning she had returned from the Hall. She shook her head to form a barrier to her thinking, then swung swiftly about to see Matthew in the doorway.

Coming and standing before her, he looked into her eyes and asked, 'Are you ready?' and she answered softly, 'Yes, I'm ready.' And at this he put out his hand and gently touched her cheek, then took her by the arm and led her away from the habitation, over the slope and down to the road to where the nine of them were seated on the cart, their faces bright and smiling; and Jimmy, still small, still dark, and still thin in spite of his fifteen years, called to her, 'Shall I get down, our Cissie, and run alongside and shout "Hoy a ha'penny oot"?' And at this they all roared with laughter; even Mr Cunningham laughed, and with his mouth wide and relaxed.

When Cissie was seated on the high box beside Matthew the small neat man reached up and, shaking first her hand and then his, said, 'I wish you both every happiness,' and they thanked him. Then Matthew cried, 'Gee-up there!' and the cart lumbered away in the direction of the church and Parson Hedley.

The girls sitting on the bundles and the boys with their legs dangling over the back of the cart waved to Mr Cunningham and he waved back, as did Bowmer from his seat high up on the coach. Then the valet entered the coach and sat stiffly on its leather seat, impatient now for it to reach the Hall so that he could inform his master that the young person was now settled – which would imply that he no longer need be concerned for her living in the makeshift dwelling; moreover, her new home would be some considerable distance from the Hall, and this fact alone would ease embarrassment as the years went on and the child grew.

*   *   *

363

It was two hours later when the cart pulled into the mill yard and even before it had come to a stop Joe, Jimmy, and William had jumped off and were calling to the girls to get down, but when the girls did alight they stood quiet and slightly subdued now, awed by the wonder of their new home.

When Matthew lifted Cissie down from the seat, he held her for a fraction of a second longer than was necessary; then, taking her arm, he led her across the yard and as he went he called to William and Joe, saying, 'See to them; give them their feed and a bit rubdown, then come along in.' And they scampered away, crying, 'Right-ho, Matthew. Right-ho.'

When the rest of the children made to run forward into the inner yard Cissie cautioned them gently, 'Behave now. Behave.' And they became quiet and curbed their excitement. Then Matthew was leading her over the threshold into her new home.

The kitchen smelled and looked the same as it had years ago. The copper and brass were shining, the fire was burning brightly, and today the long table was set for a meal; it all looked so cheerful and inviting, but her heart began to beat as if she were being threatened by an invisible presence.

She'd had her dream last night about the white house, and this one somehow didn't fit into it, but the other one would have, the one on the deed she carried in the envelope in her petticoat pocket.

There was a woman standing to the side of the table. She was a round, pleasant-faced creature, and Matthew said, 'This is Peggy. She's a good help,' and Cissie said, 'Hello, Peggy.' Peggy hesitated. She had never bowed her knee to his first wife. But then, she had been a rough piece. And he had brought the talk of the whole place about him for marrying this one, and the other one not three months dead in her grave. It was said this had been his fancy piece for years. But she was a different kettle of fish altogether from the other. And she was surprised by the look of her – she was slim and straight and had a sort of dignity about her. Her knee bent and she bobbed.

He now turned to Jimmy and said, 'Take them to the rooms I showed you. Go on.' And Jimmy, laughing and running across the kitchen, cried, 'Come on with you's!' And, their excitement getting the better of them again, they scampered after him, which made Matthew turn to the woman and say, 'They're not always like this, they'll calm down.'

She replied, 'Bairns are bairns.' And on this he led Cissie from the kitchen and into the parlour; and there he took her cape from her shoulders and untied the ribbon of her bonnet. Then, standing still, he gazed at her and said, 'Well, here we are then. It's been a long time.'

She nodded her head slowly and replied, 'Yes, Matthew. It's been a long time.'

'I never thought it would come, not really . . . Did you?' He sounded nervous, not ill at ease, but not quite sure of himself at this moment.

'No.'

'If . . . if things hadn't happened as they have, would you have married anybody else?'

She could look at him and say truthfully, 'No, I never would have, Matthew.'

At this he caught her in his arms and pressed her tightly to him, whispering into her hair, 'Aw Cissie, Cissie, I love you. Aw, how I love you! And I can't believe it, I just can't believe it. It'll be days . . . and nights afore I can take it in.'

He was looking at her again, and when he gathered her hands between his and brought them upwards towards his mouth he felt her whole body jerk and her fingers stiffen against his, and his eyes narrowed slightly as he peered at her. This is what she had done in the illness, tried to

365

prevent him from touching her hands, not wanting them washed. She wasn't really well yet; her face still looked peaky. That's one of the reasons he had pushed things to get her here, to build her up . . . and . . . and to love her. She was starved of love, as he was.

He asked gently, 'Do you love me, Cissie?'

'Yes. Yes, Matthew, I love you.' She could answer truthfully to this too, and when he said very softly, 'You'll be happy, I'll see you'll be happy,' she thought, yes, she'd be happy; during the time she didn't think of the child . . . and its father, she'd be happy.

BOOK FIVE 1853

Full Circle

1

The miller of Brockdale died on Christmas Day, 1851, aged forty-four years, and just when people said he was about to do big things.

It was around 1842 when the name of Miller Turnbull first began to be associated with causes, and not only in Shields and Jarrow and the smaller towns, but in the City of Newcastle. The miller, it was said, was a forward-looking man, quiet, stubborn, and not afraid to speak his mind. Through him, lesser men came to know the name of Lord Ashley Cooper, one of the gentry who strongly supported the Ten Hours Act, the man who in 1824 got through the Bill forbidding the employment of women and children underground in the mines, the man who was all for education, even of the poor.

With regards to education, it was said that the miller's brothers and sisters-in-law made up the best-educated family in that quarter of the countryside; it was also said that he had not only taught his wife, that is his second wife, to read and write, but had made her so damned learned she'd have no truck with ordinary folks.

Those who had visited the mill said the house was more like a mechanic's library than an ordinary home, with books in every room, and the younger girls talking of Goldsmith, Blake, Coleridge, and Shelley as if they were ladies bred, instead of one-time fell scum.

There was no doubt about it, the miller did a lot of good; but it was also said he could have done more if he had kept his wife's family on an even keel and not allowed them to get high-falutin ideas about themselves. It was this fact that made the miller suspect in the very quarters in which he should have been trusted, that of the agricultural worker.

The farm worker in the North was better off than his brother in the South and the West Country at the time, because in the North, the living-in system still prevailed; labourers were bonded for the year and paid partly in kind with milk, meat, barley, peas, and bread, and in some cases butter, cheese, and vegetables, as well as bacon at the killings, and they had all the slack coal they wanted for a few coppers, if they could carry it from the pit. Whereas in the South the wage of a man on the land still did not reach ten shillings a week, and coal was a luxury even in the depth of winter, and since the famous Tolpuddle business of '34 it would seem that gags had been put in the mouth of every man who worked on the land. In some places where a man dared to spit the gag out, the squire or the parson saw that that man was penalised. It was the fear of injustice and deportation that kept the farm labourer mute and stamped agricultural workers on the whole as a dull, half-witted lot of men.

But in the North and in the South one thing the farm workers still shared was their living conditions, and these were appalling.

It was against these conditions that Matthew worked. In 1844 he set an example by building two cottages for his workmen, with two rooms up and two down, and a fine larder and a washhouse off, and at the bottom of a good square of garden an erection of his own designing, a water closet composed of a cement hole over which stood a wooden framework, and the hole narrowed to a pipe that led to the burn. He also erected a pump that drew its water from the burn, and from which it was easy to carry sluicing water to the water closets. Matthew was very proud of this invention, and considered it very hygienic, for, as he pointed out, the burn was in constant flow.

In 1846, when William married an apothecary's daughter

from Shields, Matthew built him a fine house, standing in a half acre of land within a quarter of a mile of the mill itself. It had a large kitchen and a parlour, three bedrooms and a garret, and besides the washhouse, coalhouse, and stable there was, of course, the new sanitary arrangement – even better this one, for the effluent didn't flow back into the river as it was too far away to pipe it, but into a huge cesspool; nor was their fresh water supply drawn from the river but from a well that Matthew had caused to be sunk at the bottom of the garden.

It was around this time that Matthew became really conscious of the danger of the river water, for it was into this that the effluent flowed, that cattle paddled and went to drink, that cats and dogs were thrown, and it was from this also that most of the hamlets and the villages drew their water supplies.

The fact that the river was fast running in parts failed now to convince him of its purity, for all along its length it was being used as a dump for filth.

It was in 1844, when typhoid was sweeping both sides of the river from South Shields to Gateshead and from North Shields to Newcastle, that Matthew's mother and grannie were taken, and also Nellie. Nellie had been thirteen and bonny and bursting with health, but she had been snuffed out like a tallow-candle in the wind, whereas Annie, who had always been weakly and who, too, had lain with the fever, survived. There was no accounting, they said, for the workings of God. All man could do was to bow before His will. Matthew had let this pass, and concentrated on the river.

But in 1849 when his only daughter, the one child that Cissie had given him, died of the cholera at the age of eleven, he did not let it pass, but cursed God. He cursed Him in private and in public; he cursed Him to the face of his great friend, Parson Hedley . . . And he cursed Him to the damnation of his own soul, so said the righteous when, two years later almost to the day, after rising up from the laden Christmas table, he died.

He had left the table and staggered to the settle because of a violent pain in his chest, which he said wasn't like wind for he had hardly commenced to eat. An hour later, still sitting on the settle, strangely enough where the miller before him had drawn his last breath, he died, and more strangely still, of the same complaint . . .

Matthew's death left Cissie a rich woman, for like Miller Watson, Matthew had speculated in property. It also left her with an eight-room house, not counting the attics, and only Annie and her to occupy it. Annie was to have been married in the spring of '52 but because of the time of mourning the ceremony had been put off till the autumn.

What, Cissie asked herself time and time again during the months which followed Matthew's going, was she going to do when Annie was gone? Could she stay alone in this house? Why not? William was at hand, as were his six children, three of whom were triplets. And there was Jimmy and Ada and their four children in the wheelwright's house. Jimmy would never let her be lonely. There was Mary coming over from North Shields every Sunday, happy and contented with her shipwright husband and her three fine children. There was Joe, still working under William and married to Kitty, a fat, happy-go-lucky individual who, as yet, hadn't given him any children. They were established in a cottage a short distance away which was to have been only temporary until Matthew found a suitable piece of land on which to build them a house; but he hadn't found it before Victoria died, and from the time she went he lost interest in doing anything for anyone.

Then there were the three girls, Bella, Sarah, and Charlotte. Sarah and Charlotte were well away. Years earlier, Matthew had set them up in a little milliner's business in a side street in Newcastle. Within three years they had gravitated to Collingwood Street with a fine display-windowed shop. And now the 'Band Box' was a must for any lady of fashion. Oh yes, Sarah and Charlotte were well away, with fourteen girls in the workroom and their own apartments above the shop and a maid to look after them.

This left only Bella. As was to be expected, so was the general opinion of the family, Bella ran true to form. She was barely seventeen when she ran off and married an Irish labourer from Jarrow by the name of Shane Docherty. Shane was big, handsome, and gormless, and, as Jimmy said, that made the pair of them. Every year Bella brought a child into the world. The number had now reached nine; they were all healthy, bonny and wild, but if it hadn't been for Cissie they would have been starving and barefoot.

So, with twenty-two children visiting her, and their parents, add to this seeing to the accounts of the mill and the property – Matthew had taught her to do this in the early days – surely her time would still be fully occupied.

Part of the answer to the problem, and the answer troubled her, was that none of these things held any interest for her now. She still loved her family, but they were all set; for good or bad they had their own lives to lead. The other part of the answer was that she couldn't bear the thought of staying alone in this house.

Living in the mill had been bearable while Matthew was alive. The foreboding feeling that she had experienced when she had come into the kitchen on her wedding day had mostly, over the years, kept to the shadows; but now the shadows were lifting, and at times, especially at night, she felt there was a presence about the place, and it wasn't Matthew's presence.

Now she was alone and free . . . This last word filled her with guilt and made her turn on herself whenever it entered her mind and ask herself how she could ever think

in such a way as to consider herself free from Matthew –
Matthew who had been so good, so kind, so loving. But
she knew, in the private recess of her being, a recess of
which Matthew had been aware but had never entered,
that it wasn't his goodness, his kindness, or his loving
from which she was free but from his possessiveness.

If at sixteen she had experienced his possessiveness she
would have sunk into it gladly, but she was a woman
through hardship, although only twenty-one, when it
enfolded her, and its tangents were many and subtle.

Matthew had never denied her anything in the way of
clothes. Every year he had bought her two outfits, a heavy
winter cloak and dress with bonnet to match, and in the
summer a linen or a print; but always he chose the colours
and the material, and never did he pick anything more gay
than a light fawn. Once she had ventured to say, 'I think I
would like something pink, the colour of the fringe on the
shawl'; and to this he had said, 'It wouldn't become you.'
It took her some little time to realise that he didn't want
her to be enhanced in any way; to the outside world he
wanted her to appear neutral, not standing out from the
crowd of wives of respectable citizens. It was small
comfort to her that it was becoming the fashion among
ladies of the time to wear subdued colours and to pad their
bodies out of shape with as many as six to eight petticoats.
Decorum seeping down from the palace in London had no
meaning for her.

In his arms at night, Matthew would tell her she was
beautiful; he would become an ardent lover and cover her
body with his lips, but in the daytime he was the miller
and she his wife, and he wished her appearance and
manner to be such that she would claim respect from all.
But as the years went on and the respect began to flow in
to him and his wife in the form of invitations from his
business associates, he politely refused them. Nor, she
knew, did he like her around the yard when men were

bringing their grain in, whether they be farmer, justice, or squire.

Twice a year he took her to the theatre in Newcastle; he took them all to the theatre in Newcastle; and these were great events in their lives. But he never took her to church on Sunday, not even to please Parson Hedley.

His gifts to her were many, mostly in the form of books; but in the second year of their marriage he bought her a spinet and with delight she learned to play. He only bought her two pieces of jewellery: a plain brooch and a gold chain on which hung a pendant; neither of them was an exciting piece.

They had one serious quarrel in the first twelve years of their marriage; during the following two years they had many. The first was when they had been married but ten months. Matthew had come into the bedroom unexpectedly one afternoon and found her sitting reading the parchments.

He had thought she had returned the papers to His Lordship on their wedding morning when the valet had called, but when he found that she had kept them hidden from him and was now perusing them in secret his anger flared out at her. So this was why she had paid so much attention to her reading lessons, never failing each evening to get out the books, no matter how tired he was.

When he had made to snatch the deeds from her she had sprung away from him and put them behind her back, and the spirit that had brought her and them all through the years in the dwelling place came rising up, and she cried at him, 'Don't touch them, Matthew. I'm tellin' you, don't touch them. I didn't want to keep them but His Lordship would have none of them, he said they belonged to me. I didn't want to upset you, that's why I never let on. I don't intend to use them, but I intend to keep them. They're mine. It isn't the value of them but it's all I have for the bairn.' And at this he had cried at her, 'That's all you think about, the bairn. That's why you're not with mine. Ten months now of loving and not a sign of one. An' why? 'Cos I haven't all of you. Oh, I know, I know. I know what I know. Clive! Clive! Clive! You never ceased from calling his name all the time you were bad. God! An' after all he did. An' you know what he did, don't you? Not only rape, but murder. Aye, murder.'

'You never called it that afore,' she cried. 'An' you know it was either her or me.'

'Give them over here.' He held out his hand and it was trembling, but still she defied him, saying, 'No! No, I won't. If they're to be destroyed I'll see to it.' And when he advanced on her she yelled at him, 'I'm warning you, Matthew; if you take these from me I'll never think of you the same again, nothing will be the same again.'

After a space of time during which they had looked at each other in pain, he had flung out of the room and she had collapsed into a chair where she sat staring before her. Then, going to the empty fireplace, she had placed the deeds in it; but when the match was alight she couldn't put it to the papers. She would never claim the house or the money, there was no need to. She had all she wanted, so why couldn't she burn the deeds? She didn't really know except that these two pieces of paper seemed to hold a desire for forgiveness; they spelled reparation for a wrong, not that she held the wrong against him any more. She couldn't burn them, she couldn't.

Making sure that Matthew was in the mill she went into the attic and, finding a small wooden box, she squeezed the deeds into it; then moving the old trunk that they had brought from the dwelling, she pried up a floor board near a joist and carefully placed the box on the beam. Then she returned to the bedroom where she folded some paper to the size of the deeds, laid it in the grate, then set light to it.

Later that night she knew he had seen the ashes for he

begged her forgiveness, and she gave it him. Five weeks later she told him that she was to have his child, and Victoria was born in November 1838.

It didn't matter to Matthew that his child was a girl and that the house was full of girls; he adored her from the moment she wailed her first cry in his arms and for the following eleven years he claimed her as his own. He petted and spoiled her and indulged her every whim; no dark colours for Victoria, but soft muslins, silks, and velvets and all of rainbow hue.

Watching from the side, Cissie became fearful, more so with the years, wondering what would happen when her daughter fell in love, what would happen when young men came courting her, as they would do for she was beautiful, even breathtaking. Would Matthew let her go to another man? She was never jealous of her daughter only fearful for her, and sorry she hadn't more children. It was her fault, she supposed, that Matthew's concentration was levelled towards the one thing she had given him.

Then in 1849 the scourge swept the North again and after only five days of illness Victoria died and Matthew went mad. And that was no exaggeration; for a few days he seemed to have lost his reason, and when he returned to himself it wasn't to comfort Cissie for her loss, or to take comfort from her for his loss, but to make her feel responsible for the child's death. She had never wanted Victoria, had she? he had said. She had never loved her, had she? There was only one person she had loved. Aye, yes, perhaps two . . . aye, perhaps two. But her mind was on one all the time, wasn't it? The young upstart who rode in his carriage and on whom she tried to spy on her strolls over the fells. Oh he knew, he knew; he hadn't been deceived all these years.

With the going of Victoria the house changed. Jimmy, William, or Joe could do no right, whereas before they could do no wrong. He would not have any of the children visit the house; there was no more reading at nights, no music, no laughter. All their clothes were black, and the mourning went on for two years – in fact until the moment he died at the Christmas dinner.

And now this question: what was she going to do with herself?

The answer came in January of '53 when she had been in mourning for Matthew for thirteen months.

William had sent word that he wouldn't be able to get in for an hour or so as he was feeling low. Cissie knew he'd had a cold for some days and she tried to persuade him to stay in bed, but William was stubborn and did not take to bed easily.

It was a wet miserable day with flurries of sleet and a very high wind. She put on her cloak and some heavy boots and was on the road making her way to William's house when she met Jimmy driving the cart.

'I was going to call in on you,' he said; 'I'm on me way to Jarrow.'

'William's under the weather,' she replied. 'He couldn't get in this morning.'

'Well, jump up,' he said laughing. 'We'll visit the sick together.' Then he turned the cart around and they made their way to William's house.

Matthew had designed the house so that the window of the parlour overlooked the valley and the village and the sweep of hills beyond and so you did not approach the front door from the road but followed a curving grass path around the side of the house to it.

Above the wind they heard the cries of the children at play in the hut to the far side of the house, but even above this there rose the voice of William, and he was shouting, 'I can't do it! I tell you I can't. An' I won't!' Then Jessie's voice stopped Cissie in her tracks and she pulled on Jimmy's arm and halted him, and they listened to their sister-in-law crying, 'Eight rooms and attics. What does she want with all them, living alone, and here eight of us in these four rooms and another coming? If you don't put it to her then I will.'

Cissie and Jimmy exchanged glances. The voices were coming from the kitchen, the window of which was about three yards ahead of them.

'It's her place, she's earned it. Begod! if anybody's earned it she has. I tell you I'll not do it, not for you or God Almighty. Four rooms not big enough you say? There were ten of us in a cave out in the wilds . . .'

'Oh, my goodness gracious, not that again! Can't you forget that you once lived like a pig?'

This was followed by a ringing slap, and then silence, and quickly Cissie pulled Jimmy backwards and they made their way to the cart. Jimmy turned it again and they rode back to the mill, and they didn't speak until they were in the kitchen.

Banging a fist into the palm of his hand, Jimmy exclaimed in deep anger, 'By God! the nerve of it. The bloody upstart! Who does she think she is? Come from a potty little chemist's shop and brought up in rooms no bigger than matchboxes behind it. I'd like to give her the length of my . . .'

'It's all right, it's all right. I don't mind. And you know' – she turned and confronted Jimmy – 'she's right; what do I want with this place?'

'Don't be silly, our Cissie. If anybody's earned this place you have. It's as William said. Aye' – he nodded at her – 'an' it's a good job he did say it, or I'd have gone along there and lathered him meself.'

She laughed gently now and, turning from him, let her gaze wander slowly around the kitchen; then she said quietly, 'Do you know, Jimmy, I've never liked this house.'

There was a stunned silence before he said, 'What!' And still with her back to him she nodded her head and continued to look about her, at the brass candlesticks still shining on the mantelpiece, at the copper pans still hanging around the fireplace, at the rocking chair at one side and the leather chair and settle at the other; nothing in this kitchen had been changed from the days when Rose Watson was mistress of it. Turning swiftly to him, she said with an eagerness he hadn't seen on her face for years, 'Will you let Ada come into Newcastle with me tomorrow for a full day? Could you see to the bairns?'

He grinned slowly now, saying, 'Aye. Aye, I can see to the bairns, and she'll be tickled to death. What you up to?'

'I'm going shopping, Jimmy. Yes' – she nodded slowly at him – 'I'm going shopping . . .'

The next day, dressed in her black and driving the trap, she rode over to Jimmy's and picked up Ada, and amid waving and shouts from the children and, 'Enjoy yourselves, but mind, be careful of the traffic,' from Jimmy, they set off.

Ada, like Jimmy, was small and thin, and if there was one person she adored besides her husband it was her sister-in-law.

She had first made Cissie's acquaintance when she delivered a dress to her. For years, in fact from when she was eight years old, she had been employed in a sweat shop in Newcastle. At fourteen she had been apprenticed and gone to live in. She had worked from eight in the morning till eight at night; ten on Fridays and Saturdays. She had slept on a pallet bed on the floor with fifteen others; their food was little better than the workhouse fare; and her wage, when she was twenty, had reached the amount of five shillings a week, but that was because she was an expert cutter. The reason why she had been asked to deliver a dress to a place beyond Brockdale was that on one Sunday in a month she visited her grandmother in Jarrow and at this particular time more than half the staff were down with dysentery, they called it 'the looseness'.

The delivery of the gown was overdue and the manageress took the opportunity of making use of the cutter. She did not tell her, because she did not know, that she would have to walk three miles from her grandmother's house to the mill.

When she arrived Cissie offered the small white-faced, peaky-looking girl some refreshment and they had started talking. Jimmy had sat to the side and listened, and like his father before him, he was filled with compassion, and he had driven Miss Ada Ransome, not only back to her grannie's, but all the way to Newcastle. And every Sunday during the next three months he had gone into Newcastle and brought her to the mill, which Ada likened to heaven.

And now she was going into Newcastle with Cissie to choose material, not black or brown, or grey or fawn, but as Cissie had just described, something in a red, a soft red. She said to her, 'A crushed strawberry, that would suit you, Cissie. A crushed strawberry in a taffeta, perhaps with a sprig on it.'

Cissie, the reins in her hands, a smile on her face, glanced at Ada and, her lips pursed tight, she moved her head in small nods before saying, 'Yes, Ada, crushed strawberry, taffeta with a sprig on it.'

The family were mystified at the change in their Cissie. Sarah and Charlotte hailed it with laughter and sold her two hats and two bonnets . . . cost price of course. Bella hailed the change with sulky envy. Mary was a little shocked, William puzzled, Joe amused, and Annie didn't know what to make of . . . their Cissie – as a newlywed she was full of decorum – only Jimmy said nothing and waited and understood.

She did not wear the crushed strawberry with the sprig on it on the day she went on the special errand into town, for although it was spring and the sun was shining it was still rather chilly; but she wore the soft moss-green corded velvet suit with the short, tight jacket and a wide skirt that Ada had just finished for her, and over her shoulders a short sealskin cape; on her feet, soft brown leather boots, and, almost matching the colour of her hair, a hat with a sheen on it like that on a chestnut horse.

William and Joe gazed up at her from the yard, and Joe, still merry, said, 'By! our Cissie, you'll have the dogs after you going into Newcastle like that.' William said nothing, but he thought, What's come over her?

She smiled warmly at this particular brother: had she not him to thank for her rejuvenation? 'Gee-up there!' The sprightly cob pulling the neat trap trotted out of the yard, and Joe and William followed it to the gate and watched it along the road, after which they looked at each other, grinned, gave a little laugh, then shook their heads . . .

It was not the first time Cissie had been to the offices of Weir and Dixon. One day in '44 she had received a letter that had been sent by railway post, which was exciting in itself. When she opened it she found it was from the solicitors stating that they would be grateful for directions regarding her money, which was accumulating. Did she desire them to invest it for her?

She was thankful to God that Matthew was in Newcastle that day. She didn't answer the letter, but when she next took the girls into the city to do some shopping she left them and made her way to the offices of Weir and Dixon, and there she met Mr Weir in person and she asked him if he would be good enough to do what he thought best with the money, also to continue to let the house should it fall vacant. Finally, she had told him quietly but firmly not to communicate with her again no matter what the situation. If she wanted to give him any further instructions she would call.

Mr Weir had undoubtedly been surprised at the calm poise of his mysterious client; for he had been given to understand from private sources that the person was of low mentality, being little more than a gypsy, and had once lived wild.

Now, nine years later, she was sitting in exactly the same seat looking across the desk at the heavily jowled man who seemed to her to have grown very old in the intervening time.

Mr Weir, on his part gazing at his client, imagined that time had stood still, for she did not look a day older than when he had seen her last; in fact he could say that she almost looked younger, and she in her thirty-seventh year. She was a slightly disturbing person, he found, with her dress so gay, and he understood that her husband had been dead just over a year. Women were strange creatures, and this one before him very strange, but charming nevertheless . . . Ah, yes. Although she did not speak like a lady, her voice having a strong Northern inflection, he noted that she made use of words, and in their right context. She must, he thought, have had some form of education. And now, after all these years, seventeen years to be exact, she wished to view her property. He could not believe that she had never seen it. Surely, he would have imagined, she had gone on the quiet and looked at the house; but no, she assured him, she had never seen it.

This was a very strange affair, a very strange affair indeed. Here she was, a person of the common people, the widow of a miller who had left her quite warm, so she indicated, besides which she had been the recipient of a thousand pounds a year for the past seventeen years; and this money, under his careful supervision, had trebled itself. What was more, she owned the property that was bringing in a hundred a year, or had been up till three months before. She was a rich woman, and he told her so.

'Your estate is considerable, Mrs Turnbull,' he said. And to this she inclined her head, saying, 'That is good to know for . . . for if I like the house I may . . .' She hesitated; she was about to say 'live there', but the correct term was 'take up residence there', and on an inward laugh she said just that.

'Indeed!'

'Yes.'

'We have a client interested in it, but . . . but he hasn't made up his mind yet.'

'Well, we'll wait and see what I think about it first.'

'Of course, Mrs Turnbull, of course.'

'How much did you say that my account stands at now?'

'Around thirty thousand, give or take a few hundred; the expenses have been borne, as arranged—' he paused – 'by the donor.'

She looked at him across the desk for a moment, then said quietly, 'I would like you, Mr Weir, if you would, to take a thousand pounds by way of recompense for the work you have done on my behalf.'

He slowly rose from his seat and, coming round the desk, he stood before her, his hands joined, and he stared down at her while moving his head slowly; then he said, 'Madam, you are most generous, indeed more than generous. And I am most grateful, most grateful.'

And Mr Weir meant what he said; he was a warm man himself and not in need of a thousand or two, but in all his years of service to the public no client of his had said, 'Here is a thousand to recompense you for your work.' They paid him his charges, which weren't low, and therefore felt he was getting his due. Her donor, whose affairs he had seen to since the day he had come to this office and asked him if he could find an establishment for him, had never, when on the two visits he had paid him during the last seventeen years, said, 'There is fifty guineas extra for your services.' The gentry weren't made that way. Few people, when he came to think about it, were made that way. Those who pulled themselves up by their bootlaces held on to their money even tighter than the middle classes or

384

the gentry; yet here was this woman, not a lady according to set standards, yet not entirely of the common people; he didn't know into which class to place her, nevertheless she was offering him a thousand pounds. Now, taking her hand, he pressed it warmly, saying, 'Madam, I'm always at your service with or without your gift. Nevertheless, I'll take it gratefully and thank you again most warmly.' He bowed low over her hand and for a moment she thought he was going to kiss it, and at this she firmly withdrew it.

She drove the trap through the press near the markets, up Newgate Street, along the Gallowgate; then, asking the way, she took the road to Denton. Her heart was beating as it had not done for years, bumping in hard thuds against her rib cage. She knew what she was going to see. The house would be low and white, he had said black and white, but she knew it would appear all white when the sun shone on it, and the sun was shining sharply bright today.

And then she saw it. She had turned off the main road and gone down a tree-shaded grass track at the far end of which were two wooden gates. These were open and she drove straight through. A man was working in a bed to the side of the drive and she stopped and said, 'I have come to see the house, I have the key'; and he touched his forelock and replied, 'Aye, Ma'am.' She drove on along the short drive and around the bend, and there it was. It *was* black and white, the black standing out more than the white. It had deep-latticed windows and a black oak door with a brass knocker and knob, and in the ordinary way she would have thrilled to it and said it was a lovely house, homely looking, inviting. But it wasn't the house she saw in her dreams.

Her heart had stopped its thumping. She got down from the trap, tied the cob to a horse post on the drive, and inserting a key in the lock she entered the house, Clive's house, her house.

385

The hall was quite large for the size of the house; it had a fireplace at one end and was half panelled and the low ceiling was beamed, and the stairs went up from the middle of it. The drawing room was long and narrow and had a small conservatory leading off. There was a breakfast room and a dining room, and a nice kitchen, but only one third the size of the mill kitchen. She walked slowly up the stairs. The landing was as large as a room. There were four bedrooms each with a dressing room. Then up another flight of stairs, and there were four attic bedrooms. She descended to the landing again and stood looking down the stairs into the hall . . .

This is the house she should have been living in for the past seventeen years; this is the house in which she should have brought up her son; she could see him now, standing in the hall looking up at her as he had looked on the day she had met him on the road five years ago, in the spring.

She had felt a sense of uneasiness about that time. She wanted to get out and roam but Matthew didn't like her taking walks; he always suspected her of making her way to the fell and from the fell looking towards the wall that surrounded the Hall. When, in the early days, the girls had wanted to go back to see the dwelling place he had been firm and said no, hadn't they seen enough of the dwelling place? But on this spring day when he had business in Newcastle and had taken Victoria with him, to give her the chance to visit Sarah and Charlotte he had said, but mainly to have Victoria to himself on the drive, she had taken the trap, saying to William she was going into Shields for some odds and ends of silks and a book for Matthew's birthday. She had gone into Shields, but by way of the road that passed the North Lodge; and when she came to the slope she had stopped and, leaving the trap, had walked slowly up to the dwelling place, or what was left of it. The roof had fallen in because the wooden supports had been ripped away; the floor of the storeroom had been ripped up too. The walls were still standing, and there was the fireplace around which they had huddled for years. And as she stood and stared she was amazed that they had managed to exist in this shanty; more amazed still that her son had been born here.

Saddened, she went down the slope to the trap again. It was when she rounded the bend towards the South Lodge that she noticed two horsemen coming towards her. The road was narrow and she saw the younger rider draw his horse in and follow behind the older one. Then she was abreast of them. She was oblivious to her heart racing because she thought it had stopped; time stood still while her eyes looked into those of Lord Fischel. She wasn't aware that she had drawn the trap to a standstill, but she was aware that he was raising his hat to her, and that the younger man behind him had followed suit. Her eyes rested on the younger man, the youth. He had dark hair, a prominent nose, a wide mouth, and brown eyes. It was only when she urged the horse forward again that she realised she had stopped.

When she reached the turnpike she found her face was wet, and she was sitting with the reins slack in her hand; and the horse had stopped, not knowing which of the four strange roads to take . . .

She walked down the stairs now and into the drawing room and, standing in the middle of it, she looked about her as she thought, I'll have a rose-coloured carpet in here and pale green walls and soft gold curtains.

She had made up her mind.

The following day she took Sarah and Charlotte to see the house and asked them how they would like to live there, and they exclaimed, 'Oh, our Cissie, you can't mean it!' And when she said she did, adding, 'But of course, that's until you marry,' they had both shaken their heads.

Charlotte at twenty-six was well past the marrying age;

moreover, she was very plain. Sarah at twenty-seven was comely, but she had given her heart to a young man when she was twenty-two, and three months before the marriage he had died of the cholera. So they were both resigned, and happily so, to spinsterhood, and the thought of living with Cissie again delighted them.

Later, she brought together the boys, as she still thought of them, and when she told them her plans they were silent, Joe because he suddenly realised how much he would miss her being near, William because he was feeling unnecessary guilt, and Jimmy because he had guessed that their Cissie was up to something. And then she had said that William was to come and live at the mill and Joe was to take William's house, also that she was willing the mill, its freehold and business over to them jointly. This left Jimmy where he was and in a much poorer position; so, to level things out, she was passing on to Jimmy the Newcastle property, and at this Jimmy had exclaimed, 'Oh no! No, Cissie.' And she had silenced him.

The other property that Matthew had accumulated she was dividing among Mary, Bella, and Annie, but Bella's share, she had added with a tight grin, would be doled out to her weekly. And the tension was broken by their laughing at this.

Incoherent and shy for once, they had pressed around her and kissed her; and Jimmy, the last to leave, had taken her hand and, his voice husky and his eyes misted, he had said, 'Oh, our Cissie! Our Cissie. God surely made you when he made little apples.'

The deep, sincere, and loving compliment brought her to tears, and she pushed at him, saying, 'Get yourself away home and ask Ada would she like a new house built away from the shop.' And at this he lifted his head and gaped at her and said, 'What!' Then grinning he added, 'Now don't you put any ideas into her head; we're all right where we are.'

As he was about to go out of the door she called to him softly, and when he came back she said, 'You could, you know, Jimmy, build a nice little place, because that property in Newcastle has trebled over the years. It's in the best business part. It's worth nigh on ten thousand pounds.'

She smiled as he slowly brought his hand up to his mouth and pressed it hard, and again he said, 'Oh, our Cissie.'

Everything was settled. She was about to start a new life, and she was free and strangely excited . . . like a girl about to be married.

She had driven in the gig from 'the house' to the city. She was to meet Annie at the 'Band Box', do some shopping with her, then bring her back to the house to tea.

She found the city more than unusually crowded that day, and at the top of the Groat Market she decided to make a detour to Westgate Road and enter Collingwood Street from there. But when she turned into a side street, which was mostly taken up with large offices, she found a number of carriages drawn up to the kerb, leaving very little room for her passage. And when, about half-way down the street, she saw coming towards her at a good pace a coach and four, she hastily drew her horse into a space between what was obviously a hired coach and one which was more obviously still a private carriage.

At the moment the coach and four was galloping past her there emerged from the doorway opposite the private coach two gentlemen. One was fair and one was dark. The fair man crossing the pavement first glanced to the left of him and to a lady dressed in rose taffeta and wearing a hat of unusual shape and colour, it being made of a soft, gauzy, green material, which contrasted strongly with her brown hair.

Cissie, her lower jaw hanging slightly, stared over the distance at the fair man, as he did at her, and her eyes, still seeming to hold his, took in the figure of the young man at his side. They were both of a like height but the contrast in their colouring was sharp. A second before she jerked on the reins she let her gaze fall fully on the younger man, and it was like looking into her own eyes. She brought the horse sharply round and into the clearway again.

He was home! Well, hadn't she guessed he would come home when his father died? It was ten days since she read in the paper of Lord Fischel's death, and four days ago she had been tempted to go to the funeral, at least to view it from a distance because she felt a peculiar sorrow at his passing – he, even more than his son, seemed to have guided her life – but it was the fear of this very encounter that had dissuaded her.

Her life was running smoothly now, without pain . . . and without pleasure, except for the homely pleasure of the girls' company and the visits from the rest of the family. But she had known for a long time that there was an excitement brewing in her on which she must batten hard down. She kept telling herself that she was a mature woman, not a girl any longer; yet at times she had the fantastic idea that she was but sixteen and life was before her.

When she said to herself, 'He looks so much older,' she came back harshly with the reply, 'He would, wouldn't he?' It was eighteen years since she last saw him, but he looked more than eighteen years older. He looked a man well in his forties, although he was still thin, as thin as when she had first seen him.

She felt slightly sick, and when she reached the shop the girls were concerned for her and made her sniff some smelling salts and drink heavily sugared tea, after which she felt bound to assure them she felt a lot better.

It was the next afternoon that Ellen, the younger of the two maids that she kept, came scampering down to the bottom of the garden where she was with Ronson, the gardener, discussing the making of a new flower bed.

'Madam,' gasped the girl, 'it's a gentleman. He asked to see you. I . . . I put him in the drawing room.'

The reason for Ellen's excitement was that she had been in service in this house for nearly three months and she hadn't answered the door to one visitor, except the family, until just then. And now, what a visitor! 'Is your mistress at home?' he had enquired in the voice of a gentleman. And she knew how gentlemen should speak; she had started in service in a big house, and when she had said, 'Yes, Sir,' he had replied, 'Will you tell her that Lord Fischel would be obliged if she would see him.'

Cissie did not need to be told the name of the caller. She couldn't say that she had been waiting for him, nor would she admit that she had been hoping he would come. She could only think to herself in deep agitation, Oh God, let me pass myself when I meet him. If she had been educated in her early days instead of her twenties her thoughts would have suggested, Let me conduct myself with decorum.

She smoothed back her hair, straightened the top layer of her skirt, and wished in an aside that she had put on another petticoat and a more sober looking dress – but now she owned no sober looking dresses.

Although the day was warm she shivered as she entered the house. She paused a moment as she crossed the hall; then gripping the glass knob of the drawing-room door tightly she turned it and entered the room.

He was standing facing the door, his back to the window as if waiting for her, and having closed the door she stood still and they looked at each other down the length of the room.

When he walked towards her she moved. Her step slow, she went to meet him. He did not take her hand or give her any formal greeting. What he said was, 'It has been a long time.'

She could not answer him, her voice would not obey her. He was handsome in a cold way for his eyes were hard, yet at the same time sad; but his voice was as she remembered it, beautiful-sounding to her ears.

'You have not changed at all.'

'Not in eighteen years?' She made her lips smile. 'Won't you sit down?'

With a gesture of his hand he indicated that she should be seated first, then lifting the long tails of his black coat he sat down; and again they looked at each other in silence, until he said, 'And so you came here after all.'

'Yes, after all.' Her lips drooped slightly.

'I'm sorry the mill . . . your husband died. When did you lose him?'

'On Christmas Day of '51.' She wondered how he had come to know of Matthew's death; likely Mr Weir had told him.

'It is a pity; he was still a young man. I . . .' he bent slightly towards her now and there came a more personal note into his voice, 'I hope you were happy.'

There was a pause before she lifted her gaze to his again and said, 'Yes, I was happy.'

'Have you a family?'

'I had one daughter; she died of the typhoid when she was eleven.'

'Oh, I am sorry, I am very sorry.'

And now she in her turn said, 'I was very sorry to hear of His Lordship's death. Had he been ill long?'

'Yes, for some months. When I was informed of this I came straightaway . . . I live in Spain now.'

'In Spain?' She inclined her head. 'It is a very far country.'

'Yes, very far; but very beautiful.'

She dared to ask, 'Are you returning there?'

'Yes, I am due to sail in ten days' time.'

'Oh.' Her body felt heavy as if a weight had been tied around her middle. She wanted to ask him if he was returning to his family, to his wife and family, but she couldn't. She could not have asked this question if he had still been Mr Clive, and so much less could she take the liberty of probing with . . . Lord Fischel. She said quietly,

'Can I offer you some refreshment, a little tea?'

'That would be very nice, thank you.'

She rose and rang the bell, and when Ellen appeared she gave her the order. And he watched her the while, hardly believing that this was the same girl he had last seen incongruously sitting on the couch in the Hall drawing room dressed in heavy boots and common coarse clothes; the girl whose hands he had kissed and felt the roughness of the skin against his lips; the girl whom, against all reason, he had loved then, and whose face had continued to haunt him for years. He had lost count of the mistresses he had had since he had left this country, he only remembered that their dismissal had been preceded by bouts of black depression filled with the revived memory of this girl . . . and Isabelle, both linked and twisted, their presence shrouded like a thick vapour, penetrating his brain and thrusting him back into those three crucial months of his life that had set the pattern for his future.

He had always thought that if she were dressed correctly she would appear like a lady, and this she was proving. Her speech too was different, not refined to insipidness, not refined at all, he would say, but rounded and full of character, as was her face. And how beautiful her face. She said she had been happy with the miller?

In another silence he glanced round the room, then remarked, 'It is very tasteful'; and she inclined her head towards him and said, 'Thank you.'

'Did you put it into the hands of a designer?'

'No' – she raised her brows slightly – 'it is as I wanted it myself.'

The door opened and the two maids entered very flustered, one carrying a silver tea-tray, the other a tiered cake stand.

He watched her pouring tea from a silver pot and all the while he marvelled.

The conversation continued to be stilted during the

drinking of the tea, but when he put his cup down for the last time he drew in a long breath and, leaning against the back of the chair, slowly relaxed his body; then he startled her with his next words. 'What do you think of your son?' he asked.

One could have counted ten full seconds while she stared at him, and then she answered, 'He's a fine looking young man.'

'So think I.' For the first time his face fell into a wide smile. 'And what is more he has grown into a nice person. But I can take no credit for that as I have seen little of him over the years.' He paused here before ending, 'My father did a good job on him.'

She nodded her head twice before she said, 'Yes, I am sure he did.'

Now he was leaning towards her, one forearm on his knee, his voice low. 'Have you ever regretted your generosity?' And to this she answered simply, 'Yes, many times.'

He nodded slowly, then looked down at the floor before saying, 'It couldn't have been otherwise; yet I am not sorry you let him go, for he is fitted to the place as I never was. He will look after it as I never would. You know' – he raised his eyes to hers and smiled gently at her – 'he has your nature, warm-hearted and kindly.'

A flush swept over her body. She lowered her eyes and remained silent as he went on, 'He loves the Hall, the land. He will bring up his family there. Oh' – he gave his head a little jerk – 'you would not know. He is going to be married.'

'Married?' Her eyes were wide as she stared at him, and she experienced a new pain.

'Yes, to what you would call a childhood sweetheart, the granddaughter of my father's friend, David Bellingham. Elizabeth Rymall's her name, the Honourable Miss Elizabeth Rymall.' His lips moved up into a crooked smile. 'It's not going to take place for a year yet. I have promised to return for the wedding. In the meantime he will be getting the Hall ready.'

She was still staring at him unblinking while she told herself not to ask the question; yet she had no power to withhold it. 'Does he know about me?' she said.

His answer seemed long in coming; and then it was quiet. 'Yes, he knows about you.'

She was looking past him into a void now. Her son had known about her and never made any approach towards her.

'I told him after our recent encounter.'

'Oh.' Her eyes came back to his face. 'Only . . . only then?' Her voice faded away on the then, and he repeated, 'Only then.'

'May . . . may I ask what his reaction was?'

'He was very favourably impressed.' He did not add, 'He was also startled and disturbed.' But he continued, 'He recalled seeing you some years ago when he was a boy on holiday. He had been under the impression that his mother had died when he was a child and, thinking the subject was painful to my father, did not open it until sometime last year when he overheard two of the servants talking. It was from this conversation that he gauged that his mother was alive and living in the vicinity. He did not know exactly where, and after some consideration he put the question to my father, and the answer my father gave him was that he was not at liberty to disclose your whereabouts.' He paused here and smiled gently before going on. 'He did ask him what kind of a person you were, and part of my father's answer to this was that you were a very worthy woman. Knowing my father and his views of the female sex, I consider that high praise indeed.'

She took no notice of his compliment, or a cue from the lightness with which he was touching this delicate subject now. The ache was filling her body again, an ache that she knew could never really be eased, for it had its beginnings in a small hand slapping out at her, and so when he asked softly, 'Would you like to meet him?' she rose to her feet, saying quickly, 'No, no!' while at the same time her need shouted loud within her, 'Don't be a fool. Just once.'

'I think you're wise.' He was standing now within an arm's length of her, and he put out his hands and caught hers and felt their trembling pass through his body; and, his voice very low, he said, 'You were always wise, Cecilia.'

Slowly he raised her hands, his lips touched her knuckles lightly, then he relinquished them and, adopting his formal manner again, he said, 'I have taken up a great deal of your time.'

As always when she was deeply disturbed she could not speak. She turned from him and led the way out of the room, across the hall, and to the front door. He bowed to her. 'Goodbye,' he said; 'it's been a great pleasure meeting you again.'

Still she could not speak. It was as on that day when his father had escorted her to the door of the Hall and her emotions had kept her dumb.

He walked down the two steps and across the gravel drive to where the coachman held open the door for him. She dimly recognised the coachman; it was the one who had called for her the day she took the child back.

After the coach had disappeared round the bend of the drive she still stood at the door. She felt slightly numb now, not herself.

As she walked back across the hall, a great sadness weighing her down, she was attacked by a feeling of guilt akin to horror as she thought, Oh, how awful! How could I have forgotten? I never thanked him for the house or the money.

* * *

She told the girls about the visitor when they came home that evening, because if she hadn't Ellen would have kept dropping hints like bricks. They were equally as impressed as the servants were. Lord Fischel calling on their Cissie! Oh, they knew who Lord Fischel was, all right; they had been brought up with the scandal although they hadn't looked on it as a scandal, more as an honour in being connected with the Hall in any way. Yet they knew it hadn't got to be talked about because Matthew didn't like it. They also knew that it was the reason why Matthew kept such a tight rein on their Cissie, hardly letting her out of his sight. They thought at first that she didn't mind the restriction, but as they grew older in years and wisdom they sensed that she did . . . And now Mr Clive, who was the father of Richard, and they remembered Richard very well, had called on their Cissie, and he was no longer to be thought of as Mr Clive but as Lord Fischel. Yet in Sarah's mind a dim picture was trying to force itself to the surface, it had to do with the first time she had seen their Cissie's distinguished visitor. She clamped hard down on it; that incident belonged to the far, far past, and the past was best forgotten. Instead, she thought, when this got around the neighbourhood the ladies would forget that Mrs Turnbull's sisters ran a hat shop, and the carriages would be queuing up on them. She voiced this, and Charlotte, laughing, agreed.

Cissie made herself smile tolerantly at them while warning them not to mention anything to the others, and at this they exclaimed highly, 'Not even our Jimmy?' And she replied firmly, 'Not even our Jimmy.' It was His Lordship's first and last visit, so would they forget about it, please.

She went early to bed but not to sleep; it was almost five in the morning when she dozed off, and when the girls came in to say goodbye and reminded her they were all to meet in Newcastle and go to the theatre that night she asked why should she forget? She'd be there.

It was around twelve o'clock when the carriage drew up on the drive and one of the coachmen brought from its interior a large ornamental basket of peaches and another filled with roses, and a letter from His Lordship.

The dull day suddenly became bright; her body lost its weight. She opened the letter and once again read her name written by his hand: 'Dear Cecilia, I will be in the city tomorrow on business; could you tolerate another visit from me? I remain always, your obedient servant, Clive Fischel.' That was all.

She almost ran to the desk, took up a pen and a sheet of notepaper, then, pen poised, she stopped. How should she address him? Certainly not 'Dear Clive,' although he had called her Dear Cecilia, and she couldn't say 'Your Lordship'. The men were waiting. She wrote in a round copperplate handwriting, 'I shall be pleased to see you any time you care to call, Cecilia.' She put the letter into an envelope; and now she could write his name, Lord Fischel, Houghton Hall.

When she handed the letter to Bowmer he stared at her as if unable to believe his eyes, for he was remembering back.

'Kindly give this to His Lordship,' she said; and he replied, 'Yes, Ma'am.'

He had not said at which hour he would be coming, and when he arrived at one o'clock he apologised immediately for omitting to state a time and hoped he hadn't kept her from any other appointment. And she assured him he hadn't and asked him if he would care for a glass of wine.

It was all very formal, very polite. He sat in a chair at the side of the drawing-room window and she some distance away. He remarked that the garden was looking exceedingly pretty; he also, after observing a quantity of books about the room, asked if she enjoyed reading.

To which she answered, 'Very much.'

Who were her favourite authors?

Oh, she liked the Barrett-Brownings, and Shelley, and the writings of the sisters Brontë.

He nodded his approval but again remained silent. And in the silence he asked himself the question that had never left his mind since he had entered this room two days before. Could he do it? Should he do it? He wanted to, oh yes, he wanted to, even more so now than he had done years ago. But the same question remained now, as then; was it wise? Seven more days and he'd be gone. The first meeting could have been conclusive. He had paid her his respects, as was due to the mother of his son. He had seen to her comfort, and, although she hadn't availed herself of it until a few months before, that wasn't his fault. It had been there and waiting, and Weir informed him that his allowance to her had now grown into a very comfortable sum, and added to this there would be the miller's portion. She was happily ensconced in this house with her sisters, so why had he to dive into the past in a wild aim at unravelling the threads? What would the unravelling lead to? Would they accept her as his wife?

He breathed deeply, then gave himself the answer: Some, mostly the wrong sort, and she would be hurt. She would be cut into little pieces by the ladies' tongues and she wouldn't be able to retaliate; she wasn't that kind of woman, she would suffer in silence. But what was he thinking of? He wouldn't be staying in England, he had no intention of living in England again. He had adopted Spain, and Spain him; he had a house and friends there, and most of his friends were Spanish. With regard to the English ones, they could take her or leave her. But why should they not take her and be entranced by her, as he was? The only difference between her and them was the inflection in her voice, and once away from those of like inflection it would change. But to hell! What did her voice matter, what was he carping about? Her voice was warm and good to his ears; her presence was stirring, exciting, consuming him, making him weak. It was all he could do now not to rise from his chair and fling himself before her and bury his face in her breasts . . . But it was madness. Apart from everything else there were the conventions to be considered; his father had been dead only a matter of days. The whole thing was preposterous.

'Have you got a permanent home in Spain?'

Her unnecessary use of the word 'got' impinged on his mind, but he thrust it roughly aside and replied, 'Yes, I have a rather charming house there.'

She stared at him and a little smile crept over her lips as she asked quietly, 'Is it a long house, low, all white, quite dazzling when the sun shines on it?'

He raised his brows. 'Yes. Yes, that is a very good description. It is quite dazzling when the sun shines on it; the light is reflected from a rock face to the side of it. People have remarked about this. How strange. Have you seen a picture of such a house?'

She moved her head slowly. The smile had spread from her lips to her eyes; it had lifted her cheeks upwards and she said, almost in a whisper, 'Yes. Yes, I have seen a picture of a house like that.'

'It is a general type of house in that vicinity, but mine is rather unique in that it is built on a plateau on the hillside and has some magnificent views.'

She rose to her feet, saying, 'May I fill your glass again?'

'Thank you, it is a very good Madeira.'

She took his glass to the sideboard and from there she now dared to ask, 'Your family . . . you left your family there?'

He stared towards her straight back. He could make out the outline of her figure under her clothes. She wasn't indulging in the hideous array of skirts that were at present in vogue. She wanted to know about his family. It was a probing question. It pleased him.

A quirk came to his lips and stretched when his silence turned her sharply about and, her face unsmiling, she held his gaze. But he didn't give her the answer until she handed him the wine, and then he said, 'Unfortunately, I have no family except that which is in the Hall.'

He was grateful now for the fact that he had never housed his mistresses in the villa. The cautious, even puritanical facet of one side of the Fischel nature, he supposed, had been answerable for this discretion; and although many a time it had irked him with its inconvenience, he had adhered to it with a strictness he considered his only remaining virtue.

When she resumed her seat she asked, 'Have you been left the sea long?'

'During these past six years. Since then I have taken up painting again. I had a tendency towards it in my youth.' And what a tendency. But for raping her he would today have been an artist, a real artist, he was sure of that; but the inherent touch was developing.

And so they talked, he about the life in Spain and she, at his enquiry, of what had happened to each member of her family. And when he took his leave he again kissed her fingers and asked if he would be permitted to enjoy her company in two days' time. And as she granted his wish with an incline of her head, she thought, The day after tomorrow, and four days after that he will be gone.

She was looking for something for Jimmy's birthday and had decided on a good pipe in a case and perhaps a few special cigars. Jimmy, she knew, had never smoked a cigar, but he would be tickled by the gift and she could imagine him amusing the others by striking a pose while puffing at the symbol of the gentry.

Ransome's was the place to go to for cigars. She went

into the long male-scented shop where there were a few customers present, all men. The assistant came and offered her a chair, and when she told him what she required he brought her a number of cases holding pipes, also a selection of cigars. She chose the pipe by the look of it, but the cigars she left to his experience.

He was parcelling her purchases for her when a door opened at the far end of the room. She had heard about the special room where the gentlemen could take their ease while testing snuff. She looked towards the door. A small man was holding it wide, one arm extended, his body slightly bowed, and past him walked Clive and her son.

She remained seated as she looked down the room. Her face was straight and pale. She saw Clive glance at his son, at their son, who was looking at her with an expression in his eyes she couldn't translate.

The assistant was speaking to her and she turned to him. When she next looked down the room it was empty.

She was trembling as she left the shop, and her trembling increased when she saw them confronting her on the pavement.

'Good-day.' Clive raised his hat to her, and she answered in a whisper, 'Good-day,' all the while keeping her eyes tight on his.

'May I ask if you have a little time to spare?'

'My time is my own.' Her voice was still a whisper.

'Would it be possible for us to return to your home? The coach is just at the end of the street.'

She paused for some seconds. Her horse and trap were stabled but she could come back for them later. 'Very well,' she said.

When he took her elbow and guided her through the crowd on the pavement she didn't turn to see if her son was following; not until she was ushered into the carriage and he took his seat to the side of her was she sure that he was coming with them. She was glad of one thing: he wasn't sitting opposite her, for she would have hated to have sat all through the journey with her head bowed. She could hardly bear to look at Clive, for his face now was cold and stiff and his voice had a similar ring to it as he spoke his only words during the journey: 'We'll leave the talking until we get within doors.'

No space of time in her previous life, or in the years to come, ever appeared as long as that ride, nor was she ever again to feel more aware of a presence as that of her son sitting stiffly to her side, no part of them touching.

Clive handed her down from the carriage and she led the way into the house. In the hall she stopped for a moment, slipped the cape from her shoulders, and took off her hat and gloves while Ellen relieved the visitors of their hats and gloves. Then they were in the drawing room, and she said with forced calmness, 'Please be seated.'

But neither took the proffered seats. Clive stood straight and stiff, and his whole attitude, even his voice, was a replica of his father's as he said, 'There should be no need for embarrassment, you both know your relationship. Richard, this lady is your mother. Cecilia, your son . . .'

She was back in the dwelling place. The child was standing in the corner to the side of the fireplace. She was saying coaxingly to him, 'Come on, Richard. Come on, that's a good boy, eat your porridge.' She was putting her hand out towards him and his came out towards her, but to slap at her. 'Don't want porridge. I don't like you.' Yes, he had said that to her. 'I don't like you.' She had never admitted the words before; in all the memory she had of him she had blocked that one sentence out of her mind, 'I don't like you . . .'

But now she was looking into these same eyes, and but for the veneer and education that was imprinted on him she felt he was saying these words again, looking at this still strange woman and thinking, I don't like her. 'Well?' Again it was the voice of the old lord speaking, and the

young man, after glancing at his father, bowed towards
Cissie and said, 'I am glad at last to make your
acquaintance . . . Ma'am.'

The words were stiff, cold, and empty-sounding. But
what could she expect? She was a stranger to him. This
must be the most trying moment of his life, the most
embarrassing, as it was the most painful for her. Nothing
she had experienced before was as painful as this.

But she must carry it off . . . pass herself, and with
decorum; time enough later, all the time in the world, all
the rest of her life, for tears. She said with just a slight
tremor in her voice, 'I am aware that this must be very
embarrassing for you. I . . . I would like you to understand right away that I'm not aiming to . . .' She stopped
and searched for words, then went on . . . 'to claim an
acquaintanceship with you at this late stage. It . . . it is not
with my wish that you are here now, although . . .' Again
she paused and stopped herself from adding, 'Oh, but I'm
glad to see you.' Instead she said, 'You are welcome and
will be any time, but . . . but you need not trouble yourself that I will take advantage of this encounter.'

Her son's face was red, his whole attitude appeared
slightly shamefaced and she couldn't bear it; for this
proved to her what she had known all along, that he hadn't
wanted to meet her. His future was set, the pattern of his
life was set, he didn't want any unknown mother, and a
woman of the people besides, intruding on it, and causing
ripples of scandal in the society in which he moved.

Clive had said he was a nice person, and she believed
this, but she also knew he was human, and that she was
too; and that the longing of her arms to go out and around
him was almost unbearable, and in case the desire became
uncontrollable and she might put her hand out just to
touch him, she said on a lighter tone, 'Will you excuse me
a moment? I will order some coffee.'

She had not asked them if they would like coffee, and

Clive did not prevent her from leaving the room, and once the door had closed on her he turned on his son, his face dark with anger, and said under his breath, 'You are acting like a boor. She is no-one to be scorned.'

'I am not scorning her, Father, but . . . but she is a stranger to me.' The tone was stiff, slightly haughty.

'Then she won't be a stranger to you much longer. I have news for you; I intend to marry her.'

The young man's mouth dropped open, his brown eyes stretched wide. He looked in this moment like a child who had received a slap across the face for no apparent reason, and he whispered, 'Marry her?'

'That is what I said, marry her.'

He moved his head slowly from side to side before asking, 'You . . . you will be taking up residence in the Hall then?'

His father gave a short, hard laugh now, then said, 'Don't let that worry you, I'm not going back on my word. The Hall and all it stands for are yours, and welcome. You are my heir, it is your rightful place. You will be relieved to know that I am taking her back to Spain with me.' The Fischel in him had settled the matter, even before he knew what her answer would be. He said harshly, 'The look of relief on your face doesn't do you any credit.'

'I am sorry, Father.'

'It would please me if you could force yourself to give her some sign of affection before you leave.'

The young man again moved his head slowly, then nipped on his lower lip before he said, 'I cannot pretend what I don't feel. I . . . I am not made that way, and' – his look was direct now, his voice steady – 'it is not my fault that I have a distaste for subterfuge.'

Clive stared at his son. The irony of it, that he should have a distaste for subterfuge. He took after her in that way for she couldn't pretend either. The irony of it indeed.

When the door opened and she entered the room Clive turned to her and, his tone light now, he said, 'I was just saying to Richard that this is the house in which he should have been brought up, and but for your unselfishness and thought for his future he would have been. Perhaps he would have profited more under your care.'

She looked at her son fully now, and as if she were suddenly tired of keeping up a front, she dropped into the idiom of the family as she said, 'His Lordship made a better job of you than I would have done; that's plain to be seen. I only had you for a very short time, just over five months. Apart from giving you birth, you belonged to him. Even before you were born you were his, because he'd made up his mind to have you.'

She was staring into her son's eyes when he stepped slowly forward and, taking her hand, bowed over it and said, 'I thank you, Ma'am, for your courtesy and understanding.'

To this she answered flatly, but with a break in her voice, 'As long as you're happy that's all I ask, all I've ever asked.' Then she withdrew her hand from his and turned gratefully to the door where Ellen was entering with the tray of coffee . . .

Ten minutes later they were in the hall and she was bidding them goodbye; and when her son, again taking her hand, carried it to his lips, it meant nothing. The contact gave her no warmth, no thrill. For her the boy was back in the corner standing near the fireplace, in fact he had never left it, his hand out to her, his voice piping, 'I don't like you.'

She did not watch the carriage go down the drive, but running swiftly upstairs she threw herself on the bed and, burying her face in the pillow, wept until her body seemed awash with her tears. She wept until Mary and Ellen tapped on the door, then came into the room. She wept so that Ellen put her arms around her and rocked and patted

407

her as if she were a child, saying, 'There, Ma'am. There, Ma'am.'

And it was many weeks later that she burst out laughing when she recalled, for no apparent reason, Ellen's voice saying as she soothed her, 'To hell and damnation with all lords!'

3

It was Jimmy's birthday, the first one she had missed seeing him, but she felt she couldn't drive all the way over to the mill. The weeping of the day before had drained her; moreover, her eyes were swollen and it would be evident to anyone who saw her that she had been crying, and for some long time.

The night before, the girls had been indignant that she had been brought to this state, yet they couldn't get anything out of her. It was Ellen and Mary who informed them that it had all happened after His Lordship had left, together with the young man. And this explanation told them all Cissie had withheld.

It being Saturday, and a busy day, Sarah still found time to send word to Jimmy that their Cissie wasn't well and if he had time that night would he look over and perhaps bring Joe and William with him. She wanted cheering up.

The girls didn't close the shop until ten, yet it was nearly always eleven when they arrived home, and they came by hired coach on Friday and Saturday nights. But it was around eight o'clock, and the twilight deepening, when Cissie heard the coach on the drive and thought, That's one of them. They had come back early because they were worried over her.

She rose from the couch opposite the glowing fire, for the nights were beginning to get chilly, and went slowly down the room and into the hall, there to see Mary admitting a visitor.

Clive came straight towards her, and he spoke immediately as if he had been running, not driven in a carriage. 'I'm late; I intended returning last evening but was prevented, and I have been very busy today seeing to various things. We're sailing on Monday late, midnight . . . will we go in?' He motioned towards the drawing-room door, and, as if coming awake, she drew in a long breath, then turned about. Once inside the room he checked her walk and, taking her by the shoulders, stared into her face. His eyes, roaming over each feature, noted her puffed lids, her trembling lips. He said, 'You've been hurt yet again. Every time we meet I inflict pain on you.'

She moved her head quickly in denial, then let it droop forward but made no answer.

'This time I want, I intend, to make up for all the pain, if that is possible . . . Cecilia, look at me. Cecilia . . . Will you marry me?'

Her head came upwards. Secretly, yet not so secretly, over the past few days she had hoped and prayed for him to say these very words while at the same time she knew the desire, and its result, were utterly preposterous. Now for a second she was completely overwhelmed by the sheer wonder of them, but only for a second before she thrust them from her and him too, as she said bitterly, 'As a sort of compensation, to make up for his rejection of me?'

'No! No!' He flung one arm wide. 'It was my intention to ask you from the first day I entered this house, but it goes back much, much further than that.' His voice dropped now and he reached out and took her stiff hand. 'The motive behind buying this house for you was not purely altruistic, for I planned to visit you. I think I told you, didn't I, that when I returned from the voyages I would call. I also planned something else.' He did not say truthfully, 'To make you my mistress,' for there are some truths better left unsaid, but added, 'Even then I hoped to marry you.'

And the greater part of this was true, for he had seen himself moulding her, educating her, making her fit to be the wife of a Fischel, even a first-mate Fischel as he was then.

She forced herself now to voice another thought that had been in her mind over the past few days, a thought that had attacked her hopes with the cutting knife of reality. She said quietly, 'I'd never be able to live up to your position. You'd become ashamed of me.'

Now he came close to her and caused her whole body to quiver as he took her face tenderly between his hands. 'I'd like to gamble all I've got on the fact that I'll be the envy of every man who meets you.'

Her lids drooped. 'I . . . I can't talk properly.'

'You talk from the heart always, and you use your words well. If your inflection troubles you I can guarantee that you'll lose it within three months. But it pleases me. Anyway, that is a trivial thing, of no importance. But there is a question of importance I would ask you.' He paused here before saying below his breath, 'Have you entirely forgiven me for the wrong I did you?'

She could smile now gently at him, and, her voice soft, she said, 'It's strange, but from the moment I held him in my arms I never looked upon it as a wrong, but more like a gift.'

'Oh, Cecilia!' His arms moved tenderly around her shoulders. She was against his breast for the third time in her life, and when his mouth touched hers the strength drained from her and she leaned heavily against him.

Then the gentleness was swept away under a passion that rocked them both and she felt as she had never felt from any touch or caress of Matthew's, she felt love flowing from her; yet her body remained full of it as if it were being fed from a great rushing river. She seemed to look back down the years to the source from where sprang this flood of feeling and saw that the spring had come into being when she had first fallen to the ground with him.

When it was over they both leaned against each other, and then, their eyes meeting, he laughed and it was the sailor laughing, the young man who had given her back her child laughing. Pulling her forward now almost at a run, he sat her on the couch and, fumbling in his pockets, he brought forth an envelope and a small red velvet box. Tapping the envelope, he said, 'Guess what this is?' And between laughter and tears she said, as she might have done to one of the boys, 'You're not buying me a boat now, are you?' And his head went back and he laughed gaily, saying, 'But that is an idea.' He now pulled open the envelope and drew out a single sheet of thin paper and, putting it into her hands, he said, 'It is the deed that is going to bond you to me for life, a special licence. We are to be married on Monday morning at ten o'clock at St Nicholas'. And this' – he now handed her the box – 'is the symbol of my whole heart on it.'

As she gazed at the ring, a cluster of diamonds and rubies, it was suddenly lost to her vision in the tears that stung her eyes and pressed out from her closed lids.

Holding her gently, he soothed her, and when she brought her head from his shoulder and asked tentatively, 'But . . . but what will they say, I mean with your . . . His Lordship so recently gone?' he answered as the sailor would have done. 'I do not give a damn what they say. In any case we won't hear them. But I know what he would have said. Do you know what he told Richard when the boy asked him about you? He told him that it was the greatest pity I hadn't run off with you in the first place.' He looked deeply into her eyes as he finished, 'Richard told me that last night, after we returned home . . . I think he would like to see you again before we sail.'

When her head dropped and she made no answer, he said on a lighter and teasing note, 'What do you intend to call me?'

'Call you?' She puckered her brow.

'You, Cecilia, as yet have never called me by my name; don't you think it's about time you started?'

Her lips went into a smile; her eyes looked at him softly. How often over the years had she said his name? No, not said it, thought it. And so now, for the first time since her delirium, of which she had no real memory except that which Matthew had brought to the fore, she said it aloud, softly, tenderly; and he enfolded her again, and kissed her lips and her eyes and her hair.

Perhaps it was their engrossment in each other that made them deaf to the sounds of lowered voices in the hall, but at last they penetrated to Cissie and, drawing herself from his embrace, she looked at him and whispered, 'The boys have come, I think.'

'The boys?'

'My brothers. It's Jimmy's birthday, he's thirty-one.'

'Well then, we must congratulate him and wish him many more birthdays. Come.' He drew her hand through his arm, then firmly squeezed her fingers where they lay on his sleeve; and as he walked her with measured steps down the room she realised, and for the first time, that there was a lifetime of learning before her, not least the character of this man who one minute could be the easy-going sailor and the next Lord Fischel. When he was the latter, as now, he was very like his father. How would she like being loved by a man like his father? She would like it. Strangely, she had always pitied his father. It was the loneliness in him that called forth her pity, as it did in Clive. Without being able to think this out she had known, through her senses, the need of both of them.

When he opened the door they stood framed within it, and there before them was her family, or a good part of it. Jimmy, William, and even Joe had come, and they had collected Annie and her husband, and there was also Sarah, but not Charlotte, for she had to stay and see to the shop. But there were six of them, five of them her own, and they were staring at her in amazed silence, until, turning to the man at her side, she said, clearly and firmly, 'Clive, these are my brothers and sisters.'

Clive Fischel looked at the group before him, respectable upper working-class citizens. He smiled at them frankly and said, 'I am pleased to make your acquaintance.' Then looking down at Cissie he demanded, somewhat imperiously, 'Well!' But she remained mute and the smile she gave him had a slightly mischievous quality about it which he didn't fail to recognise. He turned his gaze upon the staring group again, gave a small cough, and said, 'Your sister has done me the honour to promise to become my wife, and I'm afraid my gain will be your loss, for we're sailing for Spain on Monday evening. We are to be married on Monday morning. And' – he finished formally – 'I hope you will give us the pleasure of your company at the ceremony.'

Jimmy, William, Joe, Sarah, and Annie gaped at the man, the man who had done their Cissie down, the man who had brought misery into her life, but the man who had also been the means of keeping the girls from hunger for years. But now he wasn't just a man, he was a lord. He was Lord Fischel, and their Cissie was going to marry him. Dear God, they thought as one, life was funny, strange . . . But they were going to lose their Cissie. Things would never be the same without her, nothing would be the same. She was the rope that held them all together. As if all were motivated by the thought of the rope snapping, they surged towards her. Ignoring the man, they crowded round her, drew her from him, exclaiming, 'Oh, our Cissie! Our Cissie . . .'

She was back in the dwelling place. She felt their need. Each one was pulling at her skirts, each one depending on her. Yet, even back there she had known that her love for them was a different love from that which she had for the child of her body, as her love for them now was from that

414

which she had for the man who had put the child into her body. Nothing or no-one really mattered but him . . .

She looked beyond them to where he was standing alone by the door, the aloneness plain to her behind his stiff-faced, haughty façade, and she pressed from them and put her hands out to him. And he gripped them tightly and drew her close to him.

Sarah, standing apart from the others, gazed at the black-clad, fashionably dressed man, the gentleman, the lord, who was going to marry their Cissie, give her his name, after which she would no longer be their Cissie, she would be . . . she could scarcely dare to think the words, Lady Fischel. Their Cissie, Lady Fischel.

She knew now that Matthew had been right to have his fears. She knew what Matthew had always known: Cissie had never been really his. She had been nobody's except this man's from the day she had watched him mate her.

They hadn't just now lost their Cissie: she had been gone from them for years, since the days back in the dwelling place.

THE END

A SELECTION OF OTHER CATHERINE COOKSON TITLES AVAILABLE FROM CORGI BOOKS

THE PRICES SHOWN BELOW WERE CORRECT AT THE TIME OF GOING TO PRESS. HOWEVER TRANSWORLD PUBLISHERS RESERVE THE RIGHT TO SHOW NEW RETAIL PRICES ON COVERS WHICH MAY DIFFER FROM THOSE PREVIOUSLY ADVERTISED IN THE TEXT OR ELSEWHERE.

☐	14624 2	BILL BAILEY OMNIBUS	£6.99
☐	14609 9	THE BLIND YEARS	£5.99
☐	14533 5	THE BONDAGE OF LOVE	£5.99
☐	14531 9	THE BONNY DAWN	£4.99
☐	14348 0	THE BRANDED MAN	£5.99
☐	14156 9	THE DESERT CROP	£5.99
☐	14705 2	THE GARMENT & SLINKY JANE	£5.99
☐	13685 9	THE GOLDEN STRAW	£5.99
☐	14703 6	THE HAMILTON TRILOGY	£6.99
☐	14704 4	HANNAH MASSEY & THE FIFTEEN STREETS	£5.99
☐	13300 0	THE HARROGATE SECRET	£5.99
☐	14701 X	HERITAGE OF FOLLY & THE FEN TIGER	£5.99
☐	14700 1	THE IRON FAÇADE & HOUSE OF MEN	£5.99
☐	13303 5	THE HOUSE OF WOMEN	£5.99
☐	13622 0	JUSTICE IS A WOMAN	£5.99
☐	14702 8	KATE HANNIGAN & THE LONG CORRIDOR	£5.99
☐	14569 6	THE LADY ON MY LEFT	£5.99
☐	14699 6	THE MALLEN TRILOGY	£6.99
☐	13684 0	THE MALTESE ANGEL	£5.99
☐	12524 5	THE MOTH	£5.99
☐	14157 7	THE OBSESSION	£5.99
☐	14073 2	PURE AS THE LILY	£5.99
☐	14155 0	RILEY	£5.99
☐	14706 0	ROONEY & THE NICE BLOKE	£5.99
☐	14039 2	A RUTHLESS NEED	£5.99
☐	10541 4	THE SLOW AWAKENING	£5.99
☐	14583 1	THE SOLACE OF SIN	£5.99
☐	14683 8	TILLY TROTTER OMNIBUS	£6.99
☐	14038 4	THE TINKER'S GIRL	£5.99
☐	14037 6	THE UPSTART	£5.99
☐	12368 4	THE WHIP	£5.99
☐	13577 1	THE WINGLESS BIRD	£5.99
☐	13247 0	THE YEAR OF THE VIRGINS	£5.99

All Transworld titles are available by post from:

Bookpost, P.O. Box 29, Douglas, Isle of Man IM99 1BQ

Credit cards accepted. Please telephone 01624 836000, fax 01624 837033, Internet http://www.bookpost.co.uk or e-mail: bookshop@enterprise.net for details.

Free postage and packing in the UK. Overseas customers allow £1 per book (paperbacks) and £3 per book (hardbacks).